ᴦate's Janitors

# Mopping up Madness at a Mental Health Clinic

## A Novel by Keith R Wilson

*Post Partum Depression* previously appeared in *The Armchair Aesthete Fall, 2000.*

Parts of *Rescue Operation* appeared in *Lynx Eye*, Winter 2000.

*Cleaning the Smoking Room* appeared in *Gargoyle #55.*

*Fate's Janitors* also appeared, in serialize form, in Fatesjanitors.com

**Acknowledgements**

I want to thank my wife, Karen Rosenbloom, for putting up with both my need for privacy and feedback as I wrote *Fate's Janitors.* Thank you, too, my other beta readers, the Night Writers: Carlos Bahr, Barb Grosh, Bob Hesselberth, David Jolkovski, Dolly Malik, Martha Price, Eric Scoles, Sally Steinmiller, Henry Williams, and Byron Wilmot.

I am also grateful to my employer for giving me a place to work and to my clients for giving me something to do, but the dysfunctional medical center of *Fate's Janitors* is a fictional setting and the clients in the book are fictional clients. To my colleagues in the psychotherapy field, thanks for your support, but you are also not in this book, for the characters come out of my own twisted imagination. That is not to say that they are not real.

To all those who have lent me their stories, especially Herman.

# Fate's Janitors
## Table of Contents

# Chapter 1 - The Forecast

"You with Behavioral Health?"

The question came from a thin man lurking near the entrance of the Iroquois Regional Medical Center. He held a quivering jumbo coffee cup of the same approximant diameter as his body. "I said, you with Behavioral Health?" repeated the man, who, himself, clearly belonged in the upper floor of the Behavioral Health wing: the mental health unit. But he was no staff member. That was for sure.

"Um, yeah. I'm an intern. I'm supposed to start today."

"Did they take away your soul yet?" he said as he quivered his cup to his lips.

"Huh?"

"Eh, maybe you don't have one. It don't matter; you can't lose what you don't have. Staff in Behavioral Health don't have a soul. They're better off without it. It's useless, anyway. Especially when all you do is categorize and control people."

"I'm sorry, I've got to get going."

"Wait," he said, placing his bony free hand upon the intern. "Have you seen Dr Ahern?"

"Dr Ahern? What Dr Ahern?"

"Dr Ahern, the new Director of Behavioral Health; Dr Ahern, the famous psychologist; Dr Ahern, the former professor. Your new boss."

"Oh, yeah, Dr Ahern. No, I haven't met him, but I read his books in school. It's pretty cool he's here."

"Oh, yeah, it's cool, all right. But you know he's touched? His university shit-canned his whole department. His wife dumped him. Then he tried to commit suicide, but the bullet missed. Now he's coming to work for The Man."

"I'm sure none of that matters. He's a good doctor and he knows psychology; he can help a lot of people."

"You pretty sure of that, aren't you? He won't be taking you down with him when he goes nuts?"

"No, I'm not worried about that."

"Well, I guess you know what you're doing. Lots of luck. I suppose someone's got to go down with him, and if it's not you, it'll just be someone else like you."

"Hey, you know, you can come with me, and we can, like, go over to Behavioral Health and, like, get your meds adjusted. I'm an intern there. I'm sure they'll see you right away if I tell them what's wrong."

"You're perfect for the job. You're already talking just like them. Categorize and control, that's what it's all about," he said as he turned away. "Go categorize and control.

# Chapter 2 – Admissions

Let's just call him Izzy.

After an eternity in college, changing his major countless times, and running out of money, Izzy switched his major one final time, to psychology. A counseling internship was required, so he took himself to the Iroquois Regional Medical Center, and started his assignment at the outpatient chemical dependency clinic.

He left the thin man and his warning and joined a crowd funneled towards an automatic sliding door. It swallowed great mouthfuls of humanity, and transformed them into workers, patients, and visitors. When he came to it, he took a deep breath and stepped inside with the rest. A blast of overheated air assaulted him and a tongue of a carpet runner captured the debris of autumn from his shoes.

A tri-colored map of The Iroquois Regional Medical Center was fastened to the wall. The Center was a three-block-long Leviathan of interconnected buildings. Outpatient Behavioral Health was at the far end, including the Chemical Dependency Clinic in the basement, and Mental Health a floor above. He had a long walk ahead through a maze of hallways. They called it the behavioral health wing at the Medical Center, but it was really a tail, tacked on as an afterthought. The real business of the Medical Center was in the units leading directly off the lobby. Oncology, Gynecology, Dermatology, Radiology, and the rest were the true medical specialties, having to do with muscles, blood, nerves, and bone. But Izzy had finally made up his mind. He would work in nothing other than psychology.

Izzy, like many blue-blooded Americans of a post boomer generation, was a natural at psychology. The good war had been won, Vietnam lost, and they put their little flag on the moon and never went back. On the TV news, between the famines and the wars, were advertisements for Prozac and Zoloft. In the courts, criminals who were once placed in the stocks were put in anger-management classes. Schools taught self-esteem alongside trigonometry and biology. As if there were no more churches and clergy, the troubled swarmed to AA meetings and therapists. There were no frontiers anymore except the one within. Instead of going westward, they went inward. Instead of butchering Indians and enslaving Blacks, they blamed their parents and called their shortcomings a disease. Instead of herding cattle across the Texas plains, Izzy, like his peers, kept a journal and rounded up every impulse in a two-toned composition book. It's what he did for perspective. It was his substitute for the gas, noose, or gun. Just as a Samurai guts himself with his sword, Izzy eviscerated his psyche.

Of course, Izzy didn't intend to go into therapy as a patient, but as a therapist. Patients have to wait for appointments and cram sixty minutes into a fifty-minute hour. They thumb old magazines in waiting rooms where they worry about who will see them there. They tell their secrets to strangers. They take strong drugs that don't get them high. They have to pay, rather than be paid.

Therapists, on the other hand, get paid, not well most of the time, but comfortably. They wear nice clothes and sit out of the wind and cold. They give people the same advice that they need, but would not take; nonetheless, they work out all their issues vicariously through their clients. They get to prop up their names with letters after, and, if they're the right letters, they get to prop the other end with doctor.

Izzy had to resign himself to starting his career as an un-paid intern. Of course, they'd give him the crap jobs and he'd have to make coffee and copies, as if Denny's moved into Kinko's and hired him to work the counter. An internship might affront his dignity, accustomed as he was to lording it over the night shift as a security guard, strutting around with a ring full of keys. The transition was a particularly keen one, considering that internships were regarded as college courses and full tuition was charged.

Change is hard, that's for certain, but doesn't everyone take a turn as an intern? Even if his nose were up someone's butt, in time, someone else's nose would be up his until they all formed a long, hunched over train. There's always some small satisfaction in that.

Izzy might've stopped at the gift shop to pick up a greeting card for his new supervisor to start things off on the right foot, but there were none appropriate, nor any suitable Mylar balloons to tie to his desk. There was a shortage of optimism at the medical center, and so he passed by the store, thinking the college cheerleaders should be on hand for the start of new internships.

In the first corridor, instead of a row of short-skirted, pom-pomed lovelies, a gauntlet of grim portraits of the board of directors guarded the passageway. They looked as though they could use a greeting card or a Mylar balloon more than most. It was as if they proclaimed, as he passed by:

"The Iroquois Regional Medical Center is a 300-bed health care provider serving the four county Finger Lakes area of New York State. We are fully accredited by the Joint Commission on the Accreditation of Hospitals and Health Care Organizations. A wide range of specialty programs and services, both inpatient and outpatient, are available at the Medical Center."

"The Iroquois Regional Medical Center was recently purchased, with five others in the state, by Medco, a for-profit medical service corporation, based in Scottsdale, Arizona. We will continue to operate as a physician-focused, comprehensive provider, striving to provide optimal satisfaction to an urban, suburban, and rural area. Our pledge is not only to continue to provide you with the service and support you've come to expect, but also to bring additional value-added opportunities for all."

"We are pleased to announce the appointment of Dr. Benjamin Ahern as Director of Behavioral Health. Dr. Ahern is a leading figure in the field of psychology and the author of many important books."

Izzy hastened away from the stares of The Board. His eyes glazed over by their proclamations, he got lost, crashed through a set of swinging doors, and found himself in ICU.

ICU seemed like an electronics store for all the monitors mounted by the nurses' station. Surrounding it, the patients slept in their rooms, crowded with machines that hovered around their beds like anxious visitors. He stepped up to the counter, populated by a squad of preoccupied medics huddled around a chart. Each wore a stethoscope around her neck like a rubber and stainless steel scarf. The intern stood open-mouthed and studied a monitor. Portentous line graphs raced across the screen, jumping at intervals like a heat of Olympic hurdlers.

There was sublimity about those line graphs that froze him. They were clearly labeled blood oxygen, heart rate, and so forth, but he knew they signified much more. It was as if they'd drilled a hole and installed a peephole in the locker room of the Fate sisters and he was watching them undress in front of him.

He would've liked to stay there until he had captured the meaning of those line graphs. If he could not determine fate, then at least he could understand it, and, if he couldn't understand it, then he could clean up after it. Go on, he said to himself, get out of ICU. You're blocking the way with your humanities degree. They only want high GPAs working here. He turned, without needing to consult the map, down the darker, less urgent hallways, for there, without doubt, would he find the chemical dependency clinic.

# Chapter 3 - The Office

At the end of a long trek through the Iroquois Regional Medical Center, the new intern arrived at last at the Behavioral Health wing and called an elevator for the nether world of drug addicts, pushers, and alcoholics. A group of young black men assembled with him, erupting in greetings and handclasps whenever a new one arrived. Izzy shrank away lest he be struck by flying elbows and chucks of gold swinging from their necks. Like most white guys, he had seldom experienced being a minority and, now that the tables were turned, he studied these men and wondered if his awkward limbs could ever move with their grace. Suddenly, it seemed important, when it never seemed important before. At last, the elevator arrived and they stepped in, Izzy among them. The group quieted in that confined space as they all turned to the door and posed, like actors waiting for the curtain to open. Out of their individual headsets pulsed beats far heavier than any elevator music he'd ever heard. At last, they reached the basement and the door released them. The group bopped out into the waiting area of the outpatient clinic, necks craning and heads bobbing to their beats.

A disapproving, rotund office manager received them as they emerged from the elevator. She ordered the men into the smoking room. "Wait there till your group starts. And hitch up your pants and don't cause no trouble." As for Izzy, when he told her he was the new intern, she peered over her glasses and sighed. "You gunna be working with Craig Creek. He not in now. We don't got no office for you, so I'm gunna have to be squeezing you in with him. You wait a minute, now. I'll get maintenance to move a desk."

"No, don't do that. I'll wait for him," said Izzy. No one likes to share an office, he thought, especially when he's had one to himself. Even married couples that've shared a bed, a bathroom, and a supper table, will fight only when they have to share their home office. And people like to be private when they're counseling. The clients certainly do. No one would want to pour out their troubles with this Craig Creek, or whatever his name was, listening in a few feet away. And, what's more, any intern would be terribly self-conscious, knowing his nascent attempts at counseling were being monitored by another. Furthermore, it would seem presumptuous to move right into his office on the questionable authority of this office manager. What if he thought it was all Izzy's idea? That would hardly be a good foot to step off on when introducing himself to a new supervisor.

"It's a big office and you'll have lots of room, but suit yourself. He be a minute. Just get some coffee and settle down a bit."

A call came in then and she answered it, so Izzy looked around for the coffee pot. He figured it would be in the smoking room, so he headed for the door that the jive patrol had passed through. A stinging cloud engulfed him when he opened it. Did the room catch fire from some stray ash? He glanced around for an extinguisher and considered the exit, but the other inhabitants didn't seem alarmed. One of the black men was chanting hip hop, pants still drooping, while the others draped themselves across chairs and held cigarettes in front of their grins. Overhead, an air purifier ran for dear life. He found the coffee urn. Sitting near it, a lone ruminating man rolled cigarettes from a yellow pouch he kept on his lap. His fingers were stained the same color as the pouch. Stacked next to him was already a cord or so of rollups and one balanced on his lips.

Izzy was intrigued by the idea of drug addicts and alcoholics. He was a ditherer, he was all about dithering. He spent his whole life orbiting earth, looking for a place to land, whereas these folks shot for the stars. They missed, of course, and many burned up on re-entry, but he admired the addicts' chutzpah. He, like many, was drawn to wild and mysterious marvels. He thought, the man who wakes up every morning, sick, homeless, and broke and, somehow, finds a way to raise hundreds of dollars for smack should be teaching MBAs at Harvard. While so many others cringe at imagined, never-materializing dangers, the crack whore, against all reason, braves the hazards of the street for a moment of pleasure. Medal of Honor winners should be saluting her. Like many, Izzy loved the very thing that he couldn't do. Whatever was most unreachable was most desirable. Many would counsel that we accept things as they are. Indeed, recovering addicts make a career out of that saying; abandoning their true nature just as West Indians brought to Spain by Columbus affected Spanish airs.

"How's the coffee?" Izzy asked the cigarette-rolling man, trying to be sociable, although the man didn't have a cup.

"It'll give you nightmares," he said. Izzy drew a cup anyway, thinking the man looked like he hadn't slept for a week, and couldn't know anything about nightmares. With his first sip, he knew the man was right. He clenched his teeth at him to show his agreement. "You come here often?" Izzy asked.

"I have group three days a week, three hours a day." After a pause, he sniggered, "And I got my three month coin the other day; three days ago. I'm Lawrence."

It might have been the most beat up room in the medical center, that smoking room. The chairs were battered; the tables rickety and ornamented with coffee rings. Yellowed posters thumb tacked to the wall proclaimed sayings as ill used as the room.

A DRUG IS A DRUG IS A DRUG
YOU CAN'T SAVE YOUR FACE AND YOUR ASS AT
 THE SAME TIME
EASY DOES IT
ONE DAY AT A TIME
FIRST THINGS FIRST
LET GO AND LET GOD

A man with a plastic badge and a face full of wrinkles came in, pumped some nicotine into his lungs, snuffed out his cigarette, and called the hip-hop club to group. Izzy asked, "Is that Craig Creek?"

"No, that's Pellegrino. Craig's got a shit load of tattoos."

Izzy went out with them and returned to the office manager. He was beginning to feel suspicious of this Craig Creek with a shit load of tattoos. When was he going to be in?

"He be here any minute," said the office manager. "He called this morning and said he'd be late. He was picking his bike up from repairs."

His supervisor was a tattooed biker tooling around on his machine in the autumn cold. He might be prone to hocking up loogies and spitting them in the wastebasket, Izzy could get his head smashed in with a tire iron if his chair squeaked too much.

Many drug and alcohol counselors were former addicts themselves, coming in as full-fledged professionals with far less education than Izzy, with ten years of college, already had as an intern. Most chemical dependency clinics preferred to hire their recent graduates, transferring from Hard Knocks University, majors in pill popping, bottle tipping, and stem sucking; to those from more conventional institutions. Izzy was a mere dilettante when it came to fucking himself up. This was no place for him, he thought.

"Do you have a phone? I'd like to call my professor," he said to the office manager.

"Sure enough." She picked up an old dial phone and placed it in front of him. The bell rang when she moved it. They weren't big on privacy here, he could see.

It took some doing to get his professor on the phone. He had to call three places and they paged him out of class. Izzy said to the phone, "Are there any other internships…. Yeah, I already knew that…. I know, I didn't make the deadline … It was all you could do to get me this placement…. Yeah, I know I was lucky they took me without having to go on an interview…No I don't want to wait for next semester…I know; it isn't too late to take an incomplete…Thank you very much. I'm sorry to, like, bother you. I won't call again like this…. Yes, I know you have office hours…. I'm sorry I told them I was your son in the emergency room and you almost had a heart attack when they paged you out of class…. Do you have your pills on you?... I'm sure your son is just fine, he'll, like, live a long life and you'll have many grandchildren…. No, I didn't know he just told you he was gay…. I'm sorry, I won't bother you again, professor. That was totally uncool…. I'm sorry… Yes, I will…. I'm sorry, professor…. Goodbye."

The office manager was trying to look as though she wasn't listening when he hung up the phone. He said, "Don't you have, like, a closet, or something, you could put me in?"

"You come back here with me. I got a room I can put you up in. It's not big, but it be all yours. "

With that, the good woman went to a door down the hall and vigorously began to haul out reams of paper and boxes of pens while talking non-stop. The supplies, staked up in the hall outside, began to teeter and tumble across the hall. She came near slipping a disk trying to move a heavy shredding machine by herself. Izzy told her to quit, for heaven's sake; he'd finish clearing it out. He didn't want her to be hurting herself on his account. So, after grabbing a fistful of post-it notes, she returned, grinning, to her desk and left him imagining his floor plan.

After getting all the supplies out and piling them by the copier, Izzy found that the light was poor, but that could be mended by bringing a desk lamp from home. It could fit a small desk, but he had to put the chair up on the desk to shut the door. There was no room for someone else to sit with him, of course, but he figured he could always steal into an empty room somewhere for an interview or therapy session. However, there was no phone, no computer, and no air circulation to speak of, so he began to think he might be harboring unwarranted preconceptions against this Craig Creek. Consequently, Izzy abandoned the scheme and hauled the supplies back in.

"Ma'am," he said to the office manager, "I've thought this over. I'd like to see Mr Creek's office." He had an idea that inspecting his space might give him an idea what to expect from him.

"I can do that. You just follow me, now; I'll have you there in a minute. And don't call me Ma'am, my name's Melvina. Craig's not usually late. He comes right on time, every day, even when he's sick or it's snowing like crazy outside. The only time he ever misses work is for his bike. That's his baby." She ushered him into a large office, big enough for four biker counselors to fit in with their desks. "You see, it's a big room. Craig won't mind." By the time Izzy turned around from scanning it, she had already disappeared.

There was nothing remarkable at all about the room, except for its unremarkableness. In fact it had the look of an inhabitant that lived so exclusively within his head that he seldom looked around to see where he was or how untidy it had become. Like a bachelor's apartment that only needs a john to piss in, an armchair to watch the game in, and a refrigerator to keep the beer in, this space was nothing more than space: a spot to write charts and sit in. It's true that Craig Creek counseled in this space, but the people he counseled were only one half step removed from the street. They slept on a mattress thrown on the floor without even a sheet to cover its loose buttons. They could feel at home in this office, a basement apartment of an office. The greenish desk bore the same coffee rings as the tables in the smoking room and Craig Creek's desk chair had a missing screw that caused the arm to rotate out like a wing. A bookcase had no books, but was stuffed with papers and loose-leaf binders and a tall filing cabinet proved when they later moved it to make room for his desk, to contain nothing more than a can of coffee. Two dog-eared posters squared off on opposite walls: a twelve-step poster on one wall and Harley-Davidson on the other.

Izzy sat on a side chair in this dingy, windowless office for some time thinking about this bike riding chemical dependency counselor who was assigned to be his role model and his mentor.

After thinking some time on that chair, he got up and took off his coat and thought some more. This room was a far cry from the glitz and forced cheerfulness of the medical center lobby, yet both were in the same building. In one wing of this medical center, cancerous tissue was cut out of patients in bright-lighted operating rooms. In another wing, patients were sent for a regular dose of carcinogens before therapy. In one wing, patients were matched with white coated, overeducated doctors. In another wing, the medical center let tattooed bikers have a go at them. How did he end up here? He had dithered, left it up to fate, and he went where they sent him, thinking it was all his idea in the first place.

# Chapter 4 - The Fates

The way Izzy imagined, it was like this:

It was the type of house that most would avoid. The lawn grown wild, paint chipped off, shutters falling loose, and inhabited by three elderly sisters. The thunder god, Zeus, climbed up to the porch, avoiding a broken step, and rang the bell. It didn't work, of course, so he knocked. He could see the piles of yarn heaped against the inside of the windows, shutting out the world. At last, he could hear one of the sisters make her way to him from within. The door creaked open.

He had more to fear from the sisters than most, but the time had come when he couldn't avoid seeing them any longer. There were too many protests and he was expected, as president of the Mt Olympus Neighborhood Association, to confront issues, such as they had with them. Being president was not all parades and beauty pageants; you should know. He's always understood that, which accounts for his long reign, going on, what, three thousand years.

The thunder god's heart tripped a little when he saw a callused hand reach by the jam. Yet, when the door swung open it revealed, not an old crone, but a young woman, pregnant about nine months.

"By Jove, it's you," she said, forcing as warm a smile as she could manage. They had a long and close association, and rivalry, back in the old days. They'd fallen out of touch, however. She hadn't heard that he preferred again to go by Zeus.

"I'm here on official business of the neighborhood association," he boomed, loud enough to substitute bombast for genuine supremacy.

"Come in then. My sisters are in the back." She extinguished her smile with a callous scowl.

"I hope you don't mind the mess," she said.

"As a matter of fact, Chloe, I do mind the mess," he rumbled. "That's why I'm here. There've been many complaints."

She didn't say a word in reply, but led him down a narrow channel between piles of yarn to the back of the house where the sisters had a workshop. The breeze from their passage and Zeus' rumbling stirred up clouds of dust that set him to sneezing. Great hurricanes hurried out of his nose, only to stir up more dust, resulting in more sneezing. The god's mighty blasts might've brought the whole house down, solving the neighborhood's problem, only the piles of yarn must've held it up.

"Excuse me," he sniffed. "Do you have a tissue?"

"No, but you can blow your nose on this," she said as she handed him a skein of yarn.

He emptied his nose and Chloe took a seat by an old spinning wheel and got it turning. As she produced a fiber, a second sister cut it at varying, arbitrary lengths and a third gathered up each strand into a skein and threw it on a pile.

"Chloe, Morticia, Moira," he declared. "I'm here on official ..."

"Yes, we heard. Haven't we paid our dues?"

"It's not about that. There've been complaints."

"There are always complaints," said Morticia as she snipped with her scissors. "We've learned to ignore them and do what we think best."

"Yes, well, there have been complaints, and I happen to agree with them."

"Go on."

"Well, for one, you're violating a zoning ordinance by having a, eh, factory in the middle of a residential area."

Moira exclaimed, "Everyone agrees they need our services, but no one wants us in their backyard. Well, we've got to be somewhere."

Chloe added, "We've been doing this for an eternity and we've been doing it right here. While you're retired, we still have work to do. More work than ever, in fact. There are more people than ever and someone has to do what we do."

"You don't have to tell me," The Cloud Gatherer conceded, "there's still a need for fate."

They had agreed, when mortals entered the scene, that someone had to decide when a life should end. Each mortal couldn't do it for his or her self, they'd all want their lives to go on forever, like the gods', and there wouldn't be any room for new people. So Morticia decides. Then, every woman wants a baby, but not everyone can have one. Furthermore, each baby can't decide what his or her temperament is going to be like because they're born with their temperament, so Chloe decides. Moira is needed because not everyone can be born in the best places, to the best parents, so she decides their lot in life.

"So, you see," Chloe continued. "This factory, as you call it, is necessary, whereas your retirement community is not."

It stung, being superfluous. It seemed that everyone had turned away from the gods, except for some right-wingers and terrorists. It bothered all the divine on Mt Olympus that they were forced into an early retirement and they knew that The Fate Sisters were behind it.

Zeus admitted, "We're all probably a little jealous of you, but seeing as though you have so much work, couldn't you at least relocate? It's clear you're running out of room in this facility. You could move to larger, more modern quarters."

"We can't afford to," said Moira. "We have a lot of work, but no one pays us anything anymore. No one believes in The Fates and we don't get any bribes or reverence. Everyone believes in Free Will, Economic Determinism, Karma, or Grace. They collect the tributes, but we still have to do the work. Go see Genetics; they have more than enough money to fund our expansion. Then we'll leave your retirement community."

Being the supreme father of the gods, he knew he wouldn't get anywhere with Genetics.

He said, "If you have to stay here, at least clean it up. I'll grant that you don't make much noise and you don't pollute the environment, but this place is a firetrap. Look at the mess you make."

"Fate is messy," said Chloe. "We can't help that."

Fate was messy and had created untold suffering, for which people then blamed the gods. The neighborhood association wouldn't let Zeus rest until he went to persuade the sisters to take care of the suffering so they could go back to enjoying their retirement.

"Just clean it up as you go. Go through these piles, sort it all out, and make some order out of it. Take up knitting."

"It wouldn't be good for us to get too close to our work," she explained. "We can do what we do only because we are impersonal and don't know these people."

The Fate Sisters have never been like the other Olympic gods. Inhuman, impersonal, inaccessible, and compassionless, they've been more a machine than spirit, more a bureaucracy than deity. They've often been tempted, but they've never been worshipped. They never could be worshipped, for they are heartless officials, unmindful of the consequences of their actions.

"In that case, get someone else to do it. Hire a janitor," Zeus looked around at the mess, "or a whole crew of janitors."

"I know what we can do," said Moira. "I've been wondering what to do with this pile; none of them seem to fit in anywhere." She pulled a fragile length of fiber from that pile and held it up. "This one will be a janitor."

"That piece of string?" he asked. "What can that do?"

"It doesn't matter what he or she is made of. A person will do anything, put in the right circumstances."

And so, thought Izzy, the Fates appointed janitors to take care of people and their suffering and get the gods off the hook. Maybe he'd be one of them.

# Chapter 5 - Craig

Izzy had just put his pens and post-it notes away in his new desk when he heard a heavy footfall in the corridor outside the office he was to share with his counseling supervisor, Craig Creek. He spun around in his chair to have a look at the man when he entered. The stranger didn't see the intern set up behind the door. He went straight for the other desk, a motorcycle helmet, like a disembodied head, tucked under his arm. He placed the helmet on his desk and, with it, a saddlebag containing his appointment book and a brown lunch sack. A long, thin, graying ponytail hung between the Harley and the Davidson of his black leather jacket. In case the stranger was an escaped convict, and not his supervisor, Izzy resolved not to say a word, least he startle him. He was eager to see his face, but the man kept it averted while he took off the jacket, revealing he wore an incongruous business shirt and tie. He had a long, spiked beard and his hands bore crude, prison tattoos that had blurred beyond recognition. Izzy began to think that flight might be his best option, but the stranger was standing near the door-way, over six feet tall, and filled out his shirt better than most. The intern regretted spending so many days of his academic career in the library instead of the gym. He was terrified of the big man and could not find it in him to address him, nor did he know what he could say.

The stranger took his plastic employee badge out of the saddlebag and carefully affixed it to his shirt. So this is my supervisor, thought Izzy.

But then the giant did something so peculiar that it captured the intern's attention and confirmed to him that the Iroquois Regional Medical Center had hired no man of science here. The supervisor sat in his chair and fumbled in the saddlebag for a well-worn devotional booklet. His thick fingers found the page and he took some time to read, his lips moving like a davening rabbi. At last, he put the booklet down and dug a large coin out of his pants pocket. He examined it for a minute, less like a coin collector and more like a priest holding the host in front of him at the altar. Then he kissed it and put it back in his pocket.

His worship completed, the giant then picked up his helmet and, to put it away, unconsciously reached for the drawer of his filing cabinet, except that the intern had moved it. He paused and began to scan the room, looking for the cabinet. The intern spent this interval deliberating on what to say, but he didn't have enough time to work out an explanation to a pissed off biker, observed in an intimate moment. The man's eyes passed right over the intern while looking for the cabinet, then, giving out a grunt of astonishment; the eyes returned right back to him.

The biker shouted, "Who the fuck are you and what the fuck are you doing in my office? Who put that desk here?"

Stammering out something about a college, the intern rose and stepped towards the door, but the man blocked his way and drew back the helmet as if to hit him with it.

The intern shrieked for the office manager, "Melvina, security, anyone, help,"

"Who are you and why are you sitting there watching me?"

At that moment, the door opened and Melvina stood there grinning. Behind her, the whole clinic: Lawrence, Pellegrino, the rappers, everyone, vied for a view of the intern's mortification. "Tell him to put down that weapon," he said to Melvina. She laughed and Craig, red faced, located the missing file cabinet, and stashed the helmet away.

The biker slammed the drawer shut and snarled, "What is this, a college kid? I didn't say I'd work with a college kid. Who the hell are you? And what're you doing in my office?"

## Chapter 6 - The Resume

"I'm Izzy, I'm, like, your intern."

"You're like my intern, huh. Are you in recovery?"

"Yes... er, no."

"Yes and no. Well, which is it?" he asked.

"I'm not an addict. I don't use drugs."

"Then you don't know anything about recovery."

"Well, not in that way, but I'm an intern, and I'll learn all about it. I've been to college and studied..."

"Fuck college. College is better at teaching people about using than about recovery. I've been to college, but I didn't learn anything in it. My school's been on the street. That's where you learn about recovery."

"I don't need to be in recovery. I don't use drugs, I don't drink."

"You can't help anybody unless you're fucked up, yourself."

"I thought you had to be psychologically healthy to be a counselor. They don't want screwed up people influencing clients. They'll, like, make them worse."

"These people can't get any worse," he said, pointing to Lawrence and the rappers, who stood and watched this interchange although with Melvina and Pellegrino. "Nothing you do can make them worse. You can't fuck them up, but you can't help them, either, unless you know what it's like to be fucked up."

"But, I know all about it. I took abnormal psychology."

"What diagnosis are you?"

"What do you mean, what diagnosis? I don't have any diagnosis."

"You mean you took abnormal psychology and you didn't find out your diagnosis? I took abnormal psychology and I had every diagnosis in the book, and then I diagnosed my friends and family."

"Yeah, I did that, too. Everyone does that, but my professor warned us not to diagnose ourselves or people we know."

"Your professor's an idiot. If I was your professor, I'd tell you to find out how fucked up you are."

"Is that what your professor told you?"

"You're damn right. He was Dr Ahern."

"Is that the same Dr Ahern that was just appointed Director of Behavioral Health?"

"Yup, that's the guy. If you want to know what counseling is, you listen to Dr Ahern."

"Is Dr Ahern fucked up, like you say he should be?"

"Fucked up? Ahern's been fucked by Moby's dick and it left him sore, dry, and bleeding on the bottom of the ocean."

Izzy was a little alarmed by his admiration of Dr Ahern. "Are you sure you have to be fucked up to be a good counselor? Is that really necessary?"

"Are you sure you've been to college?"

"Yea, I'm finishing my degree."

"Why do you want to be a counselor?"

"Why? Oh, to help people."

"You know you like to help people? Who have you helped? "

"Oh, I haven't, like, helped anyone yet, I've just been in college."

"Then, how do you know you like it?"

"Doesn't everyone like to help people?"

This got a reaction out of both Craig and Pellegrino, who broke out into laughter. Pellegrino's wrinkles formed a network around his eyes like guy wires suspending the orbs in his face.

"You can go get me and Pellegrino some coffee and donuts. Would you like to do that?" he said.

"I can do that. I can get coffee for people if they really need it. But I got years of college; I can help them a lot more by…"

"I don't like to help people. You like to help people, Pellegrino?"

"Shit."

"We don't like to help people."

Izzy asked, "Why are you counselors, then?"

"Because we're fucked up and this is all we can do," said Pellegrino.

"OK, then, you both are counselors because you are fucked up and I want to be a counselor because I want to help people who are fucked up. We all have our reasons for being counselors."

"That's right, but you got a lousy reason for being a counselor," said Craig.

"Then, I guess I'm fucked up, too."

Craig said, "I'm glad you figured that out. And, since you like to help people, I got a job for you."

He opened a desk drawer and pulled out a plastic bag of plastic cups.

"My group is starting. You can get the urine samples."

## Chapter 7 - The Pissing Contest

"See that spot there? You see it?" said Lawrence, pointing to a flicked booger in the urinal. "Suppose it's my probation officer's eye." Taking aim at the spot, he shot a golden stream of urine from a range of one yard and obliterated the booger from sight.

"Just get it in the cup, please." Izzy was not the only one losing patience. There was a line of men behind Lawrence, all waiting for their chance to perform in front of him.

"Do you have to watch?" said the next.

"I have to make sure it's your urine going in the cup. We're testing it for drugs."

"I have a shy bladder." And indeed, he did. Five minutes later they were still waiting. The line was getting restless.

"C'mon, do we have to wait all day?" they said.

"Why don't you go drink some water and go to the back of the line?" Izzy suggested.

"No, it's coming."

It wasn't.

"You heard him, go drink some water," said the man behind him.

"Fuck off. It's coming."

"Don't tell me to fuck off. You go fuck off."

"Look," the intern said. "Zip it up and get some water. There's a lot of people waiting."

He complied, but on the way out, he shoulder bumped the man behind him.

"Prick."

And they had a fight in the men's room: pushing and shoving. No punches thrown, but lots of noise. Craig and Pellegrino had to come in and break it up.

"Guys, it's a simple program," said Pellegrino. "You don't have to make it complicated. Just piss in the cup." With this advice, he and Craig each took a urinal and, thus tripling the capacity to monitor, they reached the end of the line in no time, until all that was left was shy bladder man.

"I guess you stood up to him, didn't you?" cooed Craig. "No one's going to make you piss on command. Just take your time and think about Niagara Falls. Close your eyes and think of all that water going over the falls. Now think about trying to stop it. Don't let any water go over. Not a drop. Hold it all back."

The visualization was so powerful, Izzy might have wet his pants right there, then he heard the steamy sound of urine striking a plastic cup.

"There it is, you struck gold," said Craig. Shy bladder man sheepishly put the lid on and dropped the lidded cup into a plastic bag. As he sealed the bag, Craig said, "Thank you for your contribution."

Craig, Izzy, and Pellegrino carried the urine specimens back to the staff room where there stood two refrigerators: one for staff lunches, the other for urine.

"I'm glad we got that fucking job done," said Izzy.

A buxom black woman, who he hadn't noticed was in the room, looked up from au unzipped Bible and asked, "Is this your new intern, Mr. Creek?"

"Yes, it is," said Craig.

"What do you think of him?"

"Oh, he'll do," he said. Despite his incompetence at the urinals, Izzy felt a surge of pride to hear Craig give his approval.

"I hope you'll be teaching him that such language is not appropriate in this clinic."

"Miss Bella," said Pellegrino. "Every time I see you, you're reading that book. Haven't you finished it yet?"

Miss Bella's point would not be broken off by Pellegrino's banter. She peered over her reading glasses at the intern.

"Young man," she continued, "your language belongs on the street, not in this clinic. We are asking our clients to leave their street ways behind and develop social skills that they'll need in the legitimate working world. If you can't express your frustration in a more appropriate fashion, how will you ever be able to teach the clients to?"

Despite her excessive maternal attributes, she had no warmth. Those outsized paps might have served cold milk. Izzy rarely used profanity. He was only trying to fit in with the two men. She had him all wrong, but how could he protest?

"You're being too hard on him," said Pellegrino. "He was only trying to reach the clients where they're at."

"There're no clients in this room, Mr. Pellegrino, this is the staff room. If he is going to reach the clients where they're at, he will have to be where they're at."

"If there're no clients in this room, Miss Bella, then what does it matter what language he uses? There are no clients here to corrupt."

"He corrupts himself with this language. A man's thoughts turn into his words, his words turn into his actions, and his actions become his habits. We change our habits by cleansing our actions, our words, and our thoughts. Don't you teach your clients that, Mr. Pellegrino?"

Everything was tied to everything else for this woman. There were no loose ends. She hugged her Bible, ensconced in its zippered pouch, to her bosom, ample enough for a library. A large wooden cross and a hospital badge were secured by a strap around her neck. Her reading glasses, perched on the end of her nose, were also kept in custody by its own leash. She lowered her glasses and placed them, with the badge, cross, and Bible, on her breast.

Pellegrino, answered, "My clients come here for help with their substance abuse problems, and I work with them on that. They got enough to do. I don't scare them away by forcing them to learn a foreign language."

"Mr. Pellegrino, we don't ask our clients to learn a foreign language, but we do suggest that they examine themselves for character defects. It is these character defects that, if uncorrected, lead to relapse. Have you examined yourself for character defects, Mr. Pellegrino?"

"Character defects! Why, if you knew the character defects I had, you'd want the God in your book to come back and die again just for my sins. I got enough character defects for a whole new testament. If you think swearing is a character defect, then you've lived a pretty sheltered life."

"You wouldn't think I lived a sheltered life if you knew what I've been through and what God has forgiven me for. I was as bad a person as anyone."

"Then you might forgive a person for swearing, seeing that so much of what you've done was forgiven."

"I would forgive swearing if you asked me to."

This is where Izzy stepped in and asked Miss Bella to forgive him for swearing. He wasn't really sorry, but he didn't want to watch these two have an argument over which of them was the biggest bad ass in the past. He had half a mind to give up the whole idea of this internship in a clinic with such a collection of screwballs. On the other hand, he had already learned that if these folks could be counselors, then how hard could it be?

Miss Bella broke her face into a big smile and stood up. Izzy thought she was going to hug him to her bosom, next to the cross, glasses, and badge, so he took a deep breath to prevent asphyxiation. Instead, she went to the other side of the staff room where she obtained a collection of empty urine bottles.

"I've got a group starting. You can get their urine specimens. Then you will be forgiven."

# Chapter 8 - The Cutter

The second batch of urine screens started off better than the first. There were no men with shy bladders and no fights. Izzy was beginning to feel as though he was competent at the task, a fact he was reluctant to share with anyone, because then he might be asked to do it again. It doesn't pay to know how to do everything. He knew that, at the end of the internship, there would be no line on the evaluation in which Craig would write an *A* in collecting piss. He would never put it on his resume. Just the same, there is some satisfaction in a job well done. The intern didn't need to re-create Niagara Falls in the men's room as Craig had, but the biker had shown him how to hold the bag and to test to see if the lid was on straight while it was in the bag, so as not to touch the bottle with his hands. Every bag he sealed was a triumph. The intern relaxed enough to chat it up with the people in line. Yes, he said to himself, you are a first-rate piss collector. These people will go home and say this was the best part of their day. You've done some good.

When he was about half way through he noticed that one of the toilet stalls had been occupied the whole time. This didn't seem unusual, sometimes a guy just likes to take his time taking a dump. Indeed, if you've got the newspaper and no one banging on the door, wanting to come in, it can be a pleasant experience. Perhaps it was someone in there who marveled at the work-manlike job Izzy had been doing. Maybe Craig had snuck in to supervise. But then the intern thought he heard a sob come from that stall.

"Are you all right?" he called.

The answer came, another sob, louder than the first.

Izzy looked at the men in line. They looked at him as if to say, you're the counselor, do some counseling. Izzy couldn't remember covering this in class.

"Go get Craig," he said. "Are you OK?" he asked again. He could see nothing through the cracks in the stall. The only answer was more sobbing. "Open up, I'd like to help you," Izzy said, although he didn't know what to do. Then he thought, can't a guy just cry in peace. Maybe his mother just died, or something, and he wants to stay strong in front of people, so he just went to the bathroom to cry. He'll ask for help if he needs it. So the intern said, "I'll be right here if you need me."

The messenger returned. "Craig's in group," he said.

The sobbing stopped, so Izzy collected more urine. Then, between samples, he turned towards the stall and saw a rivulet of blood running from within.

"You're bleeding!" he said, and shook the door, but it wouldn't open. "Run, get maintenance. Get something to pry this door open!"

So this is how it would be, thought Izzy, on my first day of work someone kills himself in the men's room while I collect urine a few feet away.

Certainly, that would be a terrible beginning, a black mark on his evaluation.

"Put your hand over the wound. Hold the blood back. Imagine its Niagara Falls. Go get a doctor."

A man in line offered to break the door down. Izzy said no, best not to bust the place up on my first day. He'd crawl under the door. What's the sense in coming to treatment, he wondered, only to kill yourself in the men's room. You can stay at home and do that. They ought to put a sign up; no smoking in the men's room and no suicides permitted.

Izzy squirmed halfway under and rose up on his elbows. The man was sitting on the john, pants to his ankles. His face was still wet from the sobbing he did before, but it was the same color as the porcelain, and just as impassive. He held a knife to his thigh, not his wrist, as Izzy had expected. The thigh was covered with cuts and scars of old cuts, like cuneiform. There was no reaction when Izzy said, "Hey, man, what's the matter with you?"

"At least he didn't cut off his prick," said a man in line after Izzy opened the door.

"Yes, he's alive. Please leave us alone," said the intern. "We can get your urine samples later."

"I got to take a piss," said one.

"No, I've got to get a sample later. Hold it."

"I can't hold it. I got to take a piss."

Izzy got him his bottle. "Take your fucking piss, then."

"Well, I've got to take a piss, too," said another.

"God damn you all, can't you see this guy's in trouble. Give me a fucking minute to get him out of here."

Izzy was glad Miss Bella wasn't right outside the door. The bleeding man walked right beside him, but he seemed miles away. He had his pants up, but they were still undone. Blood was smeared all over him. Melvina asked no questions when the intern said to call the ambulance, even though they were already in a hospital.

The man became more talkative before they arrived to take him away. He was a cutter, he explained. When the pain gets too great, he feels better to let out a little blood. There was no need to go to the hospital. He'd be OK now.

Izzy had no objection to whatever a person does to make himself feel better, just as long as it doesn't result in his death or harm anyone else. He could stand on his head, for all he cared. But, as he carefully explained to him, cutting in the bathroom is obviously unhygienic. There were lots of germs lurking about that could infect him. Besides, there were plenty of other things he could do to make himself feel better. Izzy went on about the advances in modern medicine, as well as tried and true ancient methods. Then there was meditation, progressive relaxation, and biofeedback. They'd be able to teach him all about it in the hospital. A pretty nurse would clean his thighs and listen to whatever was troubling him. Wouldn't that be much better than cutting himself in the bathroom?

Izzy had the man convinced and, when the medics came, he told them to take him away before he cut some more and thanked the intern for his trouble. Izzy said to himself, you had a good day. You got an office, a supervisor, collected piss, and saved someone's life. Not bad for a day's work. It'll be tough to top it tomorrow. He was sorry, though, that he missed Craig's group, but there's always tomorrow. The man went on without him while he collected Miss Bella's urine samples. Izzy waited for Craig to finish with group before he left because he wanted to tell him about the cutter.

"Did you get his piss?" Craig asked.

"What do you mean, get his piss? I saved his life."

"You didn't save his life, you saved him from having to give a piss test. Don't believe that crap about releasing the pain. He just didn't want to get caught using."

# Chapter 9 - A Flashback

Craig said no more, sat at his desk, rolled up his sleeves, as if to say, let's get to work, and began writing.

"Is there anything I can do?" asked Izzy.

"No."

The supervisor's shirt was a striped print and, when he hiked it up, his arms were so covered by tattoos it looked as though he had another shirt beneath that clashed with the one on top. Izzy regarded him as one does a gorilla at the zoo, albeit a tattooed gorilla in business casual that he's caged up with. One shouldn't blame the intern for staring, though. One didn't come across a man like Craig Creek every day. His ways were worth studying. He was a creature in transition, neither tadpole nor frog, but both simultaneously.

As they sat there, the intern's sensations were strange, to say the least. Izzy had been in a similar circumstance when he was a child. His mother had remarried a man from southern California, a rough speaking, cigar smoking defense contractor with a crew cut. How they had met and courted from across the country is another story. In any case, they all moved in with the defense contractor in his suburban tract home, bringing little more than a suitcase apiece. Izzy's big sister was there for less than a week before she lit out for Haight-Ashbury to become a flower child. Izzy discovered the kids of the neighborhood. The weather was always good, and the swirling streets seemed like a vast play yard. He spent as little time in that house as he could get away with.

One morning, he had not gotten out yet and his mother was worrying the living room carpet with the vacuum cleaner, as she did every morning. His new stepfather had gone to work, but his sweet and salty smell lingered in every room of the house. Izzy decided he would steal into his bedroom and find out more about the man. The dresser drawers held underwear and socks; briefs, but no secrets. In the top drawer of the nightstand, he found the real treasures: a cap from the American Legion, a Korean War medal, and, the best find, a Purple Heart. Izzy put all these items on and rummaged through the bottom drawer. There he discovered a cache of Playboy magazines.

The boy sat on the bed and began to leaf through the magazines. He was about twelve at the time, and he hadn't thought much about women before, but strange things were beginning to stir. It's impossible to say how long he sat there, wearing his stepfather's hat and medals, looking at pictures of naked women, but, he was so engrossed, he failed to notice that his mother had finished the living room and was vacuuming up the hall. She entered and discovered the boy decked up like an old veteran, with a stack of Playboys beside him, and his hand down his pants. She sent the child to his room without his supper, though it was only nine in the morning, on the twenty-first day of June, the longest day of the year.

Izzy lay in bed, humiliated, and dismally calculating that it would be about twenty hours before his release. This was in the days before video games and, because they had traveled so light, he possessed no toys to play with or books to read. Furthermore, it was a beautiful day outside and he could hear the sounds of the neighborhood kids begin to swell. A basketball thumped outside the window. Kids peddled their bikes down the street, baseball cards clicking in the spokes of their wheels. Sometime later he heard the crack of a bat. The boy tried to distract himself by imagining the women of the magazine and stroking his penis. It felt very good until a milky substance came out, then he got scared and began to cry. The child soaked his pillow before he got up, sought out his mother, and threw himself at her feet, beseeching her tender mercy. The punishment was too hard, he protested. "Wouldn't you rather whip me, or have me clean the house?" No, she was too conscientious a parent to let him off without a punishment, didn't believe in striking children, and the house was clean enough as it was. But she would consent to his petitioning his father for an appeal. Izzy was to march back to his room and stay there until his father came home. Then he would have to answer to him for going through his things.

"'Til my father came home?" Izzy was so astonished to hear her call this stranger his father that some valve inside shut off all his tears. He returned to his room, flipped the pillow over to the dry side, and lay there thinking. He didn't believe, come what may, that he would ever feel as miserable again. All kinds of thoughts passed through his mind, like subway trains through a station. He was sad about having to move away, losing his friends, his things, and then his sister, pain as she was sometimes. He was scared that he had hurt himself and caused the milky white substance to come out, but he was more scared of talking to his stepfather. Izzy didn't know what the strange man would do when he found out. He was mystified that his mother would call him his father, when he already had a real one, all the way across the country. For a long time, he lay there, as all these feelings, and more, came rumbling through. Then, despite his fears of the milky white substance, he turned to masturbating again, until it reappeared and he fell asleep.

The boy awoke when his stepfather arrived from work. Though their voices were muffled, Izzy could hear him and his mother talking in the kitchen. Then his heavy footfall came up the hall. By the time he opened the door, Izzy was in the closet, peeking out. He knew he would find him, he couldn't escape; but at least he could study him for a while, before having to say anything. The boy watched as he loosened his tie and rolled up his sleeves, just as Craig was later to do. A Marine Corps tattoo hid under cover of dark arm hair. Izzy held his breath, least he hear it, but he imagined his pounding heart would give him away. The stepfather only sighed and opened the closet door. He told the boy to get dressed; we're going for a ride. Izzy complied, although he imagined the man would take him out in the desert and leave him there.

Although they were alone in the car, there seemed to be many strange feelings that hitched a ride with them. An adult would understand that the stepfather was, most likely, just as humiliated at being caught with the magazines as the boy had been, just as we might suppose Craig had been humiliated at being caught in his devotions. At the time, the stepfather, a reluctant father, knew nothing about children, just as Craig had never had an intern before. The similarities were remarkable.

Izzy was the first in the car to speak. "Where are we going?" he asked.

"I'm taking you to the barbershop," the man answered. Izzy felt relieved. So this was to be my punishment, he thought, I would have to get a haircut. Izzy knew his mother and stepfather felt strongly about long hair. They kept sputtering about the longhaired freaks up in San Francisco where the sister had gone. Izzy supposed they were worried about him going, too, and they figured by cutting his hair, they'd prevent it. When they got to the barbershop, however, the stepfather took the chair instead of the boy.

He rubbed his already short hair and said to the barber, "I might as well get a trim while I'm here, Frank. This is Izzy, my new stepson."

Frank nodded at the boy over his clippers. Izzy picked up an Archie comic book and nodded back. "Show him where you keep the other magazines, Frank. He's getting too old for comic books."

Frank paused, "Are you sure he's old enough? He doesn't look that big?"

"Ah, go ahead; he's already taken an interest in Playboy. His mother caught him red handed with my collection. He's not going to see anything here that he hasn't already." Frank chuckled. In fact, everyone in the barbershop chuckled. Izzy turned red and became absorbed with Archie and Veronica.

"Look in that drawer beside you, son," said Frank, but Izzy didn't come out from behind the comic book.

"Go ahead, Izzy," said the stepfather, his voice gone stern. "You know you want to."

Izzy didn't, in fact, want to. He would have much rather been back in his room, crying in a pillow. But, if this were to be his punishment, he thought, he'd take it. He opened the drawer and began to thumb through the magazines. The men's conversation turned to the war and the election and, once Izzy was out of the center of attention, he felt very grown up, sitting there, reading Playboy in the barbershop.

Frank was done with the stepfather in a minute. He swirled the sheet off him and snapped it clear of hair. "You want to get a trim, too?" asked the stepfather. Izzy climbed up on the chair and Frank began to clip away, asking him about his opinion of baseball. Izzy decided right then that this stepfather was pretty cool, cooler than Mom, but he never did call him father.

The flashback was done in an instant, far quicker, in fact, than it takes to tell it. A tattooed woman, naked as any in Playboy, reclined on Craig's forearm and witnessed the flashback. She wiggled her ass as Craig wrote. On his other forearm, a Bengal tiger snarled at a tattooed wristwatch, which displayed a different time underneath a real wristwatch. Annoyed, Craig looked at his real wristwatch and proclaimed, "What you need to do is go to a meeting."

# Chapter 10 - The Meeting

Far more people than were needed clattered open dozens of folding chairs for the medical center's AA meeting, far more chairs than were needed. The people just needed something to do. The coffee pot had its own committee, enough humans to count the grains one by one and ladle the water out by thimbles. A platoon manned the literature rack and scrutinized anyone who dared approach. Only one volunteered to be greeter, though. Like many others, Izzy steered away from her and took a seat next to Lawrence, the ruminating, cigarette-rolling man he had met in the smoking room.

Many of these same alcoholics would have been the life of the party if this was happy hour. If this had been a smoky bar room, poorly lit by tungsten bulbs off the glistening top shelf scotch, instead of a smoky meeting room, bright lit by florescent bulbs, then there would have been no need for an automaton greeter at the door. There would be sparkling conversation, dancing, and flirting. Without their preferred social lubricant, these addicts were as stiff and self-conscious as computer geeks. Most had been to meetings before, some were partway through ninety meetings in ninety days, but many acted as though that dream of walking naked through the halls on the first day of school had actually come true, right here and now. Lawrence, for his part, was not affected by the general shyness. He whispered a running commentary in the intern's ear.

"This ain't my home group. I go to *Cleaning up the Mess*. Lots of clean time there, but this is a good one to come to. There's lots of newcomers in these rooms, so you get to see where you've been."

"We'll start now," called out a woman at the podium. "Hi, my name is Mabel, and I'm an alcoholic. We call this meeting *One Way Out* because AA is the one way out of the mess we made of our lives. Can we have a reader for the Preamble?"

Chairs scraped as everyone took a seat. Each individual surrounded himself with two or three empty ones in each direction. That's why all those chairs were necessary. Extra skin was needed, a suit of armor, a DMZ. A reader was selected.

"I never felt so alone as when I came out of rehab," said Lawrence. "They said to change people places and things, so I couldn't go around the people I used with. And my family wouldn't have me. They were sick of me; so that left no one and nothing but these meetings."

"Alcoholics Anonymous is a fellowship of men and women who share their experience, strength and hope with each other…"

For many, the extra chairs were not enough fortification to keep them safe. They put on a mask of derision to cloak their fears. They peered out of hooded sweatshirts, clutching a paper from the judge for the secretary to sign at the end of the meeting. They slumped, reclining in their chairs as if to say, "I'll sit here, but I'll be as far away from the speaker as I can. I'm not really afraid, you see, they went on. If I were, would I be flopped over this chair? Would my hood be up so I couldn't see around me? No, I'm fine."

"…We admitted we were powerless over alcohol, that our lives had become unmanageable…."

"Alcohol is not really my problem," said Lawrence. "I'm really more of a cocaine addict. But I hate going to NA meetings. There's too much chaos there, everyone talking at once. Where there are cocaine addicts, all you have to do is say the word *cocaine*, and they get excited, but the same thing doesn't happen with the word *alcohol*. Cocaine is so powerful; you only need the word to get excited. So I go to AA and whenever they say alcohol, I think drugs. It's all the same, anyway."

"Two: came to believe that a Power greater than ourselves could restore us to sanity. Three: made a decision to turn our will and our lives over to the care of God, as we understood Him...."

So that's what this is all about, Izzy speculated. They dressed up religion like therapy and snuck it into the hospital. A priest, long content with a sprinkling of widows in the pews at daily Mass, would have been ecstatic if vanloads of court mandated congregants pulled up to his church, as they do to many AA meetings. And what a diverse congregation he would have, for most churches content themselves with one slice of the ethnic pie of America. Here was the whole shebang. In one corner, the black troupe had silenced their rap, stilled their dance, and taken their seats. A smattering of Hispanic nurses who didn't care who knew, spent their lunch hour at the meeting. A doctor stood by the wall until he was paged away, and then he pushed through the homeless men gathered by the door. AA's the universal religion, but BYOG: bring your own God.

At the end of the readings, Mabel took over: "The empty chairs in the room remind us of the ones who have left us and still suffering addicts that are out there. Let's have a moment of silence for them all."

Instead of keeping silence, Lawrence began to recite the names of all he knew who died by drugs. "John, who went overboard with acid and jumped off a bridge, he was just eighteen. Then there's Bob, Wilma, Nate, Walt, Sue, and Sam who overdosed last month when that strong batch of heroin came in. Junkies are crazy, man. They were all clean, but they heard about an overdose, so they all went out to try it, thinking it must be good shit. Oh, and Hester, who was stationed in Japan and discovered how smooth Sake goes down. She drank till her liver burst."

Lawrence went on and on. Izzy didn't know if all the people in the room knew as many who had died as he had, that he began to understand they needed the extra chairs for all the ghosts that followed them. It must be that dead addicts weren't permitted to rest in a quiet grave or strum a harp in a peaceful paradise. They must be condemned to attend meetings until they save the folks they left behind. What fool claimed the dead tell no tales? Why did the insurance company pay out death benefits for those who lecture every day in these rooms? Hope feeds off the dead like maggots and faith is nourished by their decay. We hasten to speak well of the deceased, but reuse their biggest mistakes for detour signs.

"Hi, my name is Joanna," said the aged women at the podium, after having been introduced by Mabel. "I'm an alcoholic. It has been twenty years since my last drink."

The assembly broke into applause. This was her anniversary and they had come to hear her tell her story, as they had every year at this time. She was a great favorite of the alcoholics, having now spoken twenty times at that podium and having sponsored many in the crowd. They were like children, who, having found a great book for bedtime, insist on hearing it again and again. But, even one who had never heard her tell her story would've been drawn to this woman. She was in the Indian summer of old age: when, after winter crowns the head with white and the face is fissured with wrinkles, a kind of youthful bloom returns to the cheek; a glow, indicative of a state of grace.

Joanna stood silently at the podium for a while, even after the prolonged clapping ended, to enjoy the moment. As she stood there, Izzy noticed the peculiar construction of the podium in front of her. Like all podiums, it had a desk, upon which she folded her hands, supported by a tall box. However, the sides of the box were not plum, vertical supports, but rather, they went off at a slight angle, till, at a point six inches below the desk, the supports doubled back to be joined to the desk at a point directly above where they started. Astonished, Izzy whispered to Lawrence, "It's shaped like a coffin. She's speaking at a coffin." Joanna was speaking behind a podium that was nothing more than a small coffin, standing upright with a slanted desk screwed to the top.

The woman clearly enjoyed this moment. Indeed, she looked as though she enjoyed every one of them given to her in her old age. There is nothing like the smell of death to give a moment its savor, and we like our moments well seasoned. "Twenty years ago I took my last drink," she repeated. No one applauded again, but she had their attention. Nothing could be more full of meaning than for Joanna to stand behind this symbol of death and proclaim her victory, like Achilles crowing over the body of Hector.

Izzy enjoyed this moment also. He was beginning to get religion, despite the fact that no one had been able to give it to him before. This was no ordinary religion, he thought. It was not concerned with some past incident like Mount Sinai or Calvary or getting to heaven some day in the future. The Salvation these alcoholics were seeking was for today, one day at a time. The Devil was right on their heels, ready to call in his loan now. The coffin was ready. Izzy's moments hadn't mattered for him for a long time. He'd been treating his life as if it were a dress rehearsal before the real show; which some say it is, but how can they really be sure. He thought, from this point on, he would be hooked on meetings.

It's perhaps no accident that a coffin is shaped like a ship, for it's the vessel that transports us to parts unknown. All in the room were on their way, some voluntarily, others required, in this middle passage to transformation. Izzy was shackled now with all the rest. Indeed, the way he saw it, from now on, he would either have to become an alcoholic or a counselor.

Lawrence leaned over and explained, "We're grieving our drugs." True enough, too. They were grieving their drugs as well as all those who were taken by their drugs.

Then he told the intern a story. "I went to rehab once at the VA hospital. They had us go down to the woodshop and build a coffin. It was only about yay big. We put in an upholstered silk lining and the whole nine yards. They put some vodka, a syringe, a bong, and a pill bottle in that coffin and we had a funeral. The chaplain came and said a few prayers. Some of us made some speeches, saying how much we were going to miss drinking and drugging, but it was better off gone. They put the lid on top and had each of us drive a nail, closing it up. Then we took it up on the hill and buried it with military honors in the cemetery. By the time we were done, there wasn't a dry eye in the house."

"Did that help you say goodbye to drinking and drugging?"

"Naw, not at all; that night some of the guys snuck out of the unit and went up the hill and dug it up."

# Chapter 11 - Joanna's Story

"Hi, family," said Joanna from the coffin shaped podium. "I don't need to speak long. My story isn't a long one, but it's important that I tell it. There might be something important in it for you to hear. If there's only one person in the room who needs to hear my story, I'll be happy. If there isn't even one, I'll still be happy, because I need to tell it. My mother taught me that important things need to be said. One way, or another, they always come out someway.

"Any alcoholic who's been drinking will tell you her story, and it'll be a long one. She'll go on and on and on, and she'll never get to the point. Her story'll be like the man who took his dog for a walk and brought the leash, but forgot the dog." The crowd laughed.

"Alcoholics tell a lot of stories when they've been drinking," she continued, "but when they sober up, they don't have a thing to say. It was the hardest thing in the world for me to get up here the first time, but it was the best thing I ever did. I had to stand up in front of people, look them in the eye and say, I'm an alcoholic. I couldn't live my life until I did that. I didn't even know what my life was all about."

The crowd murmured their agreement. The newcomers under the hoods feared they'd be asked to speak next.

"Many alcoholics who stand up here will tell you how their drinking caused them to become homeless, lose their family, put them in jail, or ruined their health. None of that happened to me, but I was an alcoholic before anything ever happened. I was born to be an alcoholic. I was already there even before I took my first drink.

"Both my parents were alcoholics, so I was destined to become one. My Dad was the stay out all night kind, and my Mom was the kind that drank at home. Dad smashed up cars, chased women, and woke us all up when he came home in the middle of the night, sloshed. He'd be grumpy the next day and Mom would shush us all morning because he'd have to have it quiet. Sometimes she'd call in to work for him the next morning so he wouldn't have to get up. He smashed up a few cars drinking. This was before they took DWIs seriously, so he didn't get in much trouble with the law, but we were always broke because he'd have to keep fixing the car. My Mom took a part time job to help make ends meet. She did everything to make his life easier. She tried to be a good wife, almost too good.

"I was a good kid, too. I got all A's in school and I didn't make any trouble. There was already enough to worry about. When you're a kid and you have someone as unpredictable as my father around, you learn not to cause any trouble. You learn to become part of the furniture. You learn not to call too much attention to yourself because you never really knew what was going to happen next. Don't get me wrong, I loved my Dad, but I never wanted my friends to meet him, it would've been just too humiliating. I could've taken my mother by the shoulders and shook her, but I didn't. You see, alcoholism, a lot of the time, takes two: one to do the drinking, and one to pick up the pieces. Maybe it takes more than two, maybe it takes everyone else not saying anything or doing anything, either.

"I said my mother was an alcoholic, but she was a different kind. She drank secretly every day. She kept it together most days so that most people couldn't tell, but I knew. Dad was a happy drunk, he'd drink and get loud, tell stories, have a blast. Mom would drink to keep silent. But then one night she couldn't keep silent any longer.

"'Call your father,' she said to me, 'he's at the bar. There's something I want him to hear.' I often called him there. He'd be more likely to take the call if the bartender said I was on the phone than if his old lady was calling." The crowd chuckled. "Also," Joanna continued, "my Mom had been drinking more than usual that night, so she might not've been able to dial straight."

"'Here he is,' I said, and held the receiver up for her to take.

"'Tell him there's something I want him to hear.'

"'Dad,' I said, into the phone, 'There's something Mom wants you to hear.' I held up the receiver again."

Several in the room held their breath. They knew what was coming next.

"Instead of taking the phone, my Mom pulled out a handgun. My heart stopped. She put the gun up to her mouth like it was a microphone and pulled the trigger.

"Later, I heard someone under the kitchen table screaming. It was me. I had to get out of there. It was nighttime, I was in my nightgown, and barefoot. I had to walk through her blood.

The newcomers stared from out beneath their hoods like they'd been shot themselves.

Joanna was barely seventeen when she got married. She couldn't wait to get out of the house. There were two people who got roaring drunk at the wedding: her Dad, of course, and her new husband, who was just like him. She got drunk, too, but in her mother's hidden kind of way.

Even the hooded heads nodded in agreement, as she continued: "I loved it. I didn't just take a drink; it took me. It took me to a land far away where I didn't have to worry about anything or answer to anyone. I couldn't feel my mother's blood on my feet any more. My baby could be crying, and I wouldn't hear it. My husband could be chasing after women, and everyone would know, but I wouldn't care. I knew my husband wasn't treating me or the baby right and I should have said something, but I didn't have the guts. I was no better than my mother. Worse, I should have known better. Now I know that when you love someone, you have an obligation to tell them when they are hurting you and give them a chance to do better. I thought that a wife had to stick by her man, no matter what. I thought I didn't have any choice."

Years went by and she had more children. She got quieter and quieter. She kept on drinking and her husband kept right on running around. Then the most terrible thing happened. One day she'd sent all the kids out to play so she could be alone with her bottle. Her youngest had to come in the house to use the bathroom. There was something wrong with the door and it wouldn't open. The child knocked and she knocked, but Joanna was too passed out drunk to hear her. She knocked so hard she broke the glass, but Joanna still slept. The child tried to reach in to open up the door, but she was too short. She cut her wrist on the glass. She cried and cried, but Joanna went on sleeping while she was bleeding to death right on the porch. The mailman found her when he came, called the ambulance, and saved her life.

"I was still sleeping when the medics got there. One of them woke me up. 'How can you sleep?' He said, 'your child was bleeding to death on the porch.' My eyes opened to the horrible sight of my baby covered with blood, all too familiar.

"I said to myself, 'This time it's my fault.'

"I told my husband I wanted to go to rehab. I wasn't serious about quitting drinking, I just couldn't face the kids and wanted to punish myself and I could think of no better way than to go to rehab. He didn't want me to go, he didn't think my drinking was that bad and he wanted me to stay there and keep the house for him. I'd been a secret drinker, but now I began to do it out in the open. One night when he was home, I got myself completely sloshed, took off all my clothes, and ran naked down the street. He was convinced then."

The crowd sniggered.

"It was in rehab that I attended my first AA meeting. I still remember to this day, the first time I said, 'I'm Joanna, I'm an alcoholic.' I felt such freedom, so much relief to say those words. We're not supposed to like labels and categories, but I love mine. It tells me everything I need to know about me. Thank you."

# Chapter 12 - The Charts

Returning from the meeting, Izzy found Craig still in the office stooped over his desk like a monk transcribing the Holy Scriptures. In fact, he was writing in clients' charts, and not Holy Scriptures. Although, later, when he showed the intern the cabinet in which they were kept, how they kept the cabinet locked, and, after taking them out of the cabinet into their office, they weren't to leave the charts unattended, Izzy couldn't help but compare the procedure to that of taking the Torah out of the Ark. There is a suitable way to handle mysteries.

A great column of charts was stacked on his desk and, with this much documentation ahead of him, Craig kept diligently at his work and took no notice of the intern when he entered. Izzy took a seat at his desk and thought about what he had heard in the meeting. He was deeply affected by the meeting and yearned to tell Craig all about it. He craved his approval, as he had never felt of any professor before. But, he contented himself with watching him while thinking of Joanna's story and musing about the charts. Each chart in that stack contained, within its manila cover, a story similar to hers. The man who wrote in the charts also had a story. The unit they worked in, the department, the hospital; they all contained stories within stories like a huge narrating Russian doll. But that wasn't the end of it. Each of these stories affected others. Just as Craig wrote in some charts, and affected the life course of the person represented by the chart, he was also, in turn, affected by them, in the same way as Izzy was affected by Craig, Joanna, Lawrence, and all the others. He needed a chart to keep it all straight.

At this point, Craig put down his pen and it looked as though he would speak. He didn't; instead, he reached over and opened up a fat book he kept on his desk. It was the DSM, the Diagnostic Statistical Manual: the counselor's Bible, describing hundreds of mental conditions and how to diagnose them. Later they would go over this text in detail when Craig endeavored to explain the purpose of its coding of criteria. Still later, Izzy would learn that the DSM was another chart, a map of psychopathology, outlining the boundary between madness and sanity, depression and despair, brilliance and mania, imagination and psychosis. As if those qualities could be reckoned by adding things up; as if those boundaries were not like the boundary between the sea and the shore, always modified by the tides, shifting sands, and lapping waves. Craig chewed on his fingernail while consulting the book. Then, deciding on a diagnosis, he noted it in a chart, closed it up, and put it aside, starting a second pile.

Izzy would learn that all it takes is one word and we think we know a person. Alcoholic, intern, biker, stepfather; all these words provide what we think is a complete image. Joanna loved her label, but, despite what she said, a map is not the territory. It is only a bare representation of reality. While we might draw a road map, a topographical map, or a soil map - if we try to put everything on a map, roads, topography, and soil - we don't have a map at all, we have the reality. In the same way, the chart, the diagnosis, and even the story is not the person; and any chart that would pretend to be complete is not a chart anymore, it's a person, and it might as well tuck in its shirt and walk away at that point.

On the other hand, counselors know that the thicker the chart, the worse the prognosis. Although, they believe they can help people when they can say a lot about them, in actuality it's as if they become buried under a mountain of words, as a child inters his sleeping father with sand at the beach, till he can't move from the spot where he's stuck. Words both clarify and obscure, as a flashlight illuminates one object and puts another in a shadow.

If one looked at Craig in a certain light, considering his long hair, beard, and thick workingman's hands, one might have thought he was St Peter, referring to his chart of good deeds and bad as one stands before him at those pearly gates. It would be a remarkable resemblance if the light were bad enough. As Izzy thought about it, Craig's charts bore a remarkable resemblance to St Peter's chart as well. Heaven, he was told, has its assessments and keeps its progress notes and correspondence on record. It might even have a treatment plan where it carefully notes strengths and weaknesses, goals and objectives. However, Craig scrupulously had his clients review their treatment plans and sign them to prove that they've seen them. Who, on the other hand, has ever seen, in writing, God's personalized plan?

While Izzy studied Craig, the supervisor continued to pay no attention to the intern, as if it made no difference that he was there or not. He was completely occupied with his writing. Considering the fuss he made earlier that day over sharing his office, Izzy thought his indifference was very strange. But he was a strange man; that much should be plain. He, like Joanna, was clearly a man who had come a long way in his life and underwent massive revisions. He spent his time among doctors, nurses, and overeducated interns, people as odd to him as if they resided on the former planet Pluto, yet he continued to be the person he was and had no need to bow and scrape at their arrival. He conserved his store of serenity, satisfied with his own companionship. He was a true philosopher, although undoubtedly he had no use for such a fine title. He was a man you could rely on in a jam, an old sea captain, as salty as the sea itself, who had no fear of the monsters of the deep and would pilot the ship to the end of the earth. He was a wagon train scout who had been through these parts before and knew the way. He was Virgil to Izzy's Dante. The student was tremendously reassured to have such a guide for his internship, he don't know why anyone would want anyone else.

Yet, this man seemed an inscrutable mystery, one that Izzy longed to explore. It seemed that he had license to. After all, these addicts seem to think it is important to tell their story. No one else would broadcast his or her intimate secrets in public, anonymity or no. This made the intern bold enough to inquire, as a way of opening Craig up, "How long do you have clean?"

"What do you think this is? I'm not a fucking character in one of your books, college boy. Make yourself useful and get me some coffee; and a donut, plain donut. Don't give me any of that jelly crap."

# Chapter 13 - Pip

As the days went by, it seemed to Izzy that Craig got used to the idea of having an intern around to do all of his urine screens and get him his coffee and plain donuts. He also liked to lend him out to others to fulfill the same functions, thus gaining status in clinic politics. For instance, one day Miss Bella was critical of Craig's swearing, as we have already seen she could be. Later that same day, he sent Izzy out to find some Krispy Kremes at the same time as she was going to collect some piss. Craig didn't even like Krispy Kremes, but, by the time Izzy returned with a box full of them, Miss Bella had made the connection and, from then on, turned a deaf ear to his cussing. Mr. Pellegrino, who had no intern to put up for barter and did enjoy the Krispy Kremes, asked Izzy for his professor's number, so that he could get an intern of his own and be able to cuss as he wanted. But, alas, all the interns were already assigned for the semester.

The days went by at the clinic without a sighting of Dr Ahern. Most assumed that he arrived early in the morning, and stayed until late at night. He never came out of his office. Only his secretary, who spoke to no one, went in and out with folders and files. Every time Izzy had an occasion to come up from the basement, where the drug and alcohol program operated, to the first floor mental health clinic, he gazed towards The Director's office door. Izzy couldn't quiet his thoughts about this strange director who directed in absentia. Perhaps the insinuations of the thin man at the hospital entrance had burrowed into his brain and made a home there. He could not help but smile, first at his solemn pronouncements, and then at himself, for half believing them.

Despite his antisocial behavior, everyone at the clinic was very excited that Dr Ahern had come to work there. He was well known, a giant, a guru, in the field. They had all read his books, and attended his classes or conferences. Izzy's professor, when he heard, was ready to switch places with him for a month, so that he could intern under the famous Dr Ahern. He was so well regarded, in fact, that had he come to the clinic dressed like a clown, standing on his head, and had everyone barking like dogs at the clients, they'd have hailed it as a new, groundbreaking method.

One day, when Izzy was up on the first floor on some errand, Dr Ahern's door was shut as always. The only sign of an occupant was the clacking of a keyboard from within. Ahern's inscrutable secretary, a pale, lumpy woman called Mrs. Pillsbury, sat in front of it, guarding it like a watchdog. Next to her sat a black Labrador retriever with a hospital badge affixed to his collar. The dog was much friendlier than Mrs. Pillsbury. He came over for a pet, and lolled his tongue while the intern rubbed behind his ears.

"That's Dr Ahern's dog," said Mrs. Pillsbury, as if to say, don't touch him, he belongs to the boss. Izzy pulled his hand away, not afraid of the dog's bite, but Mrs Pillsbury's. The black lab rooted his nose back under the intern's hand for more petting. The dog had his photograph on his badge, just as Izzy had, as well as his name, Pip, and his title, Pet Therapist. The two visited for a spell, but, as the conversation lagged, Izzy bid adieu, finished his errand, and went back to his desk.

A little while later, as he and Craig sat in their office together, Craig, writing in charts, and the intern, filling out forms, Izzy began to grow more and more resentful. His biggest disappointment about the internship, thus far, was that he didn't get to do actual therapy with clients. He filled out forms, ran errands, and collected a swimming pool of piss, but no therapy. Once, Izzy joked that he'd move his desk and chair into the men's room, but when Craig said he thought it was a good idea, he'd have his office back, Izzy made no more jokes about it. Not once had Craig permitted him to set foot in a group or an individual session, much less have a group or individual of his own. Now here was a dog, a fine dog, but a dog, just the same, who was permitted to do therapy, while the disgruntled intern wasn't. Izzy said something about it to Craig.

"The dog's better at it than you," was his answer.

"Of course he is. His supervisor let him, like, practice at it in his internship."

"Don't be in such a hurry. Wanting is better than having," he said.

Craig being a man of few words, Izzy tended to scrutinize whatever he did say, just to get the meaning out of it. He asked him to clarify himself.

"It's like, when you're at a party and some cock tease has you all excited, but she's not putting out. You know she's holding off because she's waiting for you to get her some blow, or she wants to keep her options open to see if anyone better might come along before she goes home with you. If you know you're going to have a taste of that skank eventually, then you're willing to wait and enjoy yourself. But, if you think she's going to pass out before you get your rocks off, then you better get that quickie in the bathroom."

It took the intern a while to unravel the parable. Therapy was the skank. If the internship was going to run out, then he'd better get some therapy done before it's over. But he should enjoy himself if he still has time because a much-anticipated climax after an escalating period of foreplay is far better than a quickie in the bathroom. Wanting is better than having.

"I get it. But the trouble is I'm not enjoying myself. I'm watching people piss, for crying out loud."

"You're not here to enjoy yourself. This is work, and part of the job is watching people piss. If you didn't do it, then I would have to; and you need to do it more."

"Why do I need to watch people piss?"

"Because all you've done all your life was have people hand you things and they've watched you piss it all away. You need to watch other people piss for a while and hand that to you. Then you'll be ready to do therapy."

There wasn't much Izzy could say. Craig was right about him. It was hard, but it felt good to admit it. People had handed everything to him. And what did Izzy have to show for it? He'd think about doing urine screens in a new way: like it was getting the world back into balance. But what did that have to do with therapy?

"Because therapy is all about being real; if you don't know what real is, you're not going to help anyone else be real."

"Do you know what real is?"

And then Craig told Izzy his story.

# Chapter 14 - Cornwhacker

Craig's best buddy, Cornwhacker, got his name when they were riding through Nebraska and he developed a game of tilting at the corn with a long spear on his motorcycle, trying to impale an ear. The game ran its course and he tired of it by the time they reached the wheat lands of the Great Plains, but the name stuck. They shared a tent. Lest you think there was some greasy stuff going on between the motorcyclists in the tent, you should know there was a Mrs. Cornwhacker, also; and they shared her, too.

There were some quiet evenings on the road and some wild evenings that turned into wild nights. On quiet evenings, they'd pitch the tent and Mr. and Mrs. Cornwhacker would have their time inside first because marriage should have its prerogatives. Craig would watch the sunset with the gang and a keg of beer; then he would take his turn in the tent while Cornwhacker worked on the keg. Afterwards, they would all sit together in the tent and unwind with a doobie. More than once, they fell asleep this way and ignited the tent or the sleeping bags with the doobie. Once Mrs. Cornwhacker got some serious burns over half her face, but if you looked on the other half, she was fine, and so there was little reason to discontinue the snug routine.

On wild nights they had crank and that enabled them to stay up longer, have more turns in the tent, and go through countless kegs, maintaining a steady buzz until sunrise, when they would all pass out for the better part of the day. The wild nights were much preferred by the motorcycle gang. In fact, the wild nights were about all they talked about during the quiet ones. Looking back, however, one can affirm that it is important to keep some balance between energy and rest, action and contemplation.

They did some riding, too, all over the country. There was nothing better in this world to Craig, than flying down the road, the wind running its fingers through his hair and a Harley throbbing in his crotch. They had no particular destination; they just went this way and that. Craig generally rode behind Cornwhacker, not because The Whacker showed him the way, but because he liked to look at Mrs. Cornwhacker's tight ass straddling the seat. They had no need for money. In the small towns wherever they went, people gave them whatever they wanted. Well, not that, exactly. They roared into town on two hundred bikes, shaking everybody's windows and rattling everybody's bones, and took what they wanted, never offering to pay, and no one stopped them. In all, it was a decent life, if being like a plague of locusts can be said to be decent.

Like all good things, it had to come to an end. As is often the case, the end started with a single, innocent action, which led to an inescapable consequence, progressing remorselessly to a tragic conclusion. This single action is often very ordinary, if portentous. We can often recognize it for what it is, but are powerless to escape its trap. This is how it started: Mrs. Cornwhacker stole a bottle of peppermint schnapps. The Mrs. rarely drank. After all, she was generally busy in the tent while the kegs were being drained. It was a good thing that she rarely drank because, when she did, she turned mean. She was not a happy drunk, you see, she was a mean one. She was the most compliant person in the world when sober, put up with Cornwhacker's antics, and everyone approved of her hospitality in the tent; but, when she got some liquor in her, you knew how she really felt. Then, no man was safe from her spite and her spittle, and no bike was safe from her fury.

Craig and Cornwhacker were at the liquor store with her when they saw her do it. They'd been busy rolling kegs out of the door and strapping them on bikes when she lifted the schnapps off the shelf and tucked it under her arm. The two only had to exchange a quick, knowing glance before they marched together to the owner of the liquor store and reported the theft.

They knew she'd be pissed if she spent time in jail because they turned her in, but they'd rather have her pissed sober than pissed drunk. The owner only looked at them wide eyed and declared that he would never, never call the cops. They could take whatever they wanted, but please leave. He was a family man and had a wife and two children who depended on him. Cornwhacker's ire rose at the man's lack of self-respect, for he was, admittedly, a righteous biker. A man shouldn't let a bitch just take things, he declared, because then the bitches would just take whatever they wanted. He decided to teach the owner a lesson by smashing every bottle of liquor in the store. He didn't do it all himself, for, when the other bikers heard the commotion, they all joined in the fun. The owner cowered, crying behind the counter while every bottle was taken by the neck and smashed. When they were done, the gang exited, laughing and sucking on their cuts, leaving the floor of the store covered in broken glass and reeking like a late night lush.

At camp, while the bikers pumped up the kegs and cranked themselves up with crystal, Craig and Cornwhacker consulted with one another over a doobie because they needed to be clear headed. Come what may, they couldn't let Mrs. Cornwhacker drink the schnapps. Then Craig, who was the more intelligent of the two, came up with a brilliant idea: Cornwhacker would make his conjugal visit to the tent and steal the bottle from her.

This caper was made more complicated by the fact that, when they arrived at the tent, Mrs. Cornwhacker was within and had already started in on the bottle. The Wacker started in on her, but she wouldn't let it go. Craig assessed the situation from outside the tent. There was only one thing to do: he was going to have to go in and take it himself.

Up to this point, the two friends had always maintained separate tent visits and resisted forming a threesome. They weren't queers, after all. But now the situation was dire and sacrifices would have to be made. When Craig entered the tent, Mrs. Cornwhacker was keeping Mr. Cornwhacker's ears warm between her thighs while she took another slug on the bottle.

Craig saw he would have to occupy the upper half and so, with his tongue, he dove into her minty mouth and pinned her hands back. After a spell, she got them free and Craig thought he would have to wrestle the bottle away from her, but she let go of it and started to undo his fly. The schnapps lay on the floor of the tent, unclaimed, so Craig snatched it up. He was about to make a hasty exit, pleading that he couldn't get hard, but his penis sprang from his undone fly like a released catapult. When Mrs. Cornwhacker started to suck, Craig decided he could wait a while before he left.

The three continued in this vein until, first, Mrs. Cornwhacker came, and then came Craig. For a minute, Craig forgot his mission until Mrs. Cornwhacker, wanting a chaser, reached for the schnapps. Then Craig remembered why he had come before he came. With his pants undone, he tucked the bottle under his arm and charged out of the tent like a fullback breaking through the line. Mrs. Cornwhacker ran after him, bare assed and furious, but still not as furious as when she was fully drunk. The tent collapsed behind Mrs. Cornwhacker and Mr. Cornwhacker struggled out of it. The gang watched the scene from the kegs and cheered on all the participants. Craig reached his bike and Mrs. Cornwhacker grabbed at the seat as he kicked it to life. She couldn't hold on, though, as he sped away, clenching the schnapps between his legs.

During the get away, Mr. Cornwhacker crept towards his bike, quietly because he didn't want Mrs. Cornwhacker to see him go towards it and remember that she had a key. That was a good thing, because, as soon as she was done giving the finger to the jeering bikers by the kegs, she ran back to the tent to get the key. Mr. Cornwhacker had plenty of time to get on his bike and ride after Craig, following the plume of dust that rose up behind him, for they were on a dirt back road, out in the country.

Mr. Cornwhacker found his friend sitting under a cottonwood by a river. It was a pretty big river. It might have been the Missouri because that's where they were, in Missouri. When he shut off the bike there was no other sound but the sound of the river, no betrayed banshee could be heard stalking them on a stolen bike. Just the same, they knew it was just a matter of time before Mrs. Cornwhacker coaxed some horny biker, who had the hots for her, into letting her borrow his bike. The prudent thing to do would be to finish the bottle before she got to it. It would take some doing. Even though Mrs. Cornwhacker had already had a few swallows, this bottle was the largest on the market. They figured they were up to the task, though, because they were experienced drinkers. So they set to work in a craftsman-like manner while the big, thirsty Missouri staggered past them and their cottonwood tree.

It was autumn and nightfall, and the air was starting to get nippy. Craig had his jacket and Cornwhacker didn't so they shared it by spreading it over them like a blanket. Even though they had no woman lying between them now, it was every bit as snug as the evenings in the tent. The schnapps felt like a flame reaching down their throats into their bellies and the rest of their bodies were warm from shared body heat. Their noses were cold, though; but that made it all the more delightful, for to enjoy warmth best, some tiny part of us must be chilled.

The two continued in this cozy manner while the schnapps set to work inside them, unlocking every drawer and cupboard like a meticulous health inspector. From time to time, Craig shut his eyes to better feel the groping fingers of the schnapps on his body. Then, fighting sleep, for he had not prepared himself for a drinking binge with crank, he startled awake. One of these awakenings came, arm in arm, with a revelation. He and Cornwhacker shared one woman, one jacket, one tent, one bottle, and one friendship. They were really one person, not two. That's why they hung together. That's why they were inseparable. Of course, they didn't share everything. Whacker had the indignation and Craig had the intelligence, but that just proved the point. They didn't need everything alone, because together they shared. Of course, they had two bikes to ride, two pricks to fuck with, and two mouths to drink beer and do drugs with, but why not? If you're going to be one person, go ahead and have two bodies and have twice the fun. The whole arrangement had distinct advantages; you had to admit.

Craig no sooner had this thought than he spoke it aloud, for there is no difference between thinking a thought and speaking it aloud when schnapps has its way. Whacker didn't reply. Instead, he suddenly flung the jacket off them and stood up. Craig thought he had said some queer thing and Whacker was going to beat the shit out of him to teach him a lesson, but Whacker went to his bike. It wasn't like The Whack Man to run away in an indignant huff, thought Craig, but, when he heard the buzz of an approaching bike, he understood the situation. Mrs. Cornwhacker was coming for them.

If the friends had remained under their cottonwood tree by the river in the gathering dusk, then Mrs. Cornwhacker probably never would have found them. But, just as a squirrel treed by a dog will try to make a run for it out of stupid anxiety instead of staying put and waiting it out, Whacker took flight on his bike before Craig could stop him. Mrs. Cornwhacker easily took up the scent and chased him down the river road and Craig followed, just to see what happened. The chase continued for a mile or two and Whacker still might have gotten away because he was a good rider, but there was too much schnapps involved. While schnapps may be a brilliant hostess, good at getting a conversation going, it's a lousy driver; and Whacker, instead of holding a tight turn, rode his bike over a bank and into the river.

Mrs. Cornwhacker saw the accident and slammed on the brakes. She didn't ride much, and so she couldn't control the bike as it lay down, skidding over her pinned leg on the gravel road. Craig, following hard behind, couldn't avoid hitting her. When his bike stopped, he kept going, sailing over the handlebars and somersaulting on the road. Drunk people often walk away from accidents unharmed, and so did he, but it took him a while to collect himself. By that time, it was too late for Cornwhacker, who had been knocked unconscious and drowned in the river. Craig fished him out and tried mouth to mouth, but he didn't know mouth to mouth. Eventually he gave up, sobbed over Whacker's body, and passed out, drunk, on his chest.

# Chapter 15 - Abraham Lincoln

Some days went by, after Craig told Izzy the story, and they embarked on a glorious, multicolored autumn. The cold, crisp days were like rainbow sherbet. The nights were like snooty ladies, dressed in jewels and black velour jumpsuits. It was hard to choose between the two of them, so Izzy often awoke early in the morning, when the ladies were still out, and went to work through a crystalline exhibition, the colors of the leaves hazy in the half-light of dawn. After parking his car, he would take a long look over the ramparts of the garage at all this transitory brilliance before burrowing into the climate-controlled eternity of the medical center.

It was good for the intern to get to work before anyone else. He could make the coffee, before anyone arrived, and write client's names on the urine cups in Craig's office, without him complaining that the pen made too much noise. It was on one such morning that, papers in hand, he encountered Dr Ahern at the copier.

Other than this sighting, which we will learn more about later; Dr Ahern was never seen outside of his office and never allowed anyone except his secretary within it. There were some at the clinic who supposed that the man arrived every day before anyone else, slipped unseen behind the door of his lair, and slipped out of it every night after everyone left. Others thought he lived in his office and never went home. A few theorized that the reclusive Dr Ahern was only a figurehead and the secretary was acting as regent; however, when she began to emerge from the sanctuary now and then with orders so out of the ordinary these rumors were set to rest.

The first order decreed that the two phone lists of clinic personnel, one list for Mental Health, and the other for Chemical Dependency, the two divisions of the Department of Behavioral Health, be combined to one list. No one could discern the purpose of this; it wasted paper, and made work for the support staff. The Head Administrator of the department was so disturbed that she sought an audience with Dr Ahern, only to be turned away by the secretary.

The second order proclaimed that all new intakes be seen by an interdisciplinary team from both Mental Health and Chemical Dependency before they were admitted to either division. When as many as six people in the two divisions tried to schedule a meeting that they all could attend, it caused such uproar that the rebuffed Head Administrator had to overcome her pique and sort it all out. Craig grumbled about this new requirement more than anyone. In addition to the hassle of finding the time, he seldom felt comfortable sitting in the same room with Mental Health staff whom he regarded as privileged, overeducated Pollyannas who showered manipulative drug seekers with benzodiazepines and unconditional positive regard like indulgent grandparents when all they really needed was a good swift kick in the ass. Thinking he needed an ally, and that Izzy would be one, Craig invited the intern to join him in the first Interdisciplinary Admission Meeting.

The Head Administrator presided over the meeting, being the one person, besides Dr Ahern, his secretary, and the therapy dog, Pip, who worked for neither Mental Health nor Chemical Dependency, but both, simultaneously. Most health care is organized along two parallel chains of command so that everyone answers to two masters: administrative and clinical. There are two heads to every department, like the two Consuls of the Roman Republic, which vie for influence and control: the administrative head, which hires and fires and writes out the checks, and the clinical head that plans the treatment. Dr Ahern was the clinical head of Behavioral Health, and The Head Administrator was his administrative foil.

The Administrator's name is irrelevant. She was the perfect bureaucrat and had completely subsumed personality into function. They didn't call her by name. They called her The Head Administrator because that's all she was and if she had anything else to her that wasn't Administrator, it didn't show it at work. In fact, the only clue to her personality was the ever-present take out cup of Starbuck's coffee she carried around: a non-fat latte *grande* with no sugar, as bitter and whipped as she was. She continuously drank from it, and, when it went dry, she held it as a queen holds her scepter.

The Head Administrator was a thin, serious woman, as if she had scraped off anything superfluous from her frame. Her skin fit her as closely as an Academy Awards' gown, as if she had tucked in anything extra that might be snagged and ironed out any wrinkles in which ambiguities might hide. Looking into her eyes, one might see the images of a million perils that beset the clinic, reflected. She went on constantly that the operation might be sued, or its licenses revoked. "I will have no staff," she is famously said to have said, "That, while writing in the charts, does not imagine a lawyer looking over one shoulder and a regulator looking over the other."

"Yessiree," said the psychiatrist, Dr Staub. "Our Head Administrator is the most careful person in The Medical Center." However, we will soon wonder what the word careful means in relation to a clinician like Dr Staub.

The Head Administrator, despite being the head of a whole clinic full of agents of change, was no change agent herself. In the therapy business, flexibility and willingness to change should be bought up in advance and stored where easily accessible. They are the staples of the outfit, like tissues and copier paper, without which it could scarcely operate. The Head Administrator seemed to think that such qualities should be hoarded, so as not to waste them.

She was not fond of any of Dr Ahern's innovations, but liked the Interdisciplinary Admission Meeting least of all. Bringing Mental Health together with Chemical Dependency seemed to her like a recipe for a bomb, the two parts of the department having very different views on things. Having them meet in the presence of a client was like a bomb in a fireworks factory. She would do her best to keep that bomb from blowing.

Concerned she might run out of Starbucks early because she nervously drank it fast, she fortified herself with a *venti*. All the group rooms must have been in use, because they sat cramped in The Head Administrator's office, knee to knee: Dr Staub, representing psychiatry; the psychologist, Dave Flass; a social worker; a nurse; Craig and Izzy. The idea, as they surmised, was to get all the disciplines together, with their unique perspectives and approaches, to look at the problem, the new client, from a variety of angles; sort of like getting six blind men together to examine an elephant.

At first these six blind men seemed more intent on beating each other with their canes than identifying the elephant. Dr Flass attempted to dazzle everyone with a brilliant interpretation of the first client's hallucinations, as if to demonstrate that psychologists were as good as psychiatrists and should be paid the same. They all just rolled their eyes. If Dr Ahern had imagined they'd be conducting all night bull sessions and emerge with crystal clear diagnoses and needle sharp therapeutic interventions, he'd been around graduate students too long. The social worker oozed empathy all over the second client who had a panic attack in the room, as if to prove social workers have a better bedside manner than doctors. But all she got were sighs. They all just looked restless when Craig tried to ask questions about alcohol use that nobody thought to ask of the third, a depressed client. Once everyone stopped trying to score points, they all just wanted to reach a disposition, get out of there, and avoid picking up the difficult cases. That much, to The Head Administrator's delight, everyone agreed on, so she could have gotten by with a *grande*.

They were an hour into the process, had seen and disposed of five cases, when in came Bob. As they made room for him in the circle, the nurse read the summary of his case, like a butler announcing introductions. "Fifty-two year old, divorced, unemployed, Irish American male, supported by welfare, on Medicaid, with cirrhosis of the liver. He is referred by his PCP for outpatient chemical dependency treatment and is on the list for a transplant. The client just completed inpatient CD for the fourth time. He had failed to follow through with aftercare all the other times. He's on probation for his third DWI."

One might think Bob would hang his head sheepishly during this recital of his failures, but he glad-handed everyone like he was running for president. The Head Administrator started off with introductions and an explanation of the process of The Interdisciplinary Admission Meeting, or IAM, as she had begun to call it. Bob kept up a patter all the way through it, going from his upcoming liver transplant, to Mickey Mantle, to his favorite recipe for liver and onions, and on to why Vidalia onions were so sweet. He had certainly kissed the Blarney Stone. Craig sighed, knowing that Bob was headed his way. This was not a promising case and no one else would be able to talk in group if Bob was around. He nudged his intern, "Ask him if he's an alcoholic."

Ask him if he's an alcoholic? thought Izzy. Isn't it obvious? What else would he be? Then he thought, oh, Craig's hoping might say he wasn't an alcoholic and he would have a pretext not to admit him. Craig would declare, You can't fix something that ain't broke. Now, he went on thinking, why does he want *me* to ask him? I'm just an intern, right? Why would Craig want me to interview a client in front of the whole team? Is he trying to humiliate me? I can't ask the man, he won't stop talking. I was raised to not interrupt people.

Craig nudged the intern again.

"Er, excuse me... excuse me, sir. Are you... are you, like, an alcoholic?"

Bob stopped talking. He looked at Izzy for one, sustained beat, and said, "Are you Abraham Lincoln?"

Izzy was too stunned to know whether he was Lincoln or not. While he tried to sort it all out, Bob went on about Lincoln's presidency, slavery, the Underground Railroad, and the price of cotton in Georgia.

It was Dr Staub who rescued then all from a dissertation on the Southern economy. He squinted his eyes and leaned in until Bob stopped.

"Does your mind race?" he asked.

"Why… yes!" answered Bob, amazed that someone knew it.

Dr Staub was already scribbling on a prescription pad. "You have bipolar disorder. Take this and see me in a month."

They got Bob out of the room before he launched on to another subject. "You don't look anything like Abraham Lincoln," joked Dr Staub to Izzy.

Later, the intern told Craig he was impressed that Dr Staub, after spending five minutes with a man and asking one question, could come up with a diagnosis like that. He had a lot to learn.

"Yup," said Craig. "He's got the fastest prescription pad in the west. Anyone can go to him and get whatever drugs they want. One day I told him about my wife and he had a prescription for Valium written out before I even finished."

"Your wife? I didn't know you were married."

"I'm not any more. And I wasn't then. He gave me a prescription for someone I hadn't even seen in years and he'd never seen. Addicts have to stay away from doctors. They can't trust them and they can't trust themselves to be with them. That's all there is to it."

"Why did he think she needed Valium?"

Then, by way of an answer, he told Izzy how he met her.

# Chapter 16 - Schubert and Daughters

A long, lonely road led up to Ted Schubert's Sawmill. No one ever came by, but Craig did, because no matter how lonely a place can be, a man with nowhere left to go - broke, lonesome, and grieving - can find it.

He parked his bike by a pile of firewood logs that were turning black at the ends and growing fungus in the middles. That Ted's firewood pile was going bad was a sign of good business and an indication he might be hiring. Those logs were the tops of some fine oak Ted had cut more than two years back. The more valuable parts of the trees had long ago been sawed into squares and shipped off to some furniture mill. By the time Ted could get around to making firewood out of the tops, the oak will have been turned into a rocking chair upon which his customer may sit as he enjoys the fire from the rest of the tree.

As Craig reached the end of the pile, he sprang back suddenly as a tractor carrying some beech logs cut him off. The tractor, a blue and white Ford 9N with a homemade front-end loader, whined by in fourth gear. The logs carried in front overbalanced it so that its back wheels lifted up off the ground and spun gravel. At the wheel of the seesawing tractor was a fifteen-year-old girl just home from school with a pack of books still strapped to her back. The sign in the yard read, *Schubert & Daughters, Lumber Co.*, and this was Crystal, the younger of the two.

Years ago Schubert's wife, Sara, ran off towards less lonely roads and left him with the two girls: Crystal and Leah. Ted put up a sign that read, *Schubert & Daughters, Rabbits*, and set to building rows and rows of cages. They filled in no time, of course, and Crystal toddled from one end to the other, feeding lettuce. But the girls objected to the butchering, so they sold off the rabbits and raised goats. They made a new sign and the girls braided their blond hair to look like Heidi when they brought their cheeses to the Farmer's Market in the city. Ted built fence, but the goats kept getting out no matter how high he made it, the grass being greener and all. The girls loved the goats, but Ted, who already had a wife run off, had little patience for their capers. He became convinced that there was more money, and less chasing, in sawing logs. He repainted the sign and let the girls keep their favorite goat. One could drive by and all that would be left in the field would be the sign and the single lonely goat chewing it, as if making the sign go away would bring back the herd.

Soon the sign and the goat were joined by piles of logs that Ted had cut and Crystal skidded to the pasture. They then set up a mill that commenced to saw up the lumber for the pole barn to shelter it, like a worm spinning its own cocoon. An immense roof that could cover four sawmills now loomed over what was once the pasture. It seemed to be built as if to convince the girls that big things were coming their way, if they would only stay.

Craig picked his way around the log piles, keeping a lookout for the hyperactive teenager on the 9N. The goat was working on some weeds and a barking German shepherd pup was tied to a pole in the dusty, empty end of the barn. The structure only had one wall yet complete, sheltering the workers from the coldest wind from the west. Spare circular saws hung from nails driven into the wall. The wind, sweeping around the corner of the barn, picked up and swirled sawdust in mini tornadoes. When the machinery was silent at night, the spare saws, rung by the wind, could be heard for miles, tolling like church bells.

Ted's crew was hard at work within the barn now, and it was the rumbling of the mill that could be heard for miles. Stepping inside, Craig could see Ted working on the headsaw at a brisk pace. A gray beard flattened against his broad chest as he canted a new log onto the carriage. Holding it in place with his knee, he dogged it down with the severe efficiency of one who knows the place for everything. He then leaned on a lever and the log was winched into the spinning teeth of the headsaw. The saw's rattley breath turned into a growl as it bit into the log. Ted's eyes were steely blue and, between them, the beard, and his zeal, you might have thought he was John Brown, sawing the country in two. When the cut was complete, he threw back the lever, and the carriage returned to its place as he reached within inches of the saw teeth to clear away the slab.

"I don't need a guard on my saw," he always said, "I know where the teeth are."

As Ted began to peel off planks of clear sapwood, he pushed them on a roller table towards the eldest daughter, Leah, who shoved them through the edger. Leah, whose figure was substantial enough for Craig to enjoy through her coveralls, trimmed straight the edges of the slabs; that done, she seized the edgings and threw them like javelins into the firewood pile. The two, father and daughter, worked together as wordless as enmeshed gears, anticipating each other's every movement.

Ted motioned to Craig to fix himself a cup of coffee and, as he went below the carriage track, he found that he was not alone in his admiration of the two girls. He found a slack jawed teenage boy, leaning on a shovel, staring up at the Amazon who threw her javelins with haughty distain. The boy was no relation. No doubt he had come for the perky Crystal and discovered the remote beauty, Leah, who had quit school long ago and, rarely leaving the woods, was unknown to the young people. Not wanting to lose a daughter, Ted kept the boy close at hand, gave him a shovel, and put him to work on the sawdust pile.

Craig fixed his coffee and drank it slowly as he watched. From time to time, a gust of wind swept the mill floor above clean of sawdust. He covered the cup with his hand to protect it from flying flakes. Below the saws, the chips, undisturbed by the boy leaning on his shovel, collected in a heap. Individual chips were flung from the saw and cascaded down the pile, until, finding their place, they settled for a while. Every now and then little avalanches would start, as the weight of new chips would disrupt the balance of the pile.

Craig was so caught up in his musings he startled when Ted dashed down to the mill engine, let out the clutch, and pulled the choke. The engine lugged to a stop as the headsaw spun free. Had something gone horribly wrong?

"Sara." The man said as his face struggled between hope and anger. The headsaw was still spinning, as they looked each other up and down. Leah pulled off her gloves and shook the sawdust out. Her face was set hard and a hurt was creeping into her jaw. She looked at her mother as one might regard an old work glove with its fingers packed too full of sawdust to wear. Crystal parked the 9N nearby and bounded off it. She began to run towards her mother, but, seeing the tension in the scene, she stopped and unstrapped her backpack.

Ted asked Sara, "What do you mean by coming here?"

"Aren't these my children? I came to see them."

"Are they? They've been your children all along, you haven't wanted to see them for years."

Sara was a fine looking woman whose genes contributed to Leah's beauty and Crystal's sparkle, but Ted's look cut and stacked her as if she were no more than a pile of peckerwood thrown out back, waiting to rot. It was a look that only could mean that he was cradling a loader full of pain inside.

Craig had come for a job and had, instead, been cast in a soap opera. He was looking for a place to retreat.

Crystal unchained the German shepherd. He hunkered down on his forequarters and playfully barked. She barked back to him. He began to dash around on his four legs as Crystal had on her 9N.

"I left you, all right, and I haven't seen the girls, but I've come to see them now. I want them to know that they have choices and they don't need to stay here. You can't hold them here forever to keep you company."

Leah turned her back to them as she began to cry. She faced the swing saw, a twelve-inch blade mounted on a pendulum to cut things to length. She shoved her gloves back on, started the motor, and tugged planks down the roller table, squaring off their ends. The noise drowned out her parent's words as they continued to cut each other up.

The dog had found a rope and played tug-of-war with Crystal, his four legs locked stiff as she towed him across the floor. They stopped when Leah started the swing saw. Crystal watched her work and said between cuts, "You don't have to trim the ends of those planks. We're selling them for squares."

"I know," said Leah, and the tears came on strong.

Life has a way of changing all at once. Just like the chips on a sawdust pile, they achieve a balance for a long time until one hits in the right spot and throws everything all to hell, the whole side of the pile sliding off. Then the avalanche stops when they get back in balance.

Leah was crying so hard, she may not have seen where the saw blade was when she stuck her hand in it. Or, maybe she knew right where it was and just wanted to stop the arguing; either way, the arguing stopped when Leah turned around, holding up her injury as if she was holding a hostage. The hand was gone at the wrist, and the cuff of her work glove had slid down to her elbow. Leah turned white and might have fallen into the swing saw had Crystal not turned off the motor and steadied her. Sara bounded up the sawing platform and took off her shirt to wrap around the stump. In no time, Ted had the truck in the mill and, showing the same efficiency they had shown when sawing, Schubert and family were together again and off on the long ride to the hospital.

"I'm out of here, Dude," said the boy as he cast down his shovel. It disrupted some sawdust and Craig watched until the pile became still. Leah's hand was left on the roller table. He held the hand, stroking the fingers while it was still warm. Then, when it turned cold and gray, he buried the hand by the firewood pile and tied up the dog. By the time he was done, the roar of the mill was gone from his ears and the spare saw blades tolled on the one wall that sheltered the workers from the western wind.

# Chapter 17 - A Close Shave

Izzy was making coffee in the staff room one day, when he overheard Dr Staub, the psychiatrist, talking with Dr Flass, the psychologist. Despite the subtle difference in their titles, there seemed so little dissimilarity between the two - Staub chewing on an empty pipe, Flass chewing on his pen; Staub giving pills, and Flass giving tests - that they appeared one man looking in a mirror. Staub addressed Flass as you might talk to yourself while shaving.

"I had a strange dream last night. You know how Dr Ahern is as bald as a billiard ball? I dreamt he was shaving me, and all the rest of us, to be as bald as he. All of us in the clinic were sitting in a row of barber chairs with sheets around us, tucked into our collars, and our heads lathered up like we were wearing white helmets. Everyone was singing *Down by the Old Mill Stream* in a different key while we were waiting for Dr Ahern to come to us with his straight edge razor. As soon as he was done with one, that person would, all of a sudden, be singing in the right key, in perfect harmony, as if shaving off our hair got us in tune. When he got to me, I went on singing while he shaved my head; but when I saw the locks of hair falling on the sheet, I picked them up and tried to put then back on my head. They wouldn't stick, though. They kept falling down on the sheet and I kept trying to put them back. The more they fell off, the more desperate I was to put the hair back on. But here's the curious thing, all the while I was putting the hair back on, I was thinking, it'll grow back, it'll grow back."

"Hum, go on," said Flass, sucking on his pen.

"Well, just then, my old chief of psychiatry, the one I had when I was a resident, comes by and he takes me by the shoulders and shakes me. 'Get a grip on your countertransference,' he says to me. 'Get a grip.' I take the hair and try to put it on his head. He was balding, you see. He was the type to grow his hair long and comb it over his bald spot. I decide I'm going to give him my hair, but, when I try to put it on his head, his hair is thick and curly.

"'I guess you don't need my hair,' I say to him.

"'You'll make a good doctor someday... someday...someday...someday,' he says, like there's an echo or that his main point was I'm not a good doctor now. So, I go back to trying to put the hair on my head. He says, 'Stop it, Stop it right now. Benjamin Ahern's a great man, and if he thinks you should be bald, you should listen to him.'

"Then I wake up, and the first thing I do is reach for my head to see if I still have my hair. But it's all still there."

"Very interesting," said Dr Flass. He withdrew his pen from his mouth and pointed it as his colleague. "A totally bald head is very phallic."

"Do you think so?" said Dr Staub, sucking on his pipe.

"Yes, I do. And you seem to want to keep your phallus covered up," said Dr Flass, in all seriousness, his pen returning to his mouth.

"Yes, that's right, I do."

"And then there are the two father figures: Dr Ahern and your old chief resident."

"They are father figures because they're supervisors. That's true."

"And you are anxious about what Dr Ahern is doing to you with a razor. Why it's the old Oedipal struggle." He took a long, satisfying draw on his pen.

"That's right, I see it, now," said Dr Staub, drawing on his pipe. "The dream is about castration anxiety implicit when I place a libidinal investment on the mother object."

"Right, you compete with the father and he comes after you with a razor."

"Quite so, that's why we hide our genitalia, out of castration anxiety."

"And that's why you're trying to keep the hair on your head."

"Well, thank you. I was so close to the dream, that I couldn't see the obvious associations."

"That's understandable. Freud analyzed himself because he had to, but he didn't recommend it for anyone else."

"That's right. Well, I've got a patient waiting."

"And I have a report to write."

The two left together after placing their pen or pipe in their jacket pockets. As they went out the door, Izzy could see what they could not see when they looked in the mirror: a balding spot on the back of each of their heads.

# Chapter 18 - Dr Ahern

As was already mentioned, Izzy encountered Dr Ahern at the copier one morning when he arrived before the rest of the staff. The intermittent whir of the machine could be heard as the intern approached the room called Medical Records, where the copier was kept. Izzy was surprised that anyone was about and never expected to see Dr Ahern walking around outside of his den. He thought that a cleaning man might be secretly using the copier for some private documents, or maybe procuring a photograph of his ass to leave on his boss's desk. He also supposed that there might be some kind of espionage occurring: a man going through a divorce, copying an incriminating counseling record, or something of the sort. For that reason, Izzy sought to make himself unnoticeable, not because he was someplace where he shouldn't be, but because the other person might be. Izzy wanted to avoid the embarrassment of embarrassing someone else, the dangers of seeing something he wasn't supposed to, or the complications implicit in sharing a secret. Regardless, he was curious and Medical Records was an ideal place to lurk: the door was already open and there were many stacks of charts and files to hide behind. He found one and was able to peer through a gap and see and hear everything. When he saw what he saw, a shiver ran through him. Actuality overtook trepidation; it could be no other at the copier, than Dr Ahern with his dog, Pip.

He didn't seem to be a broken man, as the thin man at the hospital entrance suggested, or obviously fucked up, as Craig informed him. The director had not turned into a Howard Hughes, shut up in his office, growing his fingernails and his hair long. Indeed, he appeared as tan and robust as a chicken just taken off the rotisserie. Izzy wondered how this could be, he could not be getting much sun in his office, and he doubted he had a tanning bed in there. It was as though his recent adversity bronzed him, as a metalworker's fire does. Ahern didn't have a hair on his head, as if he'd been singed. A thick, white, seam, the bullet's path, went up his forehead over his right eye, like an exclamation point, giving him the aspect of one who was wide awake and would keep you up all night.

Izzy was struck by his regal posture as he stood at the copier. Most people will stoop at the copier a little, as if bowing or praying that the contraption would work correctly. Dr Ahern stood as erect as a lighthouse with the waves crashing all around it. He had placed one hand upon the copier, so that he looked like a statesman in an old portrait, with his hand upon a book. This man was a well of determination, a mountain of fortitude, and an ocean of willfulness. He was just the type to tick all the gods off.

Izzy didn't want to get caught spying again, as he had when he first met Craig, so he was about to emerge from behind his hiding place and introduce himself, when the copier jammed and Professor Ahern began to lecture to the dog.

"When will they comprehend that machines don't work? They break down, jam up, fall out of adjustment, and go kaput. They know it, but they make them anyway. Life will be easier with this machine, they say, but it doesn't work that way. You make the machine to do the work for you, and then you work for the machine, just like this machine has got me working for it, now: finding its paper jam."

Pip didn't seem particularly interested in what his master was saying. He wasn't disinterested, he just didn't seem to care one way or another, sort of how it might be if the situation was reversed and the dog was going on and on about cats.

"We love the idea of machines and are blind to their obvious flaws," said Dr Ahern, as if to a lecture hall of undergrads. "Love is blind. It's like we're honeymooning with an axe murderer. Oh, that axe? He's so considerate; he just brought it along in case a tree falls on me. We'll make a hundred excuses and rationalizations just to avoid facing up to the fact that we committed so much in something that just doesn't work.

"But that's not the worst of it. We are so much in love with machines that we'll turn people into machines. We'll program people to abandon their own needs to act in concert towards a common end, but machines don't work."

The psychologist uttered these lines while opening and slamming shut the access doors, searching for the jam. At last, he pulled out a sheet, folded like an accordion, and went on.

"Not only don't they work, but machines bite you back, too. This sheet of paper and I, we're so much alike. We both got caught in a machine; mangled, shredded, torn to bits, and good for nothing but the trash. Someone's got to get hurt when machines don't work and it's a shameful waste."

He thought he had the problem solved and started the copier up again. It whirred for a moment and went silent.

"Jammed again, damn it. Copiers work worst of all. They're always trying to make copies. They get one small thing perfect and try to make a zillion copies of it. Like McDonald's hamburgers, all the same, everywhere you go. But they're not perfect. They get worse and worse because you tried to copy them. Machines don't work and copies aren't perfect."

Pip cocked an ear in the intern's direction.

"What's that, Dog? What do you hear?" asked Dr Ahern.

Izzy was terrified. He was about to get caught again. Raging against the machine at the copier, did not seem all that much out of the ordinary to Izzy. It's what people did at copiers. Just the same, no one liked being witnessed talking to himself.

"There's no one there, Pip. It's just these shelves, groaning under the weight of documentation. Or the copier, chuckling to itself that it foiled me again."

The Director petted Pip's head. Rather than lean into it, as most dogs would, Pip pulled away and came over towards Izzy.

"Am I so far gone that my dog shuns my hand? Have I become so like a machine that you get no satisfaction from my touch? Oh, go ahead; go. Your soft fur doesn't soothe me either.

I'm incapable of comfort. I've been stroking you all this time and I might just as well have been sanding furniture. What business do I have with a dog, anyway? Dogs are meant for serenity; for an old man, sitting by the fire, dozing in his reading chair, satisfied with the life he has lived. I am charged with a mission. Get me a white stallion, instead of a dog. You don't have to worry; I won't pet you any more. Go ahead, go away! Go away, I said!"

Pip, the therapy dog, slunk out of Medical Records, tail down, misunderstood. Izzy followed quietly after, because when a man can't be cheered by a dog, he's not going to be too patient with an intern, either.

# Chapter 19 - Sandy

Izzy's professor wanted him to interview a client from his internship on audiotape. "I want you to sharpen your interview skills. Ask your client if he or she feels guilty about anything and go from there. Bring me the tape and remember to be non-judgmental."

He asked Craig if he should conduct the interview in the bathroom while he was getting urine.

"Don't be a wise ass. Your professor doesn't want to hear that on the tape. You wouldn't talk on the phone sitting on the crapper, would you?"

No, he wouldn't, but he was surprised to hear Craig be so squeamish.

"You can take Sandy out of group. He's driving me nuts, anyway. He lost his wife, his kids, and his house, all to heroin, and he won't admit it's a problem and he's got to fucking stop. See if you can get him to see that."

"I've got to be, like, non-judgmental."

"Fuck a lot of good that'll do. You can be non-judgmental all day long and these addicts will say, thank you very much, I'll go on using, just like you say, that's just what I was thinking. How are you gunna cut through their denial before they're dead with your non-judgmental shit?"

"It's just the assignment."

"You'll kill him with that assignment. But, what's the difference, he's dead anyway. Either the heroin will get him, or I will."

Sandy agreed to be interviewed. Izzy told him about the internship and the assignment. His professor would be listening to the tape and he might talk to Craig about what he said. Sandy wasn't too keen about group, anyway, and he seemed more comfortable about the audiotape than Izzy was. He wasn't getting graded on this.

When Izzy finally finished fumbling with the machine, he started. "Is there anything you, like, feel guilty about?"

"Do I feel guilty about doing smack. It that what you mean?" There was the defiance that irked Craig, right from the start.

"No, not necessarily. Is there anything at all you feel guilty about?"

He smirked. "Yeah, it's awful. I think about it every night and I can't get to sleep."

"You can tell me."

"Oh, I don't know. You might think I was an evil person."

"No, I won't. We all have things we've done that are bad."

"OK, here it goes…"

"Yes?"

"Is the tape going?"

"Yes, what is it?"

"I ah… I."

"It's OK."

"When I was a kid…"

"Uh huh."

"When I was a kid, I stole my brother's chocolate rabbit at Easter time." He grinned.

Oh, funny, thought Izzy. Did I say I was getting graded on this? "Is there anything else?"

Having had his fun with the intern, Sandy fell into a brooding silence. Izzy wondered: is he playing with me again? The only sound was the rotating of the tape. I got plenty of time, thought Izzy, there's no hurry. We can sit here and look at each other for an hour. Actually, Izzy was the only one looking. Sandy was turned away. They must have called him Sandy because his skin, hair, and eyebrows were all the same color: the color of sand. As they sat, his color darkened, as the sand on the beach does when it's wet. Then Izzy knew he wasn't playing. He had something he was guilty about and, if he could be patient, he'd hear about it.

Finally, he pronounced, "When I was a teenager, I babysat."

"Yea?"

"I had sex with an eight-year-old girl," he said.

Izzy felt his stomach clench. This was graduate level non-judgmentalism. "Go on, I'm listening."

"It didn't happen just once. I don't know how many times it happened. Little girls just turn me on. I knew it was wrong, but I couldn't stop."

He went on to say that, he joined the Navy, hoping that being shut up on a ship would keep him from temptation. But then there was shore leave. He'd go with the guys to strip joints; there wouldn't be children there. He didn't care for the women, except for the ones done up like schoolgirls, but he made a show of enjoying them, so no one would know. When he got stationed in the Philippines, where there were plenty of child prostitutes, he went wild. "I would tell myself, it's OK, they want to do it, they're in it for the money. They need to do it and I'm helping them out. They became prostitutes because they love sex and there's nothing wrong with having sex with children if they love it. I would tell myself those things, but, when I went on shore leave, I made sure nobody followed me.

"I couldn't stop thinking about young girls and couldn't stop feeling guilty and afraid of getting caught, so I took up drinking. That was good. I could go on doing what I was doing and not think about it too much, except when I got back to the ship. Then I came across heroin and tried that. It was wonderful. I could go on shore leave, score some heroin and wouldn't think about girls, or guilt, or fear, or anything. I could be normal as long as I had it.

"I quit the Navy when my hitch was up and got married. I wasn't attracted to my wife, but, you know, everyone gets married or they start thinking you're gay. My wife didn't know anything about my heroin and she certainly didn't know anything about me and girls.

They had children soon after: two girls. "It was horrible. I kept having sexual thoughts about my own kids. I couldn't tell anybody. I tried working a lot, just to stay out of the house, but my wife complained. You're never home, she said. All I could think of was to do smack to take away the urge. Then I was doing so much I was spending all our money. There's a hole in Daddy's arm where all the money goes. My wife found out about the drugs and she got pissed. She told me to quit and I said I would, but I had no intention of it. I couldn't, or I'd start screwing my own kids. Finally, she told me to get out. I was so relieved I didn't even try to talk her out of it. I didn't want to live with them and I didn't want visitation. I just wanted out. I'd just as soon my wife and kids thought I was a drug addict."

"Why are you in treatment if you don't want to stop using?"

"Probation. I stole a handbag and got probation. I'm not going to tell the judge I molest children if I don't get my heroin."

"How about getting on Methadone?"

"That'll be great, but I've got to try and fail in treatment a few times before they'll think of giving me Methadone."

Izzy had nothing more to say, and Sandy didn't, either.

"Thanks for letting me talk," he said when they were done.

When Izzy played the tape with his professor he said, "You've got to tell Mr Creek about this. He's a pedophile and he needs help."

He never asked Izzy to do another tape. "You did fine. You'll never have another interview harder than this one."

"He really had you buffaloed," said Craig when Izzy told him. "You believe that shit about molesting girls? He just wants you to say that he should go on using heroin."

"You're not concerned that he's attracted to little girls?"

"I don't believe for a minute that he molests little girls. Why would he tell you if he did? Child molesters don't go around telling people. Besides, he just met with Dr Staub and he didn't tell him anything. What makes you think he would tell an intern?"

## Chapter 12 - All Staff

Only a few days after Pip was banished from Dr Ahern's side, The Director called for an all staff meeting. All appointments they had that day were to be rescheduled. The whole clinic: Mental Health, Chemical Dependency, Pip, Pillsbury, and the Head Administrator, gathered with their morning cups of coffee in the largest group room. Dr Ahern was already present, pacing at one end. Since he had announced it, the meeting was all they talked about, speculating on what he would say in it. For now, however, everyone was silent. Except for the sipping of coffee, Dr Ahern's resolute tread was all that could be heard.

They had just started to wonder whether the man had summoned then there to watch him pace, when he stopped and turned towards the crowd.

"What's the first thing you do when you see a new client?"

There was an awkward pause while they looked around at each other. Finally, a brave few ventured a guess at what he was getting at. "We assess him," they said together.

"Good," was his hearty response. "And what do you give him when you assess him?"

More answered this time. "A diagnosis," they said.

"And according to what book do you diagnose?"

"The DSM!" Still more voices were added, curiously enthusiastic.

"Good, *The Diagnostic and Statistical Manual of Mental Disorders*." He had one with him; he picked up the fat volume.

"It has every diagnosis in the book: substance abuse, schizophrenia, depression, the whole works. In fact, it *is* the book. When you get back to your office, throw it out."

They were struck dumb. Throw out the DSM?

"As long as you have that book in your office, you will not see your clients as they are, you'll only see the symptoms and the conditions listed in the book. You'll flip through the pages until you find a diagnosis that answers your questions and you'll stop looking. You'll also stop listening, because you will think you already have the answer. That book does not help us and it certainly doesn't help the client. It helps the insurance companies limit payment. From now on in this clinic, no one diagnoses anyone."

A question shot out of the psychologist, Dr Flass, like it came from a cannon. "How will we tell the clients what they have?"

"They have what they have, it doesn't matter what we call it. If you want to tell your clients something, tell them how to get where they want to go. That's what they want to know."

Dr Staub had a question. "How will we prescribe medications without a diagnosis?"

"You can prescribe by asking them what they want to change. Do they want to be calmer? Give them an anxiolitic. Do they want to be optimistic? An anti-depressant. Pay attention? A stimulant. Make the Martians in their head go away? Then it's a neuroleptic for them. But prescribing the right medication is only a small part of treatment. Sometimes we can treat their illness very well and give them their good mental health back, but if they don't know what to do with their mental health once they've got it, they just lose it again. We have to engage them in a conversation about what they want to do and fire them up with an enthusiasm to get where they want to be. We cannot do this when we are steadily putting people in boxes and telling them all about their deficits."

The crowd was silent, no eyes rolling, no smirks. Bella's lips moved silently. She must have been praying. Nothing he said was totally unfamiliar; the DSM has always had its detractors. For instance, mental health consumer groups always bridled against giving problems the center of attention rather than giving it to strengths. But throwing out the DSM was highly radical. Then he came out with more.

"We will merge the two sections of this department into one. Each of you Chemical Dependency counselors will counsel in Mental Health if a mental health issue comes up. Every Mental Health clinician will be a drug counselor if their client wants to stop using drugs. Remember, we make no diagnoses, so we can't have two sections of the department. We will treat every client holistically, listening to his or her goals and helping them get to where they want to be, not where we want to put them. And tomorrow, we move offices. Half of Chemical Dependency comes upstairs and half of Mental Health goes downstairs."

Nervous murmurs spread through the crowd. Everyone wondered, will I have to leave my office? Then excited ones, will I get a window? One drug counselor spoke up. "But we were never trained in Mental Health."

"Do you know how to listen?" he asked.

"Of course."

"Then that's all the training you need to achieve minimal competence. You drug counselors will listen to your clients talk about their symptoms and you'll learn everything you need to know. You Mental Health clinicians will listen to your clients talk about their drug use and you'll learn everything you need to know. You already have your teachers in front of you, but you were always told that you must send them away to someone else as soon as you start to learn. Keep them with you and you'll learn everything you need to know."

They were still stunned. Everyone, that is, but Pip, the only one there who never studied the DSM. He maneuvered his head under a hand, seeking petting.

"This is why I've made the changes that I've already made: why the phone lists are combined and why I've had you sit with each other in Interdisciplinary Admission Meetings."

"Why do we have the client in those meetings?" asked a social worker.

"Because it's his life we are talking about. From now on, we will not make any decisions about care without the client being there to hear what is being said. In fact, we will not make any decisions about care. The client will. That's why he needs to be there: so he can make an informed decision."

"A client's best thinking is what made them a client in the first place," said Craig. "They need to stop talking and start listening. Take the cotton out of their ears and put it in their mouth."

"You're right when you say that some of our clients don't think too well and they've made poor decisions in the past. Some of them are delusional. But we are delusional, too, if we think that, just because we tell them to do something, they're going to go right out and do it. We prescribe medication all the time that they don't take. We tell them to go to AA meetings and they don't go. They don't eat right. They don't exercise. They keep smoking. They keep up all those bad habits until they are ready to change, just like the rest of us. It always was their decision. They should sit in the meetings we sit in and know what we know before they make their decisions."

The crowd continued to look skeptical. Dr Ahern narrowed his eyes and leaned in.

"Let me tell you why I really want to do this," he whispered. "The state regulators and the insurance companies have been pushing us around for too many years. We used to treat patients, but now we treat charts."

This got the crowd's endorsement. It was most uncommon to hear a director speak like this. Anyone there who felt they spent too much time on paperwork, and that was everyone, save, perhaps the Head Administrator, was eager to hear what he would say next.

His voice rose to clarion level. "We're not therapists anymore; we're bureaucratic administrators. Bureaucracies are inherently untherapeutic. Bureaucracies dehumanize people; they turn people into categories and numbers, symptoms and syndromes. Therapists turn people into people again; they make them all they can be, not the least they can be."

Pellegrino whispered out of the corner of his mouth, "Ain't he fucked up gloriously?"

Dr Ahern went on. "Our clients, our clients, we shouldn't even be calling them our clients. They aren't our clients. Our clients are whomever we are working for. We're working for the managed care company. That's our client. Our client is the state regulators. The person in our office is our subject. Until we start working for him, he's not our client.

"I'm telling you things you already know. You know what managed care does to people. You know how asinine the state regulations are. You're like old Southern slaveholders. You know the evils of slavery, but don't know how to live without your slaves.

"We whine, we complain. Why don't we strike? Why don't we therapists go on strike and demand the end of managed care? Don't strike for higher pay. Strike for compassion and justice towards our patients. Strike against the therapeutic bureaucracy. Oh, I forgot; we can't strike; we learned anger management." He got some laughs. "So, this is how we'll strike back. We'll create a new kind of clinic: one that does not diagnose, treats the clients holistically to help them achieve their goals, and includes them in decisions. We'll do these things and we'll achieve success, success that they can't argue with. This is why I've come here, to create a new kind of clinic that I could only write about in an academic setting. We'll put managed care out of business and kill off that Leviathan, the Beast."

They were two parts eagerness and one part fear when Dr Ahern opened up his briefcase and held it open in front of them. It was filled with hundred dollar bills.

"Do you see this briefcase of money? I've been sleeping in my office because I sold my house. I saved a little bit of money from the divorce lawyers and I cashed out my retirement fund. I have enough here to give each of you now a few thousand dollars, cash bonus. Do you see it? I have another one, just like it, that I'll give away in a year, if we accomplish the goal I set for this department."

They saw the money, all right. The fear ran away and was replaced by delight, the eagerness stayed where it was. Everyone started talking at once. They all exclaimed how they'd be spending their money. Getting bonuses was for the for-profit sector. Businessmen and salesmen got bonuses. They got the satisfaction of helping people. But they liked bonuses, too. It's just nobody ever asked them. Getting a bonus doesn't remove the satisfaction of helping one bit. In fact it may improve it, just as being digestible improves a meal.

"Whosoever of you joins with me to create a new kind of clinic will receive this bonus and another one a year from now."

The Department broke out into applause. Immediately, many crowded Dr Ahern, putting their hands out to receive their money. Only Pip was composed, wondering what treat had gotten these two-legged creatures to begging. The Director shut the briefcase and addressed the Head Administrator. Her face had blanched to the color of a latte with too much milk.

"What's the matter? Aren't you game to stick it to managed care and the regulators? Will you not spend your bonus?"

Her voice trembled. "I'm game for anything that comes across my desk if it's part of my job, but I was hired to see that we follow the regulations, not to follow the director's ambition. What good will your ambition do you, even if you achieve it, if they shut us down? What good will we do for the clients if, one day, they come for their appointments and there is a lock on the door and a notice saying we're closed? How far will your bonus go if we lose our jobs?"

"I'm not afraid of regulators. They want you to believe they will shut us down, but they won't if we are successful. If clients have fewer expensive hospitalizations, if the duration of treatment is shorter because clients are achieving their goals, then the insurance companies will praise us, not close us. I'm not afraid of them, you see, I'm counting on them and their greed."

"It's a dangerous game you're playing."

"Listen to me again. Let's get a little deeper. You see, if we're not rebelling against this dehumanization, then we're submitting. If we're submitting, then we're a collaborator with a terrible system that endangers the mental health of our clients. If you're submitting because you're afraid of losing your job, then you're doing it out of fear."

"God help us," muttered the Head Administrator. With this implicit acquiescence, Dr Ahern passed out the cash and Pillsbury brought in a breakfast buffet. After they distributed the money, the rest of the morning was spent listening to him lecture on the evils of the DSM, managed care, and the regulators.

## Chapter 21 - Dr Ahern by the Window, Gazing Out at Traffic and Thinking

I'm like an eighteen-wheeler, leaving a turbulent wake wherever I go. Follow close behind and you might cruise in the still zone of my aerodynamics; but try to pass, and you will be hit by the gathered force of my disruption. Stand still, like litter upon the macadam, and you will be lifted and moved.

The highway goes on and on into infinity; all we think we see is but a fragment of the whole. There was once a time when I couldn't wait to go down that road and see it all, but I've traveled many miles since then and what I've found is nothing other than that endless loop of farm, cows, suburbs, city, and suburbs, cows, and farms again. The concrete seams throbbing as regular as a heartbeat. The fragment was the whole all along. I tried to finish my interminable journey once. I tried to turn down a dead end, park, and get out, but the road was mismarked. It went on and on and on, and I couldn't find a way out. I pull a heavy burden and I'd like nothing better than to back my rig up to a dock, raise the clattering tailgate, and have the warehouse men unload me. But I carry a load that has no market, unless I make one.

The All Staff was easier than I thought it would be. I thought there'd be at least one who wouldn't budge; but they could all be appealed to on some level. Where the tractor goes the trailer follows. I'm the engine that drives them, and this hurt within me is nothing other than the internal combustion of my soul. What a waste, to empower, one needs be consumed.

They think I'm crazy; but I had them throw out the book that defines madness. Now madness will have to define itself. They think that I've taken on more than I can accomplish, to battle City Hall in person, but they don't know what I can do. I'd challenge Fate itself if it tried to boss me. Pro wrestlers, football players, even the whole dad-blamed army cowers in fear when the leviathan, that monstrous machine, comes along. A small group of dedicated people, with a strong leader, is the only thing that ever changed anything. I'll stand up to that beast. I won't whimper and cry, take on someone your own size, oh no, not me. You knock me down and I'm up again, looking for more. You think you'll make me turn? I won't veer off. The path to my fixed purpose is paved and lined with guardrails. Over gouged-out canyons, through crumpled mountains, across smashed-flat prairies I roll on cruise control. Nothing can detour me.

# Chapter 22 - The Head Administrator, Stirring her Starbucks, and Thinking

I've met my match this time with an idealist too charged up to listen to reason. In fact, he almost talked me into his dangerous project. I see where all this is going: it'll subvert all the careful gains we've made in mental health care. He hates the insurance companies, but we can't do without them. There was once a day when mental health care was not covered by insurance, we had no clinics then. The rich people could pay for their Fifth Avenue psychoanalysts to listen to them whine; but the people who really needed it had nothing. Before the DSM codified mental illnesses, the depressed were called lazy, the anxious were cowardly, and the hyperactive were just trouble-makers; but turning mental conditions into a medical issue changed all that. Now all those people have an illness that can be treated and medical insurance can pay for it. They are not blamed for having an illness; they have their dignity and respect. You stop diagnosing people and you pull out the one all-important prop that holds up the whole deck of cards. He'll bring it all down on us, if he succeeds. If he fails, then it is down on us, too.

Time is on my side. He knows this clinic cannot survive unless we bill; and, unless we have a diagnosis on the bill, it will not be paid. There must also be a treatment plan corresponding to the diagnosis, or we will not be paid. There must also be progress notes referring to the treatment plan, based on the diagnosis, or we will not be paid. He will have us create a whole system of documentation parallel to what we are actually doing with the client. We'll have to do twice as much paperwork; like the double bookkeeping that casinos do. The staff will see that their paperwork is not reduced and they'll complain. Then he'll have to abandon his whole scheme because they won't go along with it. He will have spent a briefcase full of money for nothing.

The staff burst out in merry laughter.

Oh, God, to have to depend on such idiots to operate this clinic, pulled out from under a cold rock. Whatever we carefully build up, the reckless tear down. He calls them dragon slayers and Managed Care is their dragon. Listen to them, having a good time, free of the cares of office, boasting while Ahern muses sullenly by the window. The vandals are at the gates and glorious Rome sits ready for their pillage. Oh, who wouldn't rather join them, pounding on the door? I would, just as much as anyone, but I must be off to hide the priceless artifacts where they won't find them.

## Chapter 23 - Pellegrino, at the Coffee Pot, Thinking

There, someone said it at last: the emperor's naked. It always takes a child or a fucked-up fool to speak the truth. We knew it all along, but we just couldn't say it. Now it's said. The cat's out of the bag and it's scratching the shit out of the dog.

He's bringing us back to the old days, that's what I like. Before therapy became a big business, supervised by layers of administrators with nothing to do but prevent you from doing your job, it was pure back then: just one addict helping another clean up the shit they made of their lives.

## Chapter 24 - Craig, with a Donut, Thinking

Things come around and I've joined a band of outlaws, again. Ahern's a righteous dude. I can't agree with everything he stands for, but at least he stands somewhere and stands strong; and he's willing to put his money and his balls on the line. I'll ride with a man like that to the end of the earth, wherever he goes.

But, what am I going to do with this money? That's a lot of money.

## Chapter 25 - Dr Staub, Calling his Broker, and Thinking

Buy tech stocks; anything with a dot-com after its name. That's the best answer to this curious development. Whatever happens, I'll be sitting pretty, having parlayed this bonus into a fortune.

I saw how The Head Administrator was ready to lie down on the tracks to stop him, but got up at the last minute. That was wise, and, yet, foolish, too. Why lie down if you'll just be getting up again? That makes no sense. I'll stick with these stocks, come what may.

## Chapter 26 - Cloud Gathering Zeus, Sitting on his Throne on Mt Olympus, Thinking

How I'd love to get my hands on another thunderbolt, but hurling them hasn't been any fun since people started blaming the weather. Oh, we gods have all found something to occupy our time, which we have plenty of. I, for one, took a part time job as an omniscient narrator. Even then, I've found there are only so many stories and, when you live as long as I have, you see them repeat. To stay vibrant, I like to switch things up and experiment with different narrative techniques. You would, too, if you had as much time on your hands. You know about my romantic dalliances. Well, you try being married to the same woman for all of eternity.

Convincing the Fate Sisters to have janitors clean up after them was a brilliant idea. Now that there are therapists helping people deal with their problems, few think of the gods anymore, much less blame them. We are left in peace to enjoy our retirement. Still, I have enough omnipotence to see unforeseen circumstances arising out of the creation of these janitors. I have always hoped that, given the right inducement, these janitors could even go on to subvert the Fates.

## Chapter 27 - Pip, Under the Buffet table, Thinking

Oh, what's this? A fallen bagel. Well, it's mine. Anything on the floor belongs to me. That fat lady's got her plate heaping and she's waving it around while she's talking. I think I'll go stand by her. The people are happy about something, as if they found a buried bone. Hark! What's that I hear? No one else hears it, as always. I don't mind being the watchdog, but I wish I wasn't the only one all the time. Oh, Alpha God, somewhere up on the buffet table, preserve this good dog from these creatures that have no nose for danger.

# Chapter 28 - The Diagnostic Statistical Manual

In the afternoon, the clinic broke into small groups to work out the details of how they would feed the insurance companies' unceasing appetite for documentation while following Dr Ahern's guidelines about clinical care. Our hero, Izzy, the erstwhile dithering one, attended that All Staff Meeting with the rest of them. He pledged when they pledged. He agreed to what they agreed. He put his hand in the briefcase and took a share of the bonus. Even though their fight was not his fight, he sympathized with them. He had no reason to complain about managed care, or regulations, or bureaucrats, for that matter, and he might have looked for a leviathan at the zoo. He preferred pee patrol to paperwork. Yet Ahern's antipathy became Izzy's. The intern listened with greedy ears to the history of his feud with the DSM.

The origins of the DSM, Ahern told them, lie in the inferiority complex Psychology has when it compares itself with its big brothers of the Sciences: Biology, Astronomy, Physics, and Chemistry. They all used to tease Psychology. "You're not a real science," they said. "You're not even adopted. You're really a Religion."

Now, none of the Sciences liked being called a Religion. The Religions were that family down the street that didn't mow the lawn. They were once the richest family on the block, but, since Papa Religion lost his job, his only occupation was to volunteer at election time. Mostly he just ran after young boys. Momma Religion baked bread. It smelled good, but it never rose because she wouldn't use yeast. The Religions were always fighting and you could hear them inside the house going at it, arguing about who was better. Whenever they went out, they'd wear their

Sunday best, but that didn't fool anyone. That's why Psychology didn't like being called a Religion.

Psychology decided it would classify all the mental conditions, just as Biology had with all the living things. He specified the criteria for each condition as Chemistry had when it recorded how many electrons were in each element. He constructed a table of the conditions and gave each one a number, similar to the Periodic Table of the Elements. He wrote all this in the DSM and proudly showed it off to the Sciences. The siblings sniggered, but Mama Science taped it to the refrigerator along with Newton's Law's of Gravity, Pythagoras's Theorem, and Einstein's Theory of Relativity, because, even though it looked like scribbling, she felt Psychology needed to be encouraged. That night, Papa Science argued that the unsightly junk should just disappear like Ptolemy's Solar System had, or at least they should put it away where it couldn't hurt anyone, along with Occam's Razor. Mama Science said wait for a few days. Psychology will just forget all about it and go back to playing with its pet rats. He won't even notice it when it was gone.

Then one day their neighbors, the Businesses, visited while the DSM was still up on the refrigerator and offered to buy it. The Sciences sold it without much negotiation because they always needed the money and were glad to see it out of the house. However, they regretted the sale when they saw that the Businesses displayed it in their storefront window with Psychology's name right on it. If they had just kept it on the refrigerator, eventually it would've been covered up when Physics drew its Theory of Everything. Nonetheless, they used the money to put up a stockade fence between them and the Religions.

The Businesses, of course, didn't buy the DSM for its aesthetic or scientific value. They bought it because they knew how to make more money off it. Just as a movie producer will distribute a movie so he can sell action figures, Aunt Pharmaceutical Business was interested in the DSM so it could sell drugs to people. She made a mint, doing so. She knew that if people could be convinced that their wayward thoughts were an illness, they could sell those people drugs for that illness. Just the fact that a person's thoughts or behavior was described in the DSM convinced people that they had a mental illness. After all, the book had to be scientific because Psychology was a Science. Wasn't it? It was OK to take drugs for an illness, but if you took drugs when you didn't have an illness, you were just a drug addict. Aunt Pharmaceuticals didn't want to sell drugs to drug addicts because then she would become disreputable, like that black sheep of the Businesses, The Mob, and she never would be able to sign a lease in the best malls. Aunt Pharmaceuticals even hoped to get some money out of the Governments, who are so cheap they borrowed everyone else's tools and acted like they were theirs when you asked to get them back.

Psychology, learning a thing or two from the Businesses, kept on making new versions of the DSM and adding to the numbers of conditions that could be called an illness. Having created these illnesses, he found that he had also created a need for psychotherapy. Millions of people started coming to Psychology for medical advice. He pretended he was a doctor and gave it to them. No one could say he was a Religion, now. Pharmaceuticals visited a lot and really took to Psychology's son, Psychiatry. She would bring him pens, post it notes and other trinkets. It was inevitable that Pharmaceuticals and Psychology would end up in bed together. The Sciences welcomed her as part of the family and everyone expected they would be married soon.

After a while, the most conservative of the Business siblings: Insurance, began to suspect that Psychology had made up all these illnesses. Insurance must have been reading his actuary tables too much and been scared to come out of the house because, by the time he found out, it was too late to do anything about it, and he almost had a heart attack. He couldn't die of a heart attack, of course, because he was low risk. It did cause him to retire a little earlier than he planned, though. He left his firm to his son, Managed Care.

The Businesses were glad to see that Managed Care was very different than his fretful father. Managed Care knew he was powerful and wasn't afraid to throw his weight around. He told Psychology straight away that he would only pay for so many sessions of its therapy and he was lucky that he got anything at all because, it was rumored, Psychology was not a real Science. Psychology cried and complained that Managed Care was bullying him, but his big brothers: Biology, Chemistry, and the rest, never came to his aide. As far as they were concerned, it was about time the little brat got what he deserved.

Managed Care told Psychology, "You're really good at writing," He said, "Since you're good at writing, and since I want to know what the money I spend on peoples' therapy is going for, I'm going to want you to write down which diagnostic category each person you treat is in. Furthermore, if there are all these diseases, we can't have the same therapy for every disease. I will only pay for whatever therapy most helps each disease. You'll have to write that up, too." Psychology complained some more. He was a doctor, not a writer. All the time Managed Care made him spend on writing, he couldn't spend on seeing patients.

The ultimate indignity came when, behind Psychology's back, while he was writing, Managed Care started to woo Pharmaceuticals. He whispered in her ear, "Your drugs are so much more effective at treating people than Psychology's therapy. Join with me and leave Psychology behind. We will make more money together than you have ever dreamed."

It wasn't really true; drugs weren't more effective; they were just cheaper; but Pharmaceuticals loved being told these sweet lies, so she started to cheat on Psychology.

This was all too much for Psychology. Deep within his heart he knew that the DSM was just a bunch of made up lies; but he could barely admit it to himself, much less to the world. He wanted to say, "These are all just arbitrary categories in the DSM. People are more complicated than that; they cross diagnostic lines, they have co-occurring disorders; their problems, thoughts, and behaviors changes over time. They could be ADHD as a child and bipolar by the time they become an adult. One psychologist will give a diagnosis one week and, if the person sees another one the next week and says different things, he will get a different diagnosis."

He would go on, admitting, "There is no objective test for any mental condition. No blood work will tell you have schizophrenia. No MRI detects depression. There's not an x-ray that shows anxiety. It all just goes by what people say."

Psychology wanted to scream, "Those drugs Pharmaceuticals makes aren't going to work by themselves. It takes a skilled clinician to sort out the tangled mess that people make of their lives. Science can only take you so far. Psychology is more than a science. No, it's not a Religion. It's an Art."

In a dusty, cobwebby, howling closet of his brain, Psychology knew the truth. Papa Science was not his father. Mama Science had slept with a neighbor and she became pregnant by him. This was why Psychology was so different from his siblings, the hard sciences. The neighbor that impregnated his mother was not Religion, as they all suspected. Mama Science had more pride than to sleep with Religion. The neighbor was Art. Psychology was the product of the union between Science and Art.

When regarded as a work of Art, the DSM was a thing of beauty. Oh, it's not like an impressionist's painting or a Mozart Symphony, or anything quite as expressive. It's more like a Mondrian Abstract or a Star Wars episode. In the library, it should be filed under Science Fiction. It's one of the greatest works of science fiction ever written. Imagine a world, says Psychology in the DSM, in which thoughts, behaviors, and personalities could be perfectly categorized in detail. A world in which we knew why people act the way they do and knew clearly the difference between sane and insane. Psychology imagined this world and wrote a book about it as if it were true. He wrote it so convincingly that everyone thought it was true. That's not the work of Science; it's a work of Art.

Psychology wanted to shout these things from the rooftops and be free of the secret, but, of course, he couldn't. He had too much riding on the status quo. He would lose face if he went back now.

That was the predicament Psychology was in, but don't worry. You see Psychology is not a real person. It doesn't exist. It's an abstraction. There is no Psychology, there are only psychologists and Ahern was one of them. Since Psychology couldn't tell the truth, Ahern would; and he did. Every chance he got, he wrote papers teaching everyone about the true nature of the DSM and of Psychology.

Ahern wrote his papers and they were published in all the best journals; he was very well regarded and was invited to speak everywhere at conferences. Other psychologists said it was convincing and probably true, but they went on doing what they had always done because the system could not change. The system needed the DSM, managed care, regulations, and the whole lot. It needed to maintain things the way they were for everything to work.

Dr Ahern might have gone on writing papers and speaking at conferences all his life with little to show for his work; many academics do. There would have been no shame in doing so. He could have eventually retired respectfully and given a post, therapist emeritus, and had his name on a school of therapy: The Ahernians. However, The Fate Sisters had something else in mind for Ahern.

A corporation bought out his university. Many schools seek partnerships with business and industry. His was successful at finding one. This corporation, understanding which side of their bread had the butter, poured money into the school's engineering, business, and hard science departments. It neglected the humanities and soft sciences until enrollment in them withered away and they had no choice but to lay off professors. As impersonal as a combine's blade, the indifferent steel of severance reaped Ahern from his university. It would surprise no one to hear that the professor bore grudges at the system. One may also imagine that, in his idle time, with the heat of his ire towards the corporation, he welded in his mind a fantastic monster, combining the DSM with managed care, bureaucracy, and state government until, all together; they began to identify for him all his intellectual exasperations. The DSM grew to be the symbol of all those evil forces that align themselves against man. Everything that restricts, opposes, pigeonholes, and controls was represented, in Ahern's mind, by the DSM. He imbued upon its pages all the rage that the whole race, from Darwin's monkey on down, has felt towards anything that dehumanizes the humans, and thwarts their divine aspirations.

It's hard to say when Ahern developed these ideas. Certainly, the germ was present in his earliest papers. It may have grown when the corporation began to meddle in academic affairs. It may have flowered at the same moment that Ahern was cut from the branches of learning. It certainly fermented during his unemployment. There was one day when, detenured, he put the muzzle of a gun in his mouth. He took it out again and drilled it into his ear. He extracted it and rested his chin upon it. He let it nuzzle his chest by his heart. As one will lean his temple on a finger, he leaned on the muzzle. He regarded the apparatus of the firearm. Trigger, hammer, firing pin, and powder; the mechanisms worked as indifferently as the mechanisms of the corporation. Press the trigger and he would become its victim, but his hand shook and he missed. At that moment, he concluded that humanity could win over the machine, that life would find its way.

The DSM has it laid out in tables and graphs, but human madness is a feline thing. It's a shape shifter. When you think it's gone, it's transformed into something else. Hemmed in by mountains, like a river it deepens, narrows, and quickens. Given space, and it will broaden and stifle in pestilent swamps. After his suicide attempt, none of his intellect had perished. It was concentrated into a cutting laser precision and aimed towards an implacable end.

This is as much of Ahern that we can know, but there is much, much, much more. Few would even bother to look this far, for we'll only seek until our prejudices are confirmed. Ahern knew this and counted on it, so that when he, at last changed out of his doleful pajamas and into an interview suit, everyone thought him no other than naturally stressed by the indignities of unemployment.

The whispers of his suicide attempt were attributed to this natural stress. Far from disqualifying him for a clinical position, even one of considerable responsibility and leadership, the calculating people of that prudent hospital administration harbored the conceit that the very breakdown that would impair him would also make him more qualified to maneuver around the machinations of the mad mind. Had any of the Medical Center Board known of the plan he had for Behavioral Health, he never would have gotten past the first interview. They were bent on smooth sailing, few waves, and rising units of service. He was intent on an audacious revolt against the system.

Here, then, was an iconoclastic leader paying, out of his own savings, a dispirited staff of an ignored department to destroy a book. He would have them venture into the thoughts of scores of certified insane people without the usual safe moorings that enable them to keep their direction. He would set them on a quest to jab harpoons into Job's Leviathan. He would cause them to lie to insurance companies, deceive regulators, and bamboozle auditors. How did he ever get them to do it? What was the DSM to them? When he plucked his single string, sounding one exceptional note, what resonated within them? That is far more than can be explained. Suffice it to say that there is an Ahern within us all. Rap on his hidden door and he will scratch and claw to find a way out.

# Chapter 29 -The Chase

"I was sound asleep when my wife shook me, trying to wake me up. `Hendrick's taking our canoe out for a joy ride,' she said."

Although it was in the middle of the night, in the middle of winter, and in the middle of frozen corn stubble it seemed like a perfectly reasonable dream, so Craig went on sleeping.

She kept on shaking him. "'Get up. Hendrick is dragging the canoe across the field with his snowmobile.'"

Saying the name of their infuriating neighbor, Hendrick, was all Leah needed to rouse Craig from a six-beer slumber in the middle of a clear, full-mooned night just after Christmas. It roused him today, too, years later, telling us the story at lunchtime, his tongue loosened by all the excitement of Ahern's briefcase. If Hendrick had come in through the door of Behavioral Health, Craig would have offered him ten-knuckle therapy, even today. Craig was thousands of dollars richer and pleased to have joined a gang of outlaw therapists, but talking about Hendrick made him as angry as if it were happening right now.

"She got up to piss, because she was nine months pregnant, and heard the sound of snowmobiles outside, so she peered out the window to watch. She saw that damn Hendrick and his buddies hooking the canoe up to his snowmobile, taking it for a joy ride.

"It was colder than a witch's tit. I kept the car battery by the stove at night so the old cage would start in the morning. I threw on some clothes, hooked up the battery and was going after them. Just as I was starting the car, Leah came waddling out and sits in the passenger seat. She's coming along. So off we go, chasing the son-of-a-bitch."

Leah was pregnant with their child and big changes were in store for them. They clattered down the road and turned up the next just in time to see Hendrick crossing in the aluminum canoe, sparks flying as it ground across the gravel road as if from an axe sharpening on a grindstone. The canoe hit the plowed snow on the side of the road hard and Hendrick held on to the gunwales to keep from being thrown. The snowmobile dug in; sending a plume of snow back at him as he drunkenly shouted, "Death to Moby Dick! Death to Moby Dick!"

Craig had his own reunion planned with Moby Dick as he sped down the road. The next crossing was a good four miles away going by car and about one and a half going as they were across the field. He had no time to spare if he was going to meet them there. He soon accelerated past the moonlit snowy fields bristling with chopped off cornstalks.

Craig, transported by his pursuit of Hendrick, urged, "C'mon you heap of cold metal, you frigid bitch, come alive. Give it up, you lazy battery. You've been lolling by the fire all night, now put out your spark. Light the air, you stubby plugs; you've been looking for a fight. Pump, you six pistons, fuck that cylinder's oily cunt. That's my baby. Why don't you shear off the driveshaft, you crankshaft? Bite something, you tires. That's the spirit. Now's the time to lose your cool, you radiator. Blast your farts you tailpipe. Let Hendrick know that I'm coming for him, we'll run him down."

"Honey, slow down; it's not that important," said Leah as she hung on to the armrest with her stump, bracing herself on the bench seat, and, with her heel, kicking the rattling tool box on the floor, an imaginary passenger's side brake pedal. Her belly had the off-balance elasticity of a playground kickball, within which, no doubt, the baby was dribbling her bladder.

"If it's not that important, what is she getting me up out of bed for? That's what I wanted to know," Craig asked them at the table. "That's how a squeeze is; she sets you up and knocks you down. She waits for me to haul the battery out to the car and roar off, chasing that Hendrick bastard, just getting a glimpse of his cocky face, and then she says forget it. I can't forget it, not once she gets me going. After a while, it's not about a canoe anymore. Hendrick ran off with my balls in the middle of the night, and she says forget it, you don't need them."

Although he'd like to grind that smile off his face with a dull file, the chase was not really about Hendrick. Down beneath all appearances, which are only construction paper masks, Craig was chasing after the Hendrick principle, the thing-within-Hendrick that moves him to run off with other people's canoes, not to steal them, really, but to toy with them and to laugh about it. Hendrick was the false mask of joy shoved in Craig's face and he wanted to put his fist through it. Hendrick didn't take a canoe and go slithering off into the night ashamed of what he's doing. Oh, no, he went blaring out behind a roaring snowmobile and made sport of it without a single care. Here was Craig, working morning to evening for his father-in-law, parking his bike and taking orders from a woman he knocked up. She displayed her belly all over the world, showing them what he'd done to her and he'd better stick around and be responsible now. Here he was, a lone wolf, captured and made to pull sleds, a reindeer hitched to Santa's sleigh, a trained seal, a grizzly bear dancing on a ball with a party hat, and Hendrick was running around, drinking with the boys and having fun. He was free and Craig was not. That's what it all came down to.

What he really wanted to do was to take a spin out on the canoe himself. He was sick of driving a rusting car, staying on the roads, with a nervous wife who had to piss every five minutes. He belonged out on the snowfields in a canoe with nothing over his head but the stars. Instead of going to bed early so he could get up and go to work the next morning, he wanted to stay out drinking all night, raising hell. That's what he really wanted.

Wedges of snowdrifts reached across the road. The biggest was just up ahead. He accelerated just as he hit it like a boat crashing into a wave. Snow sprayed the length of the car as it began to slide. Craig, unswerving from his purpose, spun back the wheel, into the slide, kept it pointing down the road, and sped up again for the next one.

"`Honey, please slow down! Be careful!'"

It was as if Hendrick, towed by the snowmobile, was towing him.

"This is why you woke me up and climbed in," he said, "to chase that bastard till we catch him and pull his grinning teeth out, one by one."

"I don't care about that macho biker bullshit. Just take me home. You're scaring me." But, not having the wheel, she was powerless and along for the ride. Craig drove as through he had escaped from prison and kidnapped the jailer.

A turn was coming up ahead and they were in good shape. They could hear the snowmobile engine behind them. He only had to make the turn onto the next road and find a way to stop them. Craig regretted not having a load in the back to weigh the car down, for, when it entered the turn, it started to spin.

Time has a way of extending itself at those moments when your run is over to give you a chance to settle in and accept your fate. When Craig was young, his Mom sent him upstairs to carry a chair down for Aunt Kathy at Christmas dinner. Delighted at the responsibility, he grabbed the chair and tripped headlong on the top step. The whole way down he foresaw what would meet him at the bottom, how he'd smash his face; and, how, through his whole life up to then, he'd been naively unaware of later getting a smashed face. Everything would change once he reached the bottom. Craig also had time to think about lion tamers and how they shield themselves by picking up a chair. As it turned out, the lion tamer image was the more prophetic, for, when he reached the bottom, the chair, which he held in front, absorbed most of the fall and broke into bits. His face was not smashed in the least and Aunt Kathy ate her Christmas dinner on a squeaky piano stool.

During the one and a half turns the car made on that icy intersection, in the same way as you clear a combination lock by spinning the dial, Craig managed to rid his mind of Hendrick and the purloined canoe. He knew that, by the time they stopped rotating, he would have to abandon his chase of the careless, grinning one and settle into domesticity. Leah would be angry that he didn't listen to her and would withhold all words for a time. Craig would live in a silent household for a few days like a caretaker in a Trappist monastery.

The revolving ride in the car ended with the two of them stuck in the ditch facing the opposite way. Craig got out and had Leah drive as he pushed, attempting to extract the car, yelling. "Don't spin the tires. Rock it." But it was no use. Leah shut off the car and in the distance, the snowmobile purred.

Craig roared out curses for a few minutes until, in a soft voice with wide eyes, his wife interrupted him with, "Honey, I think I have a problem." She was standing by the car, the crotch of her pants dark, moist, and steaming in the cold.

"Did you piss all over yourself?"

No.

"My water broke."

# Chapter 30 - The School Bus

Winter's deadly silence took over once the buzzing of the snowmobiles receded. The frustrated couple spied a yard light at the top of the next hill and began to walk towards it. Craig charged ahead in long strides, from time to time stopping to wait for Leah to catch up in her labored waddle. The wind blew hard. They had dressed in a hurry to leave and the cold stung at their exposed flesh. "Go on ahead," said Leah, "I'll wait in the car for you while you get help." Craig started up the hill, but he turned back when she cried out in pain.

"C'mon, I'm not leaving you. Remember your breathing."

"Don't tell me to fucking breathe."

As they reached the top of the hill, a row of conifers slowed the force of the wind. Snow, scored off the fields, piled on the lee side of the trees in a mammoth drift that almost buried one end of a retired school bus. Bales of straw lining the underside of the bus and a stovepipe cut through the roof indicated it had been converted to a home.

Hearing the crunch of snow as the couple approached, a platoon of dogs began to bark. One hound posted on the perimeter strained at his leash, his shadow cast out long by the yard light, almost reaching them. All the hounds erupted in frantic growling and teeth baring, skidding their water dishes across the yellow snow like hockey pucks, testing the strength of their chains. An unknown quantity of dogs from inside the bus took up the alarm and the vehicle began to vibrate in a way it had not since it was last packed with sixty kids going home on the last day of school.

A sliding window lowered and a muzzle of a shotgun poked out like the cannon from the gun port of a man-o-war.

"State your business," commanded a voice.

"Our car is in a ditch," began Craig, but the dogs raised an objection as he spoke.

"What?"

"I said our car is in a ditch." But it was useless. Resorting to pantomime, Craig pointed to his wife, made a belly with his hand, and said one word, "Baby."

The resident withdrew the shotgun and Leah lay down on the snow on her back and Lamazed through another series of contractions. The bus door folded halfway and, taking care not to let the dogs escape, a gaunt man, with white hair and red eyes, like a coked up Santa Claus, sidled out. They couldn't have woken him because he looked as though he hadn't slept in three days.

"Shut up. Shut up," he shouted to the dogs, who took no notice. He scuffed his unlaced work boots as he walked to the front of the bus, wiped off the snow, and opened the hood. It looked as though he would do some tinkering and get the old bus started, but it was up on blocks and some dogs were chained to the wheels.

"Howt, hoot, howt, hoot, howt, hoot..." said Leah on her back in the snow and holding her belly like one just knocked over by a medicine ball.

Seeing their master open the hood, the dogs changed the character of their barking. Their tails began to wag and they joyfully bayed when he emerged from under the hood with dog food scooped in a one-quart pot. He laboriously feed the dogs, one by one, to quiet them.

"Damn you, old man," said Leah, who had finished her contraction. "Can't you see I'm having a baby? Feed your fucking dogs later."

He'd finished with the outside dogs and was making shuttle runs to the inside when Craig scooped Leah up and ran to the man's Dodge truck. Despite his shotgun and suspicion, like most country folk, the white haired man kept the keys in the ignition. Craig turned the key, but the cold had gotten to the truck and it turned over too slowly to catch.

"Damn it," he yelled, pounded the wheel, and looked up to see the white haired man pointing the gun at him again. He flung the door open. "Shoot me if you want, but call a god damn ambulance. My wife is having a baby."

"Don't have a phone."

"Fuck. Let us in your house then, she can't have the baby out here."

"Can't let you in the house."

"How are we going to steal something? We don't have a car."

"Can't let you in."

The white haired man smiled a snaggle-toothed smile. A purple, burn scar blazed on his hand. Behind the bus, three walls of a farmhouse, the charred remains of a fire, reigned over the homestead; downwind stood a scorched pine tree, the branchless truck like the house's scepter. Propane tanks were stacked like cordwood behind the bus.

In a conspiratorial voice Craig said, "I don't give a fuck what you have in the bus, old man. If you let the baby die out here, then everybody will know."

"Howt, hoot, howt, hoot, howt, hoot…"

"What's she saying?"

"She's doing her breathing. They taught her that in the hospital. We really need to go in."

"All right, come on."

The three filed in through the bus door and were greeted by a surge of dogs, the dry heat of a woodstove, and the unmistakable smell of a meth lab. A Bluetick hit Craig in the chest with his front paws. Leah slid on to an unbolted seat, two dogs jumped on her, and the seat tipped over and they all fell together.

"Down dogs, down! Get off her!" yelled the white haired man. He grabbed a fistful of bailer twine and began to tie the dogs up.

Craig pulled Leah up and righted the seat by the stove, a converted oil drum. A red spot glowed on its side. A gutted doe, shot off-season, no doubt, hung upside down in the back of the bus. A glassy eye that knew the pain of birth stared at Leah, who pushed herself up and said, "I'm not having the baby here. We're going to the hospital."

"We can't get there, Honey. Our car is stuck and this man's truck won't start."

"Don't you know enough to keep the battery by the fire, old man! Fucking retard!" She yelled and pushed the seat over again.

Craig had an idea. "I got it. I can take the battery out of my car and put it in your truck. Then we can get it started and get out of here."

"I got some tools," said the white haired man. "What do you need?"

"Got'em all in the car," said Craig. Then, before he even knew what he was saying, he added, "But, before we go, first hit me with some of your meth. I'll pay you later."

Leah didn't say a word when she had cut off her hand. Not a whimper, not a cry. She had never complained about the pain afterwards, not even when her missing fingers throbbed. But now, in childbirth and in frustration, she let out screaming curses that sent the dogs cowering. Hendrick, miles away, might have heard it over the snowmobile's roar. Craig heard it, too, but it didn't stop him from getting a hit before going out to get the battery. Nothing could have stopped him.

When she was done screaming and he was injecting Craig, the white haired man asked, "Did they teach her that in the hospital, too?"

# Chapter 21 - Group Therapy

"Where's Craig?" they all wanted to know. But Izzy didn't know what to tell them. The day after the All Staff, Craig had come in two hours late and told the intern to take over his group by himself. He'd catch up on paperwork.

"Take over group!" exclaimed Izzy. "You haven't let me do anything but collect piss until now. Now you want me to do group myself?"

"This is what you wanted, wasn't it? What are you complaining about? You studied this stuff in school and you want to help people. Now go help people."

"What do I do? I don't know how to do group."

"You heard what Ahern said. Listen to them talk and you will learn everything you need to know."

Craig looked like hell, like he was sick, or something; worse than usual. "Are you OK?" Izzy asked.

"I'm OK, I just have a lot of paperwork to do"

"You don't look OK."

"You're the one who's not gunna look OK if you don't get out there and do some work."

"Where's Craig?" the group asked. They knew Izzy, of course; at least the men. He'd been collecting their urine. "You want us to piss now?"

"No, no one's pissing today. Craig's, like, got paperwork; he told me to do group, instead."

"He's hung over," said one.

"He can't be hung over, he's the counselor," said another.

"Counselors can get hung over, just like the rest of us."

"He's not hung over, he's in recovery."

"No one's hung over," Izzy said.

"I am. I got fucking blasted last night."

"Did you see Craig when you were out?"

"I don't remember anything about last night."

"Craig didn't go out and he's not hung over," Izzy said. "What makes you think, just because he told me to do group, that he's hung over?"

"That's what I always did. Whenever I didn't come to work, or came in late, or didn't do shit, I was hung over."

"Not everyone's like you."

"Every addict's like me. We're all the same."

"Let's, like, start group," Izzy said, not having any idea about how to start group.

"We're already started. Craig's in the hot seat."

"Craig can't be in the hot seat. He's not here."

"Who wants to be in the hot seat?"

"No one does; so let's put Craig."

"We're not putting Craig in the hot seat," Izzy said. "He's not a client. Only clients get put in the hot seat."

"You're not putting me in the fucking hot seat."

"Why not? You can take a turn like the rest of us."

"Yeah, what makes you so special?"

"OK, OK," said Izzy. This group seemed like chaos. He didn't know how anyone could benefit from it. He needed to know how Craig did group.

"I know," said the intern. "Since you miss Craig so much; how about if someone plays Craig for the day? Like, who wants to be Craig?"

"I'll be Craig," said one. He gets up to leave.

"Where are you going?" said Izzy.

"I'm going to do paperwork."

"Sit down. That's not what I meant. I meant, like, be the group leader."

"You're the group leader."

"I know. I'm leading you in a role-playing exercise. Someone play the group leader. I'll, like, watch you and make sure you're doing it right."

"OK, I'll do it," Izzy's old buddy, Lawrence, volunteered. Then he turned to the group. "Which one of you motherfuckers screwed up last night?"

"I said lead the group like Craig does it," said Izzy.

"That's how Craig does it," they answered.

He should've known. "OK, go on."

"Alright," said Lawrence. "Who is it? Did all of youse fuck up?"

"I drank."

"Tell us about it."

"What's there to tell? I drank."

"How much?"

"Just three beers."

That didn't seem like much, thought Izzy. Maybe he's making progress.

"Three cans, three forties, or three kegs?" asked Lawrence.

"Three forties."

"What made you think you could drink three forties?"

"I can drink a lot more than that."

"You know what I mean. What made you think you could drink?"

"My welfare worker hates me. She said she was going to sanction me if I didn't turn in my attendance from here. I turned it in, but they lost it. I get a letter that says I'm sanctioned and I've got to call to get a fair hearing. I tried calling, but the voicemail is always busy and I can't leave a message. Then I…"

"Aw, poor me, poor me, pour me a drink," said Lawrence. "You didn't answer my question. What made you think you could drink?"

"You're not listening. So I called the supervisor. She looked things up and found my paper right there. I got my welfare back and she's giving me a new worker."

"So, you drank because you weren't feeling sorry for yourself, for once."

"Right, I was celebrating."

"Like I said, what made you think you could drink?"

"I don't know; if I can't drink when I'm happy and I can't drink when I'm mad, when can I drink?"

"You can't drink at all."

"But my problem isn't alcohol. I use cocaine."

"It doesn't matter, you can't drink."

"Why not?"

"I'm done with this guy," Lawrence said to me. "We need Craig here. I don't know what he'd say."

Another group member inserted, "He'd say, when you quit using one drug, you can't go using other drugs. That's just switching addictions."

"Right."

"Can we take our smoke break?"

It seemed like a good idea, thought Izzy. It would give him time to think of something else to do with this group.

## Chapter 32 - Bark

"Bark!" said Pip.

"What is it, boy?" asked Izzy when he went out in the hall for break. "What are you, like, trying to say?"

"Bark!" the dog repeated, facing a closed office door.

"Is someone in there?"

Pip didn't say anything. He just wagged his tail.

"What's the matter?" said Melvina, the office manager.

"Pip's, like, barking at something in that office."

"There ain't nobody in that office, that's no one's office," she said.

Pip cocked his ears, then his head.

"Pip's barking for a reason," he said. "There's got to be something there."

"Who're ya gunna believe, me or the dog?" said Melvina.

"Pip, like, doesn't go around barking all the time for no reason. If he's going through the trouble of barking, we ought to listen."

"Bark!" said Pip.

Izzy tried the door. It was locked.

"See, no one's in there."

"I'm telling you, there's someone in there. Go get the keys."

"I'll get the keys if it means you'll stop going on about somebody being in that office," she said as she stalked away.

She got halfway down the hall when the door opened. Izzy startled back. A man and a woman appeared.

"Bark! Bark!" said Pip. "Bark!"

"Pip, that's OK," Izzy said, grabbing his collar.

"Who're you and what're you doing in that office?" said Melvina, stalking back, faster.

"I'm Pete, this is Kate. Dr Ahern said we could use this office."

"Just what're you using it for?" she asked, examining the two for signs of undress. There wasn't any.

"We're counselors. Dr Ahern hired us. We help people stop smoking."

"And are you helping anyone stop smoking while you're skulking in that office?"

"No not yet. We were just settling in."

"Well, when you're settling in, make sure the office manager and the dog knows you're here. You frightened everyone half to death."

"I'm sorry," they said together.

"Who're you going to help stop smoking?" Izzy asked.

"Why, everybody, everybody that smokes, that is," said Pete.

"Staff and clients," added Kate.

## Chapter 33 - The Family Man

"It's hard to know what to do when you got a fambly. It's even hard to know when it's good to get yourself shot. I was fixen to kill myself a month ago, but everythin' I wanted, I got it right now 'cause I got me a fambly."

"What's this got to do with your addiction?" asked a group member.

"That's OK. Let him, tell his story his way. We'll, like, get to his addiction later," Izzy said.

Truth was; Pip gave him the idea when he started barking and they found he was barking for a reason. People do things, like use drugs, for a reason. Get them to tell their story, and listen, and you'll find out what it is. The group volunteered Clifton, the newest member, who went on in his countrified manner.

"I got a woman and six chirdren. They weren't mine to start with. They belonged to another man, but he got took off to jail and a second man come and took his place. He made a few more chirdren 'til the first man come back and let himself in through the front door. The second man say, 'what you doin' in my house?' The first man say, 'This ain't your house, it's mine, and that woman you're layin' up with is my woman.' The second man say, 'you're wrong, they're all mine now,' and he made some holes in him. So the first man go in the grave, the second man go to the prison the first man just come from, and the women is left alone with all her chirdren. That's when I come along and got me a fambly.

"There's three boys and three girls. I can't remember all their names, but there's the boys and the girls. I got all the girls in one room and all the boys in th'other. I got a TV for each of their rooms, but I only run cable into the girls' room. The boys got so mad they rush into the girls' room and kick them out. I say, OK, I'll get you cable for you boys, too. You wait a minute, now. So I got a splicer and put cable in the boys' room for them to look at, too.

"I keep the chirdren in the house all day long, I don't let them go out in no street 'cause there's bad shit goin' on out there. You know there is 'cause the day I met them I was walkin' back from the bridge, all hepped up 'cause I'm out of prison with no place to stay, no woman to stay with, and no chirdren to holler at. I had all that there before I went away, but my woman weren't one to go visitin' her man in prison. She go back down south to stay with her Momma. When I get out, she gone, and I can't get to her 'cause the parole man would be lookin' for me. I went to the bridge to jump off, but I got scairt. I start thinkin' I'm gunna walk around a bit and go back to that bridge when I ain't scairt no more.

"Then, when I'm walkin' around, I get to this corner and a bullet flew up and killed a man dead in front of me. I got scairt that another bullet might fly up and kill me, before I got me a fambly. Then I got mad, sayin' to myself, you fool, you were fixen to jump off that bridge for a minute. Then a woman comes out of her house with her chirdren to stare at the body. I get to talkin' with her and I ain't mad or scairt about nothin'' no more.

"The next mornin' I'm layin' up with the woman and I'm sayin' I'm gunna hustle up some money and get TV's and cable and that there, to keep the children in the house where they're not fixen to get shot. It been a long time since I lay up with a woman and it feel nice. The kids is makin' noise in the house and that sound nice, too. I went to the bridge wantin' all that there, but now I guess I don't need to jump offen it no more.

"I'm layin' up with the woman and listenin' to her chirdren and there's a knock on the door. I go see who it is. His name is Chief and he's fixen to sell drugs from out my house. Chief's got a big ol' scar that go from the corner of his mouth back to his ear, like a smirk. Behind him, on the sidewalk there's three boys laughin' around the white chalk mark where the man got shot last night. I take some reefer from time to time, that and a forty; but I won't have nothin' to do with no drugs 'cause I gots me a fambly here.

"'Lookee here, I'm carryin' paper on me right now,' I say, `I gots a parole man that keeps stoppin' by.'

"He say, all right, he'll have his boys stand on the corner outside my window and they won't be comin' in.

"I keeps the radio on in the front room all day and all night long and I keeps the window open next to the radio. I never lock the door just like I never locked the door back home. The boys like listenin' to the radio when they're standin' there, so they watch the house for me when I'm gone. When I'm home they watch it, too. Just in case that second man come home from prison one day.

"Then one day my woman is pickin' up the clothes from off the floor. She gunna wash the oldest boy's pants. She go in the pockets and there's a bag in there.

"'What you got here in your pants, boy?' my woman say to him. She call him Jamel, I think.

"'I don't know,' he say back.

"'Don't say you don't know when you know. What you doin' with a bag of crack cocaine in your pants, boy?'

"'I got it from Chief.'

"My woman comes to me and say, `You gots to whoop that chile's ass.'

"'I ain't whoopin' no chile's ass,' I say. `If that boy go to school and tells his teacher I done whooped his ass, I'll be back in prison. You gots to do your own ass whoopin'.'

"She whoops his ass and she whoops it good, 'cause she won't have him bringing drugs in the house. Then she say to him, `you ain't goin' to school for the rest of the week.' Then she go out the door with the bag to smoke it up and get some mo'.

"I'm sittin' up in the house with the kids for the rest of the week. Their Momma hasn't come home yet. No one want to go to school 'cause Jamel ain't goin'. We're runnin' out of food 'cause I can't get out to do a little hustle. I see Chief out the door and he look serious on one side of his face. I call his name and he turn around so I can see his smile.

"'These chirdren's Momma went up country,' I say.  Watch 'em a bit, so I can do a little hustle.'

"I get back to the house that night and I'm carryin' a bag of food. I see a man come steppin' off the porch with a gun in his hand when I turn the corner. My woman's back and she's passed on the couch. The middle girl is cryin' real bad, like to wake up her Momma.

"I say, 'Hush, chile. You wake up your Momma.' But she woke up anyway.

"'I'm scairt,' the chile say.

"'Where's Chief?' I say.

"'He left when Momma come home. After she go to sleep, a man come in and point a gun at me. He be wantin' me to give him a bag.'

"Crazy geeker, come in the door lookin' for a bag, but Chief's not there.

"'I'm gunna go talk to him,' I say.

"I wasn't goin' to fight the geeker or that there, I was just goin' to talk to him and say that I got somethin' to do with that chile. Just so he know that if he go disrespectin' a girl, she gots a man who cares.

"I'm fixen to run out the door and go find him, but the Momma is woke all the way now. These two females, the girl and her Momma, are pullin' at me tellin' me not to run off and get myself shot. I say, no, I ain't gunna get shot, I'm just gunna go talk with that geeker. They let me go and just as I run off the porch all these cop cars come up from everywhere. I don't know who called 'em, but someone did. All the cops jump out of their car and go chasin' the geeker. I step back in the door so they don't go after me. They all run up and down the street. This one cop with a big belly chases him till he's out of breath and then he stands in the middle of the street with his hands on his knees.

"The other cops run up on him and he gets caught. We all watch when they put him in the police car. His eyes is all red and his mouth gone wild.

"My woman say, 'I'm glad you didn't go talk to him like you was gunna cause you was fixen to get shot.'

"'I don't care if I do get shot,' I say to her. It weren't a month ago a man got shot in front of me and I was scairt that a bullet might fly up and kill me dead. I was scairt then 'cause I didn't have me a fambly. But I weren't scairt a bit when I was fixen to go talk to the geeker with the gun. I figure if I got shot and lived, I'd feel good 'cause I got shot for a reason. If I got shot and dead, I don't know how I'd feel 'cause I don't know how you feel when you're dead.

"'You godamn fool,' she say. 'If you get shot and dead I'd be mad as hell with you 'cause you gotsta stay and help me with these chirdren.'

"That's why I say it's hard to know what to do when you got a fambly. It's even hard to know when it's good to get yourself shot."

# Chapter 34 - Fine

The group met the next day and Craig still looked like hell. But so did the day, for that matter. Clouds had set in for the winter, like a furrowed brow, and it started to piss rain. The group shuffled into the room as gloomily as Craig and as the day. They sprawled over their seats every which way, as if they were dead and deposited there.

"Check in," Craig growled.

"Bill; clean date: September twenty-ninth; alcohol and cocaine; today, I'm tired. I don't need time."

"Where the hell's Sandy?" said Craig.

"He hasn't been here for days," said Bill. "Not since the last time you were in group."

"You know what that means," said Craig. "He went back out and used. Go on."

"Donna, tired, marijuana, October thirtieth; I don't need time."

"Clifton, alcohol and marijuana, one week; I's tied."

"Do you need time?"

"No."

A peculiar question, Izzy thought. We all need time, or want time, even if we don't need it. Who doesn't desire a long life, or at least eternal bliss? There are many who desire eternity who don't know what to do with themselves on a slow Sunday afternoon, but we crave it, all the same. These folks ought to want eternity all the more, having given over so much of their lives chasing the dragon, they find themselves lagging behind. They all need time; today they needed time to sleep. It was clear they didn't want to spend it here.

"Lawrence, cocaine, four months; I'm fine."

"You're fine, huh?" said Craig. "You know what FINE stands for?"

"Yeah, I know, fucked up, insecure, neurotic, and emotional. I'm the other kind of fine."

"If you're all tired or fine, we'll have a hell of a group today. You're all cured; I guess you can go home."

"One day at a time," said Lawrence. "I don't have to use today, so I guess I'm cured for today. I don't know what tomorrow will bring."

"Go on, check in."

"Marie, heroin, five months; I'm tired."

"What did you do to them yesterday?" Craig said to the intern. "Have them run a marathon?"

"No, Clifton, like, told us his story," Izzy said.

"I see; he probably wore himself out, thinking of lies to tell you."

"I didn't think he was lying."

"He's that good at it. You want to know how to tell when an addict is lying?"

"How?"

"His lips are moving."

Izzy wanted to argue and defend Clifton and them all, but he looked around. They sat there like beached whales, not even getting angry. It wasn't worth the bother.

"Go on, who's next?"

"Ramon, cocaine, I drank two days ago, but I don't need to talk about it."

"You drank and you don't need to talk about it?"

"We talked about it last group."

"So you're cured, too. How are we going to use this time?"

"Where were you?" Ramon asked Craig.

"I was doing paperwork. They always have piles of paperwork for us to do. I left you in the capable hands of my intern. Didn't he tell you I was doing paperwork?"

"He told us."

"Alright, then, that's what I was doing. Next question; you want to know what I had for breakfast? Are you here about me, or are you here about you?"

There was no reply.

The intern broke the silence. "The group may not have to talk about using drugs, but they all have their, like, underlying issues. Yesterday, Clifton talked about feeling suicidal and missing his family. I don't know, but I think a lot of people might drink and use drugs to deal or cover up those feelings. Maybe if people, like, tell their stories and we get to the underlying issues, they won't have to use."

"That stuff's for mental health. If they need to talk about their feelings, they got to go to mental health."

Izzy was embarrassed for Craig. He wished they weren't talking in group. "But… we're, like, combining, remember," he said out of the side of his mouth. "We're not making that distinction between chemical dependency and mental health. Dr Ahern said…"

"I heard what Dr Ahern said. You know what; I think you're doing a great job with group. I'll let you do it again today. I'll go do paperwork. You just let me know if someone uses."

Craig left. Izzy went out in the hallway with him.

"Are you OK?" I asked.

"I'm fine," he spat, and walked away.

The intern returned to group and they finished check in. Everyone was tired or fine, but no one asked the intern how he was feeling. He was confused. He wasn't sure if he did something right, or something wrong. Craig was having an off day; that was clear. Maybe he was uneasy about all the changes. He might be feeling threatened by the smoking counselors being a-round; or, the reality of what Dr Ahern was having them do settled in. Many, like children accustomed to coloring books, don't know what to do when there are no lines to color within.

"OK, who has a story to tell?"

Bill volunteered. This was his story.

# Chapter 35 - The Post Pounders

A tractor shuttled back and forth across a hillside vineyard above Keuka Lake, pulling the trailer of a post pounding crew. The tractor, in granny gear, ground mindlessly across the side hill, tipped like a cocky hat. As it paused for the workers to replace a broken post, the exhaust cap tapped impatiently. But only the tractor seemed impatient. The workers labored methodically, maintaining the grape trellis. The driver slumped, steering with two fingers. The man on the ground, following the trailer, might have been mud, formed up to hold fence pliers and a hammer. Two more men, mounted on a platform above the trailer, swung twelve-pound mauls at the posts as they rode by.

Far below the workers, the lake, bloated with its meal of two feet of melted snow, was taking its comfort between the hills. The hill was so steep, it seemed that the driver would fall straight into the lake and startle it if he were to jump from his seat. But Bill had no thought of jumping. He was enjoying the rest that driving affords. Every four rows the crew rotated its positions and he had just come from the pounding platform, his fingers still curved stiff to the diameter of the maul handle.

"My Parole Officer told me to call the vineyard and get a job," Bill told the group. "The PO had this squeaky chair and he looked straight at me and blew smoke in my face. I thought a-bout that later when I was pounding posts. Each post was the PO's head, blowing smoke at me while I brought the hammer down. 'Call the number and make yourself useful for once,' the PO said. 'You're going to learn what rules and structure are for. If you don't have them, you'll keep falling back into the slime that you came from.' The PO flipped through my file. 'Writing bad checks; making promises you can't keep. Promise me you'll call that number and keep that promise or I'll violate your ass.'

"On the day I started the job at the vineyard I learned the whole crew had the same PO. 'Welcome to the chain gang,' they said."

Rodney was the crew chief by virtue of his seniority. Although he was a penniless parolee no less than the rest of them, he was so solicitous of the vines and urged them to keep good time so frequently that you'd think he was part owner of the vineyard. As is often the case when one man is supervising another who is in every other way his superior, the one in command is apt to acquire a bitter dislike of the subordinate. This is how Rodney felt about popular, golden-haired Gus, who stood in a wide stance, on the pounding platform, his bare chest pink and dry in the cold spring wind.

The fourth of the post pounding crew was Hoppy. Days before, Gus had driven the tractor over Hoppy's foot. Hoppy just stood there and grinned as the wheel forced his steel toed boots into the mud. Hoppy was pounding with Gus now, still grinning, and as friendly with Gus as if Gus had dropped a ton of diamonds on his foot and not a tractor. Gus started calling him Hoppy, a name Hoppy liked so well, that's what he started calling himself.

Bill took the tractor out of gear at the next row. It was time to change positions. It was Gus's turn to drive and Bill would jump down and play in the mud, but Rodney said no; he wanted Gus in the mud. Bill would go on driving and he would pound with Hoppy.

Bill said, "That's all right, I've had my turn. Gus can drive."

"I'm the crew chief and I said you drive and Gus can walk."

Gus hollered, "Yes, sir, Rodney, sir! I'd be happy to slog through the mud sir! I don't need to drive, sir! I'd be happy to eat your shit, sir!"

They all laughed and kidded about what Rodney would do when he sold the vineyard, everyone but Rodney. They started their pounding again. Gus slogged behind, singing the chain gang song.

When they got to the end of the row, the end post was partly pulled out of the ground, leaning inward, the bottom glistening with moisture. The end posts of each row require special attention, for they support the whole row of grapes. In a rainy fall, when the vines are full of wet leaves and fruit, the end posts are often overcome so that the trellis collapses, spoiling much of the harvest. Bill stopped the tractor, took it out of gear, and set the brake. Hoppy and Rodney put down their mauls and waited for Gus to reach them. When he did, he hoisted a six-pack out of the trailer by its plastic yoke. Black smoke puffed from under the tractor's exhaust cap as Gus popped a can. The beer foamed and dripped down his chest as he downed half of it in a single draught. He leaned against the end post. It had as much give as a hammock and Gus might have taken a nap, but Rodney said, "Unwrap that wire, boy, and be quick about it. I want that post pulled."

Bill put his feet up on the wheel, and lit a cigarette. The lake seemed to be asleep by now, oblivious to anything going on a-round it. On the edge of the field stood a motionless herd of deer that had come out of the still snowy woods to feed on the exposed grass of the vineyard. He could barely see them against the gray trees. They stared at the crew with intense black eyes, their noses sniffing the bouquet of his cigarette, Gus' beer, and the tractor's diesel.

"Right away, Rodney, sir; just as soon as I finish my beer, sir."

The wind picked up a little, raising goose flesh on Gus' bare back.

"I said get that post ready. We don't have time to waste."

"And I said I'm going to finish my beer."

Rodney began to pick up the post maul. On the pounding platform, he loomed a good four feet higher than Gus.

"If you don't have that post ready by the time I come down with this maul, I'm going to start pounding if you're ready or not."

Gus didn't move an inch. He leaned on the post, took another sip of beer and gave Hoppy a wink. Rodney swung the maul and he brought it down on the top of the post, an inch or two from Gus' head.

Gus threw the half empty can of beer at Rodney. It missed and went sailing off towards the lake, which seemed to have woken, its face looking as though it had fallen asleep on a corduroy pillow. Rodney gave another swing with the maul; this time aiming at Gus' head. It missed and, not having struck anything, continued in its arc until it hit Hoppy in his knee; the knee of his good leg. Gus, seeing his friend injured, climbed the pounding platform and began to hack away at Rodney with the fence pliers. They have a sharp end to them, that's used to dig staples out. That end was soon embedded in Rodney's brain.

The lake seemed to have dozed back off. The sky brought iron shaped clouds and held them over the hills as if to say, this part's wrinkled, I'll straighten it out. The deer alternated their gazing with grazing. Everything was still, but Rodney was the stillest of all.

"He's dead," said Hoppy, who wasn't smiling.

A score or so of women were working a few rows uphill of the post pounders, tying vines to the newly tightened trellis. They had a good view of the lake, the deer, and of the manslaughter. Within a few moments, the stillness of the scene was broken by the women calling to each other, did you see that! They all saw it.

Gus ordered, "Put it in gear, Bill. Let's get out of here.'"

"I obeyed," said Bill to the group. "Although now I can't say why. I had no reason to obey Gus. He just was the kind of guy that, when he told you to do something, you did it, no matter what. I drove the rig out of the vineyard, towards the road. None of us had a car, we all had rides to work, but we needed one now to make our getaway. I drove to where all the cars of the tiers were parked, but none of them had left their keys in. 'We're screwed,' I said."

Gus said, "No we're not; it could take the sheriff forever to get out here. We could be in the next state by the time they respond. Drive, drive."

He might have been correct, but, as chance would have it, a Sheriff's Deputy had been visiting the wife of his best friend just down the road. He came out of her house, tightening his belt, just as the post pounding crew drove by with a tractor in fifth gear, a pounding rig, and a man, lying in the trailer with a fence pliers sticking out of his head. He gave chase and Gus directed the crew to a nearby barn, where they drove into the open doorway, and hid in the hay bales.

"Come on out of there, you murderers," said the Sheriff's Deputy from outside the barn.

"Do you promise to let us go, if we do?" called back Gus.

"I can't promise that, but I promise you'll be treated fairly."

"I think we'll stay here and burn in hell before we believe a cop's promises."

"Come on out before you make things worse."

"They can't get worse."

"Look," Bill said to Gus. "He's calling for backup and we have no way out. Let's make a run for it before any of his buddies get here. We can run in three directions and he can only chase one of us."

"Hoppy can't run."

"He can take the tractor."

Gus studied him with narrowed eyes and glanced over at Hoppy, who nodded in agreement. Gus might have been wondering if Bill's plan was to give himself up when he ran out, securing whatever leniency he could. In fact, it was his plan. By now, any spell Gus had on him was broken by the prospect of getting in trouble with the parole officer. At any rate, Hoppy's agreeing with Bill persuaded him to go through with it.

"All right, let's do it."

They got Hoppy up on the tractor, unhooked the trailer, and pushed it outside, aiming it at the cop. He jumped out of the way and the trailer crashed into the patrol car. Hoppy and Bill threw threw their hands up in the air in surrender and Gus ran off into the woods. The cop got Bill and Hoppy handcuffed and into the patrol car before they began to hear any other sirens coming their way.

Bill said to the group, "They searched those woods for the rest of the day and put up roadblocks, but they never did find Gus. He's still out there, I guess, doing whatever, and I'm here."

"What did your PO have to say about all that?" asked another group member.

"He said I was a fucking idiot and sent me back to prison for consorting with other criminals."

Back at Keuka Lake, a herd of deer was poaching grape leaves from a vineyard. They look up from time to time to sniff the air and scan for danger. They hear something, raise their tails, and consider running away but decide it's not worth it and go back to eating. The lake gives them all a stare as blank as a guard's shades. The sky brings a few clouds by to see. They hover for a while, take a few pictures, and move on.

# Chapter 36 - Clean Time

Craig was on his third day of looking like hell. The naked, tattooed woman on his arm, green, as she was, looked better than he did. But at least they had donuts, plain donuts, at this meeting. He silently dunked one in his coffee and inverted it. The coffee seeped down into the donut, darkening it as it spread. He took a bite and sucked the coffee out before he began to chew.

"Half of all addicts will end up dying because they smoke cigarettes, not of their alcohol, cocaine, heroin, marijuana, or any other drug use," lectured Pete, the tobacco counselor, to the staff the next morning.

Kate added, "Tobacco is sneaky, it's not as intoxicating as the other drugs, it's more socially acceptable, but the health problems it causes are legion: emphysema, heart trouble, cancer…"

"We've all got to die sometime," said Pellegrino.

"We do," said Pete. "But, most of the time, when we know something is going to kill us, we fight it like heck. Except when we're addicted, then we make excuses for it and say it doesn't matter."

Pellegrino corrected him. "We fight like hell. If you're going to fight, fight like hell. When you fight like heck, you lose the fight."

Bella asked, "Are we going to tell the clients that it's all right if they use mood altering chemicals, just don't smoke cigarettes?"

Kate answered, "No, of course not. Tobacco is a drug just like all the others. It's mood altering also. Also, research has shown that addicts who quit smoking at the same time as they quit their other drugs have a lower rate of relapse with all their addiction than those who retain their tobacco use when they quit everything else. Tobacco use is associated with their other drug use. What do you do when you go to a bar? You get a drink and light a cigarette. The same part of the brain gets stimulated as cocaine and crystal meth."

"We tell addicts to change people, places, and things associated with their drug use. Well, tobacco is one of those things," said Pete.

The Head Administrator took a long draught from her Starbucks and said, "We can't bill for tobacco counseling. Insurance companies don't pay for it and the regulations don't permit it," as if the All Staff Meeting didn't happen. Maybe she thought that, if she went on talking like it never happened, they would forget it happened.

"That shows you the insanity of all the regulations and the insurance companies," said Dr Ahern. "Here's a condition that kills half of all addicts prematurely and causes untold amounts of insurance payments for cancer surgery, heart surgery, and oxygen tanks, and they won't pay for treatment. And the regulations; don't get me started on the regulations. Why do you think tobacco use is not mentioned in the state regulations? Because the tobacco lobby pays off the state government, that's why."

"I hired Pete and Kate," continued Dr Ahern, "simply because so many of our clients smoke and, since we are disregarding the regulations and going it alone anyway, we are free to provide treatment for tobacco use to any clients who are interested.

We can provide it to the staff, also, because the clients are never going to be able to quit if the staff are still using right in front of them or smelling like smoke."

"Right," said Pete, "it would be like expecting an alcoholic to stop drinking in a bar."

"So we have to stop smoking, now?" said Pellegrino.

"You can smoke all you want at home," said Ahern, "but not at work. It's just like the rules we have about drinking. A counselor can use alcohol at home, but not at work, and he can't smell like booze at work; and if he drinks at home and is still impaired when he goes to work, there will be problems, too."

"I need a fucking smoke," said Pellegrino when the meeting ended. "I don't care what they do to me. They can fire me if they want, I'm going to smoke."

Craig hadn't said a word through the whole meeting. He didn't even appear to listen; he just ate all the plain donuts in the box.

"You coming to group?' Izzy asked him.

Craig didn't answer. He supposed he thought that if he walked to the group room and let everyone in, that would be answer enough.

"Check in," he barked before they sat down.

"Are you in group?" asked Bill.

"I'm here, aren't I? Check in."

"Donna, marijuana, October thirteenth. I feel…"

"Marijuana and tobacco," interrupted Craig.

"Tobacco?"

"Yeah, you smoke cigarettes, don't you? I've seen you."

"So what? Are we counting that now, too?"

"A drug is a drug is a drug."

"Cigarettes ain't a drug," said Clifton. "They're natural."

"They're a drug and we're counting them now."

"Then, shit, we all just lost our clean time."

"Like hell, I've got four months."

"I'm not quitting cigarettes, its all I've got left."

Izzy told the group some of the things that Pete and Kate had just said. They listened, in a jittery sort of way, but their focus was really on Craig. The intern was talking as if it was his group, but Craig's gloomy presence sucked the attention out of them as if he was a black hole.

"How're you going to counsel us, Craig? You smoke. All the Chemical Dependency Counselors smoke."

Craig went on looking like hell; like a smoked up cigarette butt, thrown on the sidewalk, smashed by a shoe, and soaked by the rain. If Pellegrino was right, counselors had to be fucked up, but not in the particular way their clients were fucked up at the time of their counseling. Craig looked fucked up every which way. He may have been the one group member who most needed time today, but he wasn't going to take it. He would never do that, he was too ethical. The burned up biker was too ethical.

"I'm not going to counsel you; Izzy's taking over the group for good. Have a nice life."

"You quitting?"

He didn't answer. He must have thought leaving them with the intern for the third time was answer enough. Izzy followed him out. "What's going on?" he asked.

Craig walked on. The intern overtook him and stopped him from going further.

"You're not leaving me again until you tell me what's going on."

"I don't have to tell you nothing."

It must be Izzy had learned something by then. He must have hung around that clinic long enough to begin to pick up the signs. The signs Craig feared the group and his colleagues would see if he stayed around, spoke, or let anyone see anything but his anger.

"You've gone back to using, haven't you, Craig?"

"So what're you going to do? Ask me to tell you my underlying issues?"

"You've got to tell someone," Izzy heard himself say. "Let it out. Your secrets will make you sick."

"You just passed your course. You got a fucking A, now leave me alone."

The intern wanted to stop him, but he knew Craig wasn't ready. He knew that the same way he knew Craig had been using. Izzy was a counselor now, and he had to use his skills, such as they were, with the people who wanted them, such as they were. It's only the wannabe counselors who counsel folks who don't want counseling. They headshrink their friends and family, and force change from an alcoholic spouse who hasn't changed, but for the worse, in ten years. Amateurs give it away for free, professionals ask for your insurance card. Izzy was a professional now, or he would be once they paid him. That would be a simple matter, he thought, they had a vacancy now, and Dr Ahern wasn't one to get hung up on regulations and make him wait until graduation.

It was a bittersweet sight, seeing Craig go off. I'll miss him, Izzy told himself, but I got a job to do now.

Come to think of it, it wasn't bittersweet at all, Izzy answered himself. I won't miss Craig, he was a pain in the neck. He wouldn't let me do anything but watch clients piss for a month.

Oh, but I learned so much from him, he debated.

You didn't learn a thing except how to get piss from them, said the other side of him. Craig never did anything with clients in group except to bark at them.

The first side said, you learned that, no matter how bad a counselor you are, you could never be as bad as Craig.

And so, with all this steadfastness Izzy returned to the group, his group. They hadn't stopped talking since the two left: talking about Craig, tobacco, their clean time. Everyone had a lot to say. Izzy listened to the music of their talk for a while without hearing the words. They played outrage, excitement, loss, and rejection, all mixed up, with no orchestration, a jumble, no, a jungle of feelings.

Izzy listened, but he knew he had to do more than listen; he was a counselor now, so he had to act. They might talk, but it isn't a group until the counselor acts and makes it therapeutic; until he does, it's only a conversation. Therapy is more, so much more, than a conversation. It's a conversation you always wanted to have, but were afraid to, or couldn't, or didn't know the words. It's the questions that never get asked, the answers that had never been listened to; it's supposed to be a corrective experience. Izzy had to say something to turn this group into a corrective experience.

"How does it, like, make you feel to lose Craig and cigarettes all in the same day?"

The conversation sank; not as if it had sprung a leak and submerged till the sea overtook the gunwales, not as if someone had rocked the boat till it capsized, not as if it were torpedoed and blown all asunder. It sank as if a great fish's tail had swatted it and scattered everything, oarsmen and oarlocks, all over the sea. It took them a few minutes before they rose to the surface, caught their breath, and clung to whatever flotsam they could find.

"How does it make me feel?"

"Yes"

"Bad."

"Shitty."

"I'd howl at the moon if it was out."

# Chapter 37 - Howl

As we have seen, Dr Ahern had rejected his black Lab, Pip. It was a little more complicated than that: the therapy dog had actually lost interest in Dr Ahern after coming to the clinic. Having been brought here opened up Pip to new possibilities, innumerable hands to be petted by, and scores of donut breaks and lunch tables. Pip was in doggie heaven. He was living to his full potential, and may have been the most self-actualized creature walking around on any number of legs at Behavioral Health. Dr Ahern's rejection only wounded his psyche temporarily, the black Lab had plenty of others to attach himself to, and, although there were none of his species around, he was never at a loss for human companionship.

It appeared that pale Ms Pillsbury had taken up ownership of the dog; if feeding, watering, walking, brushing, and occasionally scolding comprise ownership. In some ways, they made a good match; they had a similar function, although dissimilar in appearance and manner. Like salt and pepper, one was black and the other was white. Both were accustomed to serving Dr Ahern, in their own ways; by nature, Ms Pillsbury was as suspicious and distrustful as Pip was friendly and sociable. Although the Labrador retriever was a dog and, inescapably, had a dog's brain, he was the brighter of the two and clearly more creatively flexible and adaptable to changing conditions, within limits, of course, as we shall see. Pip loved life with a genial, jolly, gregariousness peculiar to his species. A few crumbs fallen to the floor could make any day Christmas, given him a plate to lick, and it might as well be Thanksgiving, every arrival of a new client was a christening. Pip's calendar might as well have had 365 ¼ holidays, except that he hated weekends.

There were few people around on the weekends, only the cleaning crew and security, and Pip yearned for the bustle of the working day at the clinic. The dog had a lot in common with the cleaning crew and may have related to them on a professional level and discussed the fine points of going through garbage and cleaning floors, but they brought vacuums. More than weekends, and even more than cats, squirrels, and birds right outside the window, Pip hated vacuums. He wasn't too wild about security guards, either. Their jangling keys annoyed him, even though with them, too, he shared a common interest in guarding. Pip slept through most of the weekends, his only diversion was following the cleaning crew around when they weren't operating those infernal vacuums.

It came to pass that one weekend Pip was following the cleaning crew around for a diversion. He really had to take a walk and asked different cleaning people several times to take him. Several felt it shouldn't have to be their job to walk the dog, others were afraid of the creature, and the rest thought someone else would do it. That's another thing Pip hated about the weekends. When he wasn't sleeping, he patrolled the hallways so he wouldn't have to think about his full bladder. Anyway, that was the situation one weekend when he was following the cleaning crew around.

On Ahern's orders, many staff had moved their offices that week and, in doing so, placed some spare furniture out in the hallways. The cleaners discussed what to do about these impediments to their cleaning and, together, they decided to store them in the basement of Behavioral Health. Of course, Chemical dependency was in the basement, but sometimes even basements have basements and that's where they put the spare furniture. Pip followed them; back and forth, back and forth, hoping that one would notice his need, set down the burden, and take him for that walk. He followed them until the last bookcase was carried to the basement's basement and then, distracted by the scent of mouse; he lingered and got locked in when they left.

This was a fine situation for a dog to be. Upon apprising himself of his circumstances, Pip did what all dogs do: he scratched at the door and whined, and whined and whined, and scratched and scratched, but, alas, no one heard him because the cleaning crew had started up their vacuums. His bladder, by now, had grown to the size of a Pomeranian; the state of affairs was dire. Another whiff of mouse engrossed him for a while, but, when the track grew cold, there was nothing left for him to do but sit, consider his options, and exercise his sphincter. There comes a time, however, when even the Hoover Dam will not hold. That time came now. His bladder did not burst open like a Lab released from the car at the dog park; it seeped out in a disinclined trickle, like that same dog, exiting the car to visit the vet. Nonetheless, in no time, there was an incriminating puddle on the floor of the basement.

"I'm a bad dog," thought Pip, "a bad, bad dog."

Although he did a bad thing, Pip was not a bad dog. He was a highly competent therapy dog; but, even though that was the case, he made an error more serious than the puddling ever could have been. Anyone understanding the circumstances could excuse the puddling. He made an error common to humans and dogs, therapists and non-therapists alike. Psychologists call it The Fundamental Attribution Error: the mistake of confusing the guilt of something he did, with the shame of who he was. This common mistake would prove to be his undoing.

At times like these, our feelings are complex, often more complex than they need to be. He felt guilty and ashamed; unwarranted, but he felt them, just the same. He also felt sheer joy. Let's face it; even highly trained therapists would admit there is nothing better, upon having a full bladder, than taking a good piss. You might imagine this joy could chase away the shame and guilt, as a Boxer may intimidate a Chihuahua. The trouble is, Chihuahuas, and shame and guilt, don't intimidate that easily. Chihuahuas can put up a good fight when they have to, and shame and guilt are no different. In other words, the joy Pip felt at having pissed only made the shame and guilt worse.

After an interval, Pip, taking into account that he had already transgressed, deposited a few turds to go along with the puddles. His shame and joy compounded like a credit card balance. His body, very much relieved from the labor of holding it all in, turned over the shift to his mind, which began to manufacture associations.

It is a basic operation of all minds, even dogs' minds, when placed in a predicament, to remember similar experiences, like trying to retrace your steps to find your keys. Pip's mind began to search for a match of when, in the past, he had been this miserable. There was the time when he had been neutered. Likewise, he had pissed indoors and felt ashamed. Moreover, there was a tightness around his abdomen then and he couldn't lick it because of a humiliating Elizabethan collar, but the feeling wasn't the same. There were many other dogs around, for a cage in a kennel had been his recovery room, and he had the benefit of society to help his convalescence pass. This was different; he hadn't felt this miserable since when, in that shadowy past, he was taken away from his mother and his litter.

Every mind has its memories, and it has its deep, deep, numinous memories. The ones on the surface are memories associated with words. We people have many and dogs have a few. These are easily captured and devoured. We gnaw on them like bones, bury them for a while and dig them up again. We cherish them for a time and then easily abandon them for bare feet to step on in the night. Other memories are memories of sights, sounds, and smells. We come upon these unawares; the crayon takes us back to kindergarten as abruptly and instinctively as a hound will chase a rabbit that crosses his path. The deep, deep, numinous memories are those that are associated with feelings and such was Pip's memory of his mother and his litter. They are like the woodchuck that disappears in the burrow. You can dig and dig and never reach it. Try as he might, at the mature age of five man years, Pip could not remember the sight, sound, or the smell of his mother. He could not tell us the story of how he was taken away, which sibling went first, the box he was put it, or any of that. What he could remember was the feeling, the despondent, dreadful feeling of being alone. This was the feeling that came over Pip now, as adamantly as his full bladder had been, and he began to howl.

"Hoooowlllll"

Every feeling insists on its expression, indeed, some theorists say that feeling is an expression; that is, a primitive attempt to communicate some message to another, and that attempting to stifle the expression of a feeling is as pointless as trying not to sweat. The despondent, dreadful feeling of being alone has its expression, one that was unsuspectingly passed on to Pip all the way from his wolf, fox, and coyote forebears, and that expression is the howl, a quite functional expression meant to reunite the scattered members of a pack. His howl was just as forlorn as any heard across arctic wastelands. He might have howled at the moon, but there was no moon, so he howled at the silver crack of light shining under the closed door at the top of the stairs. He howled and howled, but no one heard.

No one heard because, at first, the cleaning people had finished their vacuuming and gone home. The jangling security guard, who was supposed to check the basement's basement every time he made his rounds, failed to do so because, on the weekends, there was nobody who would check to see if he checked; there was no guard for the guard. Then no one heard because it was nighttime and there was no one there to hear. On Sunday, no one heard because that same lackadaisical security guard was on duty and he spent his whole shift watching football. Then no one heard because it was nighttime. On Monday, people heard, but they didn't listen. The staff heard, but they thought the heating system was making funky sounds. Clients heard, but they didn't tell anyone because no one else seemed to hear and they didn't want anyone to think they were hallucinating wolves. Dr Ahern didn't hear because he was engrossed with his quest. Ms Pillsbury might have heard, because she was wondering why the dog had not come to her for walks, but she was two floors away and she thought someone else had begun to walk him. On

Tuesday she wondered why he hadn't eaten any food or drunk
any water, but Dr Ahern had given her a pile of typing to do and
he could look after his own dog, for one day. On Wednesday, the
typing was done, so she wondered some more and called a
search, but by then Pip had stopped howling because he didn't
see much more point in it. Thursday, no one had seen the dog
and they all thought he had given them the slip and gone for a
romp in the great outdoors.

It wasn't until Friday, after six days locked the basement of the
basement, that Pip was discovered by a woman going down in
search of a floor lamp. When she opened the door she was not
greeted by the friendly, AKC certified, Labrador retriever
bounding up the stairs, licking her face in gratitude. No, she was
greeted by the smell of puddles and turds. Nonetheless, she
wrinkled her nose, flipped on the light, and descended the stairs.
The woman heard a growl that she, at first, thought was a step
groaning, but, as she continued down the stairs, the growl grew
deeper and more ominous. She ran up the stairs.

"There's something down there," she called to anyone that
would listen.

The security guard, the same lackadaisical security guard that
was on duty last weekend, figured she had watched too many
horror movies, smirked at her, and bravely went down to check.
The Lab growled when he went down, too, but the man was a
security guard, after all, and, no matter how negligent he might
be when no one was looking, when there was an audience he
could be quite conscientious. He continued down the stairs and
approached the source of the growl. Pip growled until he got
closer, then he darted up the stairs, in search of his food and
water dish. Subsisting on his own puddles, turds, and horrific,
numinous memories; as if he had chased his tail, caught it, and
went on to devour himself, Pip had preserved his finite body, but
starved his infinite soul. He had regressed from being a highly
trained therapy dog, to a matted, emaciated, mad dog. People
screamed when they saw him in the hallways and darted into
doorways. He found his dishes, slaked his thirst, and wolfed

down his food. Ms Pillsbury approached him with the hairbrush and he bit her. Dr Ahern came out of his office to take charge and he bit him, also. The Lab, they said, was deranged, and although you couldn't throw a cat through the department sideways without hitting three therapists, none would treat Pip, so they called animal control and had him taken out and put to sleep.

The event affected everyone in the clinic profoundly, staff and clients alike, for Pip was a popular and highly regarded therapist, albeit a dog. Clients already knew of the wild wolf that dwelt within them. They, especially the addicts, had already shitted and pissed all over their most cherished values. They had already committed The Fundamental Attribution Error and castigated themselves when they should have blamed circumstances. They had already faced the terrible isolation on the bleak Arctic steppes of alienation and humiliation. What they didn't know was that therapists, even AKC registered therapists, had that wolf within them, also. The therapists should have known it, too, but they forgot.

# Chapter 38 – Nature and Nurture

"Dr Staub," Izzy asked. "Does this kind of thing happen often?"

Dr Staub closed the door to his office, inspected the intern for discretion, and decided to pack his pipe full of tobacco, despite the prohibition against it. Izzy needed someone to turn to, since he lost his supervisor and he was still full of admiration of Dr Staub after witnessing him diagnose Bob, the bipolar, so quickly.

"Yes, it happens quite often. People will act according to their natures. No matter how hard they try to cover it up by getting degrees, certificates, a job, and all that, they will always go back to who they are at their core; especially when they are under stress." Having packed his pipe sufficiently, he lit it, leaned back in his chair, thought about what he had just said, and gave his pipe some satisfied puffs.

"Craig had been clean for years," Izzy said. "I don't know what the point is of trying to treat these addicts if they just go back to using; and I've got to, like, do this group now and I don't know what helps."

The psychiatrist puffed a few more times while he thought about what Izzy said. Dr Staub's furniture was better than Craig's, and there was a window. The bookcases held rows of darkened texts by Freud, Alder, and Sullivan, gathering dust; but the decor was as dominated by scores of brand names as a racing car: calendars, pens, post its, and posters shouting out Prozac, Zyprexa, and Neurontin.

"The standard treatment for substance use is just not very effective, that's why they relapse. All they essentially do at Chemical Dependency is replace one addiction with another.

Instead of using drugs, they have them go to meetings. They replace an infantile dependence on substances with an infantile dependence on a higher power. Nothing is really changed, nothing in the person's essential nature. To change anything, we have to get right into the biochemistry of the brain and change that. That'll change the addict's nature and everything will be different."

"You would, like, give people drugs to cure addiction?"

"Not drugs – medication. It's a foreign idea to most drug counselors, I know. The recovery community grudgingly accepts Methadone, but Methadone also just replaces one serious addiction with a less serious one. What I'm talking about are promising medications that are coming that reduce the reinforcing properties of street drugs. You take it and it will reduce the craving for heroin and alcohol, and if you use those drugs when you are on it, you won't get high. Once we get these medications, everything will be different."

"So, in the future, you will prescribe medications for addicts and they won't need counseling and programs, or any of that."

"Oh, I wouldn't say that. You still need counselors to convince people to take their medication and stay on it when they have minor side effects. Also, people will just want to talk, even if the talking doesn't do them any good; and we'll have to listen, just to make them think we care, even if we really do care, because they won't take the medication if they don't think we care."

Izzy thought, counseling is like the raw meat you hide the pill in that you're trying to get your cat to take. He came up with a new slogan for the walls of Chemical Dependency: A drug is a drug is a drug, unless it's a medication. "So, what do I do with the group? Is there anything I can do that will help them?"

"No, there isn't much we can do with an addict until we get these medications. We can keep them alive while they're detoxing, but, other than that, they are pretty much on their own. Of course, we have no idea how many addicts have an underlying, treatable mental illness that they are self-medicating with their street drugs, like Bob, for instance."

# Chapter 39 - The Birds

Winter had arrived; it spread its drop cloths over the ground, and went on break before continuing the job. The sun had come out with its clipboard, as if to inspect, and extended icicles formed on the eaves of the building, dripping fast, creating slick ice underneath. The smokers came out, too, gathering away from the ice slicks and away from the area Dr Ahern had prohibited, their shadows cast long on the snow behind them, so that the snow seemed to have smokers, also; a parallel world of silhouettes. Smoke gamboled from the ends of the humans' cigarettes and puffed from their mouths. There was no such smoke coming from the silhouettes, though; which may account for why they die of darkness and not of cancer each day.

Izzy saw his group had gathered out in the snow and so he went to join them. He was still a long way off when one figure reached down and picked something up from the ground. They had just gotten out there on break, were lighting up, when one looked down and saw the object. The others gathered around to see. Some were gesturing excitedly, but they stopped when they spotted the intern. As soon as word spread that he was near, the group threw their arms to their sides and tried to act as though nothing happened. Izzy knew better and asked them what they found when he got close enough to do so. The one with the object quickly stuffed it in his pocket.

"Oh, nothing."

"Don't say that," said Izzy. "There was something. I saw how excited you all got. What's in your pocket?"

They had shuffled themselves like a shell game when he came up, but he knew who had the thing in his pocket. It was Ramon. The client sheepishly pulled out an ounce of marijuana.

"What are you doing with that?" Izzy asked.

"Hey, Homes, it wasn't mine. I just found it laying there on the ground. I just picked it up and I was going to throw it away in case one of these addicts found it. It wouldn't be good for them to see it. They'd want to go smoking again."

"That was good of you, Ramon. You can give it to me. I'll take care of it."

"Yeah, right. I give it to you and you'll take it to your college and all your buddies will go puff, puff, puff, puff."

"No, I won't do that. Wait, we'll get rid of it right here so no one can use it."

The intern took the bag of weed and turned towards the pristine field of snow where the silhouettes were having their convention. The silhouettes clustered and watched as he dipped his hand in the bag and sowed the field with the marijuana. Izzy couldn't see their faces, silhouettes have no faces, but he imagined they all wore expressions of regret and sadness.

"Goodbye Mary Jane, we barely knew you."

"Oh, look at it go, that's so sad."

The breeze captured the finest leaves and a distinctive, skunky smell reached their noses.

"Oh, that smells so good. Now I want to use."

"It's not good stuff. It looks like it was mostly seeds."

"I don't care. I would've smoked the seeds"

A flock of sparrows had stayed the winter in the lee of the hospital. With the sunny weather, they were out, looking for food by the man with the hot dog cart. One came over when he saw the intern throw the weed on the field and, in a couple minutes, by whatever means they had to communicate, the whole sparrow community was on the field, pecking at the weed.

"Look at that," said Lawrence. "You've done made a whole new flock of addicts. Now those birds are going to get high and they'll be flying to the worst parts of town, looking for more."

"They'll be flying, all right."

"Yeah, some counselor you are, spreading the disease."

"They're pecking the seeds," said Lawrence. "Now the seed's going to get in their shit and, when they go to dive bomb some guy's windshield, they'll miss because they're high and the seed will plant itself outside a school. The plants will grow and all the kids will see it until one of them pulls off its bud and gives it to all his school buddies to smoke. One little bag of weed, that you would not let Ramon dispose of, will cause all that trouble."

"Yeah, we're going to need some new counselors," said Ramon. "The ones we have won't be enough."

"I think we ought to make Clifton a counselor," said Lawrence. "Cliff, you're the counselor to the birds."

"I don't know nothing 'bout no counseling," said Cliff.

"Oh, sure you do," said Lawrence. You've gotten enough counseling, you could do it yourself by now."

"I don't have no diploma."

"That won't matter. You just counsel the birds. If they ask you for your diploma, we'll go get you one."

With this encouragement, Cliff went and sat down on the bench near the birds because he'd never seen anyone counsel standing up. He crossed his legs, put his hands on his lap, and said, "Now, lookee here, birds. Stop that peckin' at that weed, you hear? It's not good for you. It'll make you fly silly, flying into windows, and that there."

"There," said Lawrence. "What did I say? You're a natural born shrink. Go on, go on, do it."

"Lookee here, when you're peckin' at that there weed, you're not feedin' you fambly. They're back home at their nest worried 'bout you while you're out here peckin' at that there weed."

"They're not listening to you, Cliff. Make 'em listen."

"You there, stop flying away when I'm talkin' to you. I know you're flighty, that there's your nature and you can't help it, but try an' control that nature. You birds, but you can be angels. Y'already got the wings. A angel ain't nothing but a bird with self control. An' you, fightin' with your friend over a little bit of weed, try to share. Weed ain't no good no how unlessen it's shared."

"You're supposed to be counseling them, Cliff, not teaching them to pass a joint."

"There's no use counseling these birds. They're gunna do what they're gunna do."

"I guess you're right. They'll just have to hit bottom before they'll listen. Go ahead and discharge them as non-compliant with treatment recommendations."

"Lookee here, birds, you just go on peckin' at that there weed like you wanna do and come back when you wanna stop. We be here. Don't be too long, though, 'lessen the hawk'll get you."

# Chapter 40 - The Ties that Bind

In the business of behavioral health, the staff are always coming and going. Many will remain at their posts for decades, but the ones who don't are often gone within a few months, as soon as they come to the fretful realization that this job is not for them and they find a way out. Craig had not been at the clinic for decades, nor was he a newcomer; he was a fully ripened counselor, in the prime of his career, so his out of season departure was surprising. Just the same, the staff, inured to turnover, scarcely said a word about it. The Harley poster he left behind in his office was the only sign he'd been there. The plain donuts growing stale on the staff room table were his only memorial. His last will, that Izzy had completed his internship, was lost and the poor intern had only his own testimony to rely on in probate court.

The staff had no objection to Izzy taking Craig's caseload. Indeed, it seemed to be a better arrangement all around than adding those clients to theirs. However, The Head Administrator made an objection: something about Izzy not having any kind of a degree, a license, and not even finishing his internship. She brought the matter to Dr Ahern, who, to everyone's surprise, said that counselors had to be qualified. Dr Ahern was an academic, after all, and had an academic's faith that schooling mattered.

Hearing that Izzy still needed a supervisor, Bella and Pellegrino fell all over themselves volunteering their services. Although they didn't want Craig's caseload, they would take his intern if it meant the student would get them their donuts and collect their urine. If he had his choice, Izzy would have selected Pellegrino on the assumption that a supervisor who thinks you're qualified for a job if you're fucked up would not be too hard on you when you make a mistake. However, he expected that Bella would be assigned, if only because her prayers to God were more likely to be answered than those of the profane Pellegrino.

Alas, the choice of supervisor would belong to neither Izzy nor God; the intern's professor would be the arbitrator. When Izzy went to see his professor, he learned that the University had an agreement with Craig to supervise and that was the end of it. Craig had to sign off, not only to Izzy's competence, but also saying that he worked his thousand hours. Of course, Izzy only had three hundred-and-some of his thousand hours and he didn't have Craig's signature on anything other than a birthday card that had been passed around the office and languished in someone's mailbox after the birthday passed. It didn't matter, though, that Craig had left the clinic, the professor explained, he could still supervise you if you meet with him regularly. The only other choice would be to start your internship all over again with someone new.

For better or for worse, the intern and the biker were wedded for a thousand hours. Like mountain climbers held together by a rope, should one fall, the other would have to either hold or go down with him. Craig was Izzy's inseparable conjoined twin; it was not possible to get rid of the dependency that their academic bond entailed.

The intern ruminated bitterly on this gloomy situation. It seemed like his precious individuality had been exchanged, when he wasn't looking, for a precarious partnership with an unstable drug addict. His free will had sprung a leak, had lost headway, and was sinking. It was highly unjust that another's mistake could set poor, poor innocent him back so far in his career, just as he was getting started. There must have been an interregnum in heaven, when God's fair reign was interrupted by a lapse in the rule of law.

The group echoed Izzy's feelings about abandonment. "Every time I get a counselor and tell him my shit, he leaves and I get another and I got to tell it all over again."

"Yeah, Craig was all right. He was grouchy as hell," said another, "but you could feel him. He was real, if you know what I mean."

"I don't know what the point of recovery is, if someone like Craig can just go out and use."

"My sponsor has twenty years clean, but he keeps his one day coin in his pocket to remind him that he's just one day from his next drink. He says that the only thing that keeps him clean some days, is knowing that he's not just doing it for himself. If he relapses, then he's putting other people at risk."

"Then what the hell's the matter with Craig, then? Didn't he know that he'd want to make us go back out?"

"No one can make you go out, if you don't want to. It's your decision; just like it was his."

"You don't understand the power of addiction then," Lawrence explained, "I've used a hundred times when I didn't want to."

"That's you. How could addiction finally get to someone like Craig?"

"I don't know," said Lawrence. "Addiction uses whatever it can use. Maybe women, maybe good news, maybe bad news, maybe he came into a pile of money."

"Money?" asked Izzy. "How could money make you relapse?"

"Just from the excitement of getting it and wondering what to do with it; addiction is cunning, baffling, and… and patient. It's very patient. All the while Craig was going to college and counseling us, his addiction was doing pushups in the dark, getting ready to take him on when it had its chance. It knew that, if it took him down, it would take a bunch of other people down with him. That made it worth all the trouble."

After an hour of this discussion, one-one thousandth of his approved internship, Izzy learned the valuable lesson that we were all irrevocably linked with one another. He wasn't the only one. The Fate sisters tangled Izzy up with Craig as well as they tangled Craig up with these clients.

"What makes you guys think Craig relapsed?" asked Izzy. "He, like, never said he relapsed, I never said he relapsed. How do you know he just didn't get fed up with all the paperwork and, like, got another job? It happens, you know; you were just saying counselors, like, leave all the time."

"I've seen him," said Ramon. "He's a bouncer at a titty bar. I've seen him with a drink in his hand when the manager wasn't looking, and they say he's the man to talk to if you want cocaine."

"What were you doing at a titty bar?" someone asked.

"What's anyone do at a titty bar? I was looking at tittys."

"Keep going to a barbershop and you'll get a haircut."

Then, I'll keep going to a titty bar. Maybe I'll get tittys."

When group ended, Izzy asked Lawrence to stay behind. "I want you to, like, take me there," he said. "Right now, let's go to that titty bar and get him."

# Chapter 41 - Rescue Operation

The day was brilliant outside and, when Izzy and Lawrence opened the door to the titty bar, they stepped into a cave of seeming absolute darkness. They stumbled around like blind men for a moment, with their hands in front of them, until their eyes adjusted to the gloom. The first thing they could make out was the twin orbs of a dancer's magnificent breasts. In the same way that a full moon will emerge from an eclipse, they appeared when she pulled a veil away from her chest. Despite their size, they were not the kind that, like bowling balls in a laundry bag, clanked and sagged together. The dancer's breasts seemed supported by a marvelous cantilever, just as magically as the moon is suspended in the sky without any ropes, chains, or wires. Moreover, they were as white as the full moon and, seeing these two spheres glowing in the bar's gloom, Izzy thought of what the night might look like on other planets with more than a solitary satellite circling them.

"Boys," said an electronic voice as the song ended, "give it up for Luna! We allow tipping, but no touching!"

"Do you see him?" Izzy asked Lawrence, having returned to earth. "Do you see Craig?"

"Craig, you want me to look for Craig when she's showing us those. You go look for Craig if you want. I'm going to the moon."

As Izzy's eyes adjusted to the light, he began to see dim shadows of men skulking around the bar. A waitress, wearing clothes three sizes too small, brought them beers; and a few women, waiting their turn to dance, plied drinks from them. In the far corner, billiard balls clicked, and a pair of men, habituated to Luna's charms, bent at the pool table, intent on their game. Luna, having finished her set and gathering her discarded clothes, lingered to have Lawrence delicately place a dollar in her G-string. She swallowed his head between her breasts, tousled his hair, and clomped off to the dressing room in platform heels. The swinging door almost hit her in the face when a fully dressed woman with a duffle bag broke out and the unmistakable sounds of a cat fight overcame the music.

"Bitch," said Luna.

The door halfway swung open again, as another woman, less dressed than the first, attempted to go after the first, but was blocked and restrained by Craig, who had gone in the dressing room when the fight broke out.

"Go back in and settle down," he said. "She's not coming back."

"You want a drink?" the waitress asked Izzy. He looked at her sixth grade Catholic Schoolgirl uniform for a minute while he thought of his answer. "No, just get me a Coke. I'm working."

"What; are you a cop?"

"No, I'm, like, a counselor."

She laughed, "That's just what we need here."

"What was up with that woman who left?"

"She's just a bitch and she's better off gone. Really, everyone's nice here, except her. We're like family. Is this your first time?"

"Yeah, you see that guy with the messed up hair? Whatever he orders, I'll pay for it, but just get him a Coke. Don't let him have anything else."

"Sure," she said. "Is this some kind of a weird counseling technique?"

"Yeah, it's, like, something new."

A rap song started to pound from the speakers and a new dancer in a business suit strutted up on the stage. The commotion in the dressing room must have settled down because by the time the woman had kicked off her pinstriped skirt, Craig was out, folding his arms, leaning against a wall. The second song was quieter, so Izzy sidled up to him.

"What're you doing here?" asked Craig.

"I might say the same thing."

"And why the fuck d'you bring Lawrence?"

"We came to get you and, like, bring you back."

"What do you care what I do?"

"It's part of my internship. I, like, need you to graduate. The group needs you or they'll all go back to using."

"This is on me? I'm responsible for their recovery? I'm responsible for you graduating? Get the fuck out of here."

"Alright, you're not. But you're responsible for you and look what you're doing to yourself. A bouncer in a strip joint, aw, c'mon. You've become a caricature of a messed up biker."

A pale arm rested on Izzy's shoulder. It was Luna, having come out of the dressing room. "Is this man bothering you, Craig?" she said. "You want me to take care of him? I'll protect you."

"Yeah, get him away from me."

"What d'you do to Craig? You calling him names? Don't you know he's sensitive? C'mon with me. You won't get anywhere once he gets pissed off."

"Where're we going?"

"You're gunna buy me a drink and we're gunna have a good time."

Izzy left Craig glowering by the wall. Lawrence panted at the stage, a wad of singles in his hand and an untouched Coke beside him. The business woman was playing peek-a-boo with her briefcase. Izzy figured he'd let Craig think about things for a while. No reason to force the issue. Luna wore a blazer slung over her shoulders like a cape, her breasts bulging past the lapels. A piece of glitter sparkled from its perch on her nipple. No harm in buying a pretty lady a drink.

"What do you, like, do when you're not dancing?" he asked, trying to strike up a conversation.

She took a long sip from a narrow straw while looking into his eyes. She finished and licked her lips before saying, "Not a thing. Each night I die when the bar closes. When it opens, I'm born again."

Izzy smiled and felt his loins stir. She wanted him, or at least acted as though she did. Sometimes that's good enough. "Maybe you could tell me what happens after you die. I've always wanted to know, but I've never, like, been in a hurry to find out for myself."

"Death is incredibly sensual; like taking off shoes that you've worn all day."

She leaned on him and whispered in his ear, her breasts flattened on his chest, and went on. "You find yourself. Your outer shell, the persona that you build around you to protect you, gets shed; you go back to who you really are: what's in your core."

She had a view of the afterlife only a stripper could have. Heaven's where you take it off, take it all off.

"That's interesting," said Izzy. "I, like, knew there was more to you as soon as I saw you."

"You're wrong. There's nothing to me. I'm as simple as can be. I wasn't born yesterday, I was born today."

The business woman's set was done, the music stopped, and she was gathering the dollar bills littering the stage, and stuffing them in her suitcase. The next dancer was with the DJ, picking out her songs.

"Alright," Izzy said. "Now that you've told me what it's like to die, tell me what it's like to be born. I don't remember."

"You come to life and the people around you see you there naked. They rush around getting clothes on you. People never let things be just simple. You've got to die again just to get you back."

The music started and the new dancer began with an acrobatic spin on the pole. She hung upside down like a bat and untied her long hair so that it spilled out onto the stage. Lawrence jumped up from his seat and yelled, "You go, girl. I got a corner here you can sweep."

"I would never do that," leered Izzy. "I'd never, like, put clothes on you if I saw you naked; unless you were cold."

"Aren't you a gentleman," purred Luna. "You know, I like you and I'd like to do something for you."

She finished her drink and pulled him by the hand to a small room. Lawrence saw them go. He called out, "Go get'er, Izzy. She'll complete your education."

The dancer pushed the intern down on an easy chair, straddled him, and pushed his head between her bosoms where Lawrence's had been. The breasts were taut as a drum and smelled of baby powder. When she let him out he said, "What are you doing?"

"You're getting a lap dance, silly. They're twenty bucks."

She swiveled her hips until she located his stiffened penis pressing against his pants and ground her crotch against it. She half closed her eyes and made a moan, Izzy made one, too. His hips had a mind of their own and pushed up against hers, his penis seeking out its objective. A thin layer of clothing separated him from possessing the dancer's exquisite body. This is how addiction starts, he thought. It's great in the beginning, but I've seen plenty of how it ends. This was a fine way of spending an afternoon and he had plenty of Ahern's briefcase cash at hand, but he was still a poor student with few prospects and, once this exquisite lap dance was over, then what? He would just want another one, and another, getting more numb with each as he tries to re-experience the excitement of this first. Luna unhorsed herself from his lap and slid down his chest. Her mouth hovered by the bulge in his pants. This part of addiction's not so bad, but then he'd have to go to all those meetings. "Hi, I'm Izzy, and I'm a sex addict," he'd have to say, as he looked into the eyes of the lovelies who had gone down with him into the church basement. We'll hook up after the meeting, his eyes would say. Theirs would say, yes, we will, and they would, but it would all be so lifeless. That's what bothered Izzy most about the addicts, the lifelessness of it all, as if the bottle, needle, or pipe was sucking the life fluid out of the people while the substance was going into them.

By now, Luna was curled up on his lap and running her breath up and down his neck, the edge of her teeth grazing his skin. He thought, she only comes out at night; she dies at the break of day. It was clear to him; she was a vampire who would suck him dry. With a great heave, he threw the dancer off him and left the little room.

"Where're you going? You owe me twenty bucks."

"I don't owe you anything," claimed Izzy. "I never said I wanted a lap dance."

Craig's big hand was on his shoulder. He had been outside the door. "Pay her the twenty bucks. You wanted it."

Izzy gave her the twenty bucks. "There, happy?" he said to Craig, "Now can we talk?"

"You throw me off and you'd rather talk to him?" said Luna. "What, are you, queer?"

"He's not queer, he's just mixed up," said Craig. "I'll take care of him. You're up next."

Luna tugged at the intern's crotch. "See me if you get it figured out, queer boy."

"You're gunna get me in trouble," Craig said to Izzy when she left. "I'm not supposed to talk to people. I'm supposed to crack their skulls if they don't pay, or if they touch the girls."

"I need you back, Craig. I can't finish this internship unless you sign off on…" his words were drowned out by the heavy bass of the next song.

Craig waved his hand by his ear and took up his bouncer position by the wall. Izzy sat alone at a table, looking in the general direction of the stage, but not watching the dancer in graduation gown and mortarboard strutting back and forth. Umpteen years of college and I'm dumber than when I graduated from high school, he thought. I'd have to change my major again. Either that, or go work at McDonalds.

The waitress came over. "How's the counseling coming?" she asked.

"Not so great," he said. "I'm thinking of quitting and doing something else."

"Your patient's having a good time," she said. Lawrence had moved away from the stage and was holding court with two dancers on his lap. "He's not drinking a lot of Cokes, but he's getting along with the girls. I don't know what you're counseling him for, but if it's shyness, he's overcome that all right."

"Yeah, he's doing fine."

"Can I get you something?"

"Get me a shot of something, something strong. I don't give a shit anymore."

The dancer on the stage was prowling on her hands and knees, the academic had revealed herself as a cat. Lawrence was wearing her mortarboard and her gown was lying in a heap. Luna was right, he thought, the mortarboard, the gown, the diploma, the job: it's all just stuff that covers you up and hides what's in your core. It doesn't really matter. What matters is who you are. But who the hell am I? thought Izzy. I'm nothing more than the sum total of all my experiences; an old desk top that's taken the engravings of a pen through the paper.

The set ended and Luna took the stage again.

"Here you go," said the waitress. "Here's your drink."

"What d'you get me?"

"Peppermint schnapps," she said.

Izzy threw the schnapps down his throat. It set him on fire. He thought of Craig and Cornwhacker drinking this same poison by the Missouri. At least Craig could say he lived fully. Whatever he did, he did it with his might, he grabbed for all of the gusto he could.

Luna had her breasts in her hand and played her tongue on her nipples.

That's what I got to do, thought Izzy. Whatever I've got, I've got to use it. I won't give up on this internship until I've tried everything.

He rose up and, bearing a dollar bill in his hand, approached the stage. Luna came over when she finished a pirouette.

"Have you decided to go straight? Huh? Did these make you change your mind?"

"Yeah, they did," he said. "Let me have them." Izzy boldly grabbed her breasts in his hands.

She screamed, "You can't touch!"

Craig was on him in a moment. "C'mon, you're outta here." He grabbed him by the collar and dragged him to the door.

Outside, Izzy made a last effort to enlist Craig. "Look, you can't just go back to using and doing this to yourself. That's not who you are anymore. You've already been clean and you've been a counselor."

"I can't go back there."

"You don't have to come back right away. I just have to meet with you regularly for supervision and have you sign off. You made a promise to me. You said you'd supervise my internship."

"I don't give a shit about your internship," he said, and went back in and shut the door.

Izzy sat on the step. Blinded by the brightness of the outdoors, he thought he'd wait a while before moving on. He also didn't know where to go and what to do now. It was over.

Just then the door to the titty bar opened again and Craig came out with Lawrence by the collar.

"I didn't do anything," said Lawrence. "Why're you doing me like this?"

"You're in recovery," said Craig. "You have no business in there. Stay the hell out of bars. And you; don't go fucking bringing people in recovery to bars. It's not good for them."

"I thought you didn't care," said Izzy.

"I fucking care."

"Then when will I be seeing you?"

"Next week. I open this joint at eleven. Come at ten. And don't bring him."

# Chapter 42 - Finding Himself

For days afterwards, Izzy could not stop thinking about Luna, although, the truth be known, he was not thinking about her breasts. They were spectacular breasts, to be sure, and during her dances, both on the stage and on his lap, he experienced her breasts with all his senses: the sight of those orbs suspended over his face, their powdery smell, the taughtness of a swollen balloon, even the sound of them slapping together. These sensations gave him pleasure, certainly, but, deep inside, his stomach flipped and pulled away from the pleasure. The reason had nothing to do with his perception of danger of getting hooked on lap dances. It had more to do with his sister. It had more to do with the instinctual recoil from incest.

The last time Izzy saw his sister, she had stopped at his parent's house with a shaved head and her girlfriend, a big bold black butch named Bessie, who did most of the talking. Bessie called his sister Julietta like a Mexican: Hueyetta, although her name was Julia.

"Will you be in town long?" said Izzy's mother, placing chips and dip on the coffee table.

"We're just coming up from Mexico and going back to the Bay area. We've been gone for a few years; living with the Mexicans. The men there were all hot, hot for Julietta. Julietta shaved her head to keep the boys away. They were paying her too much attention. She couldn't even think straight. Now she's thinking straight," she said. "Aren't you, my Julietta?"

Julietta smiled.

His mother sat on her couch and looked uncomfortable in her own pristine living room.

"Have you known Julia, er, Julietta, for long?"

"A few years," said Bessie. "She was coming out of work one night and a man was following her. He had seen her dancing and wanted to get to know her better, if you know what I mean. I got in his face and he didn't bother her no more."

"You were in a show, Julia?" asked Izzy's mom.

"She was the star of the show," answered Bessie, "and making good money, although all in dollar bills. But the men were driving her crazy. I said her, 'Honey, there's more to this world than men. Come with me to Mexico.'"

"And so you went?" the mom said sweetly.

"And so we went."

Izzy's big sister, as we have seen, had run off when she was very young to Haight-Ashbury to become a flower child less than a week after the family moved to California. It seemed sudden at the time, but it wasn't. She had begun to dress up like a hippie for months prior. His mom was preoccupied with her new romance and Izzy was ensconced in the protective self-centeredness of boyhood and barely noticed. All the while, his sister groomed herself, trying on a peasant blouse, long, straight hair, and going barefoot, as one would put on a Halloween costume. She tried on new words, too, whispering them in her little brother's ear as if they were planning a jailbreak, turning him against the establishment. "Do your own thing... Today's the first day of the rest of your life...You've got to find yourself." When they drove across the country to their new home, her head turned at hundreds of hitchhiking kids wearing the same nonconformist uniform. The news on the radio was all about the summer of love. His stepfather repeated Governor Ronald Reagan's joke: a hippie dresses like Tarzan, has hair like Jane, and smells like Cheetah. Meanwhile, a cheetah was in the back seat, unbeknownst. She rolled her eyes and kept her peace. When they arrived and unpacked their suitcases, she never unpacked hers and no one noticed that, either.

Then at the breakfast table one day, Izzy's mom said, "What are you going to do today, honey?"

His sister answered, "Oh, I don't know. I guess I'll hitchhike to San Francisco."

They had a good laugh. "Be sure to wear some flowers in your hair," said his stepfather.

Izzy chewed his Captain Crunch and read the cereal box, his stepfather folded the newspaper and went to work, his mother collected the dishes, and his sister stepped out the door and put out her thumb, leaving her packed suitcase behind.

A few weeks later, after Izzy had gotten his haircut, his stepfather submitted to his mother's pleas to go to San Francisco to find her. Izzy fidgeted in the back seat as they drove past avocado fields and hitchhiking kids. This time the parents were turning their heads. They crept up and down the streets of the Haight; Izzy staring out the back window with his new crew cut, his stepfather staring out the front window with his old crew cut, and his mother staring with her flowered dress, searching for Julia's face amid the throngs of feral youth. They parked the car and combed Golden Gate Park. Some offered them pot, others, flowers, others, acid. "Don't touch anything they give you," commanded his stepfather. They found his sister sitting with a grown man, feeling his face like a blind girl, her expression blank, and her hair, filled with dying blossoms.

When they entered her line of sight, she smiled a vacant smile and said to the man. "Cool, man, I see my mom and brother, and they're all different colors."

Izzy's mom snatched her by the hand. "Julia, you're coming home," she said.

Julia screamed, freed herself, and pulled away.

"What're you doing?" said the man.

"She's my daughter. She's coming home with me."

"Mom?"

"She's not going anywhere unless she wants to. She doesn't belong to you."

"She's fourteen."

"Mom, what're you doing here?"

"Quit hasseling her," said the man. "She's just trying to find herself."

Julia's eyes darted and she screamed again, as if she was witnessing a massacre.

"Look buddy," said the stepfather, approaching the man ominously. "She's just a child, half your age."

"Those are just numbers."

The other hippies closed ranks around the stepfather. "Everyone's freaking out now. Look man, you do your thing, let us do ours."

Julia ran off into the woods. "Julia," screamed her mother. "Julia… Julia… Julia." The man ran off after her.

"She's having a bad trip, man," said a hippie. "Let us take care of it. You're just making things worse."

"You're freaks," screamed the mother. "You're freaks, you're freaks, you're freaks."

The stepfather held her. "C'mon let's go to the car. We'll get her. We'll wait for her."

They sat in the car for hours, the mother crying, the stepfather muttering, and Izzy fidgeting, until it got dark. Then they patrolled the streets of the Haight, looking for Julia. "I'm tired," whined Izzy.

His mom turned around and looked him straight in the eye. "Promise me something," she said. "Promise me you'll never do this. Promise me you'll never run off and find yourself."

Izzy started crying. He could see how much it hurt her. "I promise, Mom. I won't find myself."

"Promise me," she repeated and fell to weeping again. He continued crying, as well, until he fell asleep. When he awoke, they were pulling in the driveway at home.

# Chapter 43 - The Waiting Room

Ed Lockhart arrived an hour early for his appointment, Izzy's first with a mental health client. Izzy didn't even have much time to get nervous before Melvina called and said Mr Lockhart was waiting for him. In any case, it doesn't take long to get nervous. Melvina, for instance, got nervous the instant a mental health client stepped into her waiting room. She much preferred the company of junkies, pushers, prostitutes, and thieves because she knew what they were thinking. The mentally ill were a different matter. "I can't deal with these split personalities; you never know who you're talking to," she said. "They're not wrapped too tight. They could go postal just when you scold them to take their feet offen the table."

Everyone agreed things were much simpler before Dr Ahern came along and put chemical dependency, mental health, patients, clients, counselors, office managers, and therapists alike, in a big bowl and tossed. Melvina had kept a firm dominion over her waiting room. Magazines were fresh, bus schedules were sorted, and no one put their feet on the furniture. It was a different matter when mental health clients began to wait in what was previously the chemical dependency waiting room. Melvina no longer came from behind the safety of her counter to straighten anything. In fact, she didn't even like to say, as she often had, "don't make me come out there." Consequently, the waiting room was going to hell.

Melvina always was one to see the latent possibilities that passed through her waiting room, whether they were really there or not. From the addicts, she demanded, and often received, respect that no one else got. It wasn't the uniform of a minimum wage rent-a-cop that kept the peace in the waiting room when scores of addicts and drug dealers, many with debts and grudges, gathered for their groups; it was the threat of censure from Melvina, mother of them all. She was unnerved by the mentally ill, on the other hand, who generally came bearing no chips on their shoulders and only wanting to please.

Perhaps this trait was able to develop in the office manager precisely because she understood waiting rooms so well. There seems to be a waiting room in our psyche where all our potentialities gather for their appointments and present themselves when called upon. We see this all the time when we exhibit qualities we didn't think we had. When a shy mouse belts it out in a Karaoke bar; when The Tin Man finds his heart, The Lion, his courage, and The Scarecrow, his brains; they, all the while, had been in this waiting room, thumbing through magazines.

Izzy saw it also when he sat down with Mr Lockhart and started acting like a therapist. He didn't know he'd start acting like a therapist; he never had before. The words involved in building rapport, reflecting feelings, and communicating authentic positive regard just fell out of his mouth like an old lady's dentures. Midway through the session, he looked down at his folded hands and crossed legs and didn't recognize them. He wasn't sure whose they were, but he'll keep them. They might come in handy some other day, like today, when someone needs to think he's a therapist. The words, hands, and legs did what they needed to do today. Mr Lockhart came in, sat down and told his story to Izzy, just like he was talking to a real therapist.

# Chapter 44 - Lockhart's Place

The Lockhart daughters were beauty queens. They were literally beauty queens. They went to beauty pageants and won them. They put their trophies on the Endusted mantle of the living room that no one ever entered, except to clean. First, one would win a pageant, and then the other would win the next. You never suspected either one got jealous, because they smiled so prettily whether they won or no.

Ed Lockhart milked between forty and fifty Holsteins for a living. He loved milking cows. After getting back from running to a beauty pageant, he always said that, once the compressor started chugging and he got the milkers on, he was right where he belonged. Even the heifers never kicked, because Ed Lockhart was so calm and at peace, they thought having their teats squeezed by a milker was the most natural thing in the world. When milking was done, Ed turned his cows out to pasture. You could watch them lumber out the barn door, and the black on their massive sides would be so black and the white would be so white, it would give you a toothache to look at it. The Holsteins would lumber out the barn door and loiter in a pasture that was so green it would make an Arab's eyes water.

The cows, themselves, were beauty queens. Every year at the county fair, he would show the best of them and bring home trophies. He tried to put the trophies on the Endusted mantle, but his wife said she would have no cow trophies in her living room. So Ed built a trophy case for the milk house, next to the gestation chart and the refrigerator that kept the sperm bank.

Ed Lockhart had a teenage son to help him with the chores. Every chance the boy got, he put himself up on the tractor pulling something or pushing something else. The boy had a passion for pulling or pushing things. Since the boy became old enough to pull and push things on that tractor, Ed never had to climb up on it.

Ed also never had to fuss around the house, inside or out, as many husbands do. He had a wife who had been a beauty queen herself in her younger days. Those days were long past and so, instead of always doing her hair, she groomed the house and gardens. All around the house, the roses had their plot, the dahlias theirs, and the weeds had their pile behind the barn. Lockhart's boots and coveralls also had their place, and that was out of the house, with him in them or out of them, although he was in them through all the daylight hours. Nothing was ever out of place on the Lockhart farm.

The farm was so beautiful and perfect that a farmer's magazine wanted to come and photograph it. They wanted to photograph the farm and put it on the cover because, it looked so tidy, farmers would want to buy the magazine so it could be their farm for a while. When Ed heard about the photographer, he spent a week painting the barn, which didn't need painting. His son moved the manure pile with his tractor and his wife planted flowers where it had been.

When the photographer arrived, he set up his tripod while Ed drove his cows out to the pasture. The picture was going to be perfect. The barn with a new coat of paint framed the left side of the photograph. On the right was the house with Ed's beauty queen wife trimming the roses out front. His beauty queen daughters sat on the porch swing looking as if they were waiting for beaus to come by. His son plowed in the distance on an orange Allis-Chalmers, a streak of black plow strip like a wisp of an eyebrow across the top of the picture. Below the field was a farm pond, a diving pier jutting out towards the middle and a rowboat at rest next to the pier. In the middle of the picture stood Ed's cows, knee-deep in clover, the pink veins of their udders bulging.

The photographer straightened up and said to Ed, who was standing pretty straight already, "It's no good, I can't get an angle where you don't see it, and we can't have it in the picture."

"Can't see what?" Ed demanded. "What could possibly be wrong with my farm?"

"You've got a cow having her calf right in the middle of the field. We can't have that in the picture. No one wants to look at all that blood and slime. You're going to have to move it."

As proud as Ed was about the photographer taking a picture of his farm, he was still a humane man. He wasn't about to try to move a cow in labor, no matter if she was in the middle of the perfect picture. "I can't move the cow, but don't go away. I'll get my son to park the tractor in front of the cow. That'll look good in the picture."

"Yes, it would. I'll wait, but make sure he leaves the dirty plows up on the hill or clean them off." So off went Ed to get his son to leave off his plowing and come and put the tractor in the middle of the picture.

When they got back, the photographer was packing up his lenses and tripod. "You said you'd wait," complained Ed.

"I waited as long as I could," said the photographer, "but I can't take the picture now. The light's gotten bad."

Ed didn't say a word. He only gazed out towards the field of cows. A new bull calf lay with his legs folded up, his fur shiny with birth slime. Nearby, his mother grazed, an elongated sack of bloody afterbirth dangled from her back end.

Ed could tell you something about working with cows. If you spend any time around them, you become cow-like. For one thing, their placid personality tends to rub off. For another, becoming cow-like is often the best way of communicating with them. Either way, a true herdsman will become indistinguishable from the herd. In his best cow-like manner, Ed didn't say a word; but his boy was a different matter. The boy began to pull the photographer around the farm, telling him to look at this light and that light. The photographer kept shaking his head. "No, that won't do," he said. Lockhart's daughters and wife then came over and tried to coax the photographer with their sunny smiles, but, as bright and pleasant as they may have been to look at, they didn't change the light any. Ed let his eyes graze over the field until the photographer left. By that time the herd was gathered by the barn door, waiting for their evening milking. His wife and daughters' smiles had darkened by then, but he ignored them, opened the door, and followed the cows in.

One day followed another just as they had done before the photographer came and left without taking a picture. Lockhart's wife grew flowers just as she had done before; and the son finished his plowing and put that hillside field in wheat. Ed weaned the new bull calf just as he had weaned all the others he raised. After milking, he'd go out to the calf barn with pails of warm milk. He'd dip his fingers in the milk to cover them and let the calves suck on his fingers as he led their noses into the pail. This calf, like all the others, would butt the pail, sloshing the milk all over Ed. The daughters continued to win beauty pageants as they had before. The pageants being won, they also won the attention of some young men who asked them to marry them.

They planned a double wedding to occur down by the farm pond. In no time at all, the family was fixing up the place just as they had done for the photographer. Ed got to work building picnic tables for the guests to eat on after the wedding. That being done, he knocked together an arched trellis on the dock. Lockhart's wife would cut her roses with long stems to twine in the new trellis. Everyone would get married under the trellis. Afterwards, they would place the wedding cake underneath so that the little wedding cake brides and grooms would stand where the live brides and grooms stood a little bit before. "We hope you're going to keep the cows in the barn for the wedding," his daughters kidded Ed. "We don't want them having calves in the middle of the reception when everyone's trying to eat."

When the wedding day arrived, Ed finished his milking early and fed his cows an extra helping of hay to keep them quiet in the barn. He tried to take a long bath to soak the cow smell off him, but his daughters kept wanting to use the bathroom to fix their hair. When he was finished getting dressed, he went out and saw long lines of parked cars and pickup trucks up and down his road. The ushers had herded the guests down to the pond where the caterer was setting up and the minister was peering into the water, looking for fish.

The wedding went perfectly, without those disasters that new brides dread. The minister did his marrying; the best men their speech making, and Ed's wife cried a new pond. After dinner, the married couples cut their share of the cake and smashed it in each other's faces on cue. All the guests got a piece of cake and a cup of coffee, but then something seemed very wrong. Ed's face turned red. Was he having a heart attack? "What's wrong, dear?" asked his wife.

Ed didn't answer her just yet. He wasn't having a heart attack. "This is a farm, gull darn it," he shouted to the caterer, shaking a fist full of non-dairy creamer cups. "What blankety-blank caterer would bring non-dairy creamer to a farm?" He flung the non-dairy creamer cups into the water where they bobbed like buoys. Turning to his daughters, his wife, his son, and his guests, he shouted: "This is a dairy farm, and we're all going to know it."

Ed Lockhart spent the rest of the wedding reception fussing in the milk house in his good clothes. The guests finished their cake quickly, while Lockhart's cows, released from the barn, grazed between the picnic tables at which they sat.

# Chapter 45 - Treatment Planning

"I don't know what to do now," said Izzy. "He came in and told me his story. When he was done, he looked at me as if to say, here I am, fix me."

Craig was an hour late for their first supervisory session at the titty bar and didn't look like he wanted to hear any bit of the story the intern was so full of: his first client, Mr Lockhart. Sometimes, however, it costs more energy to stop a conversation than to let it run its course.

"What did you do?" asked Craig.

"I set up another appointment," said Izzy, "but I don't know what to do when he, like, comes back."

"You better hope he has another crisis that he has to tell you about," he snarled.

All the lights were on at the titty bar when they went in. It was better lit when it was closed than when it was open. Craig went around and turned most of them off.

"Aren't we supposed to, like, fix people?" asked Izzy.

"The only fixing we do is we make them see they can fix themselves, or that they don't need fixing at all."

Craig sank into a chair and held his head. "Who told him he had to get counseling?" he asked.

"His wife; his wife told him he had to, like, get his head examined."

"Well you done that. But the problem's not his head. It's his balls. She had them, he took them back, and she don't like it, so she sends him to you to get them back for her. I say we let him keep his balls."

"Is that, like, the treatment plan goal? To keep his balls?"

"That's everyone's treatment plan goal," said Craig. "Everyone who walks in your door has someone or something that's holding his balls hostage. Trouble is, you can't be a hostage negotiator and get his balls back for him. Even if you succeed, he still won't have them; you will. He's got to get them back, his own self."

"I thought you said he already got them back?"

"Bingo; he took them back when he let the cows out, but then he gave them up again when his wife convinced him to come to see you. He handed them to you when he told you that story and looked at you and said fix me, I'm broken. He ain't broken. Letting those cows out was the best thing he ever did."

"He disrupted the wedding," cried Izzy. "Like, his whole family's mad at him, and all the neighbors are talking like he lost it."

"He didn't disrupt the wedding by letting the cows out," growled Craig, "he disrupted it by letting everyone run all over him and turn his farm into a pretty postcard. He should've said something a long time ago if that wasn't what he wanted, but he couldn't because he didn't have the balls. He needs his balls back so it won't happen again."

"So, what do I do when he comes back?" asked Izzy.

"You ask him what his goals are."

"I thought his goals were to get his balls back?"

"He's not going to say that," he spat. "He's going to say some shit like, I've got to learn to manage my anger, or, I want to save my marriage. He's going to say what he thinks he's supposed to say because he doesn't have his balls."

Craig took his hand away from the steadying influence of his head. When he did, Izzy could see a tremor.

"Anything this pussy-whipped, shit-for-brains says, or thinks, is going to be from the perspective of a person with a problem. It's like Christopher Columbus, he's poor and he comes up with this plan to head west to get to the East Indies and get filthy rich. You know he's running right into The New World, but you don't say anything because he'd never set sail if he knew there was a whole friggen continent in the way."

"I don't understand," said Izzy, "Christopher Columbus?"

"It's like this, Einstein, right now I'm hung over; that's my problem," Craig admitted. "I want to feel better. So, from my perspective, what's the solution?"

"Stop drinking and you'll feel better," said Izzy.

"From my perspective," he snapped. "I want to feel better right now."

"You better go get a beer, then. But is that what you really want?"

Craig got up and went to the bar. He returned with a beer. "Does this answer your question?" he said.

"It does. But what do you really want?"

"I want to finish my beer."

"And then?"

"Get me another one and finish that."

"And then?"

"Get you to stop saying, and then."

"You really just want to finish one beer after another and, like, not do anything else?"

"I really just want to make you and everything else go away."

"What are you trying to escape from?"

"Who the fuck are you," said Craig, "my intern or my therapist?"

"I'm your intern," said Izzy, "but maybe you need, like, a therapist more."

"Like hell, I'm not going to you for therapy."

"Who're you going to?"

"I don't need it, I'm fine."

"Yeah, fucked up, insecure, neurotic, and emotional; you're fine," said Izzy. "And that beer's, like, got you by the balls."

"Shit."

"What'd you say?"

"I said shit," said Craig. "You think I like this? You think I like being who I am?"

"No, I don't."

"Alright, college boy; we'll have it your way. You be my therapist. That'll be your internship. If you fix me, you'll pass."

"Shit."

# Chapter 46 - The Library

Izzy left the bar that day in a fretful agitation. Had he been a drinking man, like Craig, he would have sought out a drink. But not at that bar, for there was Craig, the source of his agitation. He wanted to put as much distance as possible between himself and the biker, for what he proposed seemed so outlandish that, had Izzy stayed, the next proposal Craig might have made would be, take my bike and jump it over the Grand Canyon. Now of course, Craig would never say take my bike, he would much sooner commit his tender psyche to an intern than his bike to him.

Izzy was not a drinking man, so he didn't go to a bar; he was a perpetual student, so he went to the library. Not any library would do to soothe his agitation; he had to go to none other than The University Library. In the dusty stacks under that titanic dome was his deliverance. He was not a drinking man, but he would go to the nipple of knowledge and suck on that tit until he got his fill.

What Izzy was looking for was a counseling theory or therapy technique that would work on Craig. He studied that weekend as he had studied at no time during his previous decade of college, carrying great piles of books to his table and pouring over them as if he were an alchemist, searching for the formula to turn lead into gold. In a sense, he was an alchemist, trying to turn words, noisy breath exhaled, the cheapest substance in the universe, into a precious healing salve. He was trying to find i-deas that would repair broken bridges across the synaptic gap: non-substantial thoughts that would replace depleted serotonin and bankrupt dopamine. If only he had a license to do so, he would've given Craig a pill. He would've searched for the medication under development that Dr Staub had told him about and gotten it some illegal way and brought it back to Craig. Oh, for a chemical to solve all his problems. But then, Craig already thought of that. There had to be a method somewhere in these books that would make him, the callow intern that he recognized himself to be, into an effective therapist.

The smoke and mirrors game that worked on the group or on Ed Lockhart would never work on Craig. Mr Lockhart might be fooled into thinking he was a therapist by Izzy's parroted phrases and aped carriage, but an experienced therapist would see right through the pretense. Many group members were happy to put the intern into the role as expert in recovery even though he had no authority to claim himself as one because they knew themselves to be only playing a role. They knew they just had to act as though they were in recovery for a time until they got off parole or on disability. The intern and the group were all actors alike in a bad regional dinner theater production and, if no one from the audience was going to rise up and point out flaws in their acting, they wouldn't point out each other's, for sure. Even Lawrence, whom Izzy regarded as being sincere about changing his life and taught the intern as much as anyone about addiction, deferred to him, not because he knew anything, but because he wasn't an addict and anyone who hadn't messed up his life ought to be able to tell a person who had how to set things right. In short, Izzy never had to do anything with the clients to be a therapist, he just had to be a therapist and wear the badge, the Chinos, and make all the proper noises at the right times.

Izzy reflected, Craig was going to be a tougher client. He knew the game better than Izzy. He studied at the same school. Furthermore, Craig, studied at two more schools Izzy had never paid tuition to: The School of Hard Knocks and Psychotic State. He was one well-educated sonofabitch. A chess master who might just as well rap you upside the head with a tire iron; a point guard, moving in more directions than a dried out rocking chair sideways on a sloped porch, who might, anytime, switch up and play rugby on your ass. What's more, Craig had been in recovery, been in and ran AA meetings, studied psychology, therapized himself as he was therapizing others and was still messed up. He was going to need some serious therapy, from a serious therapist. That's how come Izzy decided to get serious all of a sudden and crack the books in the university library. That's how come he was sitting at a heavily laden table in a climate controlled hall, dripping sweat into Beck, Jung, and Rogers.

While he was thus employed, the light from the stained glass windows swung across the room like the beam of a searchlight so that it seemed that it, too, was aiding in the hunt. There were no lack of solutions to Izzy's problem in the books he stacked around him. Indeed, the problem was he had too many solutions, and they all seemed to contradict each other. He wasn't looking for a needle in a haystack; that would've been easier. He was looking for a particular, not very distinguishable, needle in a pile of needles. He worked at this all day, and night, for when at closing time, he found he wasn't any closer to completing than when he started, he hid in the stacks until they locked the door behind him and searched some more by the light of a flashlight. At last, when he could go on no longer, he collapsed and, using the tomes of psychology as a pillow, slept a fitful sleep in which he searched no less hard than when he was awake.

Izzy must have been resting his head on a volume of Adler because that's who came to him first in the dream. The rest came to him in turn, like scary features of a house of horrors.

"The problem is that Craig thinks he has an incurable illness called addiction. He does, but the illness is that he thinks he has an illness," said Adler. "The illness is that he doesn't believe in his own abilities, so he looks for a substance to do what he thinks he can't. He's like The Scarecrow, The Lion, The Tin Man, and Dorothy, all traipsing through Oz hoping that The Wizard will give them what they've had all along."

A bell rang and Dr Pavlov interrupted, saying, "The goal of therapy is to modify maladaptive stimulus-response connections. The beer is less filling and tastes great. Therefore make it more filling and taste bad."

"You only go around once in life," said Sartre, "so you have to grab for all the gusto you can."

"More filling," said Watson. "Rewards are more effective reinforcers than punishment."

"Tastes bad," said BF Skinner. "Nothing gets their attention better than pain."

Lawrence led the therapy group in a chorus line. They sang, "We're off to see the lizard, the wonderful lizard of Oz."

Carl Jung stopped them from going further, "Once in a while," he said, "alcoholics are cured by a spiritual awakening. To me these phenomena appear to be in the nature of huge emotional displacements and rearrangements. Ideas, emotions, and attitudes which were once the guiding forces are suddenly cast to one side, and a completely new set of conceptions and motives begin to dominate."

"More filling," said Watson, administering an electric shock to Skinner.

"Tastes bad," said BF Skinner, stuffing pigeon food down Watson's throat.

A man in a concentration camp uniform, Viktor Frankl, declared, "All human beings have a will to find meaning, and serious behavioral problems develop when they can't find it. By helping them decide what gives life meaning, therapy helps patients handle the responsibility of choices and the pain of unavoidable suffering."

"Less filling," said Watson, picking Skinner up by the ears like a rabbit.

"Tastes great," said BF Skinner, picking Watson up by the tail like a rat.

"I found meaning in the concentration camp," said Frankl, "that's why I survived."

Albert Bandura came on with an inflatable rocking clown. "Go ahead, hit this Bobo doll," he said, "You know you want to."

"Hey," said Frankl, "What gives?" He hit it. It rocked and hit him back. "Why did I do that?"

"You see, I proved the effects of modeling on behavior. Children who were shown an adult who fed and nurtured the Bobo doll, did not hit the Bobo doll."

Freud came by and looked at the Bobo doll for a long time. Then he burned a hole in it with his cigar and it deflated. "Ve must speak zee language of z'unconscious mind," said Freud, waving the cigar. "Relief from zymptoms is accomplished ven ve translate zee symbols of z'unconscious mind into avarness."

Albert Ellis, tattooed like Craig, stepped up and slapped Freud. "You idiot, you have a gene for inefficiency." Freud rocks like the Bobo doll. "It's as simple as ABC," said Ellis. "A- Shit happens all the time. B- But it ain't shit unless your thinking makes it so. C- When you completely make shit out of everything, everything turns to shit. All you have to do is, D- dispute the source of the shit, and E- enjoy a shit free, rational existence."

Carl Jung comes back on. "There are more things in heaven and earth than are dreamt of in your philosophy," he says.

Albert Ellis slaps him also, and he rocks like the Bobo doll. "You have irrational beliefs," says Ellis.

Carl Rogers comes on, patiently takes off his jacket, hangs it up, and puts on a cardigan sweater. He sits in an easy chair. "Hello, neighbors. We could all get along better together if we realize that each of us is right. Each counseling theory is just as good as another is as long as the counselor communicates authenticity and unconditional positive regard. This allows the client to be himself when he and the therapist are together and to get in touch with his real dreams and wishes."

"Do you have to be loved by everyone?" asked Ellis, shoving Rogers, so that both he and his chair rock like the Bobo doll.

"You are asking if I must have everyone love me," said Rogers as he rocked back.

"That's what I said, damn it," as he gave him another push.

Rocking back, he said, "You are angry that I correctly paraphrased your question."

With another push, "Answer the question, damn it."

Still rocking, "When you push me on my chest like that, it makes me rock back and forth, and I get dizzy. If you were to continue pushing me, I might get nauseous and throw up all over you."

Without saying another word, Ellis glared and gave him a final, deliberate push that was harder than all the rest. Rogers rocked so hard he and the chair begin to rotate. He put his head down and vomited. All the words anyone has ever said to him came out in his vomit. He continued to vomit. With each puke, more words came out, and Rogers began to deflate like the inflatable, and deflatable, clown. Finally, he puked out all the words and there was nothing left but the cardigan sweater sitting on the chair and the words spread all over the floor. All the other psychologists saw Rogers vomiting and they got nauseous and vomited also. Izzy saw himself with a spoon greedily eating up all the vomit, puking it, and eating it again just as quickly.

Fritz Perls, the Gestalt master, came, placed a hand on Izzy's shoulder, and said, "You're not spending enough time in contact with these theories. You must chew them and digest them first before they become yours." Perls helped Izzy up and set an elegant table for him with cloth napkins, silver utensils, and candles. He served him the vomit in a china bowl. Izzy ate slowly and carefully, savoring every bite. When he finished he patted his lips with the cloth napkin, pushed himself back from the table, and rubbed his stomach in satisfaction. "I have my counseling theory," he said to himself.

Just then, in a manner peculiar to dreaming sleep, Izzy awoke full of wonder and excitement. He had the answer to his problem! He knew just what counseling theory would work best for Craig. He found his style, his technique. But of course, in the manner peculiar to dreams, he had the excitement of the dream, but he couldn't quite remember the dream. He thought and thought, but nothing came to him, not the Bobo doll, the sweater, the chorus line, or his precious, precious answer: nothing. All he could remember was something about pearls; pearls, that didn't make any sense. The whole thing had slipped away from him when he awoke and he couldn't get it back. Izzy tried to go back to sleep to find his eureka moment again, but he was too excited to sleep and when they came to open up the library and put the lights back on, he gave up and went home.

Izzy left with a stack of more books to study, but none of them had what he was looking for. He had overlooked one slim volume in the library. In it, Fritz Perls spoke to him in a voice he couldn't hear. "You are you, and I am I," said Perls, "and if by chance we find each other, it's beautiful. If not, it can't be helped."

# Chapter 47 - The Tree Sitting Contest

"Vern would tell you that I enter a lot of contests," Betsy said, as she stabbed a needle through her needlepoint hoop. Even though it had nothing to do with the question Izzy asked, she kept on talking and Izzy let her. He just let her talk, even though it told him nothing about why she came and what kind of help she needed. He wasn't a good enough therapist yet to have her tell her story and give the information he needed for the psychosocial assessment, all while thinking it's her idea. He'd figure it out later, he thought.

"I entered the contest you see at the County Fair where you guess at the number of rocks in a water cooler jug. The winner gets water enough for the year. I didn't win no water, but I was only five off. It's OK though, we get plenty of water from our well. When they drilled it, the drilling man only went down thirty feet and he got soaked when he hit a vein and it came up like a geyser. It was all he could do to get a cap on it and now we don't need no pump because the water comes out of the ground on its own.

"I entered my grape pie in that same County Fair. I didn't win, but the pie got ate up by the judges. My friends all went to The Fair and they said to me, 'I thought you put your grape pie in the fair?' I said, 'I did, but the judges ate it all up.' You couldn't see even a single piece on the shelf with my name, Betsy Campbell, on a tag next to it. My friends said, 'Betsy, if they ate it, every bit, how come they didn't give you no prize?' I said, 'I don't know, maybe they didn't like it.'

"I even enter those contests that say I might have already won. I like them the best because when I peel the sticker off that says on it that I'm interested and place it carefully on the outlined box on the reply card, I'm thinking all the while about the money I already won, and how I'm rich, but no one knows it. Wouldn't Vern be surprised? He's always going on about needing to put a garage next to our doublewide, but we don't got the money. Even if he had his garage, he wouldn't have nothing to put in it, so he'd have to go on about that. I don't need much money. I like doing hair so much I do it for free, but I would like a new set of rollers to do the hair with.

"I enter a lot of contests, but I never entered no contest like the Tree-Sitting Contest at the Fall Foliage Festival. I was having a cup of coffee with my friend, Becky, and we saw the notice of it in the paper. I said, 'Now that doesn't look so hard. I can sit under a tree with the best of them. Just get me my needlepoint and there I go.' The winner gets their picture in the paper and a hundred dollars. So I filled out the entry blank and sent it in.

"They were gunna have the contest during the Fall Foliage Festival. Becky and I go every year to look at all the crafts. It's during bow season and Vern couldn't care less what I do during bow season. Becky said they needed something to bring the people in to the festival. 'Why would anyone come to watch people sit under a tree?' I said. 'They don't want something people would want to watch,' Becky said. 'They need something cute to put in the ad so that people know there's a festival going on. Then they'll come in and say, there's the tree-sitting contest, and when they turn away to buy the crafts, they won't miss none of the contest because there's nothing to miss.'

"We got to the festival and everyone that entered the contest gets shown a big maple tree alongside Maple Street. 'This is your tree,' they say. 'When we blow the whistle, you get up in it, because that's the start of the contest.' I didn't quite hear them because the wind was blowing and the trees were making too much noise. I thought, well, that's silly, I don't have to wait for no whistle to start sitting under a tree. I can get started right a-way. Becky had helped me bring my lawn chair and I set it up under my tree on a flat spot where the roots wouldn't make it rock and made myself comfortable in my winter clothes and my needlepoint right there on my lap.

"I just got settled down and looked around and saw none of the other contestants brought their lawn chairs. I said to Becky, 'Now you look at that, none of them come prepared to sit. How do they think they're gunna win?' Just then, before she answers, the whistle blows and I see all the other contestants climbing up their trees. I just sit and stare because I can't figure out what's going on. Becky figures it out before I do and she yells, 'Betsy, get up in the tree! You're supposed to sit up in the tree, not under it!'

"'Now, why would I want to sit up in a tree?' I said, 'I'm no squirrel.'

"'I know you're no squirrel. That's just what the contest is,' she said. 'It's a tree sitting contest.'

"'Boost me up, then,' I said. "And hand me my needlepoint.'"

All the while Betsy had been talking; her eyes had been down on her needlepoint project, which she pierced repeatedly. Izzy's eyes were on it too, for that matter, and although he couldn't make out the face of it, he could see the back. She was working with one color thread at a time and it was difficult to tell from the back what the image was because they formed no clear outline, loose ends dangled, and a thread connected one blotch of color to the next. Watching the needlepoint pattern form from the back of the work was a lot like sitting in these therapy sessions as a therapist, he thought. For a couple weeks now, people had been going in and out of his office, sharing their stories with him. Not all of them were good storytellers: they used indefinite pronouns, jumped topics, assumed he, the listener, knew what they knew, and failed to lay the groundwork of understanding. It was all just a lot of noise, but little meaning. Of course, he could interrupt and clarify, but more often than not, those attempts just muddied the waters even more. Izzy practiced listening to the music of what people were saying when he couldn't follow the words because the inflections and tone often revealed the clearest meanings.

"I wasn't up there more than an hour when I dropped my needlepoint. It fell down to the ground through the tree and sat there right where my lawn chair had been. I knew I couldn't come down out of the tree without losing the contest. Becky was gone. She'd taken the chair away so it won't get stole and went to look at the crafts. I called to people to hand my work up to me, but they couldn't hear me any better than I could hear them and the needlepoint just looked like more leaves on the ground that the wind took down, so nobody even noticed it there.

"There was nothing I could do but stay up in that tree and listen to the noise it was making. I like people, and I'm always talking with somebody, but there was nobody up there but me and the tree. I'm ashamed to say I tried talking to the tree, but the only thing it said back to me was, 'Foom.' Anything I say, and it's only got one answer: 'Foom.' Sort of like talking to Vern when his mind is on something else and he's not listening, except then Vern'll start to talking and I won't listen. I listened mighty hard to this foom, and it got to where I didn't have nothing more to say because I knew foom was the answer to everything. Everything else just disappeared. No more Becky, no more festival, no more Vern saying after I got home, 'You entered what?'"

For the rest of the day, Betsy suffered privations up above that would've sent Simon Stylites down from his column. Her hasty roost with no hammock or padding on the swaying branch of a wind tossed maple might have been more comfortable if she was sitting on a deer's antlers. In her snorkel coat and snowmobile pants, she was as prepared as she could be for the wind and cold. The trouble is, she hadn't brought a bathroom up with her in her parka, and she couldn't very well get up and walk back and forth on the tree limb.

Despite all the hardships, they were counterbalanced by the pleasures of towering over the rest of the world. She had as good a view of the fall foliage festival on her maple stilts as Nelson has over London from his Piccadilly post. She had the foom to listen to; and there was something about seeing the tops of people's heads, and not the bottoms or sides, that put her in a different frame of mind. When dinnertime came and passed, she didn't even care that Vern would come home from tromping through the woods, after ineffectually stalking deer with a compound bow, and be upset that dinner wasn't on the table. When the whistle blew for the contestants to come down out of the their trees for a bathroom break, she came down. All the serenity in the world can't stop a bladder from filling. But she didn't even look for her needlepoint in the mess of leaves under her tree before she got back up.

When it got dark and everyone went home from the festival, the tree sitters were still holding out in their trees. There wasn't much to see down below, but the stars came out all above. Looking down at the tops of heads milling around the festival and looking up at the pinpricks of stars circling heaven was much the same thing, except in black and white. Some of the contestants tried talking with one another, helloing from one tree to the next like seafarers eager for a gam, but the noisy wind blew away most of their words. That's what Betsy liked best about being up in the tree: there were no more words, every word another prick, another stitch, in her otherwise clean canvas.

Throughout that day and the night and the next day, contestants gave up and came down from the trees like the red and yellow leaves that released their hold from the branches. After a while, Betsy paid no attention. Indeed, a delegation had to come to the base of her tree to call her down when the last other contestant gave up.

"'Come on down,' they said to me, 'you won the contest. You don't have to sit up there no more.' But I wasn't ready to come down. Oh, I was hungry and I had to go potty, but I was afraid if I came down, they'd be all over me, congratulating me, and I wouldn't be able to go back up there again."

"You must have, like, come down eventually," Izzy said. "You're, like, here now."

"Yea, they all went away; everyone but Becky. She brought out the lawn chair and sat under the tree where I was going to. I hardly paid her any mind. Here I was, the winner of the contest, but it was like I never even existed. It was like I was part of the whole world and the whole world was part of me."

Just then, up in the tree, Betsy moved her foot an inch, lost hold of the trunk, and, in horror, all her identity returned as she grabbed for the nearest branch and hovered over actual non-existence.

"I came down right fast then. I was ready to go back to my life, but not all the time. I started climbing trees and sitting up in them, till Becky told me I ought to see a counselor. She said I was touched."

Izzy leaned towards the needlepoint. "What are you working on there?" he asked.

"I don't know yet," said Betsy, showing him the front. "I don't like getting needlepoint kits with the outline already printed on them no more. I like making up my own picture. It's like drawing, except with thread."

"Looks like it's going to be a maple tree," said Izzy.

"Yes," Betsy smiled. "I suppose you're right. That's what it's gunna be."

# Chapter 48 - The Briefcase

For all his seclusion before the All Staff Meeting, Dr Ahern was seldom in his office after it. He could generally be found pacing the halls of the clinic, stepping in and out of offices, checking to see how his momentous change was going. Few staff members took it seriously when he said that they should throw out their DSMs. They thought he was speaking figuratively. However, a counselor only had to have Dr Ahern visit his office once to learn that there was nothing figurative about his pronouncement. The first thing he generally did when stepping into an office would be to go over to the bookshelf, take up the volumes in his hands, and speak to the authors as if they were old friends meeting him for dinner at a trendy, yet restrained restaurant. That was not the case when he came across the DSM in the bookshelves. Then it was like the town marshal swinging through the doors of a saloon to find a notorious gunfighter. The clinic wasn't big enough for the two of them. One would have to go. A few brave souls, if the truth be told, hid their DSMs away in their desk like orthodox peasants hiding their icons from the Leninists. But no one could do it without suffering from the pangs of conscience and waking up with a start in the cold sweat of night, dreaming of a bald headed monomaniac rifling through their drawers. Since it was Dr Ahern bringing in briefcases of money and not the DSM, more often than not, the book was tossed, ringing, into the trashcan. So many, in fact, that the maintenance people complained of the weight and the waste; they should have been recycled like the phonebooks, they said. But, to no avail; Dr Ahern would have rather have had a good old fashioned book burning than to know that the very paper of the cursed volumes was spawning novels, textbooks, and the daily newspaper.

Once the clinic was purged of the hated book, The Director knew that he had to do something to keep the staff's eye on their goal. He was a good enough psychologist to know that just getting rid of something was not enough; one had to replace it with something as compelling. Lest they forget they had a second briefcase full of money waiting for them; he had that very briefcase, presumably filled and locked with cash, mounted on the staff room wall, to remind them.

Every day, in his walks through the clinic, Dr Ahern was bound to stop at the staff room and shoot a glance at his briefcase. Whether passing by on his way to a meeting, going to the lobby to greet a visitor, or getting tea, he'd stop and check in on the briefcase, again and again. One might imagine him on his sleepless nights, rising from the twisted sheets of his cot, and stalking the halls until he came upon the staff room, then stepping in to gaze at the briefcase, as a worried mother might look in on a sleeping child. Many staff witnessed the look he gave to that piece of luggage because they visited it often, as well. His stare riveted it to the wall more firmly than any self-tapping, dry wall screws ever could. Just as the case remained unmoving, fastened to the wall, tipped a little off balance, but not enough that most would notice; Dr Ahern stood, fastened to the floor, fixed on his purpose, and secured to a feral craving, if not anticipation of its fulfillment.

One morning, turning in to the break room on his way to medical records, he seemed newly attracted to the pattern of the leather's grain on the side of the bag, as if he'd just come upon a new interpretation of the significance seen there. To be sure, interpretations proliferate in all things, ready for the reading, and without the solemn significance we affix to them, most of the objects we adorn our walls with would have no more worth than the dust we wipe off them.

Of course, this was an ordinary briefcase, such as lawyers and accountants carry to their jobs. The inside was said to contain stacks of the mighty dollar, easily exchanged for all the delights of the world. The outside was enjoying a reincarnation from its first life as the hide of a lumbering cow. Not many months before, the very material that was screwed to the wall of the staff room had been grazing on a verdant hillside, warding off flies. Now, tanned and anointed with oil, it had become a holy talisman. The briefcase had become a favorite topic of conversation for the staff during breaks, speculating on whether it actually had cash within, and how they were going to spend it. Placed in full sight among a group of not so recently ex-addicts, many not so far from their pilfering ex-ways, it was a wonder that every morning the object was still screwed to the wall where it was the night before. But, however wanton the staff were, the case was a sanctified and revered symbol of whatever it was they hoped, and thus, not to be messed with.

Dr Ahern peered closely at the bag and then he stepped away and turned to the staff who were there at the time, getting coffee, reading the paper, catching up on gossip. Pointed to the bag as if it were a PowerPoint screen in a lecture hall, The Director began to speak.

"Come on up and look at the pattern on the side of the bag," he said. They all got up and peered closer, some putting on their glasses, others squinting, not ready to admit that they needed glasses.

Dr Ahern continued, before anyone had a chance to answer, "Whatever you see in the pattern will be what is already in the contents of your mind. The side of this bag is a veritable Rorschach in leather, rather than ink. The leather itself, although tanned, processed by whatever process they use on leather, still has the markings of the original cow that it came from. Look closely. See the wrinkles that reveal bovine worries. They are still there, just as the lines on your palms remain for years, despite all the uses you turn your hands to. Bend your fingers and see where the wrinkles form. Why, the wrinkles form where the wrinkles had formed before! Straighten out your fingers now. The wrinkles are still there, etched into your palm after a lifetime of clenching. Now look at the leather again. There are the same wrinkles preserved, long after the cow is converted into hamburger, eaten, and digested. The cow has long since passed on to cow heaven, where alfalfa abounds and flies are banned. She doesn't have a care in the world, but here her wrinkles remain.

"Listen to your clients and you'll discover where their minds are wrinkled. You'll find the creases that bend their thoughts one way or another. You'll see the ruts they fall in, time and time again. You'll recognize the paths they take and you can point out new paths, straddle the ruts, and bend their thoughts in new direction. It's important that we know the wrinkles of our clients' minds because those etchings are the very things that must be changed for healing to occur. The schizophrenic who turns more easily to fantasy than reality is following his path of least resistance. The addict has fallen into a familiar rut that he can't get out of. Even an absent, uncaring father will engrave his pattern upon the mind of his daughter so deeply that she will duplicate a lifetime of relationships with distant men.

"Our minds are imprinted with expectations and prejudices, as well. The DSM was just one of them. We can never know the client's until we discard our own. I had you throw out the book; now dispose it from your mind!

"Remember this if you remember nothing else: every counseling session is a two person, fifty minute revolt against the way things are, the way we figure they have to be. We show the schizophrenic a new path, pull the addict out of his rut, and help the lonely woman engrave what she wants. We are revolutionaries, one by one, not just us in this clinic, although we are especially, but every therapist is a revolutionary. In our sessions we hope to ignite a revolution one spark at a time."

Ahern stopped and, pleased with his lecture just as it was, did not stay for questions. There wouldn't have been any, anyway; for none of the staff were bold enough to challenge the great man to his face and in front of everyone. For revolutionaries they were a timid bunch.

During the harangue, The Head Administrator attempted to form a crease in the tab of the top of her Starbucks cup because it was annoying her whenever she tried to drink. Failing that, she yanked it off. Then, rather than it tearing neatly at the fold, it produced a jagged dagger, dissecting the lid. "The Professor's been in his ivory tower too long," she said to those whom she could trust. "He fancies himself as a revolutionary and thinks all therapists are revolutionaries, too. But for the rest of the world, they are agents of social control. Why do you think probation and the courts send us so many? We know how to manage them. Let this talk of revolution get out and our referral sources will dry up. Who would go to treatment, except the ones that have to?"

"The Old Man talks of wrinkles," said Pellegrino, the wrinkled man, "but what's a guy with a smooth, bald head know about wrinkles? Maybe I like my wrinkles, maybe they're fine just the way they are, like an old pair of pants that fits just right. Each one of these lines is another bit of living I did, so don't ask me to straighten them out now. I'd much sooner make wrinkles on top of wrinkles. When I get done with it, I hope someone skins, tans this old hide, and puts it up on that wall to show you all what living does to a person. You know what wrinkles are good for? They help you sop up shit. Ever take a piece of paper, crumple it and straighten it, and crumple it again? You'll turn it into a towel. That's me; I sop it up, absorb it all, and wring it all out. That's why I became an alcoholic; I just couldn't see a half glass of beer sitting on the bar without drinking it up."

After Dr Ahern left, Izzy alone continued to scrutinize the briefcase, as if he was trying to find his counseling theory there also. The comments of the staff around him only deepened his despair. None of them agreed, either. The leather bag seemed to him a complex map of a labyrinth, an endless array of choices, forks in the road that, once taken, could not be retraced and retaken without getting lost. He turned away. He had enough of choices. Oh, for someone who could just point him the way!

# Chapter 49 - The Narrative Imperative

Izzy gagged as a wild haired man entered his office accompanied by a cloud of fumes. The intern showed him where to sit, making a mental note to have it cleaned afterwards, and pushed his chair away, hoping to get beyond the reach of the vapors.

"I go, you go, we all go scream for ice cream," said the man, his eyes steady on Izzy, as if he'd come out with something weighty and was looking for help carrying it.

"Pardon me?"

"Pardonnez-moi. Esperanto sancto, omnibus, make a fuss."

"I'm sorry, I don't understand."

"I can't stand understand, kick stand, bike stand, withstand the witness stand. I'm witless, hit list, fitness. Not fit for wit. Got a zit on my mitt. Gotta quit and split." He stood up to leave.

"No don't go. You're here for an intake. I hear you need a therapist."

"Make ache and break cake. Take in an intake. Gotta shake and bake."

"You can, like, go when we're done. I have some questions I want to ask you. Why do you need a therapist?"

His too-large pants drooped as he stood, revealing browned skivvies: the source of the odor, no doubt. "The rapist needs a why. You ask, I quest the best dressed stress test."

"I see you like to rhyme, are you, like, a poet?"

"The poet doesn't know it, but he can show it and grow it and throw it." He sat back down. Izzy was glad; every time the man stirred, the cloud of gas diffused in the room more.

"What can I help you with?"

He rocked, as he rhymed. "With your help, I yelp. He belt a welt and I felt."

"Did someone hurt you? Were you beaten?"

"Beaten, sweetened, and eaten. A dead horse at the source, of course I'm hoarse."

"I don't want to beat a dead horse. We don't, like, have to talk about it if you don't want to."

He stopped rocking and answered with passion demanding acknowledgement.

"Nurse likes the verse. Converse, curse the hearse, rehearse and disperse. Fill your purse, it's not perverse,"

"We're not getting anywhere," said Izzy. "I need to know what you want from me."

"Getting knots, slots, lots of ink blots in the plots."

"You want me to understand you? But I can't. You're not making any sense to me."

"Sense a tense fence. Condense the pretense. Can't the rant recant a chant and replant?

"Anything is possible. You can do it if you try."

"Try, guy. Don't sigh. Ask why or I fry."

"Don't turn it back to me. I'm not to blame if I can't understand you. You're, like, barely speaking English."

"English speaking bear swear and glare and not repair."

Izzy said, "I'm sorry, I didn't mean to get upset. I'm just frustrated that we can't communicate better."

Resuming rocking, he said, "Better communicate than fornicate. Take the bait, create a big estate."

"I couldn't agree with you more."

"More door than four is a chore. Pour, roar, and bore; snore and ignore."

"You're right, I get overwhelmed with all your words and I, like, give up."

"Words are herds of birds, a blight plight on a night flight."

"It's just, I'm an intern, you see, and I don't know what I'm doing. I've been going to college for umpteen years and it's about time I frigging graduated, but my supervisor is, like, an alcoholic biker, working as a bouncer in a strip club. He won't help me, but he wants me to help him. I'm just under a lot of stress, you see."

"See the knee in the tree, bumblebee, let it be, princess and the pea."

Izzy knew it was wrong to burden the client with his woes, but it just felt so good. He continued, "And it's not just you I don't know how to help. I don't know how to help, like, anybody. I can't even help myself. I guess I need a therapist. But I don't even know what I'd say if I had one. What do you say?"

"Say hey, without delay. Play in the hay, convey and pay."

"Yeah, you're probably right. Just let it out. Whatever's in there, just let it out."

"Out the spout, scream and shout, cry and pout, eat the trout."

"We all need to do that, I guess. Like, stuff happens and we're not done with it until we put it into words and tell someone the story about it. It's set up that way so when stuff happens and we learn from it, we can't help but tell someone about it so they can learn. If we don't tell anyone, then, like, all the words stay with us and make us sick."

"A sick chick licks my dick, brick a hick."

"I guess you'd call it the narrative imperative," said Izzy, smiling.

He answered, rocking and laughing much too much, "Narrative imperative, narrative imperative, comparative narrative imperative."

# Chapter 50 - The Writing on the Wall

Though behavioral health opens its doors to the very members of society most people cross the street to avoid: killers, rapists, and drug addled individuals who would rob you blind for a ten-dollar hit, there are seldom any crimes committed within its holy precincts. Far more students fight in high school algebra than in anger management class. The therapist treating kleptomaniacs may prudently lock her purse in her desk, but her knick knacks remain on her shelf untouched. Street fighters hand their knives over when they check in at the front before group, like gunfighters turning in their firearms to the marshal of Dodge City. Murderers, though they shuffle around prison for decades in shackles with four guards, the day they are released on parole, will sit quietly in a small room alone with a counselor armed with no weapon other than a pen. There had briefly been a run on toilet paper from the women's stalls as one individual, receiving less in her welfare check than could cover household expenses, helped herself to a few rolls, but, other than that, Izzy had not been aware of any thefts or assaults since his internship began. That made it all the more strange when graffiti was scrawled on the waiting room wall right in front of Melvina.

The graffiti was not a simple scratching of initials that might be achieved on the sly, behind the back or sheltered by a pant leg. No, it was a daring declaration covering the entire wall, just in front of the office manager, in bubble shaped forms, cleverly utilizing in its design the discount store prints of flowers that were hung there. Melvina had her back turned, cussing at a fax that had jammed, and there it was when she looked up, boldly defacing her room in front of a dozen or so clients reading magazines.

"Who did that?" she hollered at the stunned innocents looking up from their reading. No one had seen anything, but the hollering brought in the Head Administrator, who was nearby, worrying over the latest office supply invoice. She was annoyed to lose count of the paperclips and strode up to the desk to reprimand Melvina for hollering, when she caught sight of the artwork on the wall. The Starbucks she had consumed that day must have given her a jump on the sauntering, cannabis inspired artist, for, she sprang up two flights of stairs on a hunch and met him exiting the elevator, as he stowed a can of paint in the trash. She grabbed him by his baggy pants and, missing hold of his jeans, which were drooping, had him by his boxers, which, when he attempted to break free, stretched to their utmost, giving him a painful wedgie. The Head Administrator hollered louder than Melvina ever did, and so did the baggy panted man, though for different reasons. The hollering was just enough to stir the security guard who had been sweet-talking a female janitor by her cart just down the hall, but not before he had shown her his gold capped teeth in his best smooth operator smile. At first glance, he wasn't sure who needed security more: the thin screaming woman giving a young man a wedgie, or the young dreadlocked man suffering a ball binding, but he wisely detained the man when he recognized the Head Administrator. No matter how securely the brawny guard had the dreadlocked artist in his grasp, the Head Administrator wouldn't let go of his boxers. She pulled the two men into the elevator and marched them both right to the scene of the crime.

By this point, the room was filled with clients and staff who had heard the hollering and come to view the new artwork and watch Melvina throw a fit. The Head Administrator pulled the dreadlocked man through the crowd, up to the graffiti, with the guard still attached, and demanded, "Did you do this? Did you?"

The man drew himself up as proud and dignified as he could with his boxers hanging out, their elastic all stretched to hell, and answered, "Yes, Mon."

"You're going to pay for this, you know. Just wait until the police get here. Did you call the police?"

Melvina cut her fit short and called the police.

Dr Ahern was among the crowd. He had been studying the artwork, one elbow resting on a folded arm, as one stands in a museum. He approached and asked the man, "What are you trying to say? I can't read it."

"It's wild style," said the artist.

"It's very good. Distinctively shaped," pronounced the Director. "Striking."

"Oh, it's just a throw up."

"No, it's very good. You shouldn't put yourself down like that. You're a very good artist. But what does it say."

"It's my tag, Mon."

"Yes, yes, I've seen it before. You put this design everywhere?"

"No, Mon, not everywhere. I like the daring spots. Anyone can tag on a dark street. I like to paint where's there's people and I can get caught."

"Well, you're caught now," said the Head Administrator. "You're going to jail and then we're going to paint over it. So, how do you like that?"

"I like it all right, Mon. If I get caught, it's all for Jah's glory."

"What does the writing on the wall say, though," squinted Dr Ahern. "I can't make out the letters. What is that? ADD? OCD? Do you have a diagnosis?"

"I don't keep a diagnosis; it's my name, Mon."

"I'm glad of that. For too many people," lectured Ahern, "their diagnosis becomes their name: what others know them by and how they know themselves. They carry their diagnosis around like a surname, and have more in common with other bipolars, other panic disorders, or addicts, than their own family. The community of the sick becomes a new family, all staying sick together. So, who are you?"

"Dat's who I am, mon. Dat's my name," he pointed to his work. "You can't say it. It's unpronounceable."

"Oh, like the name of God is unpronounceable."

"Yea, when Abraham talk to Him at the burning bush, Jah say, I am who I am. So that's me, I am who I am."

"He's Popeye," said someone in the crowd.

"So, do you think you're God?" asked the Head Administrator.

"I am not Jah, himself, but I have a part of Jah in me. This makes me as unknowable and unpronounceable as Jah."

"I see," she said. "So, because you're part God you think you can go around defacing walls."

"No, mon. I'm just putting my tag on the wall to let people know I'm here."

"You're no different than a dog spraying the fire hydrant," she said. "A dog writes in piss, a man in paint."

"When I have Jah, I have everything, so I got dog in me, too. And Jah leave his sign everywhere, too, 'cause he has the dog in him."

"I think we should keep his tag up on the wall," said Dr Ahern. "It's good for us to see."

"You've got to be kidding me," said the Head Administrator. "And I suppose you'll have us let him go, too."

"Well, it wouldn't be right to keep the art and throw the artist in jail."

"Then what's going to stop everyone from writing on the walls?"

"Maybe everyone should write on the walls, put their ineffable tag up there, if that'll make them better. You keep forgetting what we're trying to do here: we're trying to heal people. This art he put up here heals people who have been made too little and limited by their illnesses and circumstances, it can remind them of all the possibilities that are before them. See, the letters could mean anything, just like you, you can be anything. They cleverly bend and incorporate the environment, the paintings of flowers that are next to them, just like we are part of our environment. But, unlike the paintings of flowers, they are not bounded by a frame. Just so, a man's spirit cannot be kept in a box. This man's Jah, he's not a god that shrinks us, like a lot of gods do. This god expands us. And Kilroy here put up his art when no one was looking. Now you don't see it, then you do. In the same way change happens. In the blink of an eye you decide to do something different and, if you don't forget, it happens."

And so, just like that, the graffiti remained on the wall in front of Melvina, who scowled, all the more, whenever she looked up. The Head Administrator never returned to her invoice. Instead of counting supplies, she began to count the days until that second briefcase would be opened and they'd be free of Ahern's experiment. Clients, and even a few staff, began to write on the walls, just as she predicted, though none as boldly as the tagger, and none proclaimed the ineffable name of their god, unless their god was called *fuck* or *suck my balls*. Dr Ahern, pleased with his new acquisition, made the waiting room another stop in his pacing rounds, where he would examine the art just as he often examined the briefcase and would frequently lecture the confused occupants of the waiting room as to its meaning. Churchy big-breasted Bella, offended by the fucks and sucks written on the walls, was convinced that the graffiti was nothing other than idolatry and the Director an idolater. She handed in her resignation and left the clinic faster than she could flee a golden calf. The remaining staff began to grumble that the larger share of the briefcase was not large enough to make up for the extra work necessitated by her resignation. Grumbling, whether at the water cooler, coffee pot, or the hallways, is a verbal form of graffiti. Dr Ahern was being weighed by the staff and found wanting.

# Chapter 51 - Sue

The smell didn't disappear when the rhyming man left Izzy's office; it lingered even long after Izzy carried the tainted chair out in the hallway. However, the intern really didn't mind it so much. It was just the price to pay for an epiphany: a long awaited epiphany that could direct him, he thought, not only through this internship, but also through an illustrious career. He might even write books and be as famous as Dr Ahern, someday. He would explain that people just needed to tell their stories because their stories made them sick when they didn't tell them. That's all there was to it. Also, and sometimes they needed someone trained to help tell them tell the stories and to listen when they told them. He would be that trained, professional story listener. How hard could it be? After all, the crazy, smelly, rhyming man facilitated Izzy telling his story, and he barely spoke comprehensible English. Just the same, Izzy felt so much better after letting it out, it didn't even matter to whom he told it. He hadn't felt this good since he woke up in the library, but he had a lot more to show for it.

This epiphany served Izzy well through the next few sessions he had with clients as he masterfully drew their stories out of them. They all seemed grateful after they left even though many cried throughout the procedure. Indeed, the more they cried, the more grateful they seemed. Izzy thought, as he restocked his office with tissues, that maybe the best therapists went through the most tissues, a point he'd have to remember later when he became a supervisor, or a director. A surgeon can't operate without there being blood, he would say, and a therapist can't without there being tears.

Meanwhile, when Izzy was busy forecasting the rest of his life, The Fate sisters were making other plans for the intern. Just as tradesmen scoff at do-it-yourselfers, doctors ridicule medicine men, and lawyers consider those who have themselves for clients, fools; it seems to tick off the Fate sisters whenever people attempt to do their job for them and take fate into their own hands. The cruel deities must have had a good laugh, might have cackled about it after work, over drinks, when they prearranged Sue's therapist to have a heart attack and set up an appointment for her clinical care to be taken over by Izzy.

By the time Sue entered Izzy's office, he had every surface graced with a box of tissues, the first tissue of every box pulled up for easy access. A tear didn't stand a chance in that office.

In truth, Sue wasn't about to lose any tears over the death of her old therapist, or anything else, for that matter. She wasn't old, but, having been in therapy since age three, almost as long as she could talk, she had had dozens of therapists by then, all of them more experienced and skilled than Izzy, despite the efficacy of his new counseling theory. By now, she had no more use for a therapist than Izzy had for those cardboard cutouts he had punched out of the top of the tissue boxes. She attended her sessions regularly anyway, never missing one with any of her therapists, not because she sought their healing arts, but because the group home van picked her up and brought her there and was waiting in the parking lot for her to leave. The group home required her to attend those sessions; it didn't, she had learned over time, require her to participate.

Izzy welcomed Sue with his usual greetings and tried to make her comfortable. She stared at him. He attempted to coax her story out of her, using the methods he had learned to employ over his brief career. She stared at him. He tried to show her the way to tell a story by giving a jolly version of his first time in that very office, getting up and acting out the parts of himself, Craig, and the Office Manager. She stared at him. In fact it seemed the harder he worked the more she stared. It was not the vacant stare of the dissociated, nor the actress' stare at the back wall of a theater, nor even the fearful stare of a headlighted deer; it was the concentrated stare of a statue; the kind of stare not broken by weather, earthquakes, or roosting pigeons. It was a stare, he found, that didn't require a reply. It was not an invitation to a staring contest. In fact, Izzy felt comfortable with the stare, as if the client was not a client at all, but a sculpture of a client that had been installed in his office. He stopped trying to get the statue to tell her story, but instead, picked up her chart and had it tell her story for her.

In his lectures to the staff, Dr Ahern was almost as adamant against reading charts as he was against the DSM. "Learn from your clients by their own words, not someone else's," he would say and discouraged clinicians from reading the charts of patients before their first session. He conceded that the charts were a necessary evil to keep track of medicines prescribed, correspondence, and basic identifying data. He even recommended that all staff carefully record the client's goals and progress they made towards those goals, but he forever threatened to have the charts purged of prior assessments that would prejudice the minds of his revolutionaries. The medical records staff had even begun to do this, but, with thousands of patients passing through the clinic's doors every month, and tens of thousands more in the archives, it was an impossible task.

Upon seeing Izzy pick up her chart, Sue broke her silence as suddenly as if a cadaver had spoken. The intern almost dropped the chart when he jolted at the sound. He even looked around the office to see if anyone else was there.

Sue said, "They're telling me to stop smoking."

"What! Who wants you to stop smoking? Your doctor?"

"No one in particular."

"Well, want do you think? Do you, like, want to stop smoking?"

Sue said, "I want to stop smoking."

"That's great. How long have you been smoking?" said Izzy, still looking for a story out of her.

It wasn't going to happen, for no sooner had she declared her goal, than she resumed her silent staring; this time while resting her left ear upon her shoulder, as if she had worked hard all day and now was going to rest.

It was harder for Izzy not to be self-conscious with Sue resting her head upon her shoulder while staring at him. For one, he was afraid she'd get a crook in her neck. He was starting to get one in his, just looking at her. For another, it seemed that, by this young woman thus reclining, she had included him in an affectionate intimacy far beyond the bounds of their prescribed roles. It seemed as if she was nuzzling his shoulder, and it gave him the creeps.

"Well," he said at last, "If you want to stop smoking. You should see Pete and Kate. They're special staff just hired to help people stop smoking. I'm really glad you came here today and told me this because we can get you back on the road to recovery."

Sue continued to stare, giving Izzy no acknowledgement that he had said anything to her.

"The most important thing is to be very determined. Like there's nothing you won't do to stop smoking."

"There's nothing I won't do to stop smoking," she said, encouraging him.

"That's it; keep on saying that. Say it over and over."

If she said it over, it was within. To Izzy, she only kept staring. He rose and opened the door. It wasn't until he gently pulled at her hand that she stood and left his office, saying, at the door to the waiting room, to no one in particular, "There's nothing I won't do to stop smoking."

# Chapter 52 - Boundaries

Winter burst upon the Medical Center like a bomb, spreading its white shrapnel all over. A group of smokers huddled against the building with their heads in and back turned to the blast, just as soldiers turn against artillery. Few were brave enough to expose themselves to winter's fury. Doctors rushed to and from their cars as if they were dashing across a snipered square. Nurses carefully stepped their sneakered feet where others had trod before as if traversing a minefield. Patients struggled through unshoveled drifts in their wheelchairs and on their crutches like the wounded returning to the back lines through a shelled field. Only the most devoted visitors came to the medical center, the majority remained home to wring their hands by the phone, awaiting word of a survival, a maiming, or a death. Despite the war winter waged against the denizens of the medical center, the small crowd, like assembled refugees, clustered near the door, shielding their precious smokes from the greedy wind.

By this point in history, there were few surviving smokers left, their numbers having been reduced by a holocaust of posted prohibitions and stern stares. Like gypsies run out of one village after another, the smokers had been banned from every public place until all that was left was the ghetto of butt-strewn entrances. They were a tattered remnant, few smoked anymore except those who were society's outcasts already and those who tended to the outcasts: the clients and staff of Behavioral Health. The latest pogrom was a disregarded sign banning tobacco use fifty feet from the very door they hovered near.

"I'd like to quit," said Bill, bumming from Lawrence's cache of rollies, "but the craving has its way with me every time. I can't fight it. It's like the craving had a head start. It began its training way back when I was a snot nosed kid and my Ma was changing my diaper with a fag hanging off her lips. I wasn't even on solid food before I was already breathing in two packs a day of her second hand smoke. The smoke found all the hidden passages inside me, stealing the keys to my desires, and making copies before I even said my first word. Now it knows me better than I know myself and it whispers sweet nothings in my ears twenty times a day. When I wake up, I have to smoke, when I go to bed, I have to smoke, I have to smoke in the john and in the car, after sex, after meals, after group, whenever. It's worse than the other drugs. Them I can do without these days. They say the first thing you pick up is the last thing you put down. I'd like to quit, but, oh well, we all have to die someday from something."

"Oh, c'mon, if you're gunna smoke, smoke, and if you're gunna quit, quit," said Lawrence. "Don't come out here and talk about quitting right while you're lighting up. It ruins it for the rest of us, hearing you go on."

Bill replied, "Can't a man be of two minds, or six or eight minds if he has them? I can't shut off the desire to quit any better than I can pull the plug on the urge to smoke. They're both in there with me. First, one's greater, then the other. I've quit smoking almost as many times as I've lit up and, when I'm done with this one, it'll be equal."

"You can think about quitting if you want, just don't talk about it, and poison the experience for the rest of us. We came out here to take in smoke, not guilt. Just like the sign says: no talking about quitting within fifty feet."

Pellegrino, the wrinkled counselor, backed through the door, carrying a cardboard box. He lobbed the box in the snow and reached in his inside coat pocket for a cigarette. The lines on his face had darkened, so that he looked as if a child had scribbled on him. He lit up without a word to any of the clients standing there. Seeing the sign, he became enraged and, gripping the cigarette between his teeth, he tried to pull the sign out of the ground; but it was frozen in. He contented himself with bending the post until the sign lay face down and flat. He jumped on the sign a few times, pulled his cigarette out, and blew a long exhale, full of vapor and smoke, into the winter air.

"Whoa, there. You OK, man?" asked Lawrence.

"Fucking sign."

"Hey, aren't you a counselor, man?"

"I was a counselor, but I'm fucking fired."

"Oh, how come, anger management problems?"

"No, smoking, they fucking fired me for smoking."

"They can't do that."

"They did. We got this new rule that counselors can't smoke on the job any more than they can drink or use drugs. They say it's bad for the clients to see us smoking when we're supposed to be helping them quit."

"Man what a bitch. That's fucked up."

"Yea, you didn't make us smoke," said Bill. "We did it all by ourselves."

Sue came out of the building then, finished with her session with Izzy. She twisted her mouth at the smokers and hurried to the group home van waiting by the road. High above, the sun was peeking out from behind a cloud, to see what the cloud had done to the landscape below.

"So how did they catch you smoking?" Lawrence asked Pellegrino. "Did they give you a piss test?"

"No, I kept on going out for breaks, right in front of them," said Pellegrino. "I wasn't about to stop. It's none of their bee's wax if I smoke, or not."

"So you dared them to fire you."

"I didn't think anyone cared enough about the goddamn rule. It's one of Dr Ahern's big ideas. No one else gives a shit and he's got his head so far up his ass, he doesn't know what's going on half the time."

"So, what happened? He pull his head out of his ass and catch you?"

"No, it's still up there. The Head Administrator up and fired me."

"That the bitch that's always drinking the Starbucks?"

"Yea, you know what I told her? I said, 'Just you wait, when they're done with nicotine, they'll be going after caffeine next.'"

"You got that shit right."

"I asked her, 'What the hell do you care if I smoke? You were against the rule in the first place.'"

"What'd she say?"

"She said rules, 'Rules are rules. If you won't follow this rule, then how do we know you'll follow the others? You might break confidentiality, sleep with a client, or you might tell the authorities all about our little experiment and blow us in about the briefcase of money. Now we can't trust you to maintain boundaries.'"

"What briefcase of money?"

"I'm not supposed to tell anyone, but Ahern bought us all off with a briefcase of money to make a few changes. There's another briefcase full of money screwed to the staff room wall that we're supposed to get when we're all done."

Lawrence brightened, "Say, has he got a briefcase of money for us clients? We've put up with changes, too. First Craig goes, then Miss Bella, now you. There won't be any counselors left to share that money, anyway. We ought to get some."

Pellegrino continued, "So I say to her, 'Yeah, well maybe I'll just call those authorities anyway, seeing as though you fired me.'"

"How much money do you think is in that briefcase?"

"The damn thing might be empty for all I know. If you want it, you can have it. Go right in there and pull it off the wall, I think it's got a curse on it and we'd all be better off with it gone."

"I'm not touching anything with no curse on it, man."

Pellegrino lifted his collar against a gust that blew snow off the roof above. "I don't need this job anyway. I bought a plow with the money from the first briefcase, so I can plow driveways. If it keeps snowing like this, there'll be good money this year and I won't have to put up with all the bullshit."

"So, what did she say when you said you'd call the authorities?"

"Nothing; she just said boundaries. 'We can't trust you to maintain proper boundaries.'"

# Chapter 53 - Cleaning the Smoking Room

When Sue returned to the group home from her therapy appointment, the chore chart was up and it said it was her turn to clean the smoking room. The House Manager prepared the chart once a week and posted it outside of the staff office for all at the residents to see. It always drew a crowd when she did, residents craning to see what they'd be doing for the next week and making deals with each other, trading washing dishes for vacuuming the living room, bathrooms for the lawn, or whatever.

Sue preferred to wait until everyone cleared out before she inspected the chore chart. She needed time to examine whether someone had erased her name under a more desirable chore and put it in under a harder one. She could easily imagine someone doing it, even in the middle of the crowd, saying I'm going to put Sue's name under cleaning the smoking room, and everybody laughing at the irony because, after all, Sue was the only one in the group home who didn't smoke.

After the crowd cleared, she went up to the board to inspect it and, sure enough, there was her name, Sue, under the heading, Smoking Room. She studied it for changes in the handwriting, smudge marks and the like. Chemicals from the dry erase markers were just starting to go to her head when she heard a voice say, "I'll trade you for washing the kitchen floor on Thursday night."

Sue didn't turn towards the voice in case it was just her illness or the dry erase fumes talking to her; but then, out of the corner of her eye, she saw someone's shoes on the floor and she heard the voice repeat the offer. She turned and saw it was Tim. He had a girlfriend he wanted to see Saturday night. He explained he couldn't wait around half the night for the dishes to be done before beginning on his chore so he wanted to trade with Sue.

She didn't answer Tim at first. She thought she should study him for a while to find out his motivations. Tim was what they call a clean-cut young man; handsome and, unlike the rest in the group home, well dressed and groomed. His big, square head must have been hard to balance on his little neck because he seldom held it straight up. It was always tipping to one side and flopping around like a bobble-head doll. He never let his eyes meet another's. Maybe that's why he kept his head bouncing around like that, so the eyes would be a moving target. His hands were in his pockets, the left one scratching his genitals through the lining while he waited for Sue's answer.

Sue always had a hard time trusting Tim and it wasn't just her illness.

Someone, no one in particular, murmured in her head. *They can call you paranoid if they want, plenty of people have, but even hypochondriacs get sick sometimes. I always had a bad feeling about him. When everything is said and done, they won't be calling you a schizophrenic any more. No, they'd be calling you a genius.*

Sue was about to agree to trade cleaning the smoking room for doing the floor when Tim said forget it and walked away.

*It just goes to show, you can't trust him,* said no one in particular. *He asks you something and then he just changes his mind.*

What tipped Sue off about Tim was that he just didn't seem to fit in. It sounds like a pretty peculiar thing to say about someone living in a house full of seriously and persistently mentally ill people, but he seemed odd because he wasn't particularly eccentric; he was the most normal looking of the bunch. He had a car, a girlfriend, and a part time job. On some nights he'd go after work to a neighborhood bar and sit on the barstool and drink like a regular person. He'd come home smelling like alcohol and the counselors would get so upset they'd come out of their staff room to deal with it. All these things, including the drinking, made him seem so normal it was weird.

While Sue thought about all this, she lowered her left ear down on her shoulder. No one in particular murmured, *It's remarkable how, when you look at things sideways, your mind adjusts them so they seem straight up and down.*

She first came upon that discovery lying on her mother's couch watching TV when she was little. The TV made vastly more sense to her back then than anything her mother did.

*Your mother could've been certified nuts had she ever gone to the doctor*, said no one in particular. *As it was, your father and older sister took care of things and saved her the trouble. What they got for their pains was constant abuse and the contempt one can't help but have for those who let you walk all over them. The only thing she ever had to do was to throw temper tantrums.*

Sue watched a lot of TV and wore only blue clothes so as to blend in with the couch, which was blue also. She hardly watched any TV nowadays and could never get space on the couch. But that didn't stop her from assuming the TV watching position whenever she had to concentrate.

Sue kept an eye on the staff room door. If a staff came out and caught her with her head tipped, she'd start to lose privileges. Sue once tried to explain to the House Manager the benefits of tipping her head, but she'd have none of it. The House Manager went on and on about fitting in with society and acting appropriately and then set up a behavior plan so that Sue would lose privileges whenever she was caught tipping her head. By this time, she'd had the plan for ages; they reviewed it every three months, and she'd gotten really good at keeping an eye on the staff room door.

Tim's retreat left her in command of the field. She wasn't sure that anyone else would make a move on her so she stayed in position for some time after he left. She knew that, just by standing very, very still, she could freak some people out. Other residents generally took it in stride but new counselors couldn't handle it. One staff was so unhinged by Sue standing there, not moving, that she had to call 9-1-1 and have an ambulance come and cart her off to the hospital, still in position, strapped to a stretcher, before she felt better.

From her position, she had a good view of most everything going on in the group home. She stood at the foot of the stairs like a suit of armor in the hallway of an old castle. Anyone going up or down had to steer around her, like a piece of furniture that no one noticed, but no one crashed into, either. As usual, there was a lot of traffic in the house: people making the circuit from the bathrooms upstairs, to the smoking room, to the kitchen for a drink, out to the porch for another smoke, and back to the bathrooms. *It's as if the house was a body and these scurrying people were blood cells: treacherous, metastasizing blood cells; spreading their malignancy to every corner.*

Sue was just trying to will her lungs not to breathe and her heart not to pump when Becky, the neighbor, home from college, came in. Tim, his head on gimbals, bounced as close behind her and as jiggley as her high ponytail. Tim liked to call Becky his girlfriend, but he never said it to her face. Everyone knew, even Tim, although he refused to admit it to himself, that while she may have been his girlfriend, he was nothing more than a project to her. Her Dad had opposed the group home from opening next door and Becky felt sorry for everyone. She felt most sorry for Tim, who was her same age and relatively normal looking.

*Leave it to horny Tim*, said no one in particular to Sue, *He can't even tell the difference between captivation and pity.*

"I can't go out till I get my meds," Tim said as they passed through the door.

Sue tuned her ears in to hear what she could.

*A fly on the wall, that's what you are.*

"So go in the office and get your meds. Let's go sledding! It's a beautiful day, and the sun's out!"

Tim turned and dove through the office door and in half a second the House Manager said to him, "You need to knock before you come in." Tim rushed out of the door and knocked like some kind of a trained monkey with a red face.

Then House Manager said, "You can't come in. I'm on the phone."

Becky smiled at Tim, "No problem, just wait for your meds. I'll get started outside. When you're ready, I'll still be out there!"

Sue couldn't see the sky from where she was, nor could she see Tim. It may have been a beautiful, sunlit winter day outside, but she knew it was about to storm.

Said no one in particular to Sue, *When everything gets as grim as a head nurse when you've been caught cheeking your meds, then you know it's about to storm.*

It was just that portentous when Becky, the human exclamation point, bounced off the porch, past the guys smoking, and started to build a snowman. House rules said no one could leave if they didn't take their meds, so Tim stayed on the porch, watched her, and lit up.

*Tim never really caught on to the art of living in the group home,* said no one in particular to Sue. *It doesn't pay to get upset about the House Manager any more than it pays to get upset when the rain gets you all wet. The rain can't help getting you wet if you don't have the sense to get out of it when it's coming down. If a House Manager gave you everything that you want when you wanted it, she wouldn't be managing a darn thing; you'd be managing her. The solution to dealing with the House Manager is in remembering that the very moment she stops you from getting what you want, she, at the same time, is giving you the means to circumvent her.*

For instance, Sue used to ask her what she and the other staff were always writing about her in their charts and she never would tell her. Then one day the House Manager left her keys lying on the kitchen counter.

No one in particular had whispered to Sue, *It doesn't take a genius to see that the keys are there to take, unlock the staff room door, and read the charts yourself.*

The House Manager made a fine show of tearing the kitchen apart looking for them.

*But you knew that she would not ask anyone if they saw her keys because she didn't want anyone to know she lost them.*

Sue just kept them long enough to make her own copy at the hardware store and put them in the silverware basket of the dishwasher, where the House Manager could find them.

*So, you see,* said no one in particular, *you get a lot further with staff when you understand their ways.*

The other problem with Tim was that he was set in just one way of doing things.

*You've got to keep yourself flexible because you never know what's going to come up.*

For instance, when Sue got her copy of the staff room key, she had thought that she was going to be reading her own chart. She didn't read very far before she discovered it told her a lot more a-bout the staff writing it than it ever said about her.

*They said you were "Isolating…responding to inner stimuli… shows no interest in the lives of the other residents… cannot verbalize anyone's name…flat affect… exhibiting delusions about disease in the smoking room…catatonic… bizarre… I could go on, but then I'd be "rambling and tangential".*

Reading it was like having spoken with a newspaper reporter and wincing when he mangles your quotes. After a while it's just too painful to continue and you turn to the other stories.

Tim's chart was one of the first she had read. It was thicker than most, half-filled with Tim's own handwriting: "Tim loves Becky," over and over again like a schoolboy's punishment. The interesting thing was the Becky next door was not the Becky in the handwriting. The Becky in the handwriting was some chick he met at his sister's wedding reception years ago. He was dressed in a tux, having been given the job of usher. She said hello with a smile that melted his horndog heart. He had his own catatonic moment, not knowing what to say back. Finally, the band struck up the Rock Lobster and she went off to dance. He leaned back on the head table and was certain that he would marry her. The reception ended and his sister went off to her honeymoon. He was left planning his. When his sister got back, he pestered her for Becky's address. To her eternal credit, she didn't give it to him, accurately surmising that her brother, tux or no tux, was a royal creep.

Having no address and nothing more to go on but a kind hello, Tim nourished his crush with thousands of pages of declarations and dedications to the radio. Twenty therapists could do nothing with Tim's obsession until he moved into the group home and the House Manager treated him with one of her Behavioral Plans. Then, voila, he was cured.

There wasn't a word of this in the chart, but Sue knew that Tim was convinced that the Becky from next door was the very same Becky he'd been waiting for all these years. Never mind she had the wrong hair color and looked nothing like her. Never mind any of that. To Tim's warped mind it went to prove, all the more, that Becky was devoted to him. She had changed her name, her hair color, and got plastic surgery to trick all those who were trying to keep them apart. It was only a matter of time before Tim would tell her that he knows who she really is.

*Then*, said no one in particular to Sue, *Becky will whisk away his delusions like a doctor takes away your limits.*

Jim was now out on the porch, talking like a fish. Sue had read his chart, as well. It said, 'He's getting into his delusions. He's saying that someone is trying to drown him.' Jim had never stopped talking about being drowned since a gang of kids dunked him in the pool when he was eighteen. He's in his forties now. During this time, his eyes started popping out of his head, his chin's been receding, and he gargles when he speaks like he's under water.

*It's like what somebody said once,* said no one in particular to Sue, *after age forty you get the face that you deserve. Or, in Jim's case, the face he needs, because it's plain that he's turning into a fish.*

Jim was out on the porch wearing his baseball glove as if he'd grown a flipper. He was gargling with the other guys while they waited for the Longhaired Staff to take them to the Indian Reservation to buy cigarettes. Jim's father was a big league pitcher, but when Jim was in school, he threw a baseball like a girl. He was this nerdy little guy with thick glasses.

*Just looking at him makes you want to drown him to put him out of his misery, like a litter of unwanted kittens.*

Jim's father died a few year's back and he's been carrying that baseball glove around ever since.

*Like he's expecting to meet up with his father's ghost who might want a game of catch.*

Jim walked around on tiptoes all the time as if to keep his head above water. The House Manager wrote a Behavioral Plan about that too, but it made things worse because then Jim had to be on tiptoes to watch out for Staff. Then the Longhaired Staff got him a job walking around on stilts at festivals. For a while, it seemed like he was a new Jim. He left his glove hanging on his bedpost. When it fell off and it got kicked under his bed he didn't notice it for a week. He stopped his gargling and, if you looked at him carefully from the side, you might think that his chin was starting to jut out and his eyes were returning to their sockets. Then the House Manager found out about the stilt therapy and made him get rid of them because she was afraid of the house getting sued if he fell off.

No one in particular said to Sue, *Yup, it was ready to storm and, if it rained for forty days and forty nights, Jim would be ready.*

While Sue was waiting for the tempest, she got to thinking that, if everyone were leaving for the reservation, it would be a good time to get the smoking room cleaned. When everyone's in there, the smoking room's air gets so thick with cancer you can't see across to the other side, like a foggy night. They wouldn't catch Sue dead in there; she liked to keep the cells in your body orderly. Bruce was in the smoking room now, an auburn glass astray filled with butts balanced on his knee. His fingers were stained the same color as the ashtray and his lower lip had a notch in it where the cigarette rests.

*Just like I said with Jim. A person gets the face he needs. In Bruce's case, he's turning into an ashtray.*

According to his chart, Bruce had a stint in the Air Force fueling airplanes. He'd just hooked up his gas line to an F-16 and stepped away when the whole thing went up in an explosion. No one ever found the source of the spark that ignited the fuel. Bruce must've lit up when he was gassing the plane, and absentmindedly threw the match down where the fuel vapors could get to it. They tried to question him about the fire but by then he had become a stammering idiot. The half-witted Air Force doctors released him with a service-connected disability that set him up for the rest of his life.

*He gets more in VA benefits for being sick than the whole group home staff was making for getting him well.*

No one in particular went on: *The House Manager likes to keep Bruce's demons fresh in his mind. So she gave him the permanent job of mowing the lawn in the summer and running the snow blower in the winter because it meant he would have to gas up something year round.*

The snow blower was out in the driveway now with a full can of gas next to it while Bruce pumped enough nicotine into his brain to get up the nerve to do his chore.

Sue was just calculating how long she'd have to wait before the smoke cleared after Bruce left, when Ken passed her coming down the stairs dressed in his white clothes.

*This can only mean one thing. He's planning on being a prophet.*

Ken stood in the doorway and addressed the group of smokers on the porch.   He announced, "The spirit of the Lord is upon me because he hath anointed me to preach the gospel to the poor; he hath sent me to heal the brokenhearted, to preach deliverance to the captives..."

The fish called Jim gargled out a call to the House Manager, "Ken's preaching again." But, you can't make words out of spit; you have to have air.

"...recovering the sight of the blind, to set at liberty them that are bruised…"

Jim tried to get through the door to get the House Manager, but Ken the Prophet was standing in his way. "Excuse me," Jim tried to say through the gargle.

"…to preach the acceptable year of the Lord. This day is the scripture fulfilled in your ears." The smokers continued puffing as if it was the end of the world and there would be no cigarettes in heaven.

"Shut the fuck up, you lunatic," Tim said.

"Ye will surely say unto me this proverb, Physician, heal thyself."

Jim was gargling like he was trying to get through a whole bottle of Listerine.

*It apparently never occurred to Ken to heal Jim of his affliction. He could very easily pull his drowning ass out of the Sea of Galilee and give him the faith to pace the waves like a day room floor,* said no one in particular to Sue. *A real prophet could get good steady work around here.*

Ken continued, "Verily I say unto you, no prophet is accepted in his own country." Then he waded through the group of smokers and left.

*Verily, my ass*, said no one in particular to Sue, *I think he's got his calling all wrong. He'd like us to believe God has sent him to heal the sick, but I believe God has sent him to be the sick. Appearances to the contrary, it's harder work to be a patient.*

Tim, for instance, had given up on waiting for the House Manager to get off the phone. Meds be damned, he went with Becky to her garage to get the sleds.

After Tim left, Ken returned with a carton of cigarettes and, when he got to the porch, held the box over his head in both hands. The smokers crowded around him like pigeons in a park and broke the carton, saying, "This is my body which is given for you." The packs slid out and fell to the porch floor where the faithful fielded them on the first hop.

All this time, Bruce was lifting his cigarette to his mouth from the ashtray as if he was doing arm curls. The minute he heard about the windfall on the porch, he streaked through the hall with his very breath trailing death behind him. Once Bruce was gone it should have been Sue's chance to clean the room, but, in his urgency, he had left a lit cigarette behind and she wasn't going in there with that thing.

Becky's garage was not more than thirty feet from the porch, but the smokers were scrambling for their coffin nails, so they didn't hear anything. Sue heard screams though. She heard them clearly from inside the house because her ears weren't plugged with grandiosity or greed. Jim heard it, too. His ears were always in tune for someone getting into trouble. He ran off the porch, one hand in his baseball glove and the other with pack of cigarettes. There was another scream, this one cut short.

A few seconds later, the Longhaired Staff drove up in the van. Seeing what had occurred in the garage, he threw the van in park and ran straightaway into the staff room. "Call the police," he said to the House Manager, who was still on the phone, and ran back to the garage.

The porch crowd by now had moved over to the garage and stood around gawking at Tim, Becky, and Jim. The House Manager seemed to take all the time in the world to leave the staff room and go out to the garage. Sue followed her quietly and stood behind, as still and as white as the snowman.

Jim kneeled on the garage floor with Becky's head in his glove as if he had just caught it. Tim held her headless body as tenderly as the Pieta. Between them, a pool of blood cooled in the sunny winter day. A machete dropped on the floor accused the entire group home of a horrible deed.

"What have you done?" cried Ken. "Your brother's blood cries out to me from the ground!"

The House Manager said to the Longhaired Staff. "They're going to kick us out of the neighborhood; and every other group home, too. No one will ever be able to build another one."

*It's time for you to clean up*, said no one in particular to Sue.

On the way, she picked up the gas can Bruce had left by the snow blower.

*You can't have the neighbors see you leaving a mess in the yard.*

Stepping in the smoking room, she saw that the usual cloud had settled into a yellow coat on the furniture and wallpaper. A single strand of smoke meandered up from the cigarette that Bruce had left.

*Since gasoline is a solvent, you can use it to solve things.*

She emptied the can out on the couch.

*If you're going to clean up, you'll have to do something with that cigarette before it does something to you.*

She held her breath, picked the ashtray up by the end of her fingers, and dumped it out on the couch.

"There's nothing I won't do to stop smoking," she said, to no one in particular.

# Chapter 54 - Driving Off the Map

"What kind of freaks you got coming to your office now? People who sit in trees, people who rhyme, people who don't talk at all. I wouldn't put up with that shit. Either you want help or you don't. If you don't, then get the hell out of my office."

Back at the titty bar, Izzy had told Craig about his new clients, looking for some supervision. "Since we threw out the DSM," he said, "we've got all kinds of clients going to everybody because we're, like, not diagnosing anyone anymore. Mental Health's going to Chemical Dependency, and the other way around."

"Then I'm glad I'm not around to see it. I never liked those guys at mental health anyway; too much goddamn handholding and tissue passing. At CD it's straightforward; stop fucking using."

"How's that coming, anyway? Are you still using?"

Craig glared at him over his beer. "What the hell kind of a question is that? How do you think it's coming?"

"Stop fucking using."

"Look Sherlock," said Craig, "I'm not coming to your clinic, I'm not gunna cry in your tissues, and I never said I'd stop using; so don't include me in your freak parade."

"You said you didn't like being the way you are. You told me to be your therapist and I'd pass my internship."

"That's fucked up."

"Hey, like, no shit, Sherlock," said Izzy, "but it was your idea."

"OK, then, be my therapist. What do you want me to do? Sit up in a tree, make rhymes, nuzzle my ear on my shoulder?"

"Quit screwing around," said Izzy. "That's what I want you to do. Either you want help or you don't. If you want help, then get going."

Craig smiled, "That's the way to do it, kid. I'm proud of you. Don't take any shit from 'em, or me either." Then, distinctly, "So what do you want me to do?"

Izzy took a deep breath. "Tell me your story."

"You've heard my story. I told it in meetings a hundred times. What good's it gunna do me to tell it again."

"I've heard about Cornwhacker, and how you met your wife at the sawmill when she cut off her hand, and I heard about chasing the snowmobiles and the school bus, but I don't know how you got into drinking in the first place, or why you decided to stop and be a counselor. Or, what happened to your wife and your kid. Why aren't they around anymore? You left out parts. They might be the most important parts."

"You want me to tell you my life was so fucked up I had to start drinking, and then drinking fucked my life up so much I had to stop; but now I've turned my life over to a Higher Power, learned to let go and let God, found the fellowship of AA and now I'm a grateful recovering addict. Is that what you want me to tell you?"

"I want you to, like, tell me the truth."

"The truth is, I've been serving and eating that canned AA bullshit so long, I don't know the truth anymore, all I know is what they want me to say."

"That bullshit got you clean, once," said Izzy.

"Yeah, it did. But what got you clean won't be the same thing that keeps you clean."

"When you drive off the map, you need a new map."

"When you drive off the map, you get fucking lost. That's my story, if you want to know."

"What do you mean?" asked Izzy.

# Chapter 55 - The Robin's Egg

Not many hurricanes hit shoreline Connecticut, but when they do, all hell breaks loose. When Craig was a young teen, a pair of storms, Connie and Diane, strayed from the usual hurricane path from the Caribbean to the Gulf to wander up the Atlantic seaboard and make a Yankee landfall. They left in their wake terrible floods, downed trees, spilled bird's nests, and a bitter estrangement between Craig and his mother.

As far as he was concerned, Hurricane Diane was the worse. Connie was all water and no wind, but a week later, as if furious that Connie had stepped ahead of her, Diane came by and tore trees out of the ground, blew shingles off, and even, as Craig witnessed, scooped a beach cottage off its piers and flipped it upside down. He wished the storm had flipped his house, but that would have been quite a feat, for he lived in the biggest house in town, a fussy old Victorian mansion, owned by a fussy old Victorian lady, Old Lady Wightman.

Ma had been the Old Lady's maid since his Pa left them back before Craig could remember. He and Ma shared a room on the third floor. Ma was a turtle-like woman whose back was rounded by bearing the Old Lady's linens and humiliation. She justified it all by reminding Craig at every opportunity that Pa left them without one red cent. He'd never seen a red cent, so, for all he knew, it was true.

He'd been scraping the house that summer before the hurricanes struck, getting it ready for paint. He spent days standing on ladders in canvas shoes, his arches hurting and the Old Lady coming out in the yard to peer at her walls and complain that he was dropping paint scrapings on the grass. But what would you expect from his kind? She was always going on about his kind, but Craig wanted to know, just what was his kind? That was a hard thought to get under and scrape up. He suspected he was the kind whose Pa had abandoned and whose Ma was an Old Lady's maid, living on the third floor. Since there was nothing he could do about what kind he was, he went on dropping paint scrapings on the grass.

Even though the hurricanes didn't flip the fussy old Victorian house with the fussy old Victorian lady in it, Craig was thankful that they knocked down the trees and the Old Lady announced that she would not have him ruining her home and grounds with his scraping any more. Since there were trees down all over the yard, Craig would be the one to take the bucksaw out of the shed and cut them up.

Some of the money that the Old Lady paid Craig for scraping he used to buy his first cigarettes. He lit one up in the shed as he took the bucksaw down from the wall and almost sawed his leg off from the coughing. He found a loose floorboard to hide the cigarettes under. When he pried it up, he noticed a packet of letters addressed to Ma, tied in a blue ribbon. The letters were from Pa, and some were not more than a year old. The latest one read:

Mae,

…The wheat's looking pretty good this year and we should have a fine harvest. Enclosed is some more money for the boy. If you won't come back to North Dakota, at least send him out here for the summer. This is a far better place for a boy to grow up than back East. He can work on the farm and get tan and strong. Consider it….

Earl

When Craig read the letter, he had all the fury of Hurricane Connie and Diane, both. He might've flipped the Victorian house upside down all by himself. As it was, he was able to put a lot of vigor into his sawing that day. Ma and Pa's words kept binding his brain. "We have to stay with Mrs. Wightman because your Pa left us without one red cent," she had said.

"Enclosed is some more money," said the letter. "Your Pa's gone, so times are hard. You should be grateful that Mrs. Wightman lets us stay in her place," said his Ma. "Send him out here for the summer," said the letter. He sawed hard and kept taking breaks to go back in the shed and read more letters and smoke. They were all the same: Pa sending more money and pleading with her to come back to North Dakota.

That night, like every night, the Old Lady made them eat in the kitchen after she dined alone. Craig's throat hurt as Ma ladled out the pot roast, boiled potatoes, and carrots.

"Is something wrong?" said Ma.

He felt the blood rush to his head as he poked at the soggy vegetables.

"Oh, don't mind Mrs. Wightman, Honey. I know she's difficult, but she's been good to us in other ways."

"Just why do you put up with her, Ma?"

"I have to, Son. Ever since your Pa left us, I've had to work to support us."

"You're lying," said Craig. The words coming up his throat scalded as much as hot food going down ever would. "I found his letters in the shed. He didn't leave us; you left him. He's in North Dakota and he's been sending money, Ma. He's been sending money for me to go out there."

Now it was her turn to have her throat hurt and pick at her soggy vegetables. Craig didn't wait for her answer; it would just be more falsehoods. That night he stayed in the shed and raided the kitchen at night after Ma went up to the third floor. He must've read the letters a hundred times that night, trying to conjure up a picture of Pa. It was no use; there was nothing there. He couldn't remember him and Ma had kept no photos and told nothing but lies. He couldn't trust her; he couldn't trust her. If you can't trust your own mother, whom can you trust? No one. By the first light, he was out and sawing the downed trees into firewood lengths, taking some small satisfaction in how directly he could reduce the carnage of the storm into a pile of cordwood by the kitchen door.

While working his way through the trees, Craig came upon a robin's nest with one abandoned egg. The mother bird wouldn't be back by this point, so he took it and placed it on the porch table. While he was on the porch, Craig noticed so much commotion on the road that he had to go see what it was all about. The milkman had been driving down the road and, avoiding something that had darted across his path, swerved sharply and tipped his truck over. As it tipped, he fell out the open door and was pinned underneath. The neighbors all came and, together, they lifted the truck back on its wheels. The milkman remained motionless, kneeling, with his arms outstretched in an Allah-be-praised supplication, his neck broken.

Many of us can point to the moments when we lost our innocence. When our parents dismounted their pedestals and revealed themselves to be clay. When lies that we've been told and were happy to believe, proved to be illusions we might just as well do without. When we discover that life itself, thought to last an eternity, is only ours for a sort term lease. Crusty old biker Craig was a boy once who loved his mother, but for him, these moments when he lost his innocence came all at once, when Hurricane Diane blew in and everything changed forever.

That night, Ma came in while he was smoking in the shed. He hid the cigarette behind his back, the smoke curling out to peek. She said, "I love your Pa," she blubbered, for she'd been drinking and crying. "That's why I couldn't bear to throw out his letters. But I can't live in North Dakota. He paints a pretty picture of it out there, but the farm's just too far out and too lonely. The wind's always blowing, and it's brutal hot in the summer and brutal cold in the winter. I couldn't take the country, so I left him and brought you back home with me. I kept you from him, because he lies about North Dakota. I couldn't let you believe his lies."

She stepped forward and embraced him with a one armed hug, the other hand holding a tumbler of rum. He hugged her back with one arm, the other holding a cigarette. Her tears fell hot on his neck as she cried what might've been tears of guilt. He added a few hot tears of his own, and they might've been tears of forgiveness. They were tears of loss, actually. Ma's tears weren't tears of guilt because she never said she was wrong, she was crying because she'd been caught and knew she was losing her boy. His tears were for the loss of his Ma and the loss of his childhood. When the two of them realized what they were crying about, they pulled away.

Seeing the cigarette, she said, "You think you're grown now and you're smoking? You ain't grown yet. Not till you have kids of your own and you have to do the hard thing to protect them. Do that and then tell me you're grown."

He took a defiant drag from his cigarette and blew the acrid smoke in her face. It mixed with the syrupy rum fumes she was exhaling. She slapped him with her free hand. In the other, the rum jostled and spilled.

"Damn you all to hell, you defiant brat. Go ahead and go to North Dakota, if that's what you want. Go ahead and find out for yourself what it's like. You'll see. Then you'll come back and say you're sorry."

The next day, Craig found that Ma had not been so drunk that she didn't remember the conversation. She was stubborn enough that she wouldn't change her mind and she was stubborn enough so that she had passed her stubbornness on to her only son. Craig was not about to say he was sorry, or, as she had pronounced, thay you're thorry, for she had been drunk enough to lisp. Indeed, saying that he would come back and say he's sorry was a good way to guarantee that he would never do anything of the sort.

Craig had a bit of sawing left before he was done and he got paid. Then he would go. Old Lady Wightman kept eyeballing Craig's work from the porch and telling him how to stack wood. When she spied the robin's nest, you would have thought she was the mother bird, herself, for all the cooing she did. The house painting was coming along, even though she must have hired and fired half a dozen painters that week. She had last hired Leo, an itinerant French-Canadian, who had come down to the States to find work.

"I want the porch painted this exact color," she said, giving him the robin's egg. "Mix the paints and show me the shade you have before you start painting."

"*Bien, oui*," he said. "I show you right away."

Old Lady Wightman went in the house to sit in her parlor. Leo stared at the cans of paint for a minute before saying to Craig, "Bring me the blue, *s'il vous plaît*."

Leo pried open the can of paint and brushed some on a sample hunk of wood.

"*Excusez, Madam* Wightman, I have your color."

She took a quick look at the sample. "That is not robin's egg blue; that is just ordinary blue. Look at the egg I got you and compare it. You need more white."

She went back in the parlor and Craig got Leo the can of white paint.

Leo pulled a flask out of his hip pocket, took a sip, and offered some to Craig. "What am I going to do, eh? I am, how you say – *daltonien* - I cannot see the colors."

Craig gasped as the blistering hot whiskey went down his throat. Leo laughed, "*C'est bon, m' oui?* You help me mix; I teach you how to drink."

Craig helped him mix, but he knew that Old Lady Wightman was never going to be pleased with her colorblind painter, even with help from a non-colorblind teenager. The next sample was far too light. The sample after that was too dark again.

"*Mon Dieu, Madam*, this is a beautiful color. Do you like I paint your porch this color?"

"Yes, it is a beautiful color for the porch, but it is not robin's egg blue. I must have robin's egg blue."

"But, *Madam*, why does it matter, as long as you like the color?"

"I will have no more of your impertinence. Get the color right next time or I will have someone else paint my porch."

"*Oui, Madam*, I will have it right."

When the Old Lady left, Leo gave Craig a wink, took the paint they'd already mixed and dipped the egg in it.

He called the Old Lady out. "*Madam*, I have been working hard to get your color, the robin's egg blue. See the egg, it is the exact shade."

Old Lady Wightman studied the sample and the egg together. "All right, that is good enough; I will let you paint it this color. Be sure to clean up thoroughly when you are done."

Craig laughed as he had never laughed before. He felt free. Free of Old Lady Wightman, the shame of lacking a father, free of the lies he'd been told, and all the rules he had to follow. He took a longer draught from Leo's flask and felt free inside, as well, as if the whiskey had unlocked something he had caged within.

# Chapter 56 - Freedom

When a newly freed youth from heavily forested Connecticut goes to the Great Plains, the first things he notices is the sky. All his life the sky had been a limited shaft of sunlight sneaking through the leaves as if from out from a high window in a dungeon cell. The trunks of trees are like prison bars and the sentinel hills like wardens. In The Great Plains, the sky opens its arms wide and embraces him like a waiting lover outside the gates. By day she treats him to mounds of cotton candy they call clouds and, at night, she brings out her jewels and dazzles him with their glitter. Above all, the sky gives him space, space above all. Space is youth's chief craving, in any case. For a youth, raised in a fussy old Victorian house with a fussy old Victorian lady and a deceitful, possessive mother, under a sheltering canopy of leaves, space quickly becomes an intoxicating drug of choice.

For all that youth craves space, space, in turn, invites travel. Its like, when we have space, we cannot rest until we stake out the limits of the space we have. Our thoughts expand to fill the big sky above and our feet get moving to explore the region. No sooner had Craig arrived at his Pa's farm in North Dakota, than he wanted to leave it. Not for the same reason his mother did, for the moment he got there he understood the spell it had on his father. Standing atop a rolling Dakota hill with nothing but big doting sky around and rippling grain at his feet, we might excuse a man, the tallest thing in sight, for thinking he could make something of this country and be someone. A man might forget the pitifully small yield per acre, less even than that of rocky Connecticut, and the cost per acre in fuel and fertilizer appallingly large. A man may also forget that he shared this lonely countryside with hordes of pests, their eggs lying dormant underfoot, and that the big-haired sky ficklely withheld her rain and battered the crops with hail. A man may also forget that the space is just another word for loneliness, not just the loneliness of a Saturday night when you ain't got nobody, but the howling, desolate, helpless loneliness that impels a man to do target practice with his own skull.

When Craig arrived at his father's North Dakota farm, he had been heralded by a letter his Ma sent the week before. It still sat, unregarded in the mailbox, along with a fistful of payment notices. The ever-present wind played with the barn door like a loose tooth. A herd of pigs, broken out of their pens, turned over the yard, rooting for grubs. A weakened watchdog, chained to a stake by the door, hunkered down and dusted the ground with her tail, forsaking all pretense of a bark. Craig knocked and hollered at the door, but he knew no one was home. He checked the barn; a disemboweled tractor sat waiting for a mechanic to put it back together. Craig returned to the house and let himself in, after setting free the dog, who ran off immediately to lap up the water in a cattle trough by the fence. He stepped through the bachelor kitchen, sink piled high with dishes, the tractor's carburetor in pieces on the table, to a dusty living room. There sat his Pa, a tidy red mark on his forehead, like a Hindu's spot, the back of his head blown all to hell.

The sight and smell of it was enough to drive the boy out of the house, where he was joined by the rejuvenated dog who licked his hand and sniffed the alluring bouquet. Had he stayed, he would have seen an enlarged picture of his own self, prominently mounted in that living room and a host of smaller pictures documenting his growth and development. Further in, a clipping on the dresser testified to a shutout he had pitched. Indeed, the whole home, save the pile of agricultural magazines by the chair, might've been construed as a temple to the cult of Craig, with an immolated sacrifice laid on the chair, as if Abraham had, appearing at the mountain without his son, obeyed Yahweh's orders by taking his own life.

A quick jog to the neighbors, the dog following close behind, and a phone call, brought a flock of sheriff's cars and an ambulance to the farm. The medics could do little more than help herd the pigs back in the barn. Long sitting, dead in his easy chair, Pa remained sitting on the stretcher when they loaded him up and the procession filed stately back to town. The youth stayed at a neighbor's place and they all helped bring in the wheat. His Ma, who would not return to live on the farm, came out to sell it and bring her son back, but there were more debts than assets and Craig wouldn't go, so she returned home even poorer, and childless.

Craig had found an old motorcycle in the barn next to the eviscerated tractor. It was in one piece and, soon after a neighbor had shown him how to kick start it and change the gears, he was tracing ruts up and down the Dakota Hills and wallows, dodging cow chips, and frightening the stock. In one of these sorties, he came upon a gang of Prairie Hellions heading out from the Sturgis Rally, encamped by some cottonwoods. Craig showed off his riding by doing a few jumps and donuts. They were suitably impressed, but were more impressed with his bike, which they explained was a classic Indian Four. He petitioned to join them, but they told him to go back home to his Ma. However, once Craig Creek had seen the Great Plains, nothing could bring him back to his Ma and Old Lady Wightman. In the morning, when they were ready to leave, he grabbed a hold of the nearest sissy bar and vowed never to let go, even if they beat him to a pulp. A few of the bikers tried to do just that, but, even though bloody and doubled over in pain, he still hung on until a captain of the gang, stuck by his dauntless and resolute desire to ride with them, ordered his men to stop and offered to make Craig a prospect.

Regrettably, the new rider never rode his father's Indian Four again. The gang forced him to trade the Indian for an ailing Honda CV and gas money. On long rides, the humiliating Honda puttered and spat so far behind the pack that Craig was often in jeopardy of losing them. Fortunately, there were few roads on the Plains and the gang could generally be followed by spying the cloud of dust that trailed them. Craig disdained no task they set on him, whether it be washing the bikes, or worse. He happily made himself their slave so that he could live free. In the end, of course, he found that being the minion of a gang of outlaw bikers was little different than serving a Victorian lady, but by then he had made member.

"Did you ever, like, go back to Connecticut to see your mother?" asked Izzy.

"Why the hell would I give her that satisfaction?"

Izzy peered at Craig, by now on his third beer of the morning. "So," he said, "you've been looking for freedom all this time. Are you free now?"

"No one fucking really wants freedom. They think they do, but when they get it, they just go crawling back into their cell. Or they find another."

# Chapter 57 - Countertransference

The heads of the two men turned as the door opened and in came Luna, dressed in a puffy winter jacket, earmuffs, and a miniskirt, so that the top of her was bundled to the max and her legs were bare to the elements. She looked like the Michelin Man on stilts. That was soon remedied as she stripped off the puffy coat and the shirt underneath until she stood in the same bare breasted splendor as when Izzy first met her. Soon the miniskirt was gone, as well, until, with the earmuffs still holding back her long hair, the Michelin Man transformed into a nudist air traffic controller. Luna had said hi to Craig as she entered, but the intern had gone unnoticed, so that he began to suspect that the dancer was preparing for a morning jumping of the bones of her security guard. There had to be some benefits for male workers in this place, thought Izzy, one should not muzzle the ox that treads the grain, after all. Craig, however, perhaps long habituated to the charms of the titty bar, paid more attention to his beer and grunted only a reluctant reply. Luna, who had a pretty girl's unerring ability to detect which eyes were upon her, soon identified the presence of Izzy in the bar's gloom.

"Why, if it's not the queer boy," she said as she removed her earmuffs and tossed her hair. "I see you finally got with Craig, like you wanted. I hope it was as good as you expected."

"Knock it off, Luna," said Craig. "He's not queer, and I'm not, either."

"Oh, I'm just kidding, I know he's not queer, as I detected during our little lap dance. As for you, big boy," she said, as she ran her hand down his chest, "you never let me close enough to tell."

"I'm not going to go screwing a coworker," said Craig, "and if your hand goes any further, I'll sue you for sexual harassment."

"That'll be a laugh when you tell the jury that your workplace is a sexualized environment. 'Your Honor, she took her clothes off right in front of me every day.' By the way, what are you guys doing here?"

"He's my therapist," said Craig. "You're driving me so crazy I've had to get my head shrunk."

"You've got a shrink that does house calls, er, I mean, calls to a fine gentleman's club? Excellent; what do you charge to shrink a head?"

Before Izzy could say anything, say that he was just an intern, say that he preferred to see people at the clinic, say that he'd rather his clients kept their clothes on, Craig had an answer: "A hundred bucks an hour."

"He must be pretty good," marveled Luna.

"Yea, when he shrinks your head, it stays shrunk."

She stuck her considerable chest out and wiggled it. "Just as long has he doesn't miss and shrink something else that I need."

"No, he won't do that, he's very accurate. You know, he's developed his own school of psychology."

"Why, I declare," she said, in the mock accent of a southern belle. "You surprise me, doctor, doctor… what do I call you? Doctor…"

"Izzy, you can call me Izzy."

"Dr Izzy, I want to get my head shrunk by no one but you."

Izzy looked over at Craig. This would have been a good time for some supervision, he thought. A little help, here. Craig was laughing, although it wasn't clear whom he was laughing at, whom he was setting up, maybe both of them.

"Are you serious?" asked Izzy

She laughed, "Of course I'm serious. I'm as serious as a deathbed hard on. Do you always make your patients feel bad when they ask you for help? Can you imagine going to the meat counter and asking for five pounds of salami and the guy saying, are you serious? It's a meat counter, isn't it? And you're a therapist. I want therapy."

"I'm sorry, I meant, are you serious about, like, making changes in your life?"

"Well that's up to me, isn't it? If I pay a hundred bucks an hour and don't use it to good purpose, then I'm out a hundred bucks. That's like buying the salami and not eating it; although I can think of another good use of a salami that doesn't include eating it."

Izzy didn't know what to say, so he stood there and looked at her with a deer in the headlights look. Was there anything unethical about counseling a naked stripper at a titty bar for cash money with his half drunk supervisor nearby? Well, at least the half drunk supervisor was nearby. He was just an intern, after all, nothing could be his fault if his supervisor said it was good. "Is it OK?" he asked Craig.

"Oh, I'm sorry," said Luna, "I've been eating into your time. I didn't think."

"No, it's OK. We were done," said Craig. "You guys go ahead."

"There's just one thing," said Izzy. "You have to, like, put clothes on. I can't do therapy when you're naked."

"Oh," she shuddered, "I hate clothes. They just bother me. Touching me all over my body, like a hundred hands. I like to be free and open. Isn't that the idea of therapy? To bare it all?"

"Yes, that's the idea of therapy, but you don't actually have to take your clothes off."

"Well, what about if your clothes are already off? Do you have to put them back on? Will it work with your clothes off? I'd much rather have them off."

"It's just… I'll be distracted. I won't be able to listen to what you're saying."

"I thought you were a professional? Look, I get guys in here all the time that are as ugly as hell. They're fat and rough and smelly and nasty, but I still treat them like they're a hot stud that I can't live without because I'm a professional and they're paying me good money to make them think they get my juices flowing. So when I straddle their lap and get grinding, I put myself aside and do what they need me to do. That's what a professional does. Now, are you a professional, or not?"

"Yes, I am, of course."

"Then let's get going, doc."

"What did you want to talk about?"

"You want me to do it here, in front of Craig? I'm free and open, but not that free and open. Isn't there such a thing as confidentiality?"

"Of course, you're right. Where can we go?"

"We can go right in here." She led him to the same small room where she had given him the aborted lap dance.

"We'll need another chair," said Izzy.

"There's no room for another chair, Silly. I'll just sit on your lap."

"No, you can't…"

"Well you're not going to sit on my lap, I'll be crushed. Besides, you didn't mind it the other day."

"OK, but don't sit on it the same way."

"Is this OK?" she perched on his knees."

"Yes, that's good."

She drew up her knees and snuggled in his arms. "How about that?"

"Ah, I like it better the other way."

She grabbed his crotch, "Something tells me you're lying."

"Stop, don't do that! Do you go around doing that to everybody? Do you ever turn off the stripper thing and just be a regular person?"

She looked at him wide eyed, then, gradually, her face crumpled into tears. He had just gotten started and already she was crying, but this didn't seem like success, despite his theories about the correlation between tissues and therapeutic progress. He hadn't prepared the lap dance room for the inevitable crying, so she returned to her snuggling position and cried into his shirt.

Izzy thought, therapists aren't supposed to act on their feelings about clients. They're supposed to be as cold and dispassionate as a surgeon is with his knife. He had allowed himself to get angry and yell at her. He had committed the dreaded therapist's sin of countertransference, and then compounded the sin by feeling guilty about it. He further compounded it by hugging her and stroking her hair. "I'm sorry, I didn't mean to hurt your feelings," he said. "You're, like, very good at what you do and it's natural you'd want to do it all the time."

"No, you're right," she cried. "That's just the problem. I don't know who I am anymore." She rubbed her nose on his shirt. "I'm just an exotic dancer- a stripper."

The tears flowed again. Then, just as suddenly, they stopped and she sat up.

"I like doing what I do, don't get me wrong. I like it that men like me. I like it that they get hard when they see me, even if all they do with it is go away and beat off. I like to think that they go home and make love with their wives and think of me and they're so turned on that their wives come. I'm, like, performing a service for both of them, you see. To tell you the truth, I like it that I can control men. To be honest, I was trying to control you a minute ago. You see, I was nervous about therapy, what you might do to me, although I knew you'd be a gentleman. I was nervous about what therapy might do to me, so I tried to control you by grabbing your penis. I'm sorry; it didn't hurt, did it?"

"No, no, I…"

"I can turn the stripper thing off. I really can. It's just, when I turn it off; there's, like, nothing there. It's like when you turn the lights off and it's dark; you can't see. It's not like I don't know the problem. The problem is that I'm a professional, just like I was saying: I put myself aside to be who they need me to be and then, when I'm done being the professional, I've lost track of myself. How do you do it?"

"Ah, how do I do what, exactly?"

"How do you listen to people all day long, and some of them have got to be hard to listen to: whiny, selfish, boring, obnoxious. How do you listen to them all day long? And I know you listen to them. You can't pretend listening, just like you can't pretend being horny. People know, they see right through you. I'm a good dancer because I'm not pretending, I am horny when I'm performing. I just become a horny person. What I want to know is, how do you become that listening person and, when you're done listening, have someone left to be?"

Had Izzy been more experienced, or better schooled, or supervised, he would've said that he didn't put his own feelings aside when he listened to clients. On the contrary, he would say, he listened with his feelings. Or, rather, his feelings amounted to another ear that he listened to clients with. He would've known that countertransference, having feelings about clients, was inevitable, and, when it came up, and it comes up always, it should be used as the valuable tool that it is. Sadness would tell him that there was a loss nearby; anger, that he was being manipulated; dread, to watch out for danger, and so on. Had his education been one of feelings, and not of theories, he would've kept his feelings as a craftsman keeps his tools: sharp, oiled, and close at hand. Whenever a client made him want to scream, that was good information to have, because the client probably made others feel that way and that, my dear Watson, may have a lot to do with the client's problems. Izzy's feelings, had he paid any attention to them, whatsoever, would've been accurate instruments to detect bullshit, shame, or denial; whatever went unsaid, but only implied. He would have told Luna that when a therapist is providing good therapy he is fully himself. He doesn't have to pretend to be someone else, and so, there is no losing track of who he was when he was doing therapy.

As it was, Izzy was not that good a therapist, and so he identified with her because at that moment there was a big disconnect between who he really was and what he was willing to let on at that moment to her and to himself. In fact, he wasn't letting anything on to himself. All these weeks of listening to the stories of clients and Craig he never once asked himself how he felt because he didn't want to know. Had he done so, he would've been surprised: he felt envy. With all his clients, and with Craig, even the most miserable, traumatized soul among them, he felt envy. He wanted what they had because, even if they had all this misery, they at least had a story and they had a life. Izzy, on the other hand, never did anything and had nothing to tell for it.

At that moment, Izzy recognized what he had been feeling because he was no longer feeling it. Just as a fish first learns to understand water when he's lying gasping on the beach, Izzy recognized his envy because, for once, with Luna, he wasn't feeling it. He wasn't envious of Luna because he already had what she had. They were a lot alike.

No, Izzy wasn't a good therapist yet, but he might become one someday. As it was, he wasn't a bad therapist, he did ask her this question: "What were you before you became a strip…an exotic dancer?"

"I was a college student. I went to school for six years and couldn't graduate because I couldn't, like, make up my mind what I wanted to major in. Finally, my parents said get a job; they wouldn't be paying tuition anymore. Even then, I couldn't, like, decide who I was. But I always was pretty and never did like wearing clothes, so dancing came naturally."

She prattled on and on about her courses, her different professors, and what was wrong about all of them. Izzy didn't listen because he was thinking about what he'd just realized about himself. He knew the story, anyway. She didn't notice. She didn't even need him to listen. She wasn't even listening to herself. She had already come to a conclusion in her mind, but stalled for a while because to say it meant that she had to make it happen.

Finally, she stopped and announced, "You know what? I'm going to go back to school. I make good money on tips; I can afford it. I'm going to major in psychology. I can do what you do. It looks easy."

With that, she jumped off his lap, bolted out of the lap dance room, and announced to Craig, "You were right. He is a good head shrinker. It only took half an hour and I'm done." She turned back to Izzy. "Half an hour is fifty bucks, right? Oh, I'll give you a hundred, anyway; for a tip."

"Say," she asked. "Would you take it in lap dances?"

# Chapter 58 - The Ant Colony


The trees around the medical center were stripped of their snow and left bare to fight the storm on their own. A mid-day darkness descended and the wind and trees roared as they battled. The streetlights turned on and revealed branches, torn from the fight, scuttling across the campus.

Standing by the window, the Head Administrator grasped her Starbucks in both hands and watched the tempest outside. She was chilled and wore a heavy sweater that she kept in her office; a cold office that no amount of complaining and requisition tickets to maintenance could change. She was at the end of the heat zone, they said, and the water from the boilers had already spent its warmth by the time it reached her. However, as long as she had coffee and her mother's old sweater, even if it didn't match the rest of her outfit, she didn't mind. It kept her mind sharp. A mind that, at the moment, was recollecting the ants that had infested her parents' back yard when she was a child.

She had starting thinking about the ants as she watched the storm and all the small people struggling against it in the street outside, below the looming buildings. She thought of how the ants bore their great burdens, trekking across the yard, blades of grass as tall as trees to them. When she was a child, the future Head Administrator admired their organization and defended them against her brother, who called them fascists and would spend hours pounding them with rocks. Even after suffering hundreds of casualties by that cruel boy, they went on with their hauling without even stopping to grieve. She remembered a theory she had conceived at the time: that the consciousness of an ant lay not with the individual creature, but with the colony at large. In a sense, the individual was the colony, not the ant. It was right that it should be so, she thought, for the ant could not survive without the colony. Perhaps when entire colonies died, then other colonies grieved, but one ant would not grieve another anymore than a human grieves the cells of skin that slough off when she scratches an itch.

The Head Administrator had been a very pensive child, prone to deep thoughts, very, very different from her brother and everyone else around her. She had speculated that, in time, humans would lose their individual consciousness and develop a colony consciousness like the ants. It was the next, inevitable, step in human evolution: necessary, lest the humans destroy each other with their conflicts. She remembered thinking it would be a great improvement to live in an ant colony, or at least in the human equivalent. There would be no crime, for instance, not even any disagreements, and everyone would work together in concert. Of course, if she lived in an ant colony, she'd have to be the queen.

The Head Administrator hated the way people argued and discussed things forever, as they did in the group projects her teachers had always insisted she and her classmates work together on. She always had been the smartest child in the group and often already knew how to complete the project just as the rest of the group members were still trying to understand the instructions. She'd have to wait for them, or worse, try to explain everything to them. In the best case, the other group members would just let her finish the project herself while they chatted about their vapid interests. Most were happy to let her go ahead because they knew she was a brainiac and they would all share the grade she earned for them. In other cases, the Head Administrator would assign the other group members simple tasks that were drudgery, but necessary for the completion of the project. This method had the advantage of making her load lighter, of course, but they had often accused her of being bossy while they shared her grade. The situations that gave the Head Administrator the most trouble were when there had been a proud one in the group. The proud one was seldom very bright and held on to a perverse authority to compensate for his or her dull wit. Of course, the proud ones didn't know how to complete the project better than she had, but they would not let her do it herself. They wanted to have their hand in everything and, whatever they touched, they generally turned into confusion. Often very popular with others, these maddening characters often got the rest of the group to do things their way, not because theirs was the best, but because the others liked him or her better. Dr Ahern was one such individual. The Head Administrator learned long ago not to compete with the Aherns of the world on popularity, but to bide her time, wait until the project's inevitable failure, and step in at the end to set things right.

In conformity with the inexorable laws of entropy, the Starbucks was beginning to warm her chilled fingers through the cup and the mood of the staff was beginning to turn in her favor. Losing three chemical dependency counselors worsened the workload wonderfully, and daily she considered firing someone else on any pretense. The Head Administrator of course, had promptly notified human resources of the vacancies. There was a delay when she sent the notice to the wrong department and it sat in the mailbox of one who had recently left on a two week vacation. Eventually the error was caught and the notice went to HR. The Head Administrator was pleased to see that they sat on it also. For some reason, there was a hiring freeze in the entire medical center.

The fact that HR was doing no hiring gave the Head Administrator some pause. Like a skilled mechanic who can identify a problem with an engine from the slightest noise, the Head Administrator knew that something was afoot in the organization. The medical center had recently merged with other medical centers to create a humungous health corporation, a colony of colonies that seemed like a dream come true to the Head Administrator. There were, of course, the fears of layoffs that often accompany mergers, but when none were announced, the rumors died down. People figured a hiring freeze was a far preferable alternative to layoffs as a method of right-sizing the corporation after a merger. Still, the Head Administrator was uneasy, for she knew that the other medical centers in the corporation had no hiring freeze.

The rolodex on her desk was opened to the number for the state Office of Mental Health. So many times in the last months, she had fingered her rolodex and lingered on that very page.

She thought, *That idiot, Pellegrino, who I fired for smoking, hasn't called OMH as I had hoped.*

She pulled the card out of the wheel and pondered, *I should call them myself and report Ahern to the authorities.*

*No, they'll just blame you. You're the administrator, hired to insure that we follow regulations.*

*I'll just tell them that he's bribed the department,* she said to herself.

*You accepted his cash along with the rest,* she countered.

*I'll tell them he has submitted fraudulent insurance claims.*

*But those documents have your name on them as well as his.*

*He's treating staff and clients alike for nicotine dependence, outside the scope of our practice.*

*But he has hired certified professionals to do so.*

*An impractical professor can't be allowed to drag the whole clinic down with him. Am I the only one who can stop him?*

*If you made that call they'd send representatives down to investigate, and he would charm them just as he charmed the staff. He's the great Dr Ahern, after all, who we've all studied in college and admired as a great mind.*

She put the phone down; she had too many apprehensions to call today.

*Is there any other way? Should I kidnap him and tie him up with duct tape?*

*Even if you could truss him up, stuff him in the truck of your car, and drive him to a lonely cliff in the wilderness, you'd hear him thrashing in the back. He'd wail even if you stuffed his mouth with rags. You'd go insane and drive yourself, distracted into a tree.*

*What's left – assassination?*

Just then, the phone rang and the Head Administrator picked it up.

It was the Office of Mental Health. There had been a group home fire. One was dead and they were starting an inquest.

She steadied her voice as they arranged a meeting. The phone shook like a drunkard's hand as she placed it in its cradle.

# Chapter 59 - The Aficionado

Izzy had been an intern only a few months, and it had been only a few weeks since Craig left him to his own devices, but already the work had become routine. Not routine in the sense that it was boring or that the intern had already achieved a condition of burnout, but routine in that he didn't panic every time he walked out to the waiting room to pick up a new client. He no longer had to stare at himself in the mirror for a few minutes between appointments and give himself the affirmations that many therapists recommend for the fretful. He had his method, his counseling theory, and his tissue boxes in strategic locations, and, he felt, he was getting results. Some members of the therapy group continued to use drugs or alcohol, of course, but he felt they were bound to. Craig's relapse taught him as much. There were the chronic relapsers, for sure; but there was also some success in Lawrence, for instance, who was about ready to graduate from treatment, and even Bill and Clifton, who abstained from inhaling their skunky weed of choice. Why, even collecting urine itself was easier and he came to enjoy the smell of the salty, warm, and foamy piss as he zipped up bag after successful bag with their clean urine. Most remarkably, with the departure of Craig, Pellegrino, and Bella, Izzy had become one of the most experienced clinicians in the clinic when it came to chemical dependency. Occasionally, even the best-trained mental health therapists came to him to ask how long cocaine stayed in the system, for example, or how many beers would result in legal intoxication, and the like. Of course, Izzy didn't know the answers to the questions, but he answered them with the confidence of a man who knows he won't be doubted.

Of all that happened since he started, the one instance that gave him the most confidence was the short session with Luna at the titty bar. She had her eureka moment in that session, an experience that charges up client and therapist, alike; but he had his, as well. He realized in that moment that he envied clients for their stories because he had none of his own. He castigated himself at first for skimming through his life, rather than living it. He knew he avoided making any choices because to choose something meant that he would have to forgo something else. When he came to a fork in the road, he never took either of them. Instead, he pitched a tent and lived there, never experiencing either alternative in the hopes of keeping his options open.

Seldom did an hour go by, in the week after their session, when Luna didn't spring to Izzy's mind. There were signs that he was falling in love with the stripper, but it wasn't quite as you think. When he thought about her, it wasn't her perfect breasts that he imagined, nor was it the feel of her similarly globular ass on his lap, nor was it the incongruously shy smile of the nudist. All those were enticing, to be sure. The image that constantly came to his mind was not when she cuddled affectionately on his lap, but when she decisively jumped off it. It wasn't her or her body that he wished to possess, but her determination; a determination that he, ironically, helped her get in that session, and, a determination that he, just as ironically, already possessed, the very moment that he desired it.

You see, for Izzy, there was more to the eureka moment than just a recognition of lost opportunities. A new opportunity opened up before him. As if the intern, camping out by the fork in the road, awoke one morning and discerned a previously un-seen path in the underbrush: a faint trace explored by squirrels, widened by lumbering raccoons, and cleared by nibbling deer. This path was a way he could not fail to take. Everything seemed right about it, as if all the choices previously had seemed all wrong. It was a path made for him by those woodland animals, run right under his feet, and named in his honor: Izzy's Path. He had to take it and there was nothing in the other paths he would ever want. He would be a collector of stories. Much as others will collect stamps, Hummel figurines, or Depression glass, Izzy would collect stories.

Furthermore, it dawned on Izzy that a collector adds value to the items he collects simply by recognizing their value. Like any experienced collector, he imagined he would take a glance at a yard sale of tales and readily identify the fraudulent ones, mass-produced by defensive clients to satisfy any therapist so that he would ask no further. The knowledgeable story collector would quickly brush aside their spurious claims of childhood trauma, absent fathers, and grating grief and demand they put out the real goods, the stories that made them cry authentic tears. Moreover, like any good collector, he would also be better able to identify the priceless stories, jumbled in dusty cardboard boxes, unvalued by the owner. These he would lift up and, instead of buying them for a song and making himself wealthy, he would rub off the tarnish and convince the owner of the importance of what he already possessed. His clients would leave his office with their latent talents, unplumbed potentials, and hidden truths in hand, determined to demand the best price for their assets. This was to be his mission in life: to be an aficionado of stories, and a darn good mission it was.

The Fate Sisters made a point of not following the outcome of their decisions. If they had, they would've been pleased with this janitor because a cleaning person who values the junk we toss is a very good cleaning person indeed. Unfortunately, gods don't leave us alone just because we please them. On the contrary, we come to mind more frequently. Just as a coach puts his favorites in the game, The Fate Sisters once again tangled Izzy in with new strand of trouble.

# Chapter 60 - Ideation

None of the foregoing musings distracted Izzy when he sat down to listen to Inez, another new intake. Inez was a fragile, classic beauty, far more lovely than frisky Luna. Inez might have been a Greek statue, modeling perfection. The kind of woman you roped off and gaped at from a distance, not the kind that snuggled on your lap. Just the same, Izzy did not gaze at her. She was no more than three feet from him, he looked right at her, but he might as well have been looking at the wall. She spoke, began to tell her story without his prompting, but her words might as well been the heater blower in the ceiling, or the distant closing of doors down the hall. She had an exquisite story, enough to please even the most discriminating, fussy collector. She slipped her story, untouched, from its plastic case and placed it before him. But there it was, unrecognized and unregarded. Izzy smiled and nodded, the very picture of an attentive therapist, but he was still listening to his last conversation, the one he had before meeting Inez.

He had gone out to call Inez into his office from the waiting room when the Head Administrator pulled him aside in the hallway.

"You saw a client named Sue a few days ago," the Head Administrator said.

"Yea, that's right," he answered.

"Well, a couple hours after she left your office, her group home burned down in a fire."

"Oh, I heard about that. Was she in it? Is she all right?" He asked.

"No, she's dead," the Head Administrator answered, "and they think she set the fire. The Office of Mental Health is coming tomorrow to investigate, and they want to ask you some questions."

The Head Administrator didn't know what questions OMH wanted to ask, but she hoped that Izzy had followed policy and asked Sue directly about suicidality and homicidality sometime in the session and she hoped that, had she admitted to having suicidal or homicidal ideation, he had assessed these carefully and noted everything down in the chart.

"Just because we're a renegade clinic and have disregarded most of OMH's rules at Dr Ahern's insistence," she told him, "doesn't mean we can cut corners on client care. You'll be representing the whole department, which is very unusual for an intern, and if they don't like what you have to say, there may be further investigations. I don't have to tell you what that means."

Izzy swallowed hard.

"Isn't Craig Creek your supervisor?" she asked.

"Y-yes."

"Well," she continued, "Mr Creek was a seasoned clinician who undoubtedly instructed you in all our policies before he left, even those pertaining to mental health clients, who are, of course, outside his field of expertise. It doesn't matter that Mr Creek wasn't used to dealing with mental health issues because I'm sure he followed Dr Ahern's advice and had you learn everything you need to know by listening to your clients. Naturally, your clients aren't going to tell you what the policies of this department are, but Dr Ahern was sure that wouldn't be a problem."

"Dr Ahern, will he be there?"

"I'm afraid not, but I'm confident you'll know what to say to OMH," pronounced the Head Administrator.

Certainly Izzy recalled Sue, he remembered her as Inez continued to speak in his office. Sue was the one who wouldn't talk. But she did say one thing to him. She wanted to stop smoking. Yes, that was it. That's all she said. He never asked her if she was suicidal or homicidal. He's never once asked anyone. Was he supposed to? Would Sue even have told him, if he did ask? Would asking have prevented her from burning down the group home, if that's indeed what she did? Was it too late to write his note about the session with Sue and fraudulently document that she denied suicidal or homicidal ideation? The Head Administrator was fond of saying that if it's not written down, it didn't happen. Well, in this case, she's right, it didn't happen, but what would be the harm in saying that it did? Could he change history by changing his story? He could write that she explicitly stated that she had no plans of burning the group home down, or would that look too suspicious? Sue did say she wanted to stop smoking. He had taken that to mean she wanted to stop using tobacco. But what if she was saying to him that she was a pyromaniac and wanted to stop setting fires? Oh, he gasped, I missed it. She was reaching out for help and I heard it all wrong. She was talking oranges and I heard bananas, and then, frustrated by her inability to get help for this impulse to set fires, she decided to end it all by immolating herself in a final con-flagration. I'm a bad therapist, a bad, bad therapist, responsible for the death of my client, the destruction of a group home, and, now, the premature discovery of Dr Ahern's important ex-periment. I never should have gotten into this field, he thought. The world was better off when I collected piss.

Just then, he remembered he had a client in the room, Inez. From the pile of used tissues in front of her and the mascara running down her cheeks, he must've been doing a great job of therapy while he was ruminating on his incompetence. But, what has she been saying?

He interrupted her. "Are you suicidal?" he asked.

"What?" she said.

"Homicidal?"

"No, what kind of questions are these?"

"Are you going to burn down your house?"

"No, am I in the right place?"

Izzy furiously wrote her answers in his notebook. "No. Yes, you are. I'm sorry; it's just something I have to ask. Go on with what you were saying."

Inez patted the last of her tears and wiped the running mascara off her cheeks. She collected the used tissues into a pile, picked up her bag, and fussed with her makeup while looking in her compact mirror. Then still not saying a word, she began to unbutton her blouse.

Izzy thought, what's with these clients and taking their clothes off? He watched carefully in case he had to document what he saw. She unbuttoned her blouse down to her navel and chastely pulled it aside just enough to show her breasts divided by an angry scar like a zipper down her chest. Then she buttoned it back up. She took a big breath, spoke, and Izzy listened.

"I went in for a gallstone operation. My doctor told me I would only need a little incision that would quickly fade. No big deal."

Her eyes overflowed with tears and her mascara began to run again.

"I woke up from surgery feeling heavy, like someone was sitting on my chest. I couldn't even lift my head. The nurse came and said they'd have to look at the incision and removed the bandage. I could've died when I saw this scar. I thought something went wrong with the surgery, but no one would give me any answers. Much later, I learned that I had been mistaken for an open-heart surgery patient and they cracked me open. No one seemed to understand why I would be upset."

Izzy's ears had really perked up. He wouldn't let this pass by a second time. "You said you could've died when you saw that scar. Are you glad that you didn't?"

"No, I wish I was dead. I went and confronted the doctor. All I wanted was some recognition that he'd made a mistake and an apology, but I guess his lawyer got to him first and warned him not to admit he was in the wrong. All he did was stall and stonewall. He practically patted me on my head and sent me on my way. I could've killed him. So, I went to my lawyer, but he says the lawsuit could take years. I might just as well be dead, for all anyone cares."

"So you do want to die, and kill this doctor, too."

"No, not really; those are expressions. I just want someone to acknowledge how dreadful it is to have this scar."

"It is an awful scar. I've never seen anything like it, but I can't let you leave here without sending you to the psych ward."

"The psych ward! No way am I going back to the hospital! I'm not psycho! I just thought if I came here I would have someone to talk to, someone who understands."

"If you don't go on your own, I'll have to call the police and have you mental hygiene arrested. Then they'll take you to the psych emergency room. It's a locked ward where they have padding walls and straightjackets. You'll be safe."

"Arrested! You can't have me arrested; I haven't done anything wrong. I haven't even raised my voice!"

"You're screaming now. It's not like a regular arrest; it's all for your safety."

"Well, I'm not sticking around for this! I'm leaving!"

She left the office, not running, but angry and determined. Izzy followed closely behind her.

"Stop her!" he yelled. "She's homicidal!" However, self-preservation being a strong instinct, everyone in the hallway stepped aside to let her pass.

Melvina, the office manger, her ears always tuned to trouble, had already called security when she heard Incz screaming in Izzy's office. The previous security guard had been rotated to another division because he had been romancing the female clients, and they had just gotten a new guard: a former all-state high school linebacker, who didn't have the grades for a college scholarship. He spotted Inez coming through the waiting room with Izzy following behind her and knew right away that she was who he had been called for. The medical center had carefully trained its guards in restraint techniques, but seeing Inez break free of the defenders, his more primitive instincts took over and he put her to the ground in a perfect, textbook tackle.

The wind knocked clear out of her, and seeing more stars than on a clear desert night, she barely moved again until the police and ambulance arrived. Then the police had to cuff her to get her onto the stretcher, the medics had to strap her down to transport her to the ambulance, then they had to turn on the siren to make it quickly to the emergency room entrance at the other end of the building. At emergency, they wheeled her right away to an isolation room and snowed her with an injection of Haldol and Ativan. When she awoke, hours later, they carefully loosened one of the straps to see what she would do. Still being groggy, she rubbed her wrist and they undid the others. She sat up on the cot and looked down at the hospital gown that covered her chest. It failed to cover her back, which made her look like an escaped psych patient when she bolted out of the locked ward as the orderly wheeled the dinner trays out the door.

"It's a good thing you sent that patient to emergency," said the Head Administrator to Izzy. "She would've been a liability had you let her go."

# Chapter 61 - The Aristocrats

"Me and Clifton's been going to meetings," said Lawrence to the group later that day. Izzy was shaken by all that happened already with Sue and Inez, but Lawrence was shaken up more, by something else.

"We went to this meeting last night; Narcotics Anonymous," said Lawrence. "It's a pretty good one. The speakers put it all out there and let you know how bad it was when they were in their use. They keep it real. The first one stands up and says he used to steal prescription pads from his doctors when they weren't looking. Then the second says she stole ten bucks from the altar to the Virgin of Guadalupe. Another one says on Christmas Eve he swiped the presents he bought for his own kids and sold them for drugs. It's like each one was trying to top each other. They're all getting off on telling the truth. Another guy stands up and admits he fucked his own mother when he was drunk, well she was drunk, too. He keeps his head down and he can't look anyone in the eye, but he lets it out. Your secrets keep you sick. Then a woman stands up and says, 'I didn't fuck my mother, but I sold my ten year old into prostitution. Yup,' she says, 'I turned my daughter out for a bag.' No one hisses at her, or boos her or any of that. We all clap, give her a big hug, and say keep coming back. I get to thinking, I don't know what's more bizarre, them talking about the things they did or us congratulating them afterwards for telling on themselves. Anyway, me and Cliff clap and hug and listen along with the rest of them and I start wondering if I have some more truth to tell besides smoking up every paycheck I ever got.

"Then another one gets up and says, 'I used to eat shit. I got so fucked up, I didn't know what I was doing. I thought a turd was a sausage.'"

"You're grossing us out," said a group member.

"Sorry, but you've got to hear it. You've got to hear what drugs and alcohol'll do to you if you want to stay clean. I was pretty grossed out, too. But then, I thought, there, but for the grace of God, go I. Those are all just my not yets. I haven't done it- yet; but I will, too, if I keep going.

"I was just starting to get used to hearing all that shit and the next thing I know, there goes Clifton. He stands up and goes to the podium. He opens up his mouth and says to everyone, 'When I was drinking, I got my son to suck my dick, and that there.' He says, 'I's all better, now, I's stopped drinking and I got me a fambly.' Then he sits down."

"Lawrence," said Izzy. "You broke Cliff's confidentiality. If he wanted us to know about this, he would've told us."

"I know, but it doesn't matter now. Cliff's dead."

"Dead? What happened?"

"We walk out of the meeting when it was all done. At first, I didn't want to walk with him, no more. But then I thought, well, he told on himself, you gotta give him that. So we walk out and I tell him, 'that took balls.'

"He said, 'Yup, I feel good!' Like he'd just taken a hit of something. We cross the bridge and he stops to look at the water. 'This was the bridge I was fixen to jump off of for a minute,' he says, 'but now I feel good, because I got me a fambly.'

"I hear a pop. Cliff falls over the guardrail and into the water. I think to my self, why've you jumping now, when you're feeling good? I lean over, expecting to see him swimming around, but he sinks like a rock.

"I look behind me and I see the man who sold his kid's Christmas presents. He's putting a gun away. 'I've always wanted to shoot a pervert child molester,' he says, 'and now I have.'"

"Did you tell the police?"

"Shit, no. I go to a bar and order a drink. I know, I should've have done it. But at least it wasn't cocaine. I get a boilermaker: a shot and a beer, 'cause I needed to get fucked up. But I just look at it and say what the hell're you doing? So I leave and go over to Cliff's house to tell his ol' lady.

"I tell his ol' lady and she tells the kids. They start wailing like a litter of puppies that lost their mother. When I get the chance, I whisper to his ol' lady, 'you know,' I say, 'Cliff was a child molester.' She pulls away and glares at me. 'I'm just telling you in case he touched one've your kids. You might want to check 'em out and get 'em into counseling.'

"She slaps me in the face. 'Cliff didn't touch none of these chirdren. I was enough woman for him, and if'n they say he did, I'll slap 'em silly, too.'

"I say, 'I'm sorry, it's just something I heard, I didn't mean nothing by it.'

"She says, 'Now you watch these chirdren a minute, while I gets me a bag. You want me to bring you one?'

"I say, 'Sure, I'll do a bag for Cliff.' I'm not thinking then, either. I'm just opening up my mouth and words fall out I don't mean.

"The woman goes out and I got the six wailing children. Now I wish I'd had that drink. But I didn't, so I turn on the cable and tell them all to watch it. They look at it, but they're still crying. I'm thinking, hurry up with that bag. The longer I wait for it, the more I want it.

"All of a sudden, the weeping and wailing turns into glee. I think, good, the momma's back home with the bag. But then I look up, and it's this big man carrying in a suitcase and all the kids're calling him daddy. He sees me and says, 'What you doing here, honky?'

"I wonder if he's got something to put holes in me, like Cliff was saying happened to the man who came before him. I say to the man, 'Nothing, just watching the kids for their momma. She'll be right back. She heard you were coming and wanted to get you something for when you come home.'

"I don't wait around for a bag at that point. I just high tail it out of there. Three guys ask me on my way home if I'm straight. Each time, I feel my heart jump like I was already smoking it, but then I think, shit, I've had enough of the life. I'll be lucky to get home alive."

"What's the name of that meeting you went to?"

"They call themselves *The Aristocrats*."

# Chapter 62 - The Whale Watch

Horrified; Izzy was horrified.

Sue, Inez, OMH, Lawrence, Clifton, *The Aristocrats*, all of them, they were just too much. Izzy went down to the titty bar, wanting to unload on Craig. He needed some supervision. But Craig was tied up himself in his bouncing job. So, Izzy settled for a beer, but the beer tasted like piss. He asked for wine, but the wine tasted like drinking acorns. Whiskey it would be, he called to the bartender. But the whiskey felt like he was drinking fire. The bartender waited for Izzy's next order, but he couldn't make up his mind.

"A mixed drink, then," said the bartender. "Mixed drinks for mixed feelings."

"Whatever," said Izzy, "get me a mixed drink. Mix up whatever you want." But his feelings weren't mixed. He knew what he wanted. He wanted to talk with Craig, but Craig stood against the wall, watching that none of the patrons touched the dancing girls, and he couldn't be bothered until quitting time. Izzy would wait until quitting time, then, and watch the girls. He looked at them, but he didn't really watch. His mind was on Sue, Inez, OMH, Lawrence, Clifton, and *The Aristocrats*. They were his dancing girls. Izzy spun his barstool back to the bar. A pina colada sat there, under a pink umbrella. The topless girls circulated, cadging drinks and lap dances, but Izzy stuck his elbows out and drank. With one sip, the pina colada, with a little help from the beer, wine, and whiskey before, transported him back to Hawaii, where he'd vacationed as a teenager with his mother and stepfather.

Izzy hadn't wanted to go to Hawaii. He wanted his parents to leave him alone with the house, so he could be independent and imagine that he was grown and on his own. His parents had heard too many stories of teenagers having wild parties when they were gone to permit it to happen to them. Of course, Izzy was not the kind of kid that threw wild parties, or the kind that had friends who went to them. That Izzy's parents didn't know this about him both annoyed and pleased him. He liked being inscrutable, but wished they made more of an effort.

When he packed his bag for Hawaii, he considered running off, like his sister, to San Francisco, but the Summer of Love was over and the streets had turned mean. No, he'd go to Hawaii, but he'd do his best to let them know he was annoyed. When his mother carefully spread sunscreen on everyone before going out on the beach, he was annoyed. She had a big floppy hat, for god's sake. When his stepfather stood solemnly before a sunken battleship, he was annoyed. The war'd been fought and won years ago. Get over it, already. When they both, in their own way, invited him to go with them to see a volcano, he was annoyed. His mother in her chirpy, catch more flies with honey than vinegar way, annoyed him; and his stepfather, in his gruff, chuck 'im on the shoulder way, annoyed him. Quit acting so phony, he said. He pulled a random book from the resort's shelves and hid behind it. He read his book all the way to the volcano; all the while his parents gawked at it, and all the way back. By then, they knew he was annoyed. They weren't so phony in the morning.

Izzy was in a similar mood tonight. The bare breasted dancing girls were all just too forward. The music was too loud, the bartender too fawning, and Craig, standing by the door, watching the stage, just too busy doing nothing to talk to him on the most important night of his life. The umbrellaed coconut drink annoyed him, too, but he drank it down before he knew it and the bartender replaced it with another before Izzy had a chance to ask for something else.

Izzy looked up at the bartender, who pointed across the bar at Luna, leaning against a man in a dirty tractor cap. She waved. She'd bought it for him.

The book Izzy read on the day of the volcano annoyed him, too; but he had to keep reading it, so his parents would know he was annoyed. It had started off great: a mad whaling captain hijacked his own ship to go hunt for the particular whale that had chewed off his leg. But then it bogged down in the details of whales and whaling and irrelevant tales from passing ships. People just screw everything up when it could be simple. Just go get the whale, for crying out loud, and just leave me alone, and stop acting so fake.

The next day, his stepfather announced they'd be going on a whale watch and he could come if he'd like. Or he could stay in the hotel room and read about whales, if he'd rather. Izzy, who, at this moment was more annoyed with the author at not getting on with his book than he was with his parents for not letting him live his life, cast the book aside and went with them. Seeing as though the author was in no hurry to find the whale, he'd go look for one himself.

Luna led the man with the dirty tractor cap back to the lap dance room and Izzy felt a surge of jealousy. The surge returned, all the stronger, a few minutes later when Luna started her set on the stage. The men lined the stage waiting to give her their dollars. He kept his back turned so he wouldn't have to watch, but he could still hear and imagine, as he tore the paper umbrella to shreds.

The contrast between the whale watch and the whale hunt of his book couldn't be more distinct. They paid their dollars and lined up in front of a yacht, rather than a stalwart sailing vessel. The ship had a logo of a smiling, cartoon whale painted on its side. They boarded over an OSHA certified gangplank and were served pina coladas, his carefully non-alcoholic, by bland, white jacketed stewards. Izzy thought he'd rather jostle with the savage aborigines of his book's crew. The captain was a two-legged oceanographer; and the water, at least within the developed confines of the harbor, was as smooth as a new sidewalk.

That's just the problem, Izzy had thought. The world's gone soft and cautious. A hundred years ago, a guy my age could leave home and match himself against the greatest beasts in the wild ocean, then return to his parents a bronzed, bearded man. Now parents lead their teenagers on a leash. They've turned whaling into a walk in the zoo.

The ship slipped away from the pier and accelerated its engines, mercifully precluding all conversation. Izzy stood at the bow like the craft's figurehead, cleaving the wind with his face. In this manner, he gained the headlands and was out at sea before anyone else aboard. Here he felt emancipated.    The    air was as soft and clear as a pure thought, while the full-bodied sea heaved like the chest of a sleeping beast. High clouds skidded across the sky, their wispy vapors as changeable as a youth's character, the murderous urges of the deep sea lurked far below. The two were as one as heads and tails, male and female, thought and emotion, freedom and danger. Like the watchful eye of a cook, the tropical sun supervised the boiling bisque of air and sea, clouds and fish, and one frail minor, pitching in a frail shell.

Soon Izzy was crabbed by seasickness, and chucking his breakfast over the side. A dough-faced steward conducted him below decks, where his mother laid his green head on her lap.

Izzy had just started to feel better when the crew spotted some whales and reduced the speed. Below decks emptied as the passengers crowded to see. Izzy and his family went up with the rest, but the ship, not making headway, lolled all the more in the swells. His mother pointed gleefully at the whale's spouts and his stepfather fiddled with his camera, but Izzy lurched to the far, empty rail to barf again into the sea. There he stood alone, watching his chunky puke run down the side of the leaning ship, while the pod breeched, blew, and slapped on the other side.

Izzy had finished his second pina colada, as well as the whiskey, beer, and wine, when Luna came up and said she had a client named Phil to refer to him.

"You've got to see him tonight. He's a farmer from out of town and he won't be back. He really needs counseling. I tried to help him, in my own way. But seeing that you're here, you can use the lap dance room, just not for an hour, only for one or two songs."

Izzy staggered to his feet and smiled at Luna. He would've done anything she asked. He only requested that she get another chair, so the farmer wouldn't have to sit on his lap.

# Chapter 63 - Trimming

The snow fell heavy around Christmas time last year and remained ass deep for months. Phil pruned his vines all winter with Jack, the hired man, strapping snowshoes to their feet. The snowshoes allowed them to walk on top of the drifts; but their feet, not insulated by the snow, froze every day by noon. The vines were half buried in snow and they had to bend over all day to reach them. By noon, Phil's back stiffened up, also. He and Jack made their way to the house each day at lunchtime to thaw out and straighten up. Phil told his wife, Carol, he'd rather lie on the hard kitchen floor than eat.

"I'll just set a place for your man, then," she said.

"Not in the kitchen, he'll be fine eating in the basement next to the furnace." Phil believed it wasn't good to get too familiar with the hired help. "I pay him good money to trim my vines. I don't have to be friends with him, too."

The truth of the matter was that Phil believed it wasn't good to get familiar with anyone. He and Carol were of different sorts, as different as the French Hybrids that Phil grew next to the Concords. Twice a year they hired extra help for tying and picking; Carol would call up all her girlfriends and she would join them swarming over Phil's vines, chattering all day. He would skip lunch then, too. Carol would lead the droves of help to the house and Phil would fuss with the trellis during tying season or haul the bins of fruit out with his tractor during picking. Phil was never far from his vines and Carol was never far from her friends.

"I don't understand it," she said, "you're out in the grapes all day long, you won't let Jack talk to you when you're out there, I would think you'd like a little conversation when you come in for lunch. I know Jack likes to talk when he's out there. But you won't even talk to him to pass the time while you're working."

Phil didn't try to explain that a grape trimmer couldn't be carrying on two conversations at once. The grapeman has to be in conversation with his vines. In the summer the leaves tell whoever is listening their concerns about fungus and insects. In the winter he interviews the vines one by one. They tell him, if he will listen, about their health and aspirations for the year. When the trimmer steps up to a vine he notes the bark of the stump, the canes left from last trimming, where the shoots came out, and how far they grew. He misses nothing of what they say to him and his shears answer them back with a judicious balance of restraint and enthusiasm. Grapes, he knew, grew best when kept out of each other's shade. They also grow best when they are kept a little desperate.

"If you're not going to eat your lunch," Carol said, "and if you're not going to let Jack up here with us, then I hope you let me bring your lunch down to him. It's going to waste otherwise."

Phil let her go. She was right; the lunch would go to waste. Lying on the hard floor, Phil could hear very well the conversation going on beneath him between Jack and his wife. Jack had left his lunch in his car, he told her, and it froze during the morning. He was trying to thaw out an egg salad sandwich on the furnace duct, but Phil kept his house so cold it would still be frozen by the time Phil was done resting his spine and wanting to get back to work. So, thank you, he appreciates the gesture, he would have some lunch.

Each day, thereafter, Carol made lunch that would go to waste if she didn't take it down to the hired man. Their conversation came up through the floor to Phil. They started out as brief, polite exchanges that, in time, gave way to laughter.

Little marked the passing of the winter except Phil and Jack's progress through the vineyard, and Carol and Jack's progress through their acquaintance. The days followed one another like snowshoe prints up and down the vineyard rows. The most recent stood out clear and crisp in the snow, as the wind erased the older ones. On some days, the wind rattled the canes on the wires and stung their cheeks until they grew enough beard to cover them. On other days the wind was still and all they could hear was the snipping of the shears. The winter finally broke on the day that Phil could hear no conversation at all coming up through the floor after Carol took Jack's lunch down to him.

As silent as lunch was that day, the vineyard was full of noise. About four feet of snow was melting fast and the water was rushing down the gullies into the lake. It had warmed so much that, on the days that followed, the two workers could have eaten outdoors, but Phil's spine still demanded the hard kitchen floor. His vertebrae, in that silent house, snapped back into place as loudly as the traps Phil had set up in the house to catch the mice that were stirring from the spring thaw. Phil returned to work after resting briefly while Jack lingered in the basement with Carol.

Then one rainy Friday, Jack didn't return at all. When Phil got to the house that night, Carol also was gone. She hadn't even brought in the wash before she left. The line had broken with the weight of a soaked bed sheet. Phil slept that night on the kitchen floor listening to the rainfall. The rain would certainly wipe out what was left of the snow by morning and, by morning, he would conclude what to do without his wife.

At the first light, Phil sharpened his shears and walked back out to work. Without Jack he would have to hustle to finish the trimming by the time the buds popped. Just as he thought, the snow was mostly gone except where the drifts piled up. Rain still fell. Rivulets ran to the edge of the brim of Phil's hat and gathered, swelling into a drop. The drop inhaled moisture and grew like a long sob until, too heavy to hang on, it broke free of the brim and plummeted in front of his face.

The world was having a long soak. Raindrops clung to the trellis wires like Christmas lights someone forgot to take down. The shaggy bark of the vines sopped up the rain like a sponge and darkened. Pulled by gravity, the moisture ran down the trunk to a band, bare of bark, that mice, protected from the cold by the deep snow, had chewed away. The raindrops skidded down the wound that gleamed white like an exposed bone. Phil regarded his ruin.

He broke into a run through his grapes to examine the damage now revealed by the melting snow. All over the vineyard, the mice had girdled most of the vines, snacking on the cambium layer that bears the nutrients up and down the trunk between the bark and the sapwood. If the vine was partly girdled, it may be stunted. If it was girdled all the way around, it was certainly dead. As he had prepared his vines for spring, invisible disaster had nibbled below his feet.

## Chapter 64 - Carpe Diem

"Is there anything you regret, now?" asked Izzy. "If you had it to do over, what would you do?"

"I'd go down and punch Jack in the nose," said Phil. "It would've been rash, but I'd rather be sorry for doing something I shouldn't have done, than be sorry about something I should have done, but didn't."

"Why?" asked Izzy. "What difference does it make what you're sorry over?"

"It's better to try and fail than not to try at all."

A hand reached and drew the curtain open. It was Luna. "I hate to break up a good head shrinking, but I need the room. You guys can take it out to the bar."

Phil and Izzy filed past her and a red-faced kid. The kid's buddies were hooting and cheering him on. Punch'em in the nose, huh, thought Izzy. He wanted to punch the whole crew of buddies in the nose. Show some respect.

Phil kept on talking, as if they were still in the room. As if Izzy was listening, and not turned away, watching the curtain to the lap dance room.

"She sent me a letter, asking for money," said Phil. "Can you believe that? I don't have any money. The bank came and foreclosed on the farm and I've been looking for work. There's nothing I can do; all I know is grapes. Maybe I should just put an end to it all. There's no point in going on like this."

This might have been the time for Izzy to listen carefully and discern whether the farmer was a danger to self or others, or whether he was just expressing disillusionment with living his life as he'd been living it. Phil might have been poised on the brink of a precipitous change. He might have been ready to relate more intimately with others, communicate more effectively, have his aching back looked at, go back to school and make a career change, declare his love for his wife and petition for a reconciliation, or let her free in the hope that, if she belongs to him, she'll come back. He might have been ready to take medication to lift him out of the doldrums he'd been in for these months. It also might have been the time for Izzy to call the police to the titty bar and explain to the officers that Phil needed to be mental hygiene arrested. He hadn't broken any laws, he might have explained, but he should be transported to a psychiatric emergency room for a thorough evaluation. Phil might have been planning on stringing his wife and her lover up on his foreclosed grape trellis, taking out his pruning shears, and doing some trimming on their digits and extremities. He might have been ready to shoot himself in the head, jump off Clifton's bridge, buy a bag of dope, or drink himself into oblivion at that bar. He might have also just been asking for help.

As it was, Izzy was in no risk of having regrets about Phil or ruminating over what might have been because the intern never heard what he said. Izzy never heard Phil make a suicidal threat because the intern was already halfway to the lap dance room, avoiding having regrets of his own. Izzy unfalteringly brushed the curtain aside, took Luna into his arms, and lifted her off the alarmed kid. She let out a little scream of astonishment before he muffled it with a kiss.

Craig was on Izzy immediately, grabbing him by the collar, and pulling him away from Luna. The kid's buddies were close behind. "You fucking want to talk to me again?" said Craig, "you can wait till after quitting time."

"No, no," said Izzy. "I'll wait. It's not that this time. I was just…"

"He was just protecting me," said Luna. "He thought this kid was hurting me, so he came in to be my white knight. But he was mistaken, everything's all right. We're having a good time, now, aren't we, boys?"

The kid's friends looked around at everyone and laughed at Izzy thinking their buddy was a lecher. They decided that was something to cheer about, so they did. Luna offered him another lap dance and Craig released his hold on Izzy's collar.

"Wait," said Izzy, "I do want to talk with you."

"You wait," said Craig. "Sit at the bar and wait. Don't try to be a bouncer; I'm the bouncer, here. And don't drink so fucking much; you're already shit faced."

By the time the intern took his seat at the bar his third pina colada was already set up, and Phil was already gone.

# Chapter 65 - Gethsemane

In the dead of the night, Dr Ahern paced the halls of the medical center. Corridors, which in the day thronged with doctors bent over charts, rushing nurses, shuffling patients, and bewildered visitors, echoed his fretful footfall. Silence and stillness is all the greater when found in a noisy place, and reflection is all the more remarkable in a striving individual. The normally ramrod straight Dr Ahern stooped as he walked, as if he were examining the floor for clues to his troubles. He paused at a window to gaze out, but the light was too great within, so all he could see were the reflections of the hospital hallway and his dark shadow. He placed his hand on the pane and felt a startling coolness, like a sheet of ice. He leaned his forehead to the glass and relished the cold, as if a doting mother had placed a wet towel on his feverish head.

The nearby automatic door opened, a blast of cold air entered the room, and with it, the Head Administrator clomped in her heels, burdened by a Starbucks and bag. She spied Dr Ahern by the window and approached him uncertainly, as one would draw near a grieving parent. He straightened and, still facing the window, and addressed her.

"Forty years ago I met with my first patient; forty years of listening to trauma, dysfunction, and strife. I didn't need to have these stories become part of my life. I was born to privilege, comfort, and harmony. I'd been to Yale, as my father had, and his father before him. I could've been fast tracked to partner a Wall Street law firm. I could've swiveled in an overstuffed board room chair, or caucused in the cloakrooms of power. Instead, I rubbed elbows with the most powerless, and they drained me of everything I had. I studied science in college and could have spent millions to smash atoms or shoot to the moon; instead, I grappled for pennies in under-funded clinics and back wards. I could have had a Fifth Avenue practice, holding the hand of the rich and blotting their sniffles. Instead, I invited the most ignored and despised into my presence and took up their cries as if they were my own. My mother never said a cross word in her life and my father had a thousand friends, but I've had to argue and fight so that the unheard could be heard. No one listened."

"You're a very respected man, Dr Ahern," said the Head Administrator. "Your books are read by every college freshman. You're cited in thousands of scholarly papers. No one could ask for a better career than you've had."

"It's true that I packed the lecture halls and my publisher can't wait for me to write my next book. You're right, that every college freshman has to buy my books, but a year later, they're sold for a quarter in neighborhood yard sales, unread. I've talked, and lectured, and written for forty years and changed nothing. They'll line up to get my autograph, but they listen to me as much as they would a crazed homeless man, preaching in the street."

The great psychologist shifted a hand that had been leaning on the cold window. Moisture on the glass briefly glimmered, vaporized, and disappeared. The Head Administrator hiked the strap of her bag higher on her shoulder, for it had been slipping.

Dr Ahern sighed, "I feel so antiquated, old fashioned, and obsolete. I feel old, as if I were a Neanderthal who'd watched millennium go by and family, friends, and my entire species pass away before me. I feel like Lonesome George, the last surviving Galapagos tortoise, for whom there is no mate left and no one who will understand my language."

He turned to the Head Administrator and stared at her face. "Let me look in your eyes and see if there's any recognition there. One look in a human eye will tell you more than you ever could, gazing in a crystal ball. No, don't lower your eyes; meet them to mine; not pupil to teacher, but pupil to pupil. By God, I see the same vague silhouette in them that I saw in that window glass. Your eyes don't let me see into you, I can only see what you see. I see an old man who's fading away and becoming a shadow."

"Dr Ahern, I'm worried about you, as well as this clinic. Your reputation is on the line. OMH is coming tomorrow to investigate that group home fire. They're bound to find out that we haven't been diagnosing clients, threw out the DSM, and have been committing fraud with every bill we submit. They'll find out about the money you paid to the staff to buy their silence. They'll see the graffiti and the briefcase nailed to the wall. Everything will come to light before we're ready. But it's not too late. You and I can go to medical records and write a diagnosis in every chart. It'll only take a few hours. We can explain the graffiti, take the briefcase down off the wall, and tell OMH we paid the staff a bonus. No one will remember the great things you've done if this scandal breaks. You'll be ruined. You'll be like Freud smoking cocaine, Jung sleeping with clients, or Bettelheim beating little boys. Come on, let's go, before it's too late. We still have time."

Dr Ahern had broken off the gaze and began to pace. "No," he said. "It's already too late. I can't stop what I've started. I have to push on to the end, come whatever may. I can't turn my back on a lifetime of work; I've come too far."

The bag slipped off the Head Administrator's shoulder. She put her coffee down on the window ledge and took Dr Ahern by the arms. "It's never too late to do the right thing. You can change course still. You were right about the DSM, but you don't have to take it to this extreme. We have to work with the system we have and change things little by little. That's the only way."

"You're younger than I am and you talk like you have all the time in the world, but you don't; and I have even less time." he replied. "I could've taken it easy and reaped the benefits of a comfortable life, drinking martinis on a tied up yacht on Long Island Sound. But, no, I made my choice years ago and it's too late to change my mind. My whole past pushes me onward and I can't turn back. You say I've taken things to the extreme; well, you're right; but this is where I need to be. I have to shout, or no one will hear. I have to fail, or no one will pay attention. It has to be dramatic to make the headlines. Don't you understand? I have to sacrifice my career to my cause or my whole career would be for nothing."

He broke away from her grasp and resumed pacing. "I've always been driven to perform the impossible. I never sleep. The blanket on my cot is twisted like a rope. But I don't have to go on much longer. They're on their way. They'll be coming through this door and they won't have to find out. I'll meet them here and tell them. I won't even let them take off their coats. Will you wait with me? Sit down, we can tell them together."

But, the Head Administrator had already stolen away, blanched white as a ghost, to medical records to do what she could.

Dr Ahern turned to the reflection in the window and, mindless of anyone passing by, loudly and with great animation, rehearsed his speech to the regulators that he expected were to come that morning.

# Chapter 66 - The Delight

"You wanted to talk to me?" said Craig.

Izzy raised his head and focused imperfectly on a half-drained pina colada. He raised his head further. The lights were up, the music stopped, the dancers gone home, and the bartender rousting the last of the drinkers out the door. He'd fallen asleep and missed everything, missed the dancers, the mixed drinks, watching Luna flirt with the men, missed the gut gripping anxiety over what tomorrow would bring, and missed the last call for alcohol. He squinted at Craig. He wanted to ask him, is this what you alcoholics try to achieve? But he was too slow in assembling the thought and forming the words.

"C'mon, there's a diner down the street where we can get breakfast. You need some food in you."

The three AM cold of the outdoors stunned Izzy into wakefulness. Vapor capered annoyingly outside his mouth and a new fallen snow stridently squeaked under his feet. A yellow beam drew them towards windows streaked with grease, until they descried a peeling sign over a ramshackle shed: a diner misnamed *The Delight*.

Within *The Delight*, the people of the night: drunks, prostitutes, and insomniacs, thronged to the counter for a turn at petitioning a snarling waiter for heaping cardboard plates of breakfast. One man attempted to leave the counter with his plate, only to be jostled when a phalanx of bar staff arrived after clocking out. He spilled his plate on another drunk and a fight broke out between the two. The push from the crowd was so great that they didn't have room to swing their fists, so they grappled each other to the floor, where they were both kicked and trampled by the crowd.

Izzy was able to come away with his plate with no other incident other than to be separated from Craig. As he searched for a table, a homeless-looking man placed his bony hand on his shoulder. Izzy turned. The thin man from the hospital entrance, who had warned him of Dr Ahern, stood before him.

"Have they turned on you yet?" the thin man asked, shaking the plastic stirrer in his empty Styrofoam coffee cup.

"Pardon me?" said Izzy.

"I asked you have they turned on you yet?"

"I heard what you said, I just didn't understand you."

"Then, they haven't, if they had, you'd understand."

"Why're you talking riddles? Speak plainly."

"Some parents just turn on their children when they don't want 'em anymore. It happened to me, it'll happen to you."

"My parents are fine, and they haven't turned on me."

"I thought so, too. Then my father tried to kill me and my mother took his side. They just didn't want me anymore. It happened to me, it'll happen to you."

"So, you're a psychic, huh? Look, if there's something you know about what's going to happen with me tomorrow, tell me. That's what I want to know."

"Your own family will turn on you, they always do."

"You got some serious issues, man, if you think that just because it happened to you; it'll happen to everyone else. Not everyone has a family like yours. They were just dysfunctional."

"You counselors are all alike: analyze and categorize."

"Yeah, and you crazy people are all alike, too," Izzy snapped. "Blame everything on your parents and don't take any responsibility yourself. So, you've been abused, well boo hoo, let's all feel sorry for you."

"When they turn on you, you'll understand. Have a nice day."

"Have a nice day, yourself," said Izzy.

As he left, he ran into Craig, who asked, "Client of yours?"

"No, he just likes to mess with peoples' heads."

They sat, and Izzy, worrying his sausage with a plastic fork, said, "Let me tell you what happened today."

"Wait a minute, not so fast," said Craig. "Remember, you're the counselor here and I'm your client. That's the deal. We talk about what I need to talk about."

"But OMH is coming to talk to me. I had a client – clients - die. I sent someone to the hospital…"

"I don't give a rat's ass about that stuff. If they're dead, they're dead and nothing you do now can change it. And if OMH wants to come and close down the clinic, or slap you on the hand, they'll fucking do it and nothing you do can stop them. You wanted to hear my story; well, I'm fucking ready to tell it."

"Have you been drinking?" asked Izzy.

"Sober; stone cold sober. I wanted to be sober to tell you what I want to say. And you're a hell of a one to lecture me about drinking, while you're sitting there shit faced."

"You've been planning on telling me this?"

"I've been waiting for years. It's been a cancer, growing in my gut and it's time to come out. You asked for it, you're going to get it."

"Just what I've been wanting," said Izzy. "Delightful."

# Chapter 67 - Postpartum Depression

Craig didn't usually drink with sows, but it seemed like a good time to take up the practice, with everything going to hell around him. Despite her occasional grunts, his petulant companion paid little attention to what he was telling her, as she was intent on sucking up her beer as fast as she could. Joan Baez peered over at them, her wide spaced eyes envious of Janis Joplin's good fortune in getting beer, the disc of her nose angling to get the most of fumes reminiscent of ripe swill.

Things had been going to hell since before the baby was born. Craig's father-in-law paid him for working at the sawmill in lumber, pigs, and a canoe bought impulsively at auction, rather than with money. So they had no money, but they had plenty of work: working at the sawmill, putting up an addition to the house, shoveling shit for the pigs, all with Leah getting bigger and bigger and running to the john every time she turned around. Then the canoe got stolen. They got stuck in the ditch when her water broke, and woke up the man in the meth lab in the middle of night. Leah was furious that Craig had taken a hit before driving off to the hospital, but what did she have to complain about? They made it there on time, didn't they? She was no better than he was, it wasn't three days after the baby was born that she asked for some, too. She said that if he was going to be up all night, hammering on the house, and if the baby was going to be up, bawling her head off, she might as well get cranked, too.

Then one day, while he was working on the house, he placed the metal hammer on the woodpile. His wife scooped it up, not looking, and threw it in the stove with an armload of firewood. He saw her do it, but couldn't stop her. He pushed her aside and poked around in the fire for it. The fire was really going, it had a good bed of coals, and, by the time he fished it out, the rubber grip was pretty well gone. He threw it down on the floor where it scorched a hammer-shaped brand and yelled at her for her stupidity. She said she wouldn't stick around to be abused and flew out the front door, slipping on the ice at the front step and breaking her ankle.

"Now we were really fucked," he said to Janis Joplin. "We spent six hours in the emergency room with a newborn baby to get her ankle set."

Janis, done with her beer, gave a couple of grunts. Seeing that she was still not sedated, Craig got up and poured her another forty-ouncer. This was too much for Joan, in the next pen, who wanted some, too. She hitched her front legs over the pen panel and protested. Her piglets oinked their support. She came down off the panel and knocked over the water trough, an old hot water tank cut in half lengthwise with an acetylene torch. The flood spilled over the piglets' feet and they abandoned the protest to investigate the wetness. Janis' pigs, separated from their mother, called from a makeshift pen of straw bales. What was left of them, two days old, now more than eight hours without being fed. Janis still was not sedated enough to get them back.

The floor by the stove had been his pride and joy. Red oak, toe nailed, sanded smooth as a bowling alley, and varnished, it bore no sign of the work he put into it, no half-circle hammer marks, no nails poking up to catch socks. The floor might have been mistaken for a natural phenomenon, the work of God, and now it bore the brand of the tool of its construction like a scratchy tag on the neck of a new shirt.

The baby wouldn't stop crying when they got back from the hospital. They rocked her, held her, passed her back and forth between them, and gave up, finally, leaving her to cry herself to sleep face down, her bottom bare, airing out her diaper rash, glowing like an over-heated stove.

Craig had gone out to check on the pigs. Joan's pigs were six weeks old, active and playful, frolicking in the straw. Two, tired with the game, rooted at their mother's belly and she flopped on her side, exposing the rows of teats. At this signal the brood scrambled to nurse, vying for a choice spot. When the pigs settled in, Joan gave a long sigh and began grunting the nursing song that every sow sings to her pigs, drowning out the subtle, moist, noises of the barn.

Hogs are prolific creatures, having large litters and short gestation periods; three months, three weeks and three days after breeding they'll give birth; at three o'clock in the morning. You'll generally lose a few. The runt might die, for instance, another may get an infection from castration, and that sort of thing. Also, sows being large and their pigs being small, active and numerous, it's not unusual to lose one or two by their mother laying on them and crushing them. Some hog breeders keep the sow in a crate that they can't turn around in and must lie straight down instead of flopping over. Craig, who loved the freedom of riding on an open road on his hog, would never make a sow live in a crate. Instead, he built the young ones a triangular shaped sanctuary in the corners of their mothers' pens where they could get food and water and bask under the heat lamp.

In next the pen, Janis' one-day-old pigs were sleeping under the light, their eyes contentedly shut behind blond lashes. The sow, having recovered from birthing the eight pigs of her first litter, examined her trough to see if she had missed any food. Craig reached in to scratch her back. Flakes of dandruff lodged in his nails as he dug under the stiff, bristly hair. The sow barked, startled by the touch, and snapped at his hand.

"I'm sorry, girl. I didn't know you were in a bad mood," he said.

He watched the sow peevishly rearrange the straw in her pen. Hearing the nursing song from Joan, Janis' pigs awakened with the idea of a snack. Craig leaned on the pen panel and counted them. One was missing. He grabbed a pitchfork and poked through the straw, searching for the missing piglet while the litter set up a chorus of squeals, picketing for their dinner. Janis seized the nearest pig in her mouth, Godzilla-like, and killed it. Oblivious to the murder, the piglets continued to squeal for their dinner at her feet and under her belly. Craig quickly threw some corn into Janis' trough to distract her and jumped into the pen to save the pigs. His hand darted and seized their hind legs one by one. Each one tried to kick himself free, but he held on and threw them out. Just as Janis finished her corn, he had the last one dangling from his hand. The sow snorted in the trough and wheeled around to face him, the intruder, as he vaulted out of the pen.

The live pigs safe, he turned his attention to the dead one, forgotten in a corner of the sow's pen. Smelling blood, Janis rooted through her straw to add the dead pig to her dinner. Craig drove her away with a small prick from the pitchfork. She jolted back, squealing, as he scooped up the corpse.

Farmers had told him of sows turning on their pigs, but he never experienced it before. Old timers said that some new mothers are just too uptight and need to relax a bit before accepting their young. He knew just what would relax Janis. As soon as he separated her from her newborns, he went back to town to pick up some beer.

Soon after he returned, Craig and Janis were drinking together like two old friends. In no time she finished six forties to his four and they were out of beer. The empty bottles stood in a row like a line of empty teats. He picked up the weakest of her pigs and tossed it into her pen, as a test. At first the sow seemed to accept it all right, but then the pig began to nuzzle her underside and grunt to be fed. The mother had no patience for her and moved away. The doomed pig kept up her grunting until Janis spun around and seized it by its neck. She shook it until it died.

Craig needed to think about what he was going to do next. He knew he was in no condition to drive to town again for more beer. Maybe Joan would accept some foster pigs. They might be able to raise the surviving ones themselves. He picked up a fork and began to clean Joan's pen as he thought it out.

Then it occurred to him that he hadn't heard the baby crying all night.

When he got to the house, Leah was sobbing in bed. No amount of beer could have prepared him for the most unspeakable horror he'd ever seen crumpled up against the wall.

# Chapter 68 – Crying

"What the hell's the matter with you?" asked Craig as he finished his story.

Izzy was crying. He was bawling his eyes out. "It's all too much," he blubbered. "I don't know how you can take it. All that trauma. First, your mother lying and then your father dying. Then Cornwhacker, and your wife cutting her hand off, and then she killed your kid. It's no wonder you drink."

"God damn, here I am stopped drinking and you're trying to talk me back into it."

"You can drink if you want. I want to drink, too. I guess I'm not meant to be a counselor. You can flunk me if you want. It's all right. I can't take any more of this anyway. So much misery, I can't stand it."

"Hell, I'm not going to flunk you, you just helped me. I haven't told anyone about that since it happened and I needed to fucking get it out. You got me to do it with your harebrained theory of stories. Well, shit, if you can't take hearing them, what the hell're you asking for them for?"

"I can't take hearing them. I'm sorry, I never should have asked you. I, like, never knew there was so much wretchedness in the world."

"You're more wretched than I am. What are you crying for? I lived it, you only heard about it."

"I'm crying because everything's fucked up. Why aren't you crying?"

"I've done enough fucking crying. I'm sick of crying."

"You cried? When've you cried? I don't believe you've ever cried. I think when you start to feel like crying, you just, like, drink, smoke something, beat someone up, or swear."

"I've cried plenty. I just haven't told anyone why. Now that I've told you, I don't need to cry anymore."

"Tell me."

"Tell you what?"

"Tell me about just one time when you've cried."

Mrs. Anna E. Hess was ladling her clam chowder into a Tupperware container to take to the lunch meeting of the Washington County Lady's Missionary Society when she heard the motorcycle stop in front of her house. Peering out of her kitchen window, she saw a bearded man in black leather and chains came to the door. He knocked with an urgency that she took for anger. Although it was only one motorcyclist, she had heard enough about the men in black leather to have such a fright that she left the ladle and the chowder on the counter and hid in the pantry. She didn't regret her actions when, after only a few knocks, the man opened up the door and stepped in.

It was dark in the pantry with the door shut, but Mrs. Hess was so knowledgeable of the location of every item in it that she rarely ever had to turn on the light. Therefore, it was no problem for her to find two cans of corn and put them in a bag to have as a weapon in case the man should find her there while he was robbing her home. She placed the bag on the top shelf behind her and grasped it so that, if he opened the door, she could bring it down upon his head. With her other hand, she took hold of the broom handle, so that she would have a second weapon with her in case the cans of corn didn't prove sufficient.

Mrs. Hess was sorry to have to take such action based on the appearance of the man at the door. She knew it was not the Christian thing to do, but she was afraid. She would not be hiding in the pantry if Frank were still alive. No, she would be greeting the man at the door to offer him whatever he needed while Frank kept a watchful eye at a distance. If the stranger asked for a jacket, she would give him a coat, also. Mrs. Hess would also be more hospitable if her son or his boy were at the house, but they were out back, burning brush in a clearing they had made. Even arthritic Gus would give her more courage if he were here to bark at the stranger, although he would most likely remain lying by the fire while he barked. But Gus was with Frank, chasing rabbits in doggy heaven with a new body, and she was left here in the pantry with the cans of corn.

It then occurred to Mrs. Hess that she was not alone in the pantry. She was with God, although she had forgotten for a moment. She should have known. She was always with God; she talked to Him all day long. She and God were not like many old couples that had been together so long they needed no words to communicate. Mrs. Hess talked to God continuously, about everything. In fact, if God didn't have the patience of Job, he might have throttled her ceaseless chatter years ago. As it stood, God seemed to enjoy Mrs. Hess talking with Him, as she enjoyed doing the talking. She went out of her way to find things to report to God and belonged to a prayer chain that caused her phone to ring constantly with prayer requests, all of which she passed on faithfully to Him. People seemed to want Mrs. Hess to pray for them, if only because she, like a lobbyist of the spirit, was on such familiar terms with The Almighty that they could be sure their message would go through.

Prayer seemed to be in order in this situation, so Mrs. Hess began to pray. She prayed that the stranger would not find her in the pantry. She prayed that he would take what he wanted and get out. She prayed that he would fall off his motorcycle and die. She felt bad for that prayer and prayed that God would forgive her. She prayed for the stranger, that he would find whatever he was looking for, that he would find God, just as she had, and be on familiar terms with Him, also. She prayed that she would have the strength to brain him with the corn if he came close to her. It's hard to know just how to pray in frightful circumstances, so she settled on the all-purpose, Swiss army knife of prayers: Thy will be done.

Armed, thus, she was disarmed when the man called out, "Hello, anyone home! Your woods are on fire!"

Indeed, she knew that they were and imagined that, from the road, it would look as though a forest fire was threatening the home. She concluded that this man, although frightful in appearance and mistaken as to the danger, was performing a good Christian act, even if he were no Christian. Mrs. Hess might have remained in the pantry and let him do his calling through the house till he was satisfied that no one was home and left, but, as he was kind enough to stop, she thought she would be kind enough to spare him his anxieties. She opened the door, leaving behind the broom, but bringing out the cans of corn. There she met Craig, complete with the same leather, chains, beard, and tattoos that Izzy saw when he met him. He may have been as strange to her as he was to Izzy, but in the biker's eyes, she recognized grief.

"Oh, I was just in the pantry getting corn," she said, exhaling her anxieties about the stranger and thanks to God. "Bless you, but my son and his boy are back in the woods, burning brush."

"Oh," he said, and looked at his feet, embarrassed. "I'm sorry I came in like that, I just thought…"

Mrs. Hess emptied the bag and placed the cans of corn on the counter. "No, that was a very good thing to do. I'm glad I met you – Mr…"

"Creek, my name is Craig Creek," he said, backing towards the door. She could see he was profoundly uncomfortable, having little experience with polite conversation. "I'd better hit the road."

"Pleased to meet you, I'm Mrs. Anna E. Hess. Have you had lunch?" she asked.

"No, ma'am."

She could see he was a man of few words, but his needs were great; Mrs. Hess could practically read them on his face. The Lord has been busy, she thought, sending this man here.

"Then, you'll have to have lunch with us. I'm going to a luncheon meeting and you can help me carry this food," she said as she struggled to open a can of corn. "You're a big, strong man. Can you help me open this?"

Craig cranked open the cans of corns that, a minute ago, might have laid him low. In no time, the two were on their way to the Washington County Lady's Missionary Society Luncheon. Mrs. Hess drove sedately in an old Lincoln while he balanced the chowder and the corn on his knees.

"We don't send missionaries to Africa, or anything like that," she explained. "We keep an eye out for people in need right here in Washington County. When we hear of something, we call out the troops. We'll each bring them a dish, or watch the children, or do whatever is needed. We pray for people, too, but sometimes prayer needs hands and feet."

They pulled up to a restored one-room schoolhouse. "The men helped us fix up this place," she said of the ladies' husbands, jokingly referred to as The Mens' Auxiliary of The Washington County Lady's Missionary Society. She prayed everyday for these men. So many men need prayer, thought Mrs. Hess, because their insides don't match their outsides. Either they look like an animal on the outside, like this stranger, Craig, while inside is a scared child. Or, on the outside, is a compliant, bullied child; while on the inside, anger seethes. Reticence is the surest sign of the Devil and the Lord fighting within.

In the schoolhouse, the ladies stirred their potluck contributions heating on a wood stove. Heavily carved and lacquered school desks were arranged in a circle and, on the wall, watching over the whole gathering, was the county's namesake, George Washington; other than Craig, the only man in the room.

"Anna, who did you bring to our meeting?" said the ladies in alarm.

"Why, this is Mr. Craig Creek, a very nice man who was ready to save my house from a forest fire."

"A forest fire?" They said, with continued alarm.

"Frank, Jr. and Steve were only burning brush, but to someone riding by, it looked like a forest fire."

"Oh," said the ladies. They went on with astonishment, "You brought two dishes, clam chowder and corn. You only needed to bring one."

"I brought two people, didn't I? One dish per person. What did y'all bring?"   "Creamed codfish, carrots, Coke, cookies, and cake," crowed the ladies.

"And Craig Creek," cracked Mrs. Hess.

They cackled. "Just as if we said for everyone to bring C things."

"The Lord had everybody bring a thing that started with C, just to show us He's involved," said Mrs. Hess. "He wants us to open our eyes and see."

The ladies insisted on serving Craig. They had him wedge himself behind a school desk and placed a heaping plate in front of him. "Let us pray," said Mrs. Hess when they all had their seats and plates. Craig put down a half eaten forkful of codfish as she said, "Lord, we thank you for the food we are about to eat and the fellowship all around the circle. We ask you to give us sight, so we can see the needs of people around us, rather than their faults. Give us, Oh Lord, the will to do your work. Amen."

"Amen," said the ladies. Mrs. Hess looked over at Craig, who was shoveling in food like Esau downing his potage. The ladies gossiped about their neighbors till she felt embarrassed by them, then recognizing a hypercritical spirit in her own thoughts, felt embarrassed of herself.

"Would you like another plate?" she said to Craig when he finished.

He started to get up to fix it himself, but the school desk came up with him, he was wedged in so tightly.

"No, don't get up. I'll get it for you."

He couldn't meet her eye when she returned with the plate. She could see he had another need besides food, so she said, "Mr. Creek, may we pray for you?"

He couldn't take another bite, or speak; the feeling was so strong. The tears came tentative at first, until the ladies asked, "What's wrong. What would you like us to pray for?" Then unlocked a torrent of anguish that astonished them more than rage would ever have.

Mrs. Hess, who knew something about anguish, said, "No, you don't need to tell us what's wrong, we don't need to know, the Lord knows."

She added, "When we don't know how to pray, the Holy Spirit helps us in our weakness by praying for us in groanings that cannot be expressed in words. Our Father, who knows all hearts, understands what Mr. Creek is saying with his tears. That's enough for me."

# Chapter 70 - The Beast

That night, the insane, restrained in their hospital rooms, or pacing the lonely streets, or dozing in their apartments before snowy early morning TV screens, suddenly thrust out their nostrils and sniffed. Change was in the air. They alone could smell it in the still night, as God took a deep breath. Dr Ahern sensed it, too; and he declared to anyone who was listening that he had set the trap, the clinic was the bait, and the Beast was about to arrive. He was mistaken, however. For OMH had been called off. The Beast never, ever shows his face. When it kills, it kills by remote control.

What, in fact, had arrived was the morning newspaper, long before the daybreak, which lingered in its mid winter bed. The newspaper machine outside the hospital's automatic door quickly sold out as incoming dayshift employees spied the headline above the fold. Ahern scanned the bleary-eyed workers entering through the door, unfolding the news, accompanied by a blast of winter.

Izzy saw the paper, too. He and Craig had left *The Delight* at the same time as a flannel-coated deliveryman filled the newspaper box out front. Craig and Izzy parted ways, the intern assuming that they'd go on forever like this, meeting to discuss cases and filling out the corners of Craig's life. The intern also supposed that Craig would sometime lend an ear to hear Izzy tell his story: he could, at last, tell someone about his haircut, his sister, or the whale watch, and see what kind of sense he could make of it all. None of this was to be, however, for nothing lasts forever.

After Craig left, Izzy spotted the headline: IROQUOIS REGIONAL CLOSING, and hastily bought the paper.

SCOTTSDALE, ARIZ (APA) Medco announced last night that they will be closing the Iroquois Regional Medical Center in one month. They have already notified state and federal officials that new admissions will no longer be accepted at their facility. Last quarter, the company lost approximately $1.3 million at the center.

Medco recently purchased Iroquois Regional along with five other New York State hospitals. The remaining hospitals will benefit from some redirected Iroquois Regional employees while equipment and other assets will be redistributed to all Medco facilities.

"Our company is like a family of hospitals," said Richard Mobey, chairman and chief executive officer of Medco, meeting with reporters in the company's headquarters in Scottsdale, Arizona. "We regret that this action has become necessary, but the problems at Iroquois Regional are unrelated to the strength of the rest of our network in New York. We are a major employer and taxpayer in the state, and our other five hospitals in the area make up a network that provides high-quality services for patients, physicians, and managed-care companies in western New York. We look forward to continued growth in the remaining hospitals."

The orphaned intern's mouth was a gaping gulf. A great wind blew a whiteout down the street and drowned everything with its sheet. For a moment, all Izzy could see was white, a hue that, by its abstractedness, harkens the heartless voids of the universe, and guns us down with the thought of extinction.

# Epilogue

"You haven't come to the club all week," said Luna, having appeared, fully clothed, in the doorway of the intern's office. "I've been looking for you. I still owe you some lap dances."

"That's OK," said Izzy, spinning his chair toward the door. "You see, I have a confession to make. I'm, like, not really a therapist. I'm just an intern. And now, with the clinic closing, I can't even finish my internship."

"You were totally enough of a therapist for me," she said. "I've already enrolled in college. You made me see I could do it. So, I owe you those dances."

"Did you come here to give me those dances?"

"Yeah, we could do that. But I really came to give you this." She handed him an envelope. "It's from Craig. He wanted you to have it. He's going off to North Dakota, and he told me to say goodbye to you for him."

Izzy ripped it open.

"What is it? What is it? Is it a love letter?" said Luna.

"No, it's a letter documenting the completion of my internship. I guess I'm official, now. I can graduate."

"That's awesome!" said Luna, throwing herself on him with a hug.

"Yeah, that's great. But I don't know where I'm going to get a job with the medical center closing."

"You can, like, come work with me."

"Dancing? Me?"

"No, silly, you can shrink heads in the back room. Everyone who goes there is looking for something. You help them in your way, and I'll help them in mine."

"Counseling at a strip club?"

"Yeah, what's the difference? You do it now in a hospital. What's counseling got to do with doctors and being sick?"

"Won't the owners object?"

"No, as long as you give them a cut and don't bring the police there, they don't care what any of us do."

Izzy thought, that's an arrangement Dr Ahern would've approved: no regulators, no insurance, no paperwork, no need for a diagnosis. Ahern, who Dr Staub had committed to inpatient, was locked in a room next to Inez. "He's clearly bipolar," Dr Staub had said, "and in need of medication. That's what all this was about, all along."

"I have a confession to make, myself," said the stripper. "My name isn't really Luna, you know. It's Rachel."

"Awesome," said Izzy. "I guess I should apologize, too. I'm sorry I kissed you like that. I shouldn't've done it."

"I like that you kissed me. You can kiss me anytime you want. No one's kissed me in years. I've done other things with guys, but I've been saving my kisses for someone like you."

"Why, because I listened to your story?"

"Listening to my story changed everything. My life was a mess before you came along, like I had all these mismatched clothes on that didn't fit me. Then, just by listening to my story, you took them all off. You helped me get me back, and now I'm all yours."

Made in the USA
Las Vegas, NV
02 March 2022